Originally pu

This edition published February 2017

This is a work of fiction. Any similarity to real people or organisations is purely coincidental.

ISBN 978-1542903103

Copyright © Mark F Speed 2012 and 2017

Originally published in 2012 as *Appreciating Assets*
All rights reserved

The right of Mark F Speed to be identified as the author and illustrator of this work has been asserted by him in accordance with the Copyright, Designs and Patents Act, 1988.

No part of this publication may be reproduced, stored in or introduced into a retrieval system, or transmitted in any form or by any means, electronic, mechanical, photocopying, recording or otherwise without the prior written permission of the copyright owner and publisher.

Published by Terra Supra Limited
Registered in England and Wales no. 8109753

www.terrasupra.co.uk
Nothing is black and white

Cover design by Jason Anscomb
www.rawshock.co.uk

To Liz, with gratitude

Chapter One

The pink book wasn't there.

They'd had sex for the first time in three weeks last night. It was the best they'd had in years – easily.

It had slipped his mind that she'd been off the booze for a couple of weeks, so he'd got into bed a little tipsy, having had a bottle of red on his own. He'd also had a couple of sly cans whilst watching the late Friday night comedy slot. She'd been in bed a while, reading one of those novels with a pink cover and a goofy title.

She turned off the light and, as soon as he pulled the duvet over himself, his underpants were hijacked by her roving hand, which began to stroke him to life. He hooked his pants down and threw them out of the bed. But when he turned to kiss her she stuck her right breast in his face. He sucked her nipple dutifully while searching his mind for an occasion he might have forgotten. Her twenty-ninth birthday had been months ago, and he was pretty sure it wasn't their anniversary. Indeed, their relationship had been so chequered that surely even she couldn't keep track of all their anniversaries.

But he wasn't complaining – far from it. He kissed his way down her stomach, then kissed her thighs before focusing his attention between them. She moaned in a way she'd not moaned in months, bucked and writhed. Presently she raised her pelvis, quivered, and put her hand under his chin. He went back to the top of the bed to kiss her but she moved down his body. He was surprised by her hungriness for him, because he'd not showered since the morning. After a couple of minutes she straddled him. He watched her breasts bounce up and down in the silky-soft light, her eyes closed as she worked frantically. He pulled himself up on his elbows to kiss her but she shoved him back on the bed.

They came around the same time and she sat on him, eyes closed, getting her breath back. It was only when he had shrunk out of her that she opened her eyes and lay down beside him.

Again, he leaned over to kiss her. She gave him just a single kiss on the lips and said "Goodnight," as she rolled over. He lay there for a minute, looking at the back of her head. It troubled him as he waited for sleep to come. Was it a scene in the novel she was reading? He would have to look at that novel, find where she'd got to, and work it out.

It was now Saturday afternoon. The pink book with the goofy title wasn't there. He cast his mind back, through the haze of lunchtime alcohol, to the morning.

He'd heard her get up and shower around half-seven, leaving him in bed with his hangover. He'd surfaced around half-nine, showered and had a couple of slices of toast, not wanting to ruin his appetite for lunch. He went to the corner shop for the paper and spent one hour and two cups of tea reading inconsequentialities – a relaxing contrast with the weekday reading of critical facts and figures.

She'd not turned up for lunch at the Derbyshire, but that was normal. Although girlfriends, wives – *cohabiting partners* like Sarah — weren't discouraged, they got in the way of the bloke-ish banter. Sunday was family and females; Saturday belonged to the boys. When Steve's girlfriend had dropped by late in the afternoon and asked after Sarah, there was no way he could brag of the unexpected exuberance of Friday night's sex in mixed company. When he'd got back at half-four with a couple of ready meals for the microwave, he'd been hoping for an encore.

That was when he'd noticed something missing. He couldn't quite put his finger on it but his subconscious was nagging at him from behind the five pints of beer he'd drunk that afternoon. It was like looking at a set of doctored accounts: he knew one detail would reveal the whole picture. The living room looked somehow different, and it felt strangely… *quiet*. That was when he'd gone to the bedroom and seen that the book was missing.

Then he realised.

It was her, Sarah. She was missing.

And it wasn't just Sarah that was missing. All of Sarah's stuff was missing. He opened her wardrobe. Empty. Her other wardrobe in the spare bedroom-cum-study was also empty. Her CD collection was gone from the living room. Apart from his shaving kit, there was only one worn-out toothbrush, some toothpaste, his deodorant and some shower gel in the bathroom. No shampoo, no moisturiser, no tampons, no make-up.... The place was Spartan. It looked like... it looked like a bachelor's bathroom.

Things began to make sense. The washing machine had been running non-stop all week, which is why he'd been unable to launder anything of his own. It was a combi that doubled as a tumble-dryer. When she'd moved in four years ago she'd turned her nose up at it because of her Green stance, insisting they dry everything on an ugly clotheshorse in the spare bedroom. He recalled having teased her about her sudden use of the dryer on – when was it? – Wednesday evening. She must have laundered everything.

He went through to the spare room and kicked the empty clotheshorse: the only remaining symbol of her four-year occupation. His foot caught in the white plastic-coated wire and he stumbled backwards against the wall, hitting his head just hard enough to make him stop and think.

He took stock. He felt a peculiar numbness; almost guilty at not feeling shocked. Had he committed some heinous act? Was there someone else? Unlikely, given last night's – apparently valedictory – sex.

Normally he'd observe a polite, middle-class hiatus between the lunchtime session and an evening beer. But not now: no one would sigh, raise their – *her* – eyebrows or make a comment. The fridge had gone the same way as the bathroom. She'd not removed anything from it, but it had run down to the three basic bachelor Bs: beer, bread and butter. He put the two ready meals in and opened a bottle of beer. No need for a glass now.

They'd never been in love. Very fond occasionally – but never both at the same time, and never in love. They'd never felt lost without each other, never had the heady heartstring pulling of romance. The joke to his friends had always been that she was his default girlfriend. She would drift back into his life whenever he was single, like some back-up program for regular sex. Even when he'd been dating – or, more correctly, trying to get into the pants of — other women at university, she'd appear out of nowhere and they'd end up in bed. And she'd always been the one to finish the relationship weeks or months later, which he accepted without much comment, for there was never any reason for it – nothing he could fathom, anyway.

She'd never quite fitted in to the regular flow of his life and his circle of friends as he'd expected of a perfectly tailored partner. She was quite pretty – average height, average build, shoulder-length brown hair, blue eyes. That was rather the point: she fitted the bill for a 'default' girlfriend. In all those years of living together, marriage had never been seriously discussed and he had always avoided presents of jewellery.

But this was different from the times she'd dumped him during their dating years. She'd not said a word. There was no note. Nothing on the answering machine. Should he call her? His hand toyed with his mobile.

He could hardly declare his undying love. So far as he knew, there was no specific apology to be made. Unless she felt she was due one for four years – fourteen percent of their lives, he calculated – of unstimulating togetherness. But she was as much to blame as he was. What could he offer her – another forty years of the same? If he called her, was he surrendering and saying he didn't want this freedom? He sensed a turning point.

His guilt and his mobile tugged at him. He scrolled down through the directory to her name, wondering whether he was doing the right thing. He couldn't not say anything, could he? Well, clearly *she* could. But two wrongs don't…. He didn't want any acrimony, and he'd always liked her parents.

He pressed the button, more nervous than he'd expected, and held the phone up to his left ear.

"Hi."

"Sarah, hi. It's Ian."

"Yes. Caller ID. Amazing, isn't it?"

"Your stuff's not here."

"I took the last of it at lunchtime. I've been moving it out all week. You were working late."

"That's why you left?"

"There was no reason to stay."

"So that's it."

"If you say so."

"I didn't say that. I…"

"You what, Ian? What *did* you say?"

"…" He hated this. Never argue with a lawyer: all sentences were death sentences. He took a swig of beer.

"What, exactly, was keeping us together?" she asked.

"Well. That's no reason…"

"No reason to what?"

"Please don't make this difficult."

"It was remarkably easy, Ian. Shall we keep it that way?"

"But what about last night?"

"What about it?"

"Well, I enjoyed it and I think you did too."

"That's all it ever was, or at least all it had become. Be honest."

"I suppose." He felt like a naughty ten-year-old.

"And if you want that kind of thing now, you'll just have to get off your fat arse and go and get it, won't you?"

"…" He felt hot blood pulsing in his ears.

"Well?"

"Well maybe I will!"

He terminated the call. Why didn't they make mobiles you could slam down? He felt like calling her back and giving her a piece of his mind, but she'd just ring off. He could text her something hurtful. Nothing came to mind and he was dying for a pee. He put the phone back in his right trouser pocket, took another swig of beer and went to the toilet. He had just started to relieve himself when the phone burst loudly into life and vibrated against his scrotum. His penis in his left hand, a couple of fingers holding the elastic of his underpants down, he reached for the phone. The LED screen said 'Sarah'. The anger rose in him again. He stabbed the green button, hoping she'd hear the sound of him urinating.

"What?"

"I just called to wish you luck. Fat men are attractive in some cultures."

That was *it*! Instinct made him want to swap the phone to his left hand so that he could gesticulate properly. In that moment of drunken hesitation he lost his grip on his underpants. The elastic snapped back and the warm urine poured inside his trousers. He grappled with his penis and sprayed the floor around the bathroom as he got the phone back to his ear. The line was dead. He was still searching for a comeback anyway. He dismissed the thought of calling her again.

Fuming, he dabbed at the mess with a pad of toilet paper, then took a shower. The only clean trousers he could find were so uncomfortable around the waist he took them off again to check the size: thirty-four inch waist. He had changed to a thirty-six last year, but even so.... He looked at himself in the mirror and saw a twenty-nine-year-old accountant with the ghost of a double chin and a podgy stomach. Boringness personified.

Forensic accountant, he reminded himself. That counted for something.

His slight chubbiness wasn't unusual in someone of his age and profession. No sense in doing anything rash: he was a busy man. He'd figure this one out. Caution was what was needed. Sudden lifestyle changes were ill-advised.

Besides, it wasn't like he'd just gone through a divorce. The flat was his and she'd just pitched in with the odd bill. If he'd taken a lodger, four years would have seen him reduce his mortgage by around twenty-five percent. Had all that sex on tap been worth those thousands of pounds of lost revenue? He decided against calculating an average cost per fuck because he knew the figure would appal him. But he knew his monthly mortgage repayments to the penny and part of his mind instantly estimated the number of fucks per month. The cost per fuck — *CPF*: a new accounting ratio with which to benchmark the happiness of cohabiting couples – rang up in his head with a *ker-ching* like figures on an old-fashioned cash register.

It was a good job this had all happened now. Imagine if he'd married her? He'd watched his boss, Donald Peterson, going through it the last couple of years. The rage, the humiliation, the paperwork, the meetings and phone calls, the exclusion *from his own home*, having to start again at the age of sixty on the property ladder. No thanks. This was a lucky escape, and he knew it.

But why shouldn't he take Sarah up on her challenge? He'd show her. She'd held him in check in that final year at university. "Fucking default girlfriend," he muttered, remembering the merciless ribbing of even his female friends at her continual dumping of him.

With only suits left to change into, he opted for a night in wearing a dressing gown, savouring a decent bottle of red. There was a profound satisfaction to eating food that he had microwaved himself, having the washing machine on – especially as it switched to environmentally hostile tumble-dry mode at the end of the wash cycle – and watching in peace the programmes he wanted to watch, even if they were awful. Four years of cohabitation scrubbed clean, with no comeback. He felt glad to be alive and overjoyed to be single: all the sex he'd missed was out there, waiting for him. Lock up your daughters – the all-new Ian Bourne was off the leash tomorrow and he was in town to *party*. He was carefree and single, and his old inhibitions had vanished.

But then it dawned on him how much electricity the tumble-dryer was using. He turned it off and laid out his washing on the clotheshorse in the spare room before going to bed.

Chapter Two

Sunday morning put the fear of God into him.

He reached out an arm and felt cold, empty bedding. Her pillow didn't even have a dent in it. Before leaving on Saturday she must have plumped hers up in the morning, as she always did. Its unused smoothness seemed to glare at him. He felt very alone. His head ached and his tongue was furred but Murphy's Law dictated that he had an even better erection than on Friday night. The hangover enhanced his anxiety and a light, clammy sweat formed on his forehead.

The magnitude of his crisis engulfed him. He was approaching thirty, single, and there was no prospect of sex on the horizon. Furthermore, he realised that the days of condomless sex were over. From now on, he would remain sheathed – assuming he even got that far. Spontaneity would have to be planned and sensitivity was gone. Each new partner would be a gamble. Awkward questions about contraception, fumbling with a condom, the danger of deflation. He was weeks, months – perhaps even years away from a sexual partner he'd be able to trust enough.

He dealt with his morning glory the way he had in his teenage years – though at least he had fresh images of Friday night in his mind to spur him on. But four years of cohabitation meant that he didn't have any tissue to hand when the moment of climax grew near, and he had to run to the toilet to finish the job – an uncomfortable end to a less than satisfying release. The contrast with Friday night was crushing. So much for the previous night's plan to get out and grab some sex.

He dithered all morning as to whether to show up for lunch at the Derbyshire. Realising he didn't want to spend the rest of the day alone, he pulled himself together by half-eleven and made the short journey to Balham high street. He rehearsed various conversations in his head but, since he didn't know who was going to be there, it was a little pointless.

The empty pub stank of Saturday night's stale beer, and the squeak of his footsteps echoed across the wooden floor. He checked himself in the mirror. Pale, puffy face and pinhole eyes. With his new single status, he reassessed the barmaid. She caught him staring at her and he looked away too quickly. He mumbled his thanks as she handed him his pint. She gave him his change without a word and walked to the other end of the bar.

The arrangement was that whoever was first bagged some space and waited until one o'clock before ordering food. He took a mid-sized table near the fake fire and spread out a newspaper. As the pub filled up, he bought himself another pint. Time dragged and he began to get twitchy. He nodded to a few familiar faces, but there was none of his own crowd here. Other tables were packed and he was getting looks from people standing at the bar with menus. He drank quickly, toes curling. With every opening of the door he looked up. Nothing was ever pre-arranged, but someone always came. Always. At ten past one, his third pint was interrupted by his mobile. 'Stu' flashed up on the screen. He smiled.

"I've got us a table. Can I get your food ordered, avoid the wait?" Ian asked with forced jocularity.

"Lunch is being served. The invitation was for half-twelve, lunch at one."

He felt a pang. Seven years ago to the day he'd been Stu and Nina's best man. "Sorry. Sorry to Nina for me. Been a lot going on. Be there ASAP." He downed his beer in one and then regretted it on his empty stomach. He'd forgotten to tell Stu about Sarah but thought better of ringing back.

He and Stu were childhood friends. Stu was a burly Bristolian lad, just over six feet tall, son of a policeman and a nurse, who had inherited the best qualities of both professions. Whilst Ian had gone north to Newcastle, Stu had gone to university in the capital and fallen for Nina, a native Londoner on his course. Somehow, Stu had gone to the teeming metropolis and found a woman with the home-making qualities of a West Country lass, like his mother. She was sturdy, with a slightly ruddy complexion and thick, fair hair like her husband's, only longer. They had married a month after graduation.

For a pair of teachers, they'd done remarkably well thanks to her local knowledge and Stu's earthy practicality. A year after graduating they'd bought a wreck of a house on the border between a well-to-do and a down-at-heel neighbourhood. As Nina had predicted, the latter had become trendy and their house had multiplied threefold in value. Ian, the professional money-man, had not done nearly so well. He'd arrived green to the capital and spent two years studying for exams whilst the market had gone up without him. Before he was priced out altogether, he'd panic-bought into a small apartment block in an already gentrified street. His unhappiness had increased when he'd gone so far as to calculate what Stu and Nina's pensions would be for their public sector non-contributory schemes. Even factoring in the cost of a child, with another due in four months, he knew they'd do well. He was also envious of their longer holidays, and what he perceived as fewer working hours.

He queued for a card, flowers and a bottle of decent red, thereby extending a quarter-mile journey to twenty achingly slow minutes. When he arrived at their house he was dripping with sweat and reeking of beer. Stu let him in with a smirk and nodded him towards the knocked through kitchen-living-dining area. He pecked Nina on the cheek as she accepted the flowers and card. "Sarah not coming?" she asked.

As he sat down at one of the two empty seats he said, "She's left me." Looks were exchanged between husband and wife. "Yesterday. Got home and she wasn't there."

"Oh, I'm so sorry to hear that," said Stu, uncorking the red wine Ian had given him. "D'you know why?" He poured a glass and handed it to Ian.

"Just…" he waved his hands over the steaming plate of casserole and rice that had appeared in front of him. "Just, that was it, I guess. No reason." He took a sip of wine.

"How are you feeling?" asked Nina.

Rather drunk, he wanted to say. "Great," he said. "World's my oyster. Free at last. Cheers." He took a large gulp of wine and topped up his glass.

"But you've been together years," said Stu. "I can't believe you're being so flippant."

"I'm going to have a bumper sticker saying 'Accountants write it off'," said Ian.

"Except you don't have a car, you wally," said Stu.

"Ian, if that's the way you feel, get yourself on one of those internet dating sites," said Nina. "Get back on the horse that threw you."

"Horse? I'd have said fucking *moose*," said Ian, shovelling in another mouthful. "Or bitch."

"Ian!" said Stu. "Listen to yourself. And stop that swearing. Jeremy might be asleep but I want his first word to be three letters — 'Mum' or 'Dad' – not four."

"Sorry. It's just that there was no word, nothing."

"Where's she gone?" asked Stu.

"Dunno. I phoned her and she wasn't what you'd call talkative. At least not in a 'miss you' kind of way. I mean, she wouldn't be would she?"

"There must have been *some* reason," said Nina, with what Ian took to be a nod at his wine glass, which was already half-empty again. He rolled his eyes at her.

"Look, you didn't know us at university. It was just a convenient relationship in our last year-and-a-half there. It was a mistake. Really."

"Some mistake, living together four years," said Stu.

"We met at a party, ended up in bed together and it all went badly wrong after that."

"Doesn't sound bad to me at all," said Stu. "She's a lovely lass."

"You don't understand," said Ian. "It was never like that. She kept dumping me but always came back."

"A lot of men would love a woman that faithful."

"It restarted as a shag-of-convenience when she was settling in London. Except that when you're living with someone it's not so easy to dump them."

"Apparently it is, though," said Stu, finishing his casserole.

"You two make it all look so easy."

"Oh, no," said Nina. "It's not easy. You have to work at relationships."

"And how do you know Sarah wasn't the one for you if you don't know who you're looking for?" added Stu.

Ian often felt he was back at school when he was talking with these two. "Look, what I want is sex," he said. "I don't want to end up regretting for the rest of my life all the shagging I never did at college."

Stu and Nina looked at each other. "You don't think we have enjoyable sex?" asked Stu.

Ian helped himself to more red. "That's not what I mean. I want variety. I want to play the field before I get old."

"Well that's not the road to happiness," said Stu. "And my mum's been nursing Aids patients."

"You're not even thirty," said Nina. "You've got your whole life ahead. There are plenty of wonderful women around. Take my friend Betsy – she's lovely and she's newly single like you."

"Betsy? A woman called *Betsy*?" said Ian. "I don't wish to appear ungrateful, or judgemental, but even her name puts me off. She sounds either like a cow or a seventy-year-old. Or both."

"I think you've had quite enough to drink," said Stu, taking Ian's glass away from him. "How much did you have last night, and how much have you had today?"

Ian knew not to bother even reaching for the glass. Stu was his father's generation now. It was as if aliens had snatched him up and reprogrammed him. He resisted the temptation to stab him to see whether he bled red or green.

"You need fresh air," said Nina. "You've been cooped up in that flat by yourself. The pair of you take Jeremy for a walk. I'll wash up."

Ian helped clear the table while Stu went through the pilot's check-list of life-support equipment required to launch Jeremy and his pushchair for a thirty-minute orbit of the local park.

"Sure you're up to this?" asked Stu as they left the front door. Ian's withering stare was lost on Stu's serious face.

They walked in silence for a minute or two. Ian was savvy to this police procedure. He wasn't going to crack first and spill his guts.

"So have you told your parents about Sarah yet?"

"No."

"They were quite fond of her, you know."

"I know."

"And I think they had their expectations."

"I know."

"Because they're not getting any younger."

"...."

"And your sister's got two daughters. I 'xpect your dad'll be wanting you to carry on the Bourne name."

"This is *my* life, Stu. Okay, it's not glamorous: I'm an accountant. A *forensic* accountant, mind you. Remember when we were ten? I wanted to be an astronaut. From astronaut to accountant in nineteen years. Game over. I never even applied to become an astronaut. I just got the 'naut' bit of astronaut: nought; nothing. But you know what? All the major rock bands have tour accountants. Maybe NASA has mission accountants? But even then it's unlikely they'd ever blast me off to calculate the depreciation of a satellite, isn't it?

"But you, Stu. I swear I could see it when we were young. You were programmed to Do The Right Thing, to find a sensible woman like Nina and produce the next generation of Lloyds. Bingo! Mission accomplished right on schedule. Stuart Lloyd can return to Earth."

Stu stopped the pram. "Is that really what you think?" He placed a powerful hand on Ian's shoulder and looked him straight in the eyes. "You think this is all a game? You're dealing with people's lives, my friend. Your parents wiped your arse and fed you. Just be grateful. And bloody grow up."

"Sorry. It's not a criticism of you. I'm happy you're happy. I'm just not ready for this stuff yet." They resumed walking.

"Which is probably why Sarah left you," said Stu. "She's another one not getting any younger. It's different for women, you know. You ever thought of what there was for her in your relationship?"

"Well, she had a flat for free."

"Great. She didn't own a *share* of the flat. No commitment from you."

"I said the flat was for free."

"Material things again. You're a natural-born accountant, aren't you? Nothing emotional. Remember when I got that beautiful old mini Cooper when we were eighteen? You told me all the running costs and said I'd be better off with a bike. That was – hang on – *six years* before you qualified. Christ, I can't imagine what it must have been like living with you. Did you tell her how much it cost every time she put the kettle on?"

Ian's mind flicked up yesterday's CPF calculation in his head and Stu saw the hesitation in his friend's face. "Bloody Nora, you did, didn't you?"

"She paid the electricity and gas bills, that was the deal," he blurted. "I just didn't love her. And it was a two-way thing. She never loved me."

"How'd you know?"

"She never said it."

"Doesn't mean to say she didn't. Lawyers are always careful about what they say, aren't they?"

They retired to the pub, where Stu was more his old self and less the parent – though his father was evident in him. As they sat there talking, Ian envied him for this settled contentedness.

Fast-forward eighteen years and he could see Stu – same seat, same pint but with Jeremy a young man, supping bitter with his father.

He got back to his empty flat around six, with stocks to replenish the alcohol he'd consumed. He ate the microwaved meal he'd bought on the way home the previous day – Sarah's meal. He had five shirts to iron for the coming week. Each one had been chosen by her, on painfully boring shopping expeditions. She was all around him in his clothes. Wherever she was, he hoped her heart was breaking.

Nina's advice struck him as good. He took the laptop out of the spare bedroom-cum-study, sat on the sofa and booted it up. A search on the word 'dating' produced a list of candidate sites. He took a fancy to M—.com, which promised sophisticated personality matching and a money-back guarantee if he didn't meet someone 'special' in six months. Most importantly, it promised more single women than any other site. If Ian knew anything, it was that life was a numbers game.

He dithered over choosing a user name. 'IanBourne' didn't give him the necessary anonymity. 'BourneBoy' sounded too boozy and BourneAgain made him sound like a Christian fundamentalist. 'BalhamIan' gave too much away about his location, or sounded like a Bohemian, which he most definitely wasn't. The system told him that 'Ian' had been used so many times that he would have to have the suffix 832 after it. He typed in 'Forensic' and the system accepted it. He entered his credit card details then rubbed his hands together at the prospect of access to this magical world of available women.

But the system wanted to know a little about him first. Irritated, he put in his date of birth. He rounded up half an inch and put his height at five-eleven. Then he entered his weight from his student days. From a list of body types he selected 'Athletic and Toned', since he'd kept himself in good trim whilst an undergraduate. Hair: Brown, Eyes: Blue, Glasses: No, Smoker: No, Drinker: Occasional (well, he reasoned, he didn't drink that much during the week), Diet: Always Healthy (the microwaved meals were usually low-fat), Kids: None, Want Kids: No.

He hesitated and then changed his answer to Want Kids to 'Maybe'. He didn't want to put anyone off. It wasn't going to go that far without him being able to back out, was it? He clicked Next.

Hobbies and Interests, said the headline. He stared at the screen. There was a list of everything from martial arts to poetry, gardening to rock-climbing, scuba diving to sky diving, tai chi to feng shui. He estimated the number of rows and multiplied by the three columns. At least sixty hobbies and interests. And he didn't do any of them. Cinema? He'd not been in years – downloading the video a few months later was cheaper. Reading? He managed to get most of the way through a doorstop-sized airport thriller once a year on a Greek island.

He stared into the vacuous abyss of his empty life and felt very, very sorry for himself.

Sarah could have filled in any number of things: tennis, running, reading, aerobics – even the occasional horse ride, or a bit of water skiing on holiday.

Greek island beach holidays once a year. That surely qualified him to tick 'Travel'. He looked again. 'Pubs' and 'Eating out' came to his rescue. Then he thought about what sort of woman he'd meet. He didn't want someone who just ate out, went to pubs and travelled. She'd be expensive, for one thing. And she'd not have quite as good a body as Sarah. Or be as interesting. Nina was right: he had to make up his mind. What the hell *did* he want?

He saved his entry, logged out of the site and put the laptop aside. He did the only thing that any self-respecting bachelor could do in his situation. He went into the spare bedroom and reached on top of the wardrobe for the one pornographic DVD he'd smuggled back guiltily from a stag weekend in Amsterdam several years ago.

Taking it back to the living room, his blood rose as he savoured the collage of photos on the cover. This DVD was an old friend – his sure-thing date for a lonely but intimate evening when Sarah was away. He hit the eject button on the DVD player and popped open the box. There was a yellow note stuck to the disc:

> Found years ago. How long before you resorted to this, you wanker – one day or two? S.

His mood was now one of defiance: he was determined to enjoy himself. This was the kind of sex he wanted – young and perfectly toned women in athletic positions. And tomorrow he was going to go out and get it. He grabbed a beer, pressed play, settled back in the sofa and loosened his trousers.

Chapter Three

Monday morning: up at seven with a fierce hangover and a tremor in his hands. No morning glory because he'd spent the last of his libido with an American threesome – two college-age girls and an older man – just after eleven o'clock the previous night. A knot tightened in him at breakfast as he realised that he'd be coming home to an empty flat that evening.

The tube felt particularly cramped and he half-expected to see Sarah in his crowded carriage. By breaking the London Law of Commuting and examining his fellow passengers, he noticed how many attractive women there were in his age-range. He set to thinking on what his age-range was. Plus two and minus five, perhaps? So maybe thirty-two at a push, and twenty-four at the lower end. He thought back to the time when even a twenty-four-year-old had seemed mature and unobtainable. As an undergraduate, he'd longed to be taught what one of their number must know about sex. And now one of them would consider him very much the older man. He shuddered. But if he lay in bed with a thirty-two-year-old he'd probably hear her biological clock ticking, and be tricked into fatherhood. He wondered what people think of him if he dated a twenty-year-old – lucky bastard or filthy lecher?

An attractive brunette caught him staring at her a second time. He turned his attention to the posters. This whole dating business was full of pitfalls and he felt ill-equipped. He realised he'd never even started a relationship other than when he was a student. He could appreciate the certainty Sarah had provided: the shelter against a changing and hostile world. He must seek counsel from his peers.

He alighted at Chancery Lane with the other drones; the sullen clump of their shoes beating a Death March to the ticket barriers, which chirruped their greeting and slammed open with a bang that niggled his hangover. He waited his turn and was out: out into the roaring traffic of Holborn and an April shower of November intensity.

As the rain soaked through his suit he realised that his mistake was not so much to miss the forecast or to forget to bring an umbrella – indeed, an umbrella would have inverted in the squall – but to get out at Chancery Lane at all. He'd been doing it with Sarah every morning for four years, walking her the hundred yards to her office. The fifteen-minute walk from her office to his was the only regular exercise he got. Turning back and taking one stop on the tube would take just as long, and be an admission of defeat. Besides, rain of this intensity never lasted at this time of year, so he pulled his jacket around him, lowered his head and pressed on.

The security man – Ed? Ted? – smoking a cigarette outside Sarah's law firm in St Andrew Street nodded to him as he approached, and he returned the greeting. Ed/Ted thought twice and made a move to say something, but Ian waved and hurried on past against the rain. That was another relationship that would fall by the wayside. Hadn't Ed/Ted wondered why Sarah wasn't with him? She might be inside already. Perhaps the fellow was going to offer him condolences? He was sure news of her newly single status would be emailed around the office before ten o'clock. Doubtless there'd be junior partners with their eyes on a pretty young thing like her. There, he caught himself admitting it: he was still attracted to her. He swore under his breath and upped his pace to near jogging down St Bride Street, its cobbles gleaming in the rain like the skin of a snake.

As he waited to cross the wide expanse of Farringdon Street the rain became a cloudburst so heavy that the pavement disappeared beneath an effervescent layer of splashes. The wind gusted in from the exposed river-end of the street and blew his jacket open, soaking him to the skin. He clutched his jacket tight about him with his left arm and shielded his eyes from the deluge with his right. The last two hundred yards to the bottom of Queen Victoria Street afforded no protection at all. Every pedestrian light was against him so he chanced his life with the traffic in a bloody-minded dash to escape the angry gods of wind and rain. Cold water flooded into his shoes. As he passed Blackfriars station he comforted himself with the thought that it would only be a one-minute walk from tube to office from now on. This was the last indignity Sarah could wreak upon him. He was amongst his own people here. The lawyers massed to the west of Farringdon Street, except for the bear-pit of the Old Bailey. This was the outskirts of the City proper: an accountant's sanctuary. Even God was on the money-men's side, residing in St Paul's Cathedral, a couple of alleyways to the north.

The rain eased off in the last few steps to D'Arcy House and the sun burst brilliantly around him. He glanced up at the open bible carved in stone above the entrance by the building's original owners, the British and Foreign Bible Society. *The Word of the Lord Endureth For Ever* was inscribed upon its pages. It lent a certain authority and righteousness to his work, he felt. God in his Heaven kept a ledger on every mortal, but the earthly ledgers belonged to accountants. And not even God could help those who crossed *forensic* accountants.

Flushed and out of breath from the brisk walk, he shook himself off in the polished marble lobby and muttered his good morning to the security guard and receptionist, who hid their amusement well. He could have done with being earlier than ten-to-nine but he certainly wasn't late. Two people from another firm rode with him in the lift, backing away from his dripping clothing. A sideways glance in the mirror told him he looked dishevelled and pathetic. He was thankful there were no client meetings scheduled for that morning.

He got out at the fourth floor and squelched his way to the glass door. Woodcock and Tweed, said the big blue writing. *Forensic Accounting Division* was in smaller white lettering below. The office, just half a dozen people, was too small to have a full-time receptionist. Whilst the separation from Woodcock and Tweed's headquarters was to enhance the illusion of speciality, the reality was an unnecessary complexity to the administration and the development of an 'us and them' attitude. He waved his security tag over the sensor above the visitors' bell and went in. He made a desperate bid for the comfort of his desk across the open plan office but was stopped in his tracks by Peterson's voice.

"Ian, my boy! Looked at your diary, booked you in for a client meeting at half-nine." Peterson's office was situated so that he could monitor all his staff's movements.

He turned to his right, presenting his bedraggled state to Peterson with a pleading, open-handed gesture. "Morning, Donald," he said. "Bit wet out."

"Good God, man! What did you do, jump in the Thames?" Peterson surveyed him over his wire-rimmed spectacles, which perched almost at the tip of his nose.

"Might as bloody well, have. I'll go and sit under the hand-dryer in the gents' for ten minutes."

"Good idea. Don't want you catching a chill. Not our star young buck. Good weekend? See yesterday's rugger?"

Ian filled in a gap from Sunday: his regular mates at the Derbyshire had all been at Twickenham for some rugby match or other – a hospitality freebie he'd declined. He wavered over a response to Peterson, who was an avid rugby bore. It didn't do much for him, though normally he feigned a semi-interest for the sake of his career. But there was an opportunity to work an angle here. "No," he said, walking the few yards to Peterson's doorway and standing in it. He lowered his voice. "Sarah walked out on me on Saturday."

"My dear chap," Peterson raised his skinny frame from his chair, "are you alright? Come in, sit down." Ian flopped down in one of the two chairs. "Was it expected?"

"No. Came back from the pub on Saturday and she was gone. Turns out she'd been moving out all week."

"Bitch! You know what happened with Alice. No discussion, just some papers served on me. Thirty-five years and then *that*."

"It's not like a divorce. We were only living together."

"Joint mortgage?"

"My place entirely."

"Good man, that's something. I've told my sons never to marry on any account. 'Boys, keep your name on everything,' I tell them." He scratched his pepper-grey beard. "How long?"

"Living together four years, known each other a bit over seven."

"You're – what? – getting on for thirty. So that's about twenty-five percent of your life. Sixty percent of your adult life."

This was getting Ian down. He'd wanted Peterson to understand that he'd like some peace and quiet, and preferably not to be wrapped into a client meeting in – he looked at his watch – twenty-five minutes. "Who's the client and how can we help them?"

"Client? Oh, some group headquartered up in the Grim North. Look, I'm sorry – it's a bit of auditing work."

Ian gave a sigh akin to a death rattle. Auditing was for the brain-dead or the young and desperate to please. Besides, he was far too senior now to be going on this sort of thing.

"Now Ian, don't be like that. It's a key account for the Auditing division. Their finance director's an old chum of Messrs Woodcock and Tweed themselves. Needs someone heavyweight to go in there for show, you understand. Timothy Woodcock and Jonathan Tweed have even been known to go up there themselves on occasion. But Hendricks, who was going to go, is off sick and you, unfortunately for yourself, are free. Unless you're telling me you've conjured up a large money-laundering case between half-past five on Friday and nine o'clock this morning?"

"Sadly not. Go on, fill me in."

"I got the email late on Friday evening, together with PDFs of the accounts. Bit of a hoo-ha over some disappointing results I understand. The client would greatly appreciate it if he got some extra value for money by way of some gratis forensic accounting with his audit. Regional office in, let's think now, *Gosforth* is the account contact. Gosforth, now where in God's name is that?"

"Newcastle. Posh bit."

"Does Newcastle have a posh bit?" Peterson's question was genuine. To Ian's knowledge, the only time Peterson had spent outside London was at Oxford University – a move that hadn't even taken him away from Old Father Thames. Few were so provincial as native Londoners in Ian's view.

"Of course," he said. "It has some very posh bits."

"Ah. You were at university there."

"Business school."

"Quite. Old stomping ground, eh? Well, that may come in handy – speaking the lingo and all that. Now look, the chap's due any minute — William Armstrong. Get your jacket off and get yourself under the dryer."

"Just one thing's troubling me."

"Go on."

"Why's he come all the way down here, rather than just brief me at the audit?"

"You're a bit *too* suspicious sometimes, Ian. I think he was down here for the weekend and then got wind that there might be a change of staff, wanted to check you out. You know what millionaires are like, particularly self-made ones. Just watch out for the ego."

"Yes, but rule ES5 says we shouldn't be examining audited accounts that we prepared – another firm of accountants should be hired in."

"I didn't say it was the accounts we'd prepared that were suspect, my boy. You're doing an audit and looking into some suspect figures of his. As I said, it's a key account to Auditing, so it's a fair bit of kudos for thee and me if we can manage it well. You have your junior partnership to think of. And a chap like Armstrong will have a lot of contacts up there — get this one solved and we could see a lot more business coming our way from the Grim North. Think of your bonus. See you in the conference room in ten. Now get dried out."

On his way over to the gents', Ian waved a quick "Good morning" to the rest of his colleagues. This was a rude start to the week: not even a chance to check his email or grab a cup of tea. But there was the tantalising prospect of his entry into the partnership. He did a mental calculation of the percentage increase in his monthly take-home pay and made a quick stab at his first year's bonus. His heart lifted. He just hoped he wouldn't end up like Peterson, talking in a version of English which belonged to black and white films and must surely have been outdated long before Messrs Woodcock and Tweed had founded the business. But he supposed the firm's mock tradition provided some semblance of a brand image, albeit sepia in an age of silicon.

Serving such a small office, the gents' was cramped: a stall partitioned off one end of the room. To the right was a urinal and on the left was a washbasin with a mirror above it. On the wall adjacent to the washbasin and behind the door was the dryer.

He hung his jacket on the doorknob of the stall, grabbed a few wads of tissue from the dispenser, spread some on the floor under the dryer and stuffed others into his pockets. He took his shoes off and stood on the tissue, to absorb some of the water from his socks. Then he stuffed the tissue from his pockets into his shoes and put them on the floor.

The dryer was an automatic one. Rather than being able to press a button, he would have to ensure that some part of his body was underneath the nozzle. He took off his tie and put it on the top of the dryer to catch some of the heat. He undid a couple of buttons of his shirt, bent his knees and dried the front of it, his face level with the machine. The atmosphere in the small room was beginning to get clammy, even sub-tropical, but he felt much better. His trousers would be next. He undid his belt and the top button to give some slack and leant over backwards with his shoulders against the wall next to the basin. His wet socks provided good traction on the floor. He kept one hand under the machine and used the other to hold open the top of his trousers. He undid the zip to let in more air and leaned back a little more, doing the limbo.

The door swung open with considerable force, stubbing against his toes. He let out a yelp of pain and fell onto his bottom, his fall cushioned by his wet shoes. He sat there, his shirt and trousers undone, clutching his bruised toes and letting out gasps as the pain throbbed.

He looked up and saw a bald, stocky, middle-aged man in a dark blue blazer and grey trousers staring down at him. It could only be one person. He scrabbled to his feet and offered his right hand. "Ah, Mr Armstrong, I presume." Ian's trousers fell around his ankles. "Very pleased to meet you." He released Armstrong's hand and pulled his trousers up.

"Surely not *that* pleased to see me, son?" said Armstrong in a Geordie accent. "Mind if I use the loo, or have you got another performance in a minute?"

"Sure, sure! Just let me…." he took his wet jacket off the doorknob of the stall and put the collar of it over a tap on the basin. Armstrong squeezed past awkwardly and went into the stall. Ian mouthed swearwords at himself in the mirror as he fumbled with his trousers, tie and shoes. He grabbed his jacket and left the steaming hell of the gents' toilets.

He joined Peterson in the conference room next to his office. There was a black attaché case with the initials WGA embossed on it in gold. "Our chap's here," said Peterson. "Rose's bringing some tea and biscuits. They love their tea and biccies up North, don't they? Told her to bring in a big bowl of sugar, too."

"I, ah, bumped into Mr Armstrong in the loo. I think your view of Northerners is a little stereotyped, Donald."

"Five quid says he takes at least two biscuits."

"You're on."

"Another fiver says he takes sugar in his tea."

"Done."

Armstrong hesitated at the door when he saw Ian. "Come in," said Peterson, motioning him to a chair on the other side of the large blond oak conference table. "This is Ian Bourne. He's our Bright Young Thing. He's been in our forensic accounting division about four years now. Keen as mustard. Got his sights on a junior partnership."

"Aye, nice to see you with your clothes on, son," said Armstrong and sat down.

Peterson raised his eyebrows at Ian, who smiled back feebly, hoping his boss would assume it was a quaint Northern expression.

Rose, the office manager, came in with a thermos pot of tea and another of coffee, as well as an array of biscuits. She was a pretty East End girl in her late twenties who was always smartly dressed – dark blonde with big brown eyes, and a figure that would fill out later in life.

Peterson smiled as Armstrong reached for a chocolate biscuit. "Are you going to be mother, Ian, or shall I pour?" asked Rose.

"I think the lad's well qualified for the job," said Armstrong to Rose with a laugh. Confused, she left. Ian poured Armstrong a coffee, proving Peterson wrong at least on that point. Then Armstrong disappointed him by putting two sugars in his coffee and stirring it slowly.

"Good," beamed Peterson, catching Ian's eye. "So, tell us what ails you at Armstrong BioDiesel?"

"What *ails* me, as you put it, is that the bastard thing isn't making the bottom line it should, like." He opened his attaché case and half-threw a pile of accounts on the table.

"May I?" asked Ian, and reached for them.

"I had a brief glance at the PDFs this morning. I couldn't quite grasp your concerns," said Peterson.

Ian glanced over them whilst he listened to Armstrong give a potted history of his diversified group of companies and the BioDiesel offshoot. The surname Armstrong was common enough in Tyneside. He guessed the middle initial would be George, after the great engineer, and wondered if he was a descendant.

The company had been founded a few years earlier: a pioneer in the green fuels market. Armstrong had seen the change in attitudes and the margin of safety the subsidies and tax breaks would give him. As a bonus, he'd been able to label a lot of his expenses as research and development costs and write them off against tax. He was a shrewd businessman with the good sense to hire an equally shrewd accountant. From the group accounts, Ian saw that another subsidiary in Armstrong's little empire was a chain of filling stations throughout the North East, which had given him an enviable head start on any competitors. The man had a natural genius for business integration that Ian instantly respected and envied. His own father was in the cutthroat business of printing and had not taken Ian's advice to enter early into the digital market. Although the Bourne family business was still profitable, his father had missed the opportunity to step it up.

The two older men's conversation had moved on to rugby. Armstrong had a box at the Newcastle ground, which had long ago replaced Gosforth, and season tickets at Twickenham. It was obvious why the meeting in London had been convenient for him – he could write off most of the weekend's entertainment against expenses.

Ian cleared his throat. "I'm a little surprised your filling stations aren't taking more on non-fuel sales," he ventured. "Low tobacco sales due to competition from counterfeit tabs?" He curled his toes, hoping he'd pitched it right, particularly his use of 'tabs' in place of 'cigarettes', and the slight touch of his old Bristolian accent to indicate that he, too, was not a native Londoner.

Armstrong looked at him deadpan for the first time. "Aye,

right enough, son. Right enough." He took a sip of coffee. "But I can't do much over illegal competition, can I? Tell me what my *real* problem is."

Ian tensed. "I'm no consultant, but from a marketing perspective I'm surprised account sales aren't higher on the biodiesel."

"Aye, good lad," said Armstrong. He broke another biscuit and munched it slowly. Ian knew to keep quiet when a man of this ilk from Newcastle was quiet: deference was important.

Peterson wasn't so savvy. "As I say, he's our Bright Young Thing."

Armstrong ignored him. "Anything else?"

"I'd expect growth to be better than twenty-something percent." Armstong held his eyes. "For the amount you've invested in sales and marketing, and from what I understand about fuel trends. Just an opinion." Ian was conscious of curling his toes again. He was out on a limb on this one, and Peterson clearly hadn't spotted anything awry – either that or he was testing Ian's ability.

Armstrong munched the rest of his biscuit and Ian did his best to hide his unease. Peterson blurted, "Of course, Ian's still very much learning the ropes. You understand it's only an opinion. Twenty percent's pretty damned respectable."

Armstrong locked his eyes on Peterson. "*Never* undermine your own staff, they're the best asset you have. You have to let them develop their own opinions. As it happens, I agree with the lad."

"Statutory obligation, you see," said Peterson. "Opinion only, can't make judgements. Must issue strong caveats, first glance at the accounts. D'you follow?"

Armstrong ignored Peterson. "I'm off to Spain for a couple of weeks. When I get back I'd like you start on the audit. With regards to you adding some extra value by looking for fraud, keep it under wraps, do you understand? I don't want any gung-ho stuff, poncing around in flash cars and attracting attention to yourself. This is just the annual audit as far as any of my staff are concerned. Alright, son?"

"Yes," said Ian. "I'll do as much as I can from here."

"Right, gents. I'll love you and leave you." 'Armstrong took a card from Ian and examined it before pocketing it. He picked up his attaché case and turned to Ian as he reached the conference room door. "Nice meeting you, Ian." He looked him in the eye and gave him a firm handshake. He gave Peterson the briefest of handshakes and made his own way out before they could show him to the exit.

Ian followed Peterson back into the conference room and closed the door.

"What do you make of that?" said Peterson. "Bloody Northerners with their little chips on their shoulders. Still, well done — you obviously speakee el lingo. I just hope you can match his expectations. *Son*."

"I happen to like the way business is done outside London. Men like him do more for their communities than hedge funds ever did."

"Parochial, paternalistic nonsense. Well spotted though – nothing really stuck out from the page at me, I must say. You winged it pretty well, but for me I'd have preferred to let him come to me with it. I'll buy you lunch off the back of securing that bit of business. However, I'll be expecting a tenner out of you. Two biscuits, plus sugar in his tea."

"We're quits. You said he'd take sugar in his *tea*. He drank coffee."

"Bah," said Peterson. "Thank God you're away from that lawyer girlfriend. I dread to think what your offspring would have been like. Finish up on the Elmer account and help the others if they need it. Make sure you're free for when our Geordie lad gets back from Torremolinos." Ian made for the door. "Oh, look, Ian. About this Sarah stuff. You're putting on a brave face but if you need any counselling, then we do have facilities. I can have a word with personnel. We have, you know, *counsellors*, on hand for that kind of thing. Touchy-feely stuff. I, um. I found they were quite good. Just between you and me. You know, helped me reframe stuff. Anger and bitterness."

"Thanks," said Ian. "Thanks, Donald. I appreciate your concern. See you for lunch." The prospect of auditing work was far more likely to drive him to a counsellor than his loss of Sarah.

He felt heavy as he made his way to his desk, which sat in a three-sided cubicle with four-foot walls. He grunted another "Good morning" to his near-neighbours.

"New job?" asked Angela, to his left.

"Armstrong BioDiesel," said Ian. "Newcastle."

"Eee, by 'eck! I hope you enjoy your chip butties," said Angela, another one who'd never ventured out of the South East.

"That was a Yorkshire accent," said Ian. "Besides, it's *stotties* they have up there."

"Someone didn't have a good weekend."

"Sarah left me. No warning, no idea where she went."

"If you want to talk about it…."

"Then I'm sure I will. Thanks, but I'll be fine."

As soon as his PC had booted up, he checked his emails. Nothing from Sarah. He logged into his Hotmail account – just a load of junk, and a message from M—.com, addressing him as Forensic, confirming his payment and telling him to complete his registration. He realised what a lousy moniker it was, suggestive more of a serial killer than a Romeo. He resisted the temptation to log in.

What he couldn't resist was a quick email to Sarah. It was their unwritten rule at work to use company email. It was faster and allowed them to respond from their mobile phones if they were off-site.

> Just a quickie to check how you are. Hope we can still be friends. Nina and Stu were asking after you yesterday.

He pondered the sign-off before deciding that 'Take care' was suitable. He decided on a straight 'Ian' as a signature, rather than 'Ian xx'. He hit Send and opened up an email from Peterson, pointing to a folder on the server for all of the accounts of Armstrong's group of companies.

A new email came in and his spirits rose. But it was a 'system undeliverable'. He opened it up. 'Sarah Conway: address not found. Please check with your system administrator.' Surely not? He thought back to Ed/Ted that morning outside her building – he'd tried to say something.

He picked up the phone and dialled her number. "Perkins Botham, Karen Goodman speaking," said a Scottish voice. Karen was a colleague in Sarah's department.

"Karen, hi. It's Ian."

"Oh, hi Ian," Karen's voice pitched lower. "This is a bit of a surprise."

"Sorry?"

"You know, after Friday."

His felt a little adrenalin in his blood. "You mean after Saturday. She left me on Saturday."

"Oh. She left here on Friday."

"She *left*? She changed jobs?"

"Yeah."

"Where to?"

"Ian, I'm really sorry. If she hasn't told you then I can't. We have to protect people's privacy and I'd be liable if anything happened."

"What? What do you mean? What do you think I'm going to do?"

"Look, Ian. I don't know what happened between you. But she obviously doesn't want to have any further contact."

"Karen, this is *ridiculous*. You've been round the flat, for God's sake. Dozens of times. This is me: Ian."

"I just can't. You might want to approach her through her lawyers."

"She *is* a fucking lawyer."

"Ian, I'm really sorry, but you have to see it from my angle."

"Yeah, yeah. Look, tell her I was asking after her. Okay?"

"I will." She softened her tone. "I'm sorry it ended the way it did, really I am. Try to put it behind you."

"Sure. Listen, this doesn't affect business between us, does it?" Karen had referred a handful of cases his way over the years. Perkins Botham — fondly referred to as Perky Bottom by most – was a rich vein of new business for him.

"Of course not – it's my duty to recommend only the best to my clients."

"Thank you for saying that, Karen, I appreciate it. The same goes for my clients. Cheers."

"Thanks, Ian. 'Bye." She hung up.

He put his head in his hands. He didn't deserve this level of humiliation, did he? Had sharing her life with him for four years really been so bad that she would cut him off so finally and publicly? Counselling looked like an attractive proposition now.

Lunch with Peterson wasn't fun, with the older man telling him how lucky he was to be single and still young. In the afternoon he had a hushed conversation with Rose, who'd heard the news. She was one of those streetwise Cockney girls who seemed born for ancillary jobs in the City: resilient and highly organised, often far more intelligent than the middle-class graduates they tended. With his unstuffy provinciality, he and Rose had always had an affinity. If not exactly a close friendship, then at least a camaraderie. But, with the Blitz-like spirit of her ancestors, she didn't dwell on his change in circumstances. "Me Nan always said that the easiest way to get over a man was to get under another one," she said.

None of his colleagues were up for a beer or a meal that evening – too close to the weekend. He stuck his head round the door of the Derbyshire on the way back, but after the strains of the previous day's corporate hospitality at Twickenham no one was in that he knew.

After dinner he logged in to M—.com and looked at the profile he'd saved. He changed his body type to 'Normal', though he kept his weight the same. Perhaps he should lose some – thirty was looming large and he didn't want to end up a fat, middle-aged executive. He decided he'd have a night off the booze and finish off his profile. It looked like a lot of hard work.

About Yourself was the next prompt. '2,000 characters maximum,' it said. Words failed him so he clicked on the Help icon. 'Be sincere. Tell your date what interests you, what you're passionate about. What's your favourite food, or the wildest, wackiest thing you've ever done? How do you relax? What do you do at weekends? Show them what an interesting and inspiring person you are!'

He felt a sliver of fear stab his soul. No wonder she'd left him: even he didn't find himself interesting. What was there in his life but an endless succession of weekends at the Derbyshire? Even his favourite food would be the Sunday roast there. How did he relax? Jerking off to porn was hardly an answer, and with just the one DVD, he was neither a collector nor an aficionado. He opened up a Word document and typed:

> Half-hearted British male professional. Not interested in anything other than money and casual but unadventurous sex. No commitment given, none expected in return.

That was at least honest. Now, how could he improve on it?

> Easy-going guy. Dependable. Professional and ambitious. Sociable. Seeking to widen interests. Seeks similar female.

That was more like it. Five minutes later he'd worked it up to:

> I'm an easy-going south London professional who enjoys the good things in life. I have a full social life but would like to meet a special someone who will widen my interests. I'm loyal and dependable with a good sense of

humour.

He was happy with that and clicked Next.

About Your Date. His heart sank. The Help button told him to be very specific about who he was looking for. Right back to Nina's question. There was a series of multiple-choice questions, like the ones he'd filled in on himself. He set her academic standards high, and a minimum salary a few thousand below his. The age he set at 24-32, which he thought was reasonable. But after the last multiple-choice question there was a text field waiting to be filled. After a couple of minutes' thought he wrote:

Must have a good sense of humour and no hang-ups.

He clicked Next and got a patronising 'Congratulations!' message. 'Now upload a photograph – people with photographs get seven times more hits' it added in the small print. But he'd waited long enough for this moment: he wanted to see inside the gift box he'd bought. He clicked through and hit Search against the criteria he'd set. A list of contact names and photographs appeared, from as far away as Aberdeen and Torquay. He narrowed the geographic search to London and tried again.

He couldn't believe his luck – over 150 women, ranked by percentage match to his profile. And the first one – 83% – looked very attractive, too. Heartened, he clicked to view her profile.

He had no chance. She played sport 3-4 times a week, took holidays in exotic, named destinations from Machu Picchu to Marrakech, where she climbed mountains and used her fluency in three foreign languages to meet locals on their own spiritual plane.

Telling himself it was a fluke, he clicked on his number two match. If anything, she was slightly more attractive. She was short on words: 'I want a partner who can meet me on my own territory'. That territory extended from the bottom of the Red Sea, which was her favourite scuba diving destination, to the skies above Colorado for her paragliding.

Number three listed her most fun activity in the last year as having helped out at a shelter for the homeless on Christmas Day.

He hit the Next Page button several times to move down to the region of his 100-120th best matches, with 50% matching – whatever that was based on. There were few pictures here, which raised his suspicions, but he told himself not to be so shallow. After all, he had his own reservations about being seen here. He thought that one through a little. If he was seen, it would only be by someone else who'd subscribed, wouldn't it? And he could hardly be ridiculed for internet dating, could he?

He clicked on a match at random. Nothing inspiring, but nothing threatening either. A graduate his own age from south London. 'Looking for Mr Right to sweep me off my feet. Must be dependable and want to start a family soon.'

Nope.

Let them come to him, he decided. There were some digital photos on the hard drive from last summer's holiday. He had a quick look through. They were mostly of Sarah. He'd forgotten how good she'd looked back then. She always lost a few pounds for the beach and tanned beautifully. And he loved the way her hair lightened to blonde after a couple of days of sun. He reminisced about the leisurely sex they'd enjoyed at sunset one particular evening before heading out for a meal of fresh seafood.

There was one photo of him. More accurately, it was him and her. They'd taken a day-cruise to an island covered with ruins and another couple had taken a photo of them, his arm over her shoulder. His sunglasses went against the guidance in the Help menu. Nevertheless, he cropped the photo so that there was just the smallest piece of her outfit blowing in the breeze across the left of his body. Of course, his left arm was missing, cut off at the shoulder. Still, people would realise he wasn't an amputee, wouldn't they?

He clicked on the upload button. 'Thank you. Your photo will take up to 72 hours to approve.' He looked at his watch. This was no use to him at all. So much for the internet's promise of instant gratification and his visions of a date that weekend. He wondered how long it would take to manoeuvre someone into a first meeting, and to bed from there. He must be looking at weeks.

Dejected, he took a beer from the fridge and put the DVD back in the player.

He was just undoing his fly when the phone rang. He juggled his thoughts for a few seconds – should he let the answering machine take it and just get on with his entertainment? What if it was Sarah, and she was downstairs? He felt sufficiently lonely to be happy to talk to anyone. He turned the DVD player off, picked up the cordless phone and stabbed the button.

"Hello?"

"Hello darling, it's your mummy," his heart sank. He took back his generalisation about being happy to talk to anyone — this would not be an easy call.

"Hello, Mum. How are you?"

"Oh, we were just wondering how you were. Didn't hear from you at the weekend and then we remembered it was Stu and Nina's wedding anniversary, wasn't it? Did you see them and little Jeremy?"

"Yes, I saw them yesterday and they're fine. They asked me to send you their love."

"Oh, that's lovely, please give them mine. And how's Nina's baby?"

"Strangely enough, the foetus wasn't saying much." He turned the DVD back on and hit the 'mute' button. He could at least use the time to get past the compulsory copyright notice.

"Oh, don't be like that. You know what I mean."

"Nina's just fine. Everyone's fine. How's Dad?"

"Oh, he's fine."

"Good." He tried not to let the irritation creep into his voice.

"Then that's fine."

"Your sister's got a date fixed for Hannah and Natasha's christening in June." In his mother's habits, lack of an 'Oh' at the beginning of a sentence signalled the beginning of the real conversation.

Naked bodies had begun writing on the screen. Even though he'd watched the DVD countless times, it still had a hold over his imagination. "Date?"

"You know what I'm like with dates. The second Sunday, here at home. I did tell Sarah that might be the date, so I'm sure she's got it blocked off in the calendar for you."

He was cornered. "Sorry, what date?"

"Second Sunday in June. I asked Sarah to block it off."

"Sarah probably can't come."

"Oh! Why's that? Hannah and Natasha love her, and I think Jane even considered her for a godmother."

"Mum," there was no anaesthetic for this operation. "Look, Mum. Sarah left me on Saturday."

"No, it's on a *Sunday*."

"Mum, you're not listening. Sarah left me. Don't expect her to come to the christening."

"*What?*"

"She moved out on Saturday. I'm sorry."

"But *why*, Ian?"

"I think we just drifted apart." The DVD was reaching one of his favourite moments. "Look, I'm really upset and I don't want to talk about it now. Okay?"

"Now I'm worried about you. Where's she gone?"

"I have no idea. She doesn't want to talk with me and she's changed jobs." He heard her mother sniffling. "Don't worry about me, I'll be fine." He heard the phone being passed over. His heart sank further.

"Hello, son."

"Hi, Dad."

"You've upset your mother."

"No I didn't. Sarah left me, that's what upset her."

"You know she adored Sarah."

"Apparently Sarah didn't adore the family enough to want to be part of it."

"Now don't be like that," said his father in a stern voice.

"Dad, she left and she seems glad it's over. End of story. I have my own life to lead."

"You have to learn to think of people other than yourself, Ian. You're not getting any younger and neither are we." Stu had read Ian's father all too well. Perhaps they were in cahoots?

"Dad, I'm sorry. I'm really not in the mood. I've been put on a really good case at work and I can get stuck into it. If I can get this one under my belt then it's a junior partnership." He heard a quick snort from his father: real work was managing businesses, not being a parasitic bean counter. And there was the sensitive topic of succession at the family firm, in which Ian couldn't even feign an interest.

"Just be there on the tenth for your sister, will you?"

"Of course I will." His favourite girl in the DVD was fellating another actor, and he loved the scene that followed. "Look, I've got to go – I have to mug up on this case for tomorrow."

"Right. I'll let you go then. Look after yourself, okay?"

"Thanks, I will. 'Bye." He didn't wait for his father's farewell before terminating the call.

"Fuck!" he shouted, and hammered his fist into the sofa. He turned the volume back on. It took him half an hour to regain a semblance of enthusiasm. Even then, his mood wasn't quite right and he did no more than go through the motions. He was dreading the tenth of June, but no excuse in the world would be acceptable to escape the christening of his nieces in Bristol.

Chapter Four

I am sexy girl with good look. I enjoy the preparation of food. I am fit and like very much to float, making competition when girlhood. In summer I take boat on river for exercise, sometimes to fishing. Chemical engineer is my degree in final year which big potential for money.

I like very much London but am not so far gone. Its very fashion place, in particular for girl with good lookings.

Russian men not so handsome like you, and not so faith with wives. I find you fascination and interests, also good looks. You would to like me – very full of faith and loving. I look forward to expect from you soon!

Marina

There was a low-resolution image of an attractive peroxide blonde at the bottom of the email, with brief details stating that she was twenty-three and a student in Ukraine. A hyperlink urged Ian to log in to M—.com and look at the rest of her details.

He'd come in early on Tuesday morning, determined to finish the Elmer account ahead of time and get himself into Armstrong's work. The end of the financial year had seen the office deserted on days other than Mondays and Fridays, with most of his peers out with clients, though Peterson was a constant presence.

Rose had heard his snigger. "You know the rules," she said in her cheeky Cockney voice. "Share it with the rest of the class."

He automatically clicked on 'minimise' and spun round to see Rose at the open end of his cubicle, mug of tea in hand.

"A bit too late, Mr Bourne," she teased. "Was that a young

lady you was lookin' at?"

"Just an email from a friend."

"Good to see you're on the bounce from Sarah. Go on, let's 'ave a look at her."

"Really, it's nothing. My first email back from a dating site."

"Got much interest?"

"Early days."

"You could get a bit more interest if you lost weight."

"What? I'm not fat, am I?"

"I've noticed the lift gets to the ground floor a bit faster with you in it, that's all I'm saying. I bet you've got an inch on your waist for every year you've been here. If you don't take care of yourself, don't expect anyone else to."

"But I think I still have a certain sex appeal."

Rose sniggered. "I'm sorry," she said. "I just don't see you as 'sexy'."

"You can't be an arbiter of taste for *all* women. You're not my type, for a start."

"With respect, Ian, I don't think your type is a Ukrainian either. I think you ought to crack it with British women before you move onto something more exotic, don't you? Go on, let's 'ave a look at your profile."

"Absolutely not."

"Only offering to help."

"I'll let you know when I need it."

Rose's assessment of his weight gain had been painfully close to the mark and he resolved to change his ways. He'd tried gym membership before but he'd not liked the wait to use machines covered in sweat, the communal showers, or the expense.

At lunchtime he went to a specialist running store up near St Paul's. He was quite turned on by the ministrations of the attractive female shop assistant, herself obviously a keen runner. She seemed to know exactly his type and, indeed, there was another male of a similar age in the shop being fitted out for a pair of running shoes. Was he following some biologically programmed stage of ageing? What proportion of men had these awakenings? The thought of asking the shop assistant for a date went round his head a few times before he discarded it. The art of the pick-up had always eluded him, and it had been a whole seven years since he'd been successful – further ones having been thwarted by Sarah's inopportune appearances at parties. His head swum at the steepness of the learning curve he faced.

The shoes cost him twice as much as he'd expected, and that gave him an added incentive to get value from them. During a quiet patch in the afternoon he searched for advice on the internet for losing weight. Losing twenty-five pounds should put him back to the trim physique of his early twenties, when he would run three times a week to relieve academic stress. The more serious sites cautioned him to seek medical advice before so much as putting one foot in front of the other, and that a loss of two pounds per week was the safe upper limit. At that rate it would take three months, which would be late July: there was no way he could wait that long. His view was that it was all common sense – eat less and exercise more. Twenty pounds was a more realistic target but drastic measures were called for. He'd often managed on one meal a day plus snacks as a student, so surely there was no reason he couldn't do it again.

He left work on time and bypassed the Derbyshire. It took some searching, but he found his old gym kit. The bulge of his belly under the T-shirt made him self-conscious as he walked briskly over to Clapham Common, where he upped his pace to a gentle jog. The belly had a life of its own, bouncing noticeably, and his self-consciousness turned to outright shame. How had he let himself go so badly? After less than a hundred yards he was quite out of breath and eased back. A pair of women whipped past, conversing, and with no audible panting. The sight of their athletically toned bottoms spurred him on – he ached for a body like that in bed beside him again. His increase in pace lasted all of fifty yards before his vision was clouded by swarms of black dots, and there was a peculiar sensation of light-headedness at the back of his eyes. He walked for another hundred yards to recover, then jogged at a slower pace. The one-mile route he'd mapped out in his street atlas took him nearly fifteen minutes. Back at the flat he managed a few sloppy push-ups and twenty sit-ups.

Dinner was a low-fat microwaved meal that provided no comfort. He examined the label on a can of lager for its calorific content before putting it back in the fridge. He looked briefly at the attractive females on M—.com to strengthen his resolve. As he suspected, his photo had still not been uploaded onto his entry, lending the lie to the Ukrainian's comments about his good looks – she must send out dozens of emails hoping to hook an unsuspecting fool. His entry was labelled 'New'. He realised that any women who'd been looking for a man for a while would probably search for all the new men coming onto the site, and that his lack of preparation had blown his chances.

"You look like death warmed up," said Peterson. "Sure you don't want counselling?"

"I didn't sleep much last night," said Ian. He winced as he hobbled his way to his desk. He returned Rose's snigger with a deadly look. If there was no gain without pain, then last night's advance had been immense – not a single muscle in his body spared him agony. His stomach had rumbled all night but he'd resisted the temptation to eat. He'd read somewhere that after the first two or three days the body expects less. It made him wonder just how much it had been expecting in the first place. Breakfast had been a banana, and he longed for a plate of hot, buttered toast.

No email from Sarah, although he knew Karen must have told her by now of Monday's conversation. The one ray of hope was an email from M—.com telling him that his photo had been uploaded. The bad news was that, due to his sunglasses, it couldn't be used as a 'primary' photograph – his profile would still appear photo-less on the main listing. Only if someone were to click on his profile would they be able to see his image. He stood up. "Rose," he called. "Can you give me a hand, please?" She came over.

"I need a photograph," he said.

"Anyone or anything in particular? Would Sir like the Tower of London, or perhaps something more exotic like the Taj Mahal?"

"Me. For the dating site. Could you oblige, please?"

"I knew you'd come back begging for help, my boy."

"Just a photograph will do for now, thanks."

"What, *now*? Have you looked in a mirror recently?"

"I have to have *something* up. And it takes up to three days before the bloody thing's approved." He handed her his mobile phone and showed her how to work its camera function. He stood against a wall and smiled as she looked at the image on the phone.

"Love, I've seen healthier-looking corpses. Let me put some make-up on you."

"I don't want to look like a bloody transsexual."

"I think you'd look quite nice with a bit of make-up. You should lose your inhibitions."

"Please, just a straight head and shoulders job should do. You get seven times more hits if you have a photo."

"Yeah, but looking like that you're just going to attract Goths or necro-whatevers."

"I'm sure weirdos have their own specialist dating sites. I just need the photo to show that I'm not some monster. They can see from my other photo that I'm fun and go on holiday. And that I tan."

"It's all about personality too, you know."

"I'm not worried about that – once I've got them hooked I can take it from there." Rose raised an eyebrow and smirked. "Look, just take a bloody photo, will you?"

"That's better – anger brings so much more colour to your

face. Now if you'll just smile. No, that's a grimace. That's better. A couple more?"

They scrolled through the photos and settled on one, which he emailed to his Hotmail account. "Go on," she said. "Give us a look at your profile."

"I can't. You know the internet's monitored here. I can't be seen logging in to that kind of thing during office hours, can I?"

"Don't see why not. Staff welfare, isn't it? Never been any bother for me."

"You're not in line for a junior partnership. Oh, alright – maybe on your machine tomorrow. Look, thanks Rose. I appreciate it."

Lunch was a banana and an apple, which he'd brought with him. He chewed on each mouthful twenty times but still felt empty. Boredom turned his thoughts to M—.com and his ill-prepared debut on the site. With such a long approval time, the sooner that photo was loaded the better. No one had ever said anything over the use of non-work email accounts like Hotmail. And wasn't M—.com simply another communication website? He was aware of certain clauses in his employment terms, but he thought they were more geared towards gambling, pornography and conducting business other than that related to his own employment. Everyone spent hours planning holidays and buying books online. Besides, it was his lunch hour and he'd been in since eight.

He logged into his Hotmail account and clicked on the link to M—.com. If anyone did have an objection, he could say he'd pressed the link by mistake. Entering his password, he realised he'd just invalidated that excuse. With a schoolboy's trepidation, he downloaded the photo from Hotmail onto his hard disk and then uploaded it from there into his dating profile, receiving notification once more of the approval time. A click on a 'Who has viewed me' link revealed that only Marina the Ukrainian and the 50% match woman who wanted to start a family had viewed his profile, presumably after seeing that he'd viewed hers. He was confident his fortunes would change.

For the first hundred yards of that evening's run his body screamed at him to stop, but he made it a further fifty yards until he did so. The muscles warmed up and the pain receded, if only slightly. But it gave him hope. He'd remembered to time himself properly using the chrono function on his watch. With a time of 12:41, he felt like a champion. The bathroom scales said he'd lost two pounds. Although he knew that was probably accounted for by the weight of the food he'd not eaten in the last twenty-four hours, it spurred him on. He did feel somehow fresher and more clearheaded, though he had to concede that that also might be due to other factors: namely the lack of alcohol. Underneath that, there was a certain weakness from the lack of food.

After his shower, he noticed that the answering machine was blinking. He put his meal in the microwave and listened to the message. There was the sound of a crowded bar. "Ian? You there? Pick up." It was Rob, one of his Derbyshire mates. There were mutterings and laughter in the background. "Mate, we're wondering where you are. Look, sorry to hear about Sarah. Plenty more fish in the sea. And it's your fucking round, you tightwad, so get your arse down here. Get in touch, alright?"

He could be there in half an hour and enjoy a couple of hours of company. As he savoured every last morsel of his low-fat meal he thought long and hard. What would he get out of it? For a start, he'd undo some of the work he'd put in the last two days. And the odds of meeting a suitable single female were close to zero. Unless, of course, Giacomo was on the pull.

Giacomo, or Giac – pronounced 'Jack' – as he was more commonly known, was a classic ladies' man. His tall and dark Italian good looks, excellent fashion sense and gift of the gab made him irresistible. Rob and the others could teach Ian little, if nothing and, besides, they were mostly in stable relationships that were heading towards marriage. If anyone could give Ian a masterclass in the art of the pick-up it was Giac. For one thing, Ian had noticed that he didn't hang about much in the

Derbyshire, apparently using it as a safe haven from his conquests. Indeed, Ian had seen him deftly turn down occasional brazen advances when drinking there. ("Not the right quality, mate. And never shit on your own doorstep," was how he'd put it to Ian one Friday night.) That was a lesson in itself: if an expert like Giac wasn't looking for action in the Derbyshire, then nor should he be. He contemplated calling Giac for some initial counselling, but pride told him to wait until he'd at least had a go at the internet dating.

He logged in to M—.com and under his profile ticked Running as an interest. He felt a real sense of achievement at having been able to do that. Suddenly he was a much more interesting person. Indeed, he reasoned that being able to tick that one box must have bumped him up the percentage matches for dozens, if not hundreds, of women all over London, and that it must act as some kind of deterrent to the less fit amongst them. And by the time he'd got himself in a position to date, he'd be slim and trim – with an improved libido to match.

Thursday morning was less painful, though he drew more remarks from Peterson and Rose about his haggard looks. He relished those comments because they were confirmation that it wasn't just his imagination telling him that his suit felt much looser on him.

At lunchtime he bought a literary novel with a pretentious-looking front cover and credible highbrow quotes on the back. It was his first novel in God knows how long and he read it in favour of the paper on the way home. That evening's run saw his time down to 11:58 — a full forty-four seconds faster than the previous evening. He was now four pounds lighter – that couldn't all be explained away by lack of food. He felt new hope surging inside him as he logged in to the dating site. His photo had been uploaded. It wasn't his best, but at least his profile was now scientifically proven to be seven times more attractive than previously. Then he noticed that he had a new message in his

Inbox. With a tickling of adrenalin, he clicked on it. It was Marina again. He opened the message:

> I miss your email so much today. You probably too get tired to read my email, but to me my life, even in brief simply would be desirable to write to you. I will think that you to write to me, I to hope for it. I with impatience shall wait from you for the reply and the information which you to want to inform me. I to wish successful your day. I to hope that we with you is very strong to make friends. How you to consider? I shall hope that we to find out a lot of interesting the friend about the friend.
>
> Your ever friend,
>
> Marina

He was tempted to write back. A wild part of his mind wondered if any low-cost airlines flew to Ukraine, and whether he might spend a couple of weeks out there, living like a prince, being courted by desperate Ukrainian would-be émigrées. The beeping of his microwave brought him back to reality – he was light-headed with the lack of blood sugar.

His reason returned after dinner and he realised he was able to tick Reading as an interest. If he continued to fill out his character at this rate he'd be fending off love interests in a fortnight.

He struggled to the end of the second chapter of 'this challenging and witty polemic against suburban carports' before resorting to his DVD, telling himself he was too tired to appreciate subtle humour. He chose to ignore another call from Rob down at the Derbyshire. "You can run but you can't hide, fat boy," Rob said into the answering machine. Ian later lay awake wondering if it was just a turn of phrase, or whether he'd been spotted running on the Common. A certain pious resentment kept him awake. The Derbyshire crowd were stuck in unchanging lives, with the same girlfriends. He was going to break free of all that – they'd be laughing on the other side of their faces in a month's time.

Friday had him in a conundrum. Although his stomach had begun to accept the lack of food, it didn't stop him thinking about it. Nor did it stop him from thinking about the weekend, and his neglected social life. He felt tetchy and worn down. No more emails had been forwarded to his Hotmail account from M—.com, in spite of his photo being up and his extra interests having boosted his profile nearly two-fold.

Peterson hailed Ian as he walked past his office at quarter to six. "Fancy a pint?"

"No thanks, Donald. I have to get home. Stuff I have to do."

"I'm quite concerned about you, Ian. Your behaviour's been somewhat erratic this week and you're not looking well. Are you sure you don't want to have a chat with this counsellor lady? She's very good, you know. I need you to be in tip-top condition for this assignment with Armstrong, and it's only the week after next."

"Really, I'll be fine, thanks. I'm just sorting myself out. Have a good weekend."

He struggled with the carport polemic on the tube, calculating that, at the present rate, the 328 pages would take him a month to finish. The pull of the Derbyshire was strong, but he was determined not to undo the week's work. He would increase the length of his run instead. He struggled around the circuit twice, and surprised himself with a time of 22:09. He'd run double the distance in less than twice the time. The scales told him he was five pounds lighter than at the start of the week. He'd be on target in a couple of weeks – less if he redoubled his effort. As a reward, he couldn't help but pick up a four-pack in his local off-license. To offset the extra calories, he replaced dinner with a packet of dry-roasted peanuts. The alcohol would help him sleep through any hunger pangs.

He logged in to M—.com. One email in his inbox, and he knew who it was from before he opened it.

Why to not write soon? I am impatiently growing for your response.
With love,
     Marina

He resisted the temptation to write back. Even some cutting remark would be misinterpreted as a come-on and he'd surely be swamped with email.

Emboldened by the alcohol coursing through his veins on a near-empty stomach, he decided to seize the initiative. His running breakthrough had proved that he was the master of his own destiny. He would email one of these girls.

He did a new search. With his own entry altered, he noticed a different ordering in his matches, and some new faces. He remembered what Giac had said about not shitting on his own doorstep and picked one from north London. She was quite pretty – not as attractive as Sarah, but he had to start somewhere. She listed her job as marketing, and liked to visit museums, art galleries and pubs. Wine-tasting and cooking were amongst her other hobbies. On that basis, he reasoned that she couldn't object to his penchant for real ale. He clicked on the Help function for advice on writing her an email. 'Show them you read their profile by talking about their interests. Be positive and witty.'

Quarter of an hour later he'd managed to refine his message to:

> You won't gather dust with me in a museum because your picture's a real portrait. You won't W(h)INE when you're 'cooking' with a man of TASTE like me!

He clicked the send button and continued to search for suitable females. There was a button which allowed him to send a

'Wink' to anyone he fancied. He set a new set of characteristics in his search criteria, trimming down the size of the body he'd be happy for his date to have, and taking the age range to 20-30 years. The bottom line was that it was a numbers game, so he sent a Wink to the top ten in his search results.

Chapter Five

As he lay in bed the following morning with a mild hangover and a raging erection, he wondered where Sarah was and how she was feeling. He replayed in his head the last sex they'd enjoyed only a week before. After he'd masturbated — a box of tissues now strategically positioned on the bedside table – he lay back and let his mind drift.

They had met at a party in Jesmond, a trendy suburb near the university. It was before closing time and he'd gone early, equipped with half a dozen cans of lager, which he guarded jealously. The party was in one of the massive three-storey late-Victorian brick houses that had been allowed to run down as student digs in the last recession. With several bedrooms and generous, high-ceilinged communal spaces, they were affordable, and ideal for large parties.

Sarah had been wearing a black skirt that didn't quite reach her knees, and his gaze had been drawn from across the room to her black-stockinged calves. He'd noticed that she'd been hitting on the same guy – a student known for his succession of good-looking girlfriends – for quite some time, and seemed to be struggling to hold his interest. She caught him looking at her and flashed a smile.

He refocused his attention on Valerie Craven, a local girl he'd fancied since the first year of their course. Like him, her father was a small businessman who wanted her to take over the reigns of the family company – an automotive engineering firm that fed parts to the Nissan car plant in Sunderland. Although she didn't reject the possibility entirely, her plan was to earn her stripes in someone else's business first. Ian knew she was more than capable of attaining a senior management position at an early age, and they were both in a group of five students whose grades consistently outclassed those of the others on the course. Her middle-class Geordie accent was only slight, and he enjoyed her ability to think her way laterally through problems, as well as to manage the people around her – even fellow students – in a disarming way. She was a trim, sporty type with a gleaming white smile, high cheekbones and pure blue eyes. And there was something about the way she brushed her short black hair back behind her little left ear that drove him crazy. Tonight he'd finally got her interested, pulling witty comments from thin air. He was just the right side of intoxication not to get carried away, and felt about himself an aura of unstoppable good fortune that evening. Like a sportsman at the peak of his career, he was scoring point after point – and the crowd at the back of his head was cheering him on to what was sure to be a glorious victory.

He broke away to get food from the kitchen before the main body of guests slewed their way in from the pub. As he filled two paper plates Sarah sidled up to him and reached past for the last sausage roll, brushing against his left shoulder. He made some remark about loving someone enough to give them his last roll, a weak pun on a popular TV advertisement of the time. She countered with a witticism of her own and turned to face him, trapping him in the corner of the room. He couldn't work himself up to push past her towards the main party, and every time he thought he would get away she pulled him back into the conversation, pinning him in the corner with a relentless series of engaging, open-ended questions he felt obliged to answer.

Within two minutes she'd begun to pick the food off the plate he'd filled for Val. He felt powerless, as her magical field of assertiveness held him there. The crowd at the back of his head was screaming at him to sprint that last hundred metres, or to hit the ball with that extra ounce of energy and cover himself with glory. But the amateur in him played up and played the game before him at that moment, rather than the championship match that – for that night only – he could easily win in the living room. Greatness beckoned, but some self-sabotaging program forced him to play safe. He played his world-class lines on a Sunday league match.

Five minutes into the conversation he spotted Val at the top of the two steps that led down into the kitchen. She had seen enough and turned away. It took him a further twenty minutes to break away from Sarah, by which time Val was deep in conversation with the guy Sarah had been trying to chat up. Insult was added to injury by the fact that they'd both helped themselves to his supply of lager. There were two cans left and it was only half-past eleven. As he picked up the remains of his hoard he felt someone brush against him. Sarah.

"Do you love me enough to give me your last can?" she asked. Without waiting for a reply, she took one of the two remaining cans and popped it open. "Cheers," she said.

Her gall amazed him. She'd wrecked his evening, perhaps even his life, and continued to nail him in place with endless badinage. He resigned himself to it. He couldn't face the long walk back to the pavilion with the crowd booing him. There had to be a runner's up prize. Even though he didn't actively like her, he could see the potential before him. He pulled himself together and set about the task with a vengeance as they sipped their warm lager.

There was no spare booze to be found, and the best a cab firm could offer them was an hour's wait. They both lived in Fenham, a three-mile walk over the main roads that traversed the Town Moor – an area of common land still used to graze cattle. She suggested they walk it because, she said, she was enjoying his company. And so they set out in the chilly early hours of a Sunday morning in March, the bitter east wind at their backs, whistling through the leafless branches of the dormant trees along Grandstand Road.

She was from Nottingham, was the same age as him, and had also taken a gap year prior to coming to Newcastle. Whilst he had spent his working at Andrew Bishop, the small firm of accountants in Bristol that his father retained, she had used her year to work her way around Europe, with a three-month leg out to the Far East. She was reading English but planned to take a Common Professional Examination postgraduate at the university before becoming a trainee solicitor. Although he found business studies interesting, he envied the conversational range her degree would give her later in life. Whilst he'd be able to bore for Britain about Maslow's Hierarchy of Needs and the psychology of employee motivation, she'd be able to talk with authority and passion about great literature. The intensity of his course and his dedication to it meant that he'd never had time to join any clubs other than business-related ones. He'd talked to her about the family business, and the conflict with his father over whether he would take it over or pursue a profession. She'd been sympathetic, having seen the pressure there had been on her two elder brothers. What had spurred her interest in a career in law was that everyone expected her to become a teacher, which she found to be a patronising and sexist stereotyping.

With a mile to go, it began to rain. It wasn't a hard rain, but with an easterly wind behind it they were sodden and cold by the time they reached her shared house at the top of Wingrove Road. It was gone two in the morning. The walk and the rain had sobered them, and they'd huddled together on the walk to help keep the cold off.

He lived only a few hundred yards away in the maze of streets to the east of Wingrove Road, but she invited him in to dry off and get warm before continuing his journey. They made their way quietly to the cold communal kitchen and brewed tea. He remembered being surprised that it was no tidier or well-kept than that of his all-male household. If anything, it was worse.

She put a fan heater on in her bedroom and they sat next to each other on the bed, warming up. He slowly put his left arm behind her then squeezed her hip. She dropped her head onto his shoulder. He kissed the top of her head. She turned to meet him with her lips.

He'd only had a couple of relationships before, and they'd taken months of careful groundwork to initiate, and neither had lasted more than a year. As Sarah and he removed the last of their clothes and slipped under the covers of her bed he couldn't help thinking that, were it not for her, he might be enjoying the much sought-after delights of Valerie Craven's body. But then he turned his thoughts around – Val was in his tutorial group, and he'd have jeopardised the delicate balance of personalities. That had been a source of terrible anxiety to him. What if he'd crashed and burned when it had come to trying to kiss her? Sarah was a risk-free, no comeback play, safely insulated from his circle of friends. He was about to increase the number of women he'd slept with by fifty percent and, into the bargain, achieve his first-ever one-night-stand.

"Shit," she said.

"What?"

"My period's just started."

She pulled a dressing gown off the chair by the side of the bed and went to the bathroom. He stayed put, hoping she'd not want to send him away disappointed on a first night.

They kissed some more after she got back, but even in the confines of the single bed she somehow managed to avoid any physical acknowledgement of his erection.

He spent an uncomfortable night and suffered a dead right arm rather than seem disingenuous by waking her. But there was no interest in his morning glory, either. Indeed, she seemed forced out of bed early at penis-point, eager to get him out of the door before her housemates discovered she'd picked someone up so carelessly. They agreed to meet for a drink at the local pub that evening.

He arrived alone at the Prince of Wales and saw her sitting in a corner with two girls who turned out to be her housemates. It wasn't what he'd expected and he found the conversation difficult. The previous night's loquaciousness deserted him and it was only after his first quick drink that he'd relaxed enough to lose his awkwardness. He and Sarah trailed behind the other two as they walked home.

"I had to make sure you weren't some kind of nutter," she said.

"And what sort of guarantee do *I* get?"

He could never be sure, but that remark might have contributed to the two further weeks of dating that it took to get her back in bed. It rubbed salt into the wound of his resentment over the loss of his chance with Valerie Craven, and he never forgave her for it. Somehow he'd managed to go from a bird in each hand to one in the bush.

He returned to Bristol in April for another six-month placement with the accounting firm. He and Sarah had been going out for a month and been sleeping together for two weeks, during which time they'd made love five times. The sex had been great as far as he was concerned; he was getting to know her likes and dislikes, and he'd taken to holding her hand in public. On his first day back at the accounting firm he opened up his Hotmail account. There was an email from her: she was dumping him, citing upcoming second-year exam pressure. He put it down to experience, and looked forward to what Bristol in the summer could offer.

Bristol had plenty to offer, but not to him. After they'd left school, his friends had scattered to the four winds. The ones who'd not taken gap years had graduated and were stuck into their careers – either in the far-flung towns in which they'd studied, or London. Those who were in their final years were not there until early summer – and even then only fleetingly before they holidayed prior to taking jobs elsewhere. Having been working in the accountancy firm since he was eighteen, he was now very much a part of the team. He was out of synch with his friends and his generation; stranded prematurely in a career. He was best man for Stu at his marriage to Nina, and was the proverbial only spare prick at the wedding – unless he'd taken a fancy to Stu's widowed grandmother. Serious adulthood had begun and he had missed all the fun. The only social life he had was with colleagues from work – ones he might spend the rest of his working days with. Whenever they went out he would spend the evening gazing at Bristol's beauties – the luscious sun-ripened legs and cleavages of female youth. That glorious, golden summer it was all on display but tantalisingly out of reach.

That was the summer he decided he'd move to London when he graduated. He'd always had a provincial allergy to the Big Smoke, but now there was nothing left for him in Bristol. In July he was offered a proper trainee position in the accounting firm as a matter of course when he graduated. When he turned it down, the managing partner was stunned. And when his father discovered Ian's intentions, he hit the roof – at least whilst he was at the accountants in Bristol there was some hope of him joining the family business.

So when he received an email from Sarah in early August asking him to join her in France for a week, he was on a plane in 24 hours. They were with two other couples – female friends of hers with their boyfriends – sharing a villa in the Loire Valley. He didn't click until after the second day that he might have been a late substitute for another man. He never said anything to her about it – with his complete lack of an alternative sexual opportunity, he didn't want to rock the boat. And the sex was great, facilitated by the pleasant surroundings, great food and affordable wine.

They'd taken separate flights back to their local airports. Apart from a weekend in Nottingham when her parents were away, there was little other communication until they were back at Newcastle. She dumped him a fortnight into term without explanation. He was slightly more put out this time but, again, he didn't protest his case: with the extra experience from the relationship he was sure he could do better. He launched himself with renewed vigour into the social scene for his final year, convinced that his relative wealth and worldly authority would be a hit.

At the start of November it looked as though it might be a better year: Valerie Craven had taken an interest in him again. On a couple of occasions he'd been in the bar of the students' union and she'd broken away from friends to talk with him. He was neither confident nor competent with women by nature, but he'd seen her friends look over with knowing smiles. On both occasions he'd been about to move on to other pubs with his own friends and hadn't had the courage to ask her to join him but, the third time the students' union had been his destination because there was a black and white outfit night. He'd opted for a black suit, white shirt, black tie and black shades to look like one of the Blues Brothers. Val had waved at him from the other side of the room and he'd gone straight over. After a few minutes he noticed that the other girls had melted away and they were alone at last. His suit lent him confidence, and he found himself in the same flow as he had been with her several months ago.

It was like a scene from a movie when it happened. The expression on Val's face changed and then he felt an arm around his stomach, a kiss being planted on the right of his neck. The weight of the person behind him made him stagger forward and he spilt half his drink over Val, who gasped and threw her empty hand up. "Ian! How are you?" said Sarah, letting him go and pushing in front of Val. "Let me buy you another. What are you having?" And before he could even protest he felt her hand on his shoulder, guiding him towards the bar, leaving the shell-shocked Val mopping her blouse with a tissue and looking at him with a curious mixture of anger and disbelief. From that day on, he only ever acknowledged her with a wave or smile – he was too embarrassed to try again.

The part of his mind that was a single male in his twenties had welcomed the return to sex with Sarah. They opened presents from each other on Christmas morning and he called to thank her. It was her mother who'd answered the phone and she knew who he was, and they'd exchanged pleasantries. They went up to Edinburgh to see in the New Year together with friends. But after they returned to Newcastle on the second of January she dumped him. At least this time she had an explanation: it was her New Year's resolution, and a specific reason made it easier on him somehow.

But then in the small hours of the morning a few days later he'd asked himself a simple question: what, exactly, had the resolution been? If it was so that she should be single and free to concentrate on her final year, or to be with someone who shared an esoteric philosophy that she'd got into, then he could feel happy about that. But if it was to give up being with losers, ugly boyfriends or boring people, then he was very pissed off. Wounded pride kept him from asking her during occasional encounters around campus or in the Prince of Wales. He never saw her with another man, and it nagged at him that their sex might have been so unsatisfying for her to prefer celibacy.

In February he thought long and hard before popping an unsigned Valentine's card in the post. It was one of those cards that wasn't about unrequited love, but more along the lines of fond friendship. He was sure she knew his handwriting well enough to recognise it from the envelope. But it proved to be yet another year where his lifetime's ambition of receiving a Valentine's card was not fulfilled.

A few days later she invited him to dinner and took him to bed afterwards. He accepted the renewal of the relationship without question. He no longer bothered to try to understand whatever was going on inside her head. In March they marked their first anniversary in a passing comment, but without ceremony. They stayed together over Easter but she finished with him a month before their finals. His parents came to his graduation and he felt a question hanging in the air over his single status, since most of his friends were joined by partners from home or Newcastle.

A couple of days later he was surprised to be invited to Sarah's graduation, and to have lunch with her parents at an expensive restaurant that must have been reserved weeks in advance. He felt a little used but suppressed the resentment and played the loyal boyfriend. Indeed, he took a genuine liking to

Sarah's parents. They were a pleasant couple – general practitioners who'd met at medical school. As he lay next to her after they'd made love that night, he wondered what the future held for them.

They had a fortnight in the Loire Valley again. It felt comfortable and permanent, and he was less fearful of adulthood. He kept the peace at home with his father by providing cover for office employees on holiday, and streamlining some business processes.

His graduate traineeship with Woodcock and Tweed started in early September; Sarah's Common Professional Examination began a couple of weeks later back in Newcastle. He paid a peppercorn rent to Stu and Nina as they refurbished their house, helping them out occasionally with small DIY jobs. They were over a year into their marriage and working hard at their careers. He was working long hours and studying for his exams and it might have been too much for him if he'd not had them to fall back on. From September to November he and Sarah managed five weekends together – three in London, two in Newcastle. She finished with him on his last trip to Newcastle, citing exam pressure. That was one of the more disappointing times for him. He'd got a career and money, had begun to put down roots in London, and was developing a fondness for her. But it felt final. He was a dyed-in-the-wool accountant, and it was clear that her assertiveness and relentless way with words would make her an excellent lawyer.

They kept in touch loosely. He sailed through his exams and she took a position with the Nottingham branch of a national firm of solicitors for two years, and lived with her parents to get her finances in order. He bought his two-bedroom flat and had been in it just a few months when she called. She had been promoted to her firm's head office in London and needed somewhere to stay whilst she found somewhere more permanent. It had taken all of ten days before a tentative touch on the hand from Ian had turned into sex, and instant cohabitation. That one touch had meant four years of Sarah. His parents had loved her, and they'd even been allowed a double bed in the guest room at the parental home.

And there he lay alone in bed, a week after her final dumping of him, four years on. He'd been played for a fool, and he wanted the last laugh. What had he gained from the whole relationship? It had been steady sex and companionship for four years. One thought weighed heavily on him: the sex he could – and should – have had with other women in that time. Besides Valerie Craven he was convinced there were probably three or four other women he could have had had he not been in this on-off relationship. The thought of the loss of the delights of those unknown bodies distressed him.

That was when he had his brilliant idea. His trip to Newcastle to investigate Armstrong BioDiesel would be a perfect opportunity to track down those women he should have slept with all those years ago. The last he'd heard, Valerie Craven was still working in the area. And there were two or three other girls who'd been on his course with whom he'd always fancied his chances. He'd not have to go through this pretence of dating, since some kind of relationship had already been established. He could just turn up with his slim undergraduate physique and his successful London career and see who took the bait.

He skipped his morning banana to cut down further on his calories, since he wouldn't be going to work, and made do with some green tea that Sarah had left. The previous evening's two-mile run had stiffened his leg muscles somewhat, but that afternoon he was able to run the two miles in 21:47. Now that he'd reached a certain threshold of pain, and had a tangible goal, he found he was able to push himself on for a further mile at the same pace. At this rate, he'd be fighting fit in no time. He felt a new air of certainty about himself that he liked.

There were three messages on the answering machine when he got in. Two were from Derbyshire friends – Rob and Chris, both wondering whether he'd be joining them for lunch. The other was from Stu, checking to see how he was. Lunch at the Derbyshire was clearly out of the question, and he could pretend he'd been away in Bristol for the weekend. Stu was a different matter.

"Hi, Stu."

"How are you, boy?" asked Stu in his Bristolian drawl. "You been awful quiet. Y'alright?"

"Fine, really, thanks. You'd be proud of me. I'm getting fit. Running every day on the Common. And I've cut down on the booze."

"Oh, that's good." There was a pause. "Still nothing from Sarah?"

"Not a dicky bird. Given up trying to contact her. She's moved jobs too, you know. And her colleagues won't let me know where she's gone."

"Your ma was asking if I'd give Sarah a call, so that's put the lid on that one. Have you tried calling her parents to see if they can mediate?"

"I'm very touched at everyone's concern, but rumours of my suicide over this one have been greatly exaggerated. There are plenty more fish in the sea and we were clearly unsuited at some deep level. In fact, we were really unsuited at quite a shallow level, Stu. Do I miss her? Yes, like people miss a favourite sofa or a childhood toy. But we don't go around pining for them, do we? Or marrying them for that matter."

"That's quite a callous way of putting it, me old mate. It's obviously left a bitter taste in your mouth. Have you thought about talking to someone about it? You know, a professional?"

Ian groaned. "I'm doing the Ian Bourne therapeutic regime, Stu. It's a winner. It involves getting fit, getting laid and getting a promotion. It's a holistic approach that works on all parts of the mind, body, penis and paypacket. The only thing it doesn't cure is altruistic interference from well-meaning relatives and friends."

"Your ma's worried about you. She doesn't like the thought of you being alone in London."

"Stu, she's worried because my father is driving her spare. You know the story: I won't take over the business and now I refuse to sire the next generation of clones."

"I won't press you on it. But remember that me and Nina are here for you. And if you're going to get into this sleeping around business just remember to be careful."

"Look, I appreciate it, mate. I'm just a bit tired." They said their goodbyes.

He went to the supermarket by a circuitous route to avoid passing the front of the Derbyshire. He dithered when he got there because his diet meant that most of the food was off-limits. He settled on organic carrots and broccoli, as well as bananas and apples, plus a tin of tuna in brine. He ate a couple of carrots raw for lunch.

He felt exhausted, and unable to read more than another twenty pages of *Carport Cornucopia*. The author's name sounded like something used to restrict traffic, and he wondered if that had influenced his choice of subject matter. Then he remembered Sarah had bought him the book after he said he'd half-enjoyed a biographical film of the man's childhood under Japanese wartime occupation. Was it his last literary joke, and was Ian the only one to get it? After an unsatisfying early dinner of microwaved tuna and boiled broccoli, he allowed himself the luxury of turning on his laptop and logging in to M—.com.

He looked at his previous evening's email to the girl from north London and felt embarrassed. There were no emails for him, and only a couple of the women he'd winked at had even bothered to view his profile.

Sunday morning's high point was his run: ten pages of *Carport Cornucopia* emptied it of joy. The Derbyshire's draw was strong, but he wasn't yet ready to unveil the new, slimmed-down super-stud Ian Bourne; and the women he'd winked at on M—.com had evidently been too busy dating to check their accounts.

He needed to get out of the flat. His mind settled on galleries and museums – a large proportion of the women's entries had mentioned them. It would be another box to tick on his profile if he were to wander around a few. What's more, they were free, and surely offered at least some chance of meeting single women.

He ironed a clean pair of jeans, careful to make sure the crease was at the stitching, rather than the front. The shirt he chose was one Sarah had told him was a favourite, as was the jacket. His clothes felt much looser, and he drew his belt in an extra notch. If his weight loss continued he would have to invest in a new wardrobe next month, and he hoped Rose would be able to advise him. The mirror confirmed that his shadow of a double chin was less obvious, even to his newly critical eye.

He loved London on sunny spring Sundays, when it had rolled back its winter cover of grey sky. The air was fresh and the crowds were thin: not yet swollen by the teaming tourists who frustrated the natives with their sudden stops, or by clogging narrow pavements and tube entrances with chaotic groups. And the women. The women came out in force from their cold bed-sits and flats, undressing to compensate for the months of enforced insulation. There were so many of them, so attractive to Ian's eye that he scarcely knew where to look.

But not one of them was single. Or, more correctly, not one of them was solitary. Those who weren't holding the hand of some lucky man were in unapproachable pairs or trios. It was the same everywhere he looked.

However, frustrated though he was, he dutifully toured Tate Britain – although he balked at the price of a ticket to the Turner Prize exhibition, before deciding it could be a date for a lucky woman – and the National Gallery, then wandered around the British Museum.

The trip left him culturally enriched enough to tick the 'Museums and Galleries' box on his profile when he logged into

M—.com that evening. It also left him hungrier than ever for a broadening of his sexual experience. But there was nothing doing from the women of M—.com – the spring weather had evidently lured them away from their computers. He wondered whether he'd come close to any of them on his trip around town.

His single DVD had lost its allure. The same bodies, the same motions and sighs could only do so much for him. He made a mental note to take a trip to Soho in the next few days for some new films – variety was the spice of life.

Chapter Six

"Donald wants to see you in his office," said Rose, resting her arms on the top of his cubicle.

"About…?" asked Ian.

"About now," she quipped.

Ian rolled his eyes at Rose. She leaned over a little more and lowered her voice. "Well, we's all noticed you're losing weight and we're a bit worried about you. Bless 'im, I think he's worried for your 'ealth." Ian let out a sigh and got to his feet. "By the way," she asked, "'ow's it going with the dating stuff? Much luck over the weekend?"

"Not a sausage."

"Early days, eh love? They do say there's someone for everyone. My offer for help still stands. I'd love to give you a makeover, my boy."

"Thanks, again. Perhaps when it's life-threatening."

"Now, now. Don't be sarky, Mr Bourne." She led him over to Donald's office. His heart sank further: Rose's ceremonial behaviour signalled that this was bad, and weariness weighed on him with every step. She stopped at the open door and knocked gently. "Ian for you."

Peterson looked up over his specs. "Ah, Ian. Thank you, Rose."

"Would you like some tea or coffee?" she asked. Ian hoped this didn't mean a long haul ahead. Both men declined and she closed the door behind her. Peterson motioned Ian to a round meeting table in the corner. They drew up chairs.

Peterson cleared his throat. "I think this whole Sarah thing has hit you harder than you think, Ian."

"No, really I—" He was silenced by a wave of his boss's hand.

"You look terrible, you're losing weight and you're listless. Classic signs of depression."

"Really, it's just that—" Another wave, accompanied by a

stern look.

"Been through it myself. With this new European health and safety stuff we can't afford to overlook these sorts of things. And you should be starting on this whole Armstrong business next week."

"I'm sure I'll be fine, honestly."

"Anyway, we can't afford to take chances. Liability insurance over employee health and all that – I'm sure you've seen stuff in the papers. So I've arranged for you to have a little chat with a professional."

Ian's heart sank, and he felt a little flutter of fear. "Exactly what sort of professional did you have in mind?"

"Oh, I think the official title is occupational psychologist. You know, counselling. As I say, been through it myself. Look, here's the card. It's about a ten-minute walk, over in College Hill. Booked you in at four this afternoon, so early bath for you as a bit of a treat, eh? Nothing to worry about, have you right as rain in no time at all." Peterson rose and Ian followed him to his feet. "Chin up and all that. Best foot forward." He motioned Ian to the door and sat back behind his desk. "Won't go on your record."

"Um. Thanks," Peterson's lack of eye contact had done nothing to reassure him.

Ian left Peterson's office, wondering what it must be like to be one of his sons, and whose side they'd been on in their parents' divorce. He ignored inquiring looks from colleagues and slumped down at his desk, feeling stigmatised. Whatever Peterson said, it would be a blot on his record. The senior partners would perceive him to be a weakling.

The Elmer report was in its final stages and he was just mopping up now. He logged into his Hotmail account in the vain hope that someone might have sent him a decent joke.

There was an email from someone with the name WhichHazel from M—.com. He glanced around the top of his cubicle walls before clicking on the message.

> Hi Forensic,
>
> Thanks for the wink. You don't say much in your profile. What did you do with your weekend? Pub and footie with the boys? ;) What's with the funny nickname?

There was a small photo of a moderately attractive woman of thirty-one on the bottom of the email. He felt a peculiar mix of elation and panic. He glanced around again – then clicked on the link to her full profile.

She was in marketing, with a salary similar to his. She liked most of the things he purported to like, but also tennis – though probably just for those two Wimbledon weeks of the year, Ian mused – and TV soaps. He could forgive the former, but couldn't bear the latter. However, most things were a compromise and he could live with limited exposure to soap operas if there was regular sex within a reasonable timeframe. But what was the meaning of her little remark about the pub and football? Did she like her men blokeish, or was she teasing an apparent shallowness on his part? His own profile hadn't given that much away, and he'd not listed any sport as an interest, other than running.

He skimmed through what she'd written on her profile. It was the usual mish-mash of thoughts, but he did glean from it that she liked her men intelligent, humorous and truthful. Her politics she listed as 'Liberal' – whatever that meant these days. Mercifully, he'd ticked the 'Middle of the Road' box, which he interpreted as a great get-out to enable him to appeal to a broader range of women, whilst still appearing to be politically aware enough to have at least ticked a box. She had indicated that she was looking for men aged 27-39. He felt a pang of guilt when he realised he'd reset his range of suitable women to 20-30 when drunk the other night. Still, the fact that she was a year over the range he'd stated must surely mean she was keen.

He felt a surge of optimism. Today was Monday. If he

played his cards right then he could have a date at the weekend – by which time, if he applied further restrictions to his diet and pushed his exercise regime, he ought to have lost a few more pounds. He checked his watch: hours until lunchtime. He should really be working, but he had to show some early interest — who knew how many winks and emails were flying her way this morning?

> Last weekend I read some of Carport Cornucopia, a humorous polemic about the loss of London's front gardens to cars. I went for a run on Clapham Common every day, which is my routine. On Sunday I went to Tate Britain, the National and the British Museum. I found nothing British in the latter but the Tate was sweet (!). I'm a forensic accountant so that 'accounts' for my nickname!
>
> Ian :)

He hit send and hoped for the best. There was no reply by the time he left at quarter to four for his appointment with the counsellor.

College Hill was in the maze of narrow alleyways between St Paul's and the Thames. He announced his name over a speaker at the door and was buzzed in. An attractive receptionist – Hair: Blonde, Length: Shoulder, Build: Petite, Eyes: Blue, Glasses: No, twenty-three, five feet six, he noted in his newly-learnt dating shorthand – gave him a toothy smile and he accepted a cup of tea. He sat down on one of two small black leather sofas. The premises were much classier than he'd been expecting — a real oak floor and modern art prints with pencil signatures to indicate their limited number. He couldn't help wondering what the cost of this session was going to be. He hoped it had all been amortised through some policy or other – the last thing he wanted was a large cost logged against his name on his personnel record.

When the receptionist put his mug of tea on the glass-and-chrome table in front of him, he was disappointed to notice the engagement ring on her finger. She sat back behind a white counter and focused her attention on a workstation with a chic-looking screen. Numbers multiplied in his head.

"Ian?"

He looked to his right and saw the smiling face of an Asian man in a suit looking at him from a half-open door.

"Yes?" He stood up.

"Would you come this way please? I'm Dr Patel. Please, call me Raj." He shook Dr Patel's hand. The man's warm smile was contagious. "Please, do bring your tea with you."

Ian followed Dr Patel down a short corridor in the same décor as the reception room, with doors leading off it. Dr Patel held one open for Ian then closed it behind himself. He gave Ian an open-handed gesture to a soft, black leather armchair. Ian sank into it and put his tea down on a coaster on the small mahogany table between him and the doctor. This was not what he'd been expecting. He felt relaxed and comfortable.

"Welcome," said Dr Patel with another infectious smile. "So, please tell me why you've come to visit me."

His relaxation vaporised. "What?"

"Why have you come to visit me?"

"My boss told me to."

"Of course, Ian. He has your best interests at heart. Why do you think you're here?"

"Well…"

"Just relax. We have plenty of time. There are no clocks ticking here."

Dr Patel was wrong: Ian could hear a time-bomb ticking in his head. How much was this man charging per hour? Every minute he spent here was another step into the red on his record. This was a loaded gun to his temple: he had to be succinct.

He told Dr Patel that Sarah had left him nine days before, and that his boss was over-concerned because he'd misinterpreted Ian's planned weight loss as depression. He glanced at his watch. Five minutes gone. Did Dr Patel charge in quarter of an hour increments? He could wrap this all up in another five minutes and show himself to be keen by going back to the office.

"That's a very plausible story, and you're a very intelligent man, Ian," said the doctor slowly. "Of course, it's perfectly acceptable to be upset about the loss of a long-term relationship. Sometimes we hide these feelings of betrayal and disappointment away from our conscious mind, and it manifests itself in ways we don't ourselves see. These things can run very deep."

"No, really. I'm quite shallow, Doctor. Er, Raj."

Dr Patel smiled pitifully at him. "No, I think you're a very sensitive and compassionate human being, Ian." He let some silence hang. Ian found it menacing. "Tell me, it must be quite difficult being away from your family right now. They are in Bristol, I understand."

"Honestly, it's a blessing in disguise. My Dad wants me to take over his company so that he can retire, and both my parents want me to have children. They loved Sarah. Believe me, I'm more than happy to be away from all that."

"Hmm…" said Dr Patel. "I always think of Bristol and London as *opposites*, you know."

"…?"

"Both are great seafaring cities. London sits with her legs spread open to the East, and to the rising sun. Birth, you understand. Bristol faces the setting sun in the West, associating herself more perhaps with death. Don't you agree?"

"What about Newcastle?" Ian blurted desperately.

"Hmm? This is where you were at university? Dear me. I think you can take an analogy too far, don't you?"

"But I wasn't the one who…"

"What was it that you didn't do? Tell me now. Don't be shy."

"Look, I'm not depressed. I'm perfectly happy that Sarah left me."

Dr Patel stared at him meaningfully for a few seconds, holding him in an awkward gaze.

"I'd just like to put the last four years behind me and get on with my life. I really want this junior partnership."

"You're so brave, my friend." Dr Patel leant over and touched him on his forearm. "What help can we give you with this?"

Ian let out a desperate little laugh. "Help?"

"Yes, let's maybe talk over some key objectives that you want to achieve in the next few months. Get you back on your feet and functioning."

This was more like it: goal setting was something Ian understood very well. But he still felt a little guarded. "You mean, like my junior partnership?"

"Yes, but I'd like to see you more fulfilled in other areas of your life. You must have put a great deal of work into this relationship over the last few years, and now you have to fill that gap. Am I right?"

"Yes," he lied, "there's a big hole. Obviously I'm getting my physical health in order—"

"Although I'd like you to eat properly. Do go on."

"But I really think I need to work at other relationships."

"Oh, *definitely* you need help with other relationships. You are very right to say so." Ian mentally rubbed his hands with glee at the prospect of professional help in sorting out his sex life. "And I must say that it's wonderful to see that you're so excited at the prospect. I think your first goal must be to sit down with your parents this weekend. Go and spend quality time with them. Let them know your feelings."

"I'll be seeing them for the christening of my sister's children in June." Ian cleared his throat. "What I had in mind was getting back on the horse that threw me."

"That is hardly a realistic goal, Ian."

"Why not?" Ian wondered if the receptionist had given him a low attractiveness rating – or whether he was exhibiting some kind of pathological sexual condition that needed treating.

"You said Sarah was not responding to your attempts to communicate with her."

"Oh," Ian laughed. "No, I mean getting *another* girlfriend."

Dr Patel stared at him again for a few seconds. "But suppose you experience the same level of damage again? How much can you realistically sustain without jeopardising your work?"

"Look, the whole point is that I'm fine, Doctor. Raj. I want to get back out there and enjoy myself."

"That's really very commendable."

"One of my goals is to go on a date this weekend. I've not been on a date in over seven years. In fact, Sarah and I never really dated. It all just happened."

Again, Dr Patel kept his gaze for a few moments. He sighed. "Well, I can see that you're a very determined man, Ian. Please, don't get hurt. Be strong and brave."

Ian hoped his face wasn't betraying his incredulity at this man's lunatic ramblings. "Yes," he said, mustering his sincerity. "I'll be brave and strong, Raj."

"Excellent." Dr Patel rose to his feet. "I'd like to see you again in two weeks to check how you're doing. My thoughts will be with you." The infectious smile was back and Ian felt the tension of the consultation lift from him.

"Thanks, Raj. I do feel a lot better with all that off my chest," he lied.

"Good man!" said Dr Patel and opened the door for him. They shook hands and Ian walked back to reception, where he booked himself in for an appointment at the same time in a fortnight.

Once outside he checked his watch: half-past four. Perhaps he should have asked for a receipt stipulating the length of time of the appointment, just to make sure the firm wasn't overcharged? He was in a dilemma now. It was only a ten-minute walk to work. Peterson had told him to take an early trip home, perhaps also acknowledging that he was just tweaking numbers on the current job. It felt ridiculously early to be going back to the flat. Perhaps he could do a much longer run, or make a more concerted effort on M—.com?

Then he realised it was the ideal opportunity to take a trip to Soho and get that extra pornographic DVD he'd been promising himself. The Londoner's tube map in his head flashed up that he was a few minute's walk from Bank station, and the Central Line – and thus within easy reach of his objective. But he realised he might pass too close to Woodcock and Tweed's main office in St Swithin's Lane, so with a flutter of naughty schoolboy excitement in his chest, he set off for Monument entrance to Bank station. A couple of women on the tube eyed him warily before he realised that he was wearing a lascivious smile.

He got out at Tottenham Court Road and walked down past the bookshops of Charing Cross Road, in half a mind as to whether he ought to buy a less challenging novel. He could skim through the remainder of *Carport Cornucopia* and then be on to something better. He went into a branch of BookShelves, and hovered around the 'Three-for-Two' table. He gave up after a few minutes and went to the A-Z by Author section, and found himself staring at the latest William Boyd bestseller. Hadn't he just seen a Boyd title advertised in the 'Three-for-Two' pile? He stood there a moment and contemplated how much reading he was going to do. Was it better to spend more now to get a discount, taking the risk of buying a book that he'd enjoy as little as *Carport Cornucopia*? Or should his strategy be to buy one at a time? He struggled to understand whether the 'Three-for-Two' offers meant that the books were being discounted because they were of poor quality, or whether they had to be discounted because they were bestsellers that other shops were discounting in order to grab market share. Buying a book had been so much simpler in his youth, and he cursed the person who had turned the pleasure of browsing into a nightmare of consumer choice.

Harper Lee. The name popped up into his head. He'd enjoyed *To Kill a Mockingbird* at school. It would offer the additional benefit of showing him to be politically correct. And surely everyone had read it at school, which meant it would be a ready conversation piece. Relieved, he made his way over to L and quickly located several copies tucked into the shelf, spines outwards. He plucked one out.

Three-for-Two! Screamed the giant orange sticker on the front. "Fuck!" he muttered, a little too loudly. A couple of people edged away from him. He grinned an apology and wandered, defeated, back to the 'Three-for-Two' table where he picked up a Boyd and an Updike without even examining the covers.

When he paid with his credit card he noticed he was low on cash. He didn't want the pornography appearing on his credit card statement, so he went to a cash machine and made a withdrawal. It was now quarter-past five, and the streets were getting busier with commuters: he could feel prying eyes on him already. He turned west off Charing Cross Road and then realised too late that he was in Old Compton Street. He'd had a couple of gay friends at university, but felt a bit nervous about being spotted walking through the area.

He hurried along through to the junction with Wardour Street and positioned himself so that he could look down the length of Brewer Street, whilst pretending to be waiting for a gap in the traffic to cross the road.

He could see a couple of shops on either side, the blandness of their exteriors declaring their business louder than expensive signage could do. They even lacked doors – though a couple of them had multi-coloured plastic ribbons, suggestive to Ian's charged mind of the outfit of an exotic dancer. He selected a target doorway and crossed over into Brewer Street, feeling his heart thumping. What he was about to do might be acceptable on a stag weekend abroad, but was a different matter on home territory.

Pedestrians were fewer in number along Brewer Street. He affected as casual a walk as he could, with his BookShelves bag as cover. He was careful not to move his head too obviously, but scanned around as much as he could for disdainful eyes. As soon as he was alongside the predetermined doorway he sidestepped in through the ribbons without looking. He bumped straight into a large, potbellied man in builder's clothes, who was coming out. "Fucking watch out!" snarled the man, shouldering Ian back onto the pavement.

"S-sorry," said Ian. He could feel the whole street watching him.

"Wanker," spat the man.

"Fucking hypocrite," muttered Ian, pushing aside the ribbons.

"Sorry, mate. We're closed for refurbishment," said a middle-aged man in slacks and a shirt, holding a clipboard. Ian looked around and saw that the shop was indeed being fitted out. There wasn't a DVD or magazine to be seen anywhere.

He turned on his heels and exited, the long fingers of ribbon clinging to his shoulders for a second or two, covering him with guilt for all to see. Desperate not to meet the eyes of other pedestrians, he stepped off the pavement towards the shop opposite. A white van screeched to a halt in front of him and sounded its horn.

"Fucking wanker!" shouted the van's driver – a burly-looking man about Ian's age. "In a hurry to go home and watch your porn are you? You dirty fucker."

Pushed beyond his normal limits of endurance, Ian stood his ground. Shaking with rage and fear, he took the novels out of his bag. "Books," he said. "But I don't suppose you can read, can you?"

"Fucking *right*," said the van driver. He undid his seatbelt, got out of the cab and started walking purposefully round the front of the van. The fact that the driver's seat was on the other side gave Ian valuable extra seconds. The narrowness of the pavement and the number of onlookers who'd stopped to stare meant that he couldn't take advantage of his recent running practice but he ducked in through the ribboned doorway of a shop thirty yards up the street, panting.

It was another porn store. He looked around and saw nothing but magazines, videos and DVDs, from floor to ceiling.

"Come here, you fucking wanker!" said the white van driver, standing at the entrance, fists clenched. A cacophony of vehicle horns was calling him back to his van.

"Got a problem, mate?" A heavily-built man in short sleeves that revealed a collection of tattoos strolled over towards the driver. The driver thought better of it and left.

The blaring of the horns outside subsided and the low groan of traffic started again. Ian noticed there were half a dozen other men in the shop, none of whom was looking happy with the commotion. The heavily-built man, a couple of inches taller than him, with the same thickness of stubble on his head as on his face, walked towards him. "Now," he said, entering Ian's personal space. "What can I do you for?"

'Just browsing' didn't seem an appropriate response. "Got any decent movies?" asked Ian.

"Are you taking the piss?" growled the man.

"No, no. I'm genuinely interested."

The man studied Ian's face for a few moments. "Gay films are over there."

"But I'm straight."

The man snorted and went back to the cashier's desk.

The array of pornography before him was dazzling. Straight, lesbian, orgy, young, old, different races – even sex involving only specified orifices. He tried to remain cool whilst examining the back covers of a few titles, but a voice in his head nagged that he was leaving fingerprints everywhere. Then he spotted the CCTV cameras positioned in the corners of the ceiling. He had visions of the incident with the van driver being broadcast either on a late-night reality TV show, or becoming the kind of cult video clip to be emailed to every office worker in the world. He hunched his shoulders to try to mask his face.

The afternoon's events had ruined his mood and he could barely muster enthusiasm for the subject at hand. In the end, he plumped for a DVD that promised a wide variety of sex acts, strung on some exotic espionage plot.

He attempted a smile as he reached the counter. "Sure that's enough?" asked the man. "It's three for two on that series. Buy one more and you get another free."

Ian felt a surge of frustration. "I just wanted the one, really."

The man laughed. "No one wants just the *one*," he said. "Go on, make the most of it. How about I recommend a few? You want a bit of variety." He made a gesture at Ian's suit. "Clearly you're a man of taste."

Ian realised the spending power his suit indicated – especially compared to the other men in the shop. He felt a new surge of confidence and was determined to redeem himself. "How about if I were to come back? Would I get two for the price of one having paid full-price for this?"

"Sorry, the offer's only for one purchase." The man pondered the matter for a few seconds. "What about half-price on the second one if you buy two next time you're here?"

"Fair enough." Ian handed over the exact money for his one DVD, which was wrapped in a paper bag and sealed with sticky tape.

The man wrote on the receipt. "There you go, just bring that next time you're in."

"Great, thanks," said Ian, pleased that he'd been able to pull something from the wreckage of the last half-hour. The receipt was as good as cash as far as he was concerned, so he tucked it carefully into his wallet in the section he kept for five-pound notes.

He got home earlier than usual for a weekday evening and

ran his three miles at a better pace than he'd achieved thus far. Dinner was half a can of cold tuna and some broccoli. He was continuing to lose weight.

There was not one, but two emails in his M—.com inbox, and he was delighted. One was from Marina and the other from WhichHazel. To prolong the pleasure of anticipation, he read the one from Marina first.

> My love, you must be to want more information with my life. I am to live with my mother in cosy flat in Kharkov. I to make my personal room very cosy, with shelves and soft toys. I hope some day that you to like. But of my father you must to ask? He was engineer at power plant and tragical died with defeat of a current since three years. My mother and I to make closer this happens. Tonight to tell her of our relationship, which she will I to understand well certain.
>
> With love from your Marina

At the back of his mind, thoughts still lingered about flights. He clicked on the email from WhichHazel.

> Very droll. Forensic accountant sounds a bit less boring. What are you doing at the weekend? More of the same, or do you fancy a date?
>
> Cheers,
>
> Hazel

He punched the air. He was about to write back to say that any time or place would be good when he realised that he mustn't appear too desperate.

> I'm flexible for the weekend. A date would be great.

Best regards,

Ian

He clicked on send and regretted not having said more – perhaps telling her how long his runs were, or that a date would have to work around his busy schedule.

It was as near to a perfect evening as he'd had since Sarah left. Things were on the turn. He popped open a celebratory can of lager and started his new DVD. His share of sexual heaven was on order, and he might not have to wait that long for delivery.

By the time he'd finished his second lager, the doubt was growing in his troubled mind. Although he and Hazel might talk about a novel or two, he couldn't see how he was going to make all the right moves to manoeuvre her into the sort of activity he was currently observing on the DVD. Indeed, how adventurous would Hazel be? Would he end up with a stagnating sex life? How could he go about obtaining spectacular sex like that on the DVD?

First things first: Giac could offer expert guidance on getting to first base. He picked up his mobile, searched and hit the button.

"Ian, my man," said Giac. "We're all wondering where the hell you've got to. Not sitting there wanking yourself blind are you?"

"No. Don't be stupid," said Ian, a little too hotly. "I've been running and losing weight. Listen, I need a bit of a favour."

"Sure, shoot."

"I'm going on a date and I need your advice on technique."

Chapter Seven

"Jesus, you've lost weight," said Giac, shaking Ian's hand and squeezing his shoulder with the other. "Have you been ill?" Giac brought new meaning to the phrase 'smart casual'. His immaculate trousers and sports jacket made Ian's tailored suit look cheap and shabby. An ornate but discreet gold ring in his left ear set it all off.

"As I said, I've been running and dieting." Such was Ian's commitment to his programme that he'd got up at six that morning to go for his run, because meeting Giac at a bar in Fulham straight after work would have meant skipping it.

"I'm impressed, mate. Now, you must be asking yourself why we've met in this bar."

"You won't shit on your own doorstep?" ventured Ian, handing Giac the pint he'd bought him.

"Exactly," said Giac. "And I don't want you cramping my style on my territory, either. No offence, but you're a liability until you're fully trained."

Both men drank and looked around the bar. Giac had been characteristically late and Ian had arrived early, so he was on his second pint on an empty stomach. He could feel the alcohol buzz already. "Not bad, eh?" he said, nodding at a group of attractive women at a nearby table.

"Pretty good all round," said Giac. "Now, what we're looking for a is a pair of single women." He explained to Ian the supposedly foolproof psychology behind picking up women in this particular situation, as developed by an American guru. Giac would lead the way by talking to the less attractive of the two women, and would ignore the prettier one. He would give the pretty one a gentle put-down – a so-called 'neg' – when, inevitably, she tried to break into the conversation. Then he would finally turn his attention on her and make his move. It all seemed perfectly simple to Ian and he was genuinely interested to see how this little practical psychology exercise would unfold.

For his part, it would be useful practice ahead of what he hoped was an upcoming date with Hazel.

Giac nodded towards a couple of women perched on bar stools, one peroxide blonde, the other honeyed. "Don't look at them," he told Ian, who looked puzzled. "If you look at women and don't immediately approach them, they get spooked." Ian thought back to his numerous embarrassed encounters with women on the tube and curled his toes. "Okay, get ready," said Giac, as if he were commanding a platoon of elite soldiers. Ian saw one of the women catch Giac's eye. Giac smiled back and moved towards them. Ian padded behind but was cut off for a few seconds as a member of the bar staff pushed past with a tray of empty glasses.

Giac was happily conversing with the woman with honey-blonde hair by the time Ian reached them. He already felt out of place, and the only room for him was behind Giac, and to his left. "—mate Ian, who's quite shy," he managed to catch Giac saying, and raised his glass to acknowledge. He stood for a couple more minutes leaning over, earnestly trying to catch the conversation over the background noise. Giac seemed to be talking about adventure sports – about which he knew nothing – with some authority. As Giac had predicted, the peroxide blonde – left out of the conversation for the same amount of time as Ian – tried to break into it with a comment about paragliding. "And they say blondes are the dumb ones," said Giac. "But since you're only a bottle-blonde, I'll let you off!" The honeyed blonde laughed and the conversation continued.

Then it all changed. In a heartbeat, Giac had turned his attention to the peroxide blonde and had drawn in close to her. She seemed delighted to have his attention at last. This left Ian with the honey-blonde, whom he felt was out of his league.

"Sorry, I didn't get your name," he said.

She looked at him blankly. "So you're the runner's-up prize, are you?" she said.

He remembered Giac's tip on using the so-called 'neg' to get an attractive woman's attentions. "How do you think *I* feel – you're not even much of a runner-up are you?" he said.

For a moment he thought she'd slap him. She fixed him with a cold stare, slammed her glass down, grabbed her friend and made for the door. The puzzled peroxide blonde turned her head back towards Giac, gave him a beaming smile, waved Giac's card at him and made a telephone gesture.

"What the fuck did you do?" asked Giac. "I was on a sure thing there."

Ian explained his brief dialogue and Giac groaned. "No, Ian. You can only use the neg when you're in conversation with a *couple*. You know, to play on her insecurity. Don't you listen to anything? If it's a woman by herself, you have to make sure she's interested in you first."

"Sorry," said Ian sheepishly. "Hey, I've not seen that business card before."

"This?" Giac pulled out a fresh card from his wallet and handed it to Ian. "This isn't a business card, buddy. More like a calling card. Or a 'call me' card."

Ian examined the card and whistled. It was laminated and printed with a colour photo of Giac on the back. "Expensive."

"Look, if you're serious about this game, then you have to invest in the tools of the trade."

"Mind if I…?" asked Ian.

"Hang on," said Giac. He took the card back and wrote on it. "That's the website of the printer who makes them for me." Ian thanked him and tucked the card away in his wallet.

After a few more drinks they made their separate ways home. Ian cheered himself up with the thought that he might have a date that weekend. He was tired, and drunker than he'd been in quite a while, so it took him a couple of attempts to get his key in his front door. He flopped down on the sofa and turned the laptop on, then logged in to see if there was any word from Hazel on M——.com.

There were two messages – one from WhichHazel with the

subject matter 'What's your phone number?' and the other from Marina, entitled 'Missing you xxx'. He scrolled his cursor drunkenly across the screen and clicked. There was no message, just a subject header, so he simply clicked Reply, typed in his home phone number and clicked Send. He realised he was falling asleep and turned the computer off before making his way straight to bed.

His hangover was bad on Wednesday morning. He had skipped breakfast because he wanted to lose more weight by Saturday. If he could lose weight whilst still eating, then without food he could knock off a few extra pounds in three days. But an empty stomach with that kind of hangover was not pleasant, and he felt weak. He felt even worse when Peterson dumped some more files about Armstrong on him. "By the way," asked Peterson. "The counselling the other night? Of course, it's a private matter, but did it go well?"

"As well as can be expected."

"Great man, Dr Patel, isn't he? Really helps to clarify one's thoughts."

"Early days, Donald." He saw an inquisitive but concerned look on his boss's face. "But I felt so much better. I have a much clearer sense of direction now. Seeing him again in a couple of weeks."

"Excellent, excellent. Well, mind how you go," said Peterson, and went back to his office.

The thought that Peterson had got anything valuable out of any counselling with Dr Patel beggared belief.

"You look rough, love," said Rose, leaning over the wall of his cubicle. "Out with the boys, or was you with a young lady?"

"Sort of both. My mate tried to show me how to pick up women. He's got all these techniques."

"You either got it or you ain't. No offence, but you chatting up a woman using some fancy technique would be like me trying to reproduce one of them old masters using a paint-by-numbers set."

"Thanks for that vote of confidence."

"I'm just saying that you need to stick to what you're good at. You strike me as the kind of bloke who'd never be any good trying to be a ladies' man. I bet you'd just get too shy or nervous. You'd be much better off sticking with women you just meet in some situation like work or whatever."

"Great advice. Thanks." A sub-routine deep in his brain wondered whether she might be putting herself forward for his attentions.

"Any luck with the lovely ladies of M—.com?"

"Yes, as it happens."

"Go on, then. Give us a look." Rose sidled round into his cubicle.

He sighed wearily and went to the M—.com website, where he had tagged WhichHazel as a Favourite. "She's in marketing, and I think we're going on a date sometime this weekend," he said.

"Very nice. Why don't you reply to her email? You haven't even opened it. She says in the subject that she wants your phone number. I wouldn't leave it much longer if I were you."

"Eh? But I replied to that last night. Unless…" The thought didn't bear thinking about. He looked more closely at his inbox. The message from WhichHazel was still unopened, but the one from Marina had been opened and replied to.

"What's up?" asked Rose.

"Nothing," he groaned. "You're right, I'd better reply to Hazel. See you later." He opened WhichHazel's email which, like Marina's, consisted just of a subject header and no message. He sent her his number, with an apology about his lateness and a suggestion that they talk that evening about a date. He calmed his fears about Marina by telling himself that international telephone calls from the Ukraine would be prohibitively expensive.

His thoughts turned back to what Rose had said about

meeting women through some activity, and he realised that he could be up in Newcastle in a week, with time to spare in the evenings. Hadn't he resolved to track down the women he thought he could have had when he was a student?

He skipped lunch and went for a brisk walk along the Embankment. How had he not seen this before? No food, but a little bit of exercise at lunchtime would see him slim in double-quick time.

That evening's run marked a significant improvement, so he added another mile at the end. The bathroom scales told him he'd now lost over twelve pounds. Just a few more days on this accelerated regime and he'd be back to his student physique.

He was flicking through his address book when the phone rang. The sound jangled his nerves. There was only one person he wanted to speak to right now. He picked it up from the base station and clicked it on.

"Hello?" he said.

"Hello?" said a female voice.

"Yes, hello," said Ian.

"Hello?"

It must be the Ukrainian – a native English speaker would have got on with the conversation. He terminated the call and went back to his address book. Then he realised he couldn't dial out and have a long conversation with any of his friends because he might prevent Hazel from getting through. He considered his mobile as an option but ruled it out on the grounds of cost.

The phone rang again.

"Hello?" he said.

"Hello?" said the female voice, with what he could now recognise as a foreign accent. He terminated the call. She'd give up soon enough.

He turned the laptop on. Last weekend's campaign of sending Winks had clearly worked, and he and Hazel weren't in an exclusive relationship. It was a numbers game. He logged in to M—.com

The phone rang.

"Hello?" he said.

"Ian it's your mother."

"Hi, Mum." He rolled his eyes.

"I'm just calling about June the tenth."

"That's the christening. It's in my diary."

"Oh, I'm glad to hear that. Now, how are you? We were worried when you didn't call at the weekend."

"Really, I'm fine. I need to go."

"We were going to invite you down this weekend as well."

"Mum, I'm actually quite busy. In fact, I have a date this weekend and I'm waiting for a call to arrange it." There was a silence on the other end of the line, then a sob. "Look, Mum. I really don't have time for this. I'll talk to you later in the week. Cheers." He hung up.

The phone rang again. He clicked the button.

"Hello?" he said.

"Hello?" said the female voice. Definitely a foreign accent. He terminated the call.

Just as he was hitting the Search button to find his next batch of prospective dates to send a Wink to, the phone rang.

"Hello?" he said, trying not to sound weary, in case it was Hazel.

"Hello? Forensic?" the caller announced the last syllable of the name as an 'itch'. He terminated the call – definitely the Ukrainian. The phone rang once more.

"Hello?" he said, making a face at the handset.

"Hello?" said the female voice. He terminated the call. Then he realised that it couldn't have been the Ukrainian because it would have taken her longer to dial back. What's more, the Ukrainian had had a different voice. Realising it could only have been Hazel, he picked up the phone so that he could dial 1471 to get her number. Just as he hit the button to talk, it rang.

"Hi. Hazel?" he said.

"I suppose Hazel's this new girl, is she?" said his father. "I must say you didn't waste your time, did you? Four years of living together and you're straight on to the next one. It's *appalling*."

"Hazel's a friend," he said in a voice that told his father he was lying.

"You've upset your mother again."

"She upsets herself, Dad. She should focus on things that make her happy."

"You make her unhappy. She's worried about you and wants to see you. Stuart doesn't think you're looking after yourself. We'd like you to come down and spend the weekend with us."

He spent the next five minutes placating his father, then another ten reassuring his mother. When he finally got off the phone he knew his chance to talk with Hazel that evening had gone because the last number to have rung would have been his parents'. Unless she were to ring again.

The phone rang. He picked it up and listened.

"Forensic?" said the accented voice. He ended the call and turned on the answering machine. He sent an email to Hazel with his mobile number. He didn't like to give it out, but at least it could be turned off and couldn't be traced geographically. He heard a couple of "Forensic?" calls come through, and he idly wondered what time it was in Ukraine, and how much it was costing this deluded woman.

He got the call from Hazel on his mobile at lunchtime on Thursday. He'd expected some casual talk to check out their compatibility but it was short and business-like, which was a relief given that he was in the office. She accepted his explanation of a faulty line for the previous evening's missed conversation. They would meet for a coffee and, if things went well, they would move on to lunch. The enthusiasm of the professional marketing manager left him feeling warm and happy, and he was conscious of a spring in his step, even though he'd been fasting since Tuesday evening.

After more questioning, Peterson seemed to conclude that the therapy was working, and that he was the perfect manager for having arranged it. Ian was happy to let him believe it, hoping it would keep him off his back for the Armstrong job.

It was Peterson who found him asleep, face down on his desk at ten-to-five. He shook him awake.

"Ian, are you alright?"

"Hmm?"

"You're looking awful. Rose? I need help."

"Hello, what's up?" said Ian, lacking the energy to make sense of his circumstances.

"Pull yourself together man."

"Shh, Donald," said Rose. "It's alright. I think he's just hungry."

"*Hungry*? Surely to God he can afford to *eat*?"

"He's been on a bit of a diet. I've seen this kind of thing before. But not with a man, though."

"Christ Almighty," said Peterson. "He's anorexic. Must be all this stuff with losing his girlfriend. Can't you do something? Don't we need a doctor?"

"He'll be alright. Leave him with me." She gave Ian some full-sugar cola.

"I'm not sure what happened there," said Ian.

"You stupid plonker," said Rose. "You know I have to note this in the medical book, don't you?"

"Really, it's not necessary."

"You know Donald – he'll insist. Now he thinks you're anorexic as well."

"Fuck and damn. Sorry."

"You just bleedin' look after yourself, alright? One of us will have to accompany you home – them's the rules. Trouble is you've got no one to go back to, have you?"

"Don't rub it in."

"What about them friends of yours?"

"Stu and Nina?"

"Yeah, them. Come on, I'll get us a taxi."

And so Rose accompanied him in a taxi to Stuart and Nina's house, making sure he was safely inside before leaving. The embarrassment was almost too much to bear.

"So, I was right," said Stuart. "Can't look after yourself. Look at you – you're wasting away. Your eyes are all sunken in and your face is gaunt."

"No, really," Ian protested. "I'm getting back to the weight I was when I was a student."

"Well you were a stick insect back then. Men are supposed to get a bit heavier as they get older."

His hosts made sure he ate a full meal but he declined a bed for the night. The conversation was awkward as Stuart walked him back to his flat. Ian cursed himself – no run that day, plus all those extra calories.

He ignored a couple of emails from Marina but there were four messages from her on his answering machine. Just how persistent was this woman going to be?

The internet was a wonderful thing, he thought. How the single man could ever have lived without it amazed him. He could partake of any vice from the comfort and privacy of his own home. Where women and sex were concerned, any whim was catered for, from the repulsive and illegal right up to the genuine search for a spouse.

Precisely where on that spectrum Ian's activities lay that evening was a matter of opinion. To the majority of men, he thought, it would be down at the innocent end. Women, though, might feel differently about it. But, as his mother had demonstrated so clearly the other evening, it was because they chose to upset themselves.

There were four women he was curious to catch up on, and who could make his trip to Newcastle all the more entertaining. Valerie was the most tantalising unfinished business, but there were also Patsy, Debbie and Tamara. Each of them occupied her own space in his imagination. Over the four years of his degree, each had had vignettes of memories tucked into her file.

There was Patsy smiling at him over a coffee, touching his arm tenderly, shyly after a break-up from Sarah; her fingers tipped by manicured, red-varnished nails. Patsy was a classic Geordie lass – always well turned-out in a trendy top and a mini-skirt which suited her petite figure. Her light-honey hair was highlighted with streaks of blonde, and he marvelled at the expense of frequent salon appointments on her student's income. Her smell was always enticingly fresh – a mix of fabric softener, hairspray, and the whiff of some perfume whose name eluded him. When he sat down next to her in lectures he'd take a few deep breaths with his eyes half-closed and draw in her essence, wishing he could wake up enveloped in it one morning after a night of passion. But despite her obvious sexuality, there was always something attractively prim about her, even when she traded smutty *double entendres* with him in a giggling, girlish way. Even if he'd had the courage to make a move, there'd always been a man in her life whenever he'd been single.

Debbie's breasts filled most of the available space allocated for her in his head. More specifically, she was jiggling them suggestively at him at the Friday night disco in the student's union, just for one fleeting moment after she'd caught him transfixed by them. "I didn't know ye was a breast man, Ian," she shouted in her broad Geordie voice, deepened by her taste for spirits and rough-smelling Regal cigarettes – a brand he'd never seen south of Newcastle. She flipped up her impossibly-stretched T-shirt to reveal the two magnificent globes tethered by what to him looked like an industrial-strength bra, and pushed them to within a foot of his face, flicking her long black hair back over her shoulder to make sure his view was unobscured. "Fancy — —, do ya?" she shouted over the music. He'd never been able to fill in the words that the music had rendered incomprehsible – though his imagination had provided some likely or wishful substitutes — and he'd always wondered what might have happened if he had simply said yes, instead of scurrying off to get a round of drinks.

Then there was Tamara. What could he say about Tamara? Even her name suggested it all: a wild rock chick with the leather trousers to match and a body to die for.

He had yearned for them all in his fantasy world, and he was quite convinced that at some time or another he could have made a move on each of them. But he'd always lacked the nous. The embarrassment of rejection would have carried over into lectures, seminars, presentations and exams. Of course, he was free of that now, and he'd kicked himself in retrospect so many times. Any mistaken, drunken advances would have been long forgotten. He'd played a long game with the short sightedness of the amateur. He was no Giac.

And the nicknames, how he loved to play with their nicknames, fondly remembered from those halcyon days. Plush Patsy, Pristine Patsy and Patsy Please had had their day with the boys. Dumb Debbie with her Do-me-Debbie eyes. Debbie-dee-*Dawg* had been a drunken indiscretion from a fellow student who'd experienced her intimately in their final year, boasting of her preference for the doggie position and a tendency to howl when close to orgasm. From that day on, he'd always smiled inwardly when he'd seen her – imagining those magnificent breasts swinging free beneath her as she was pounded from behind, loins slapping on buttocks.

Tamara eclipsed the other two. She'd barely socialised on the course, preferring to find her men in the sex-starved ranks of the heavy-metal worshipping Engineering faculty. She would always have a longhaired, black T-shirted, pale-faced youth trotting around after her, as if on a leash. The generic appearance of these chosen men made it difficult to tell the frequency with which they burnt out and were replaced, but someone guessed their lifespan to be one to two months. The subject of Tamara's sex life had provided a rich vein of humour during a particularly cruel drinking session one Saturday afternoon in a cheap pub called the Trent House, fuelled by jealousy for those lucky engineers. What had they, the savvy businessmen of the future, not got that the engineers had?

"She must have a pile of spent ones at home," someone had quipped.

"Shame on her for not recycling," said another.

"Doesn't she know there's a shortage of Engineering graduates in this country?"

"Yeah, and she's the cause of it!"

"Why do they burn out so quickly?" someone asked. He answered their blank faces by singing, "*Tamara never comes*."

"Will you still love me *Tamara*?" sang another, with the crowd joining in on the last word.

Ian had fond memories of Tamara and her skin-tight leather trousers. He'd once gone to a heavy metal night at a local club. She'd recognised him and dragged him onto the dance floor for a head-banging and air-guitar session. So far as he was concerned it had been the single event that had done most for his street cred during his whole four years. But on the Monday morning she'd just smiled at him – though he'd treasured that rare acknowledgement. In the depths of his imagination her nickname was Tie-me-up-Tamara. If only he'd made a move on that dance-floor, how different his life would have been. To have been one of those lucky sex-slaves on his way to burnout – what a way to go.

These were the fantasies that drove him through the tiresome business of entering his details on the university's alumnus database and registering his interest in tracking down Valerie, Patsy, Debbie and Tamara – the fantasy women he knew still to be in Newcastle.

Tamara belongs to the people who prepare for her today, he chuckled, as he entered her name into the search tool.

Rose had prepped him for Saturday's date over a couple of after-work drinks on Friday evening. "Don't take her no flowers on a first date," she'd said. "You'll freak her out."

"Thanks, useful tip," he said. The thought of buying flowers had never crossed his mind. He wondered whether he might be better at this dating game than he'd realised.

"Just keep the conversation light-hearted and casual. Try to come across as deeper than you are."

"Fuck, I can't believe *you're* telling *me* I'm shallow."

"I'm sure you've got hidden depths, love. But I must say the camouflage is fucking world-class."

"Anyhow, she likes soap operas, so she can't be that deep."

"Dangerous talk, Mr Bourne. Culture is what the masses say it is, not some poncey upper-class twits. It's a proven fact that children learn to socialise by watching television drama. And it's not watching some minority arts programme what binds society together, is it? Record viewing figures and all the gossip belongs to the soap operas, don't it?"

Ian was continually surprised by Rose. "Where d'you get all this stuff about socialising and television?"

"You people get the newspapers delivered to the office every day, but I'm the only one with the time to read them. Perhaps if you made more of an effort?" She wished him luck and gave him a parting peck on his cheek, which made him wonder once more.

There was only one message from Marina on the answering machine when he got home, her slender means perhaps proving a better kerb on her enthusiasm than any email he could write. He kept the machine on all evening to guard his privacy. At around nine o'clock it intercepted a half-drunken call from Rob and Chris, snickering about his forthcoming date, and how he'd ruined Tuesday night for Giac. He'd show them, thought Ian. Before going to bed he skim-read the final two-hundred pages of *Carport Cornucopia*.

With Rose's comment fresh in his mind on Saturday morning, he bought the *Guardian* instead of the *Telegraph* because he believed that was what Marketing people read. He also bought a copy of *Suds!,* a magazine given over to soap opera news, with a condensed summary of the week's happenings on each of the shows. He was lost in a minute and bewildered in two. It was an alien world of peculiar names and unlikely events. For one thing, he found himself unable to grasp where the characters and their storylines finished and the lives of the actors who played them began. It seemed to him that the socialisation of children from television soaps had actually been responsible for the apparent collapse of society. He penned a letter to the editor of the *Telegraph* in his head, urging a clampdown on plotlines and that viewing be restricted until after the watershed.

He was in a quandary about the day's run. Should he run in the morning and turn up glowing, or should he save it until the evening, in case they had a calorific lunch? In the end, he decided on the latter. Again, he wore clothes that Sarah had said looked good on him. He logged in to M——.com one final time to memorise Hazel's face and then he was on his way, with his copy of *To Kill a Mockingbird* to read on the tube. He'd kept the 'Three-for-Two' sticker on in the hope that it would mark him out as a prolific reader.

They'd arranged to meet at a trendy café off Tottenham Court Road, he guessed because she could always have retail therapy in Oxford Street afterwards if it didn't work out. He arrived ten minutes early and had a quick scan inside before deciding he was best waiting at the door for her, trying to relax.

"Ian?" said a woman's voice. He looked up and saw Hazel. Or, rather, what looked like a discernibly older version of Hazel than he'd seen on the website. Her reddish-brown hair was in a different style; tied back loosely over her shoulders.

"Hazel," he said, flustered by the look of her in the flesh, wondering whether it was the loss of definition on screen that was the cause of the apparent mismatch. He shook her hand.

"I see your left arm's grown back," she said.

"Sorry?"

"You looked like an amputee in that holiday snap. But I

suppose it's only the girlfriend you're missing. Come on, let's go in."

She had wrong-footed him. All he could think of was Sarah now: it was her behaviour to a tee. But there was something in her assertiveness that he rather liked. She even insisted on paying for the drinks.

"Forensic accountant. Sounds rather glamorous," she prompted, smiling.

He wondered to what extent he could lie about his job. "Demanding," he said. "You need an eye for the details, and the tenacity to follow something through. And you have to be able to get into the head of the perpetrator."

"It really does sound quite exciting," she said.

He liked her ability to make him feel important, and her interest – however real – in his job. To his surprise, he found himself telling her a story about a recent case involving a pizza restaurant that had been making about half the money it should have been. The restaurant had been on a busy high street in a resort town. The firm of accountants from the parent company had been in and checked the receipts for the amount of ingredients going into the restaurant, and they had tallied perfectly with the receipts going out for the pizzas.

"But sometimes shops or restaurants are set up in the wrong place," she said. "I'll tell you a story about that after you're done. By the way, all this talk of food – I'm starving. Fancy some lunch?" She was already on her feet before he could reply. "I'm meeting a friend in an hour, so we'll have to hurry."

Ian was thrilled that he'd passed whatever criteria she'd set in order to get to lunch. And he was impressed with her logistical planning – there was an upmarket pizza restaurant three doors along. Just two weeks since Sarah had left, and he was already on a successful date. This was easier than he'd thought – Rose was right: he should just be himself and pretend he'd met this woman through work.

"So tell me – what was the answer?" she asked.

"Easy when you step back," said Ian. "My suspicions were aroused by the levels of perishable stock they were holding – you know, salad and the like. You never hold more than two days' worth in that game. With stock levels that high there'd have been wastage like no one's business — except there was hardly any, just like you'd expect in a busy restaurant. That was what made me suspicious."

"Go on, I'm intrigued."

"Then I realised they had two cash registers," he said triumphantly.

She giggled at his playful teasing. "Yes, *and*..."

"The couple who managed the place were running an additional set of accounts. They were buying in extra ingredients from a *different* supplier so that they could keep the receipts of those separate from the legitimate business. Then they were running half the sales through the other till, which they had bought themselves. What no one had twigged was that almost every outlet like that – apart from the really huge ones in Central London – normally have just the one till. How could a restaurant with half the trade have two tills?"

"I see," said Hazel. "In other words they were able to manufacture and sell pizzas at cost-price and sell them to customers at full price?"

"Precisely." He liked a woman who could understand the basics of cost accounting. "The ingredients were about an eighth of the selling price, so it was hugely profitable because the staff were cooking and serving them – and even washing the dishes afterwards."

"So what happened?"

"After they got the business under legitimate managers again, it became one of their most profitable outlets."

"And the couple? What was it – theft or fraud?"

"Fraud against their employer. But worse for them it was also VAT fraud – they never paid VAT on the pizzas they made and sold. Defrauding the tax man is what racks up your prison time in this country." He was really enjoying himself. He bit into a starter of garlic bread – it was flatbread, dripping with real butter: his favourite. A few small pieces of fresh garlic crunched between his teeth and his taste buds felt like they would explode with pleasure. How long was it since he'd eaten this well? He took another slice.

"Are you alright?" asked Hazel.

"Yes, really. Delicious garlic bread, don't you think?"

"You must be quite hungry. Shall I order some more?" the smile had gone and she looked genuinely concerned.

Alarm bells rang in his head as he realised he'd taken far more than his fair share of the plate. "No, no," he said with his mouth full. A masticated piece of bread flew out sideways. It missed the table and stuck to the black trousers of a passing waiter. "Excuse me. I do apologise. Been working late. You were going to tell me a story?"

She finished her mouthful before speaking. "All the retail chains measure the foot traffic past potential sites. It's grown to be quite a science. So when one of the big American burger chains wanted to enter the German market they brought over their experts and did an expensive survey. They bought a busy corner location with plenty of visibility, at what seemed like quite a decent price."

"And?"

"It had practically no customers. They tried everything – adverts, money-off coupons distributed on the street: the whole shebang. Nothing worked."

"So what was it? Don't tell me they'd built it in a Hindu area?"

She chuckled at his joke as she prepared for her own punch line. "No, they'd built it in the red light district. No one was ever going to stop for a burger there." They both laughed heartily, though at the back of his mind was a recent experience that chimed far too well with her story.

He realised she'd been letting him do too much of the

talking. Giac had told him that it flattered women to listen attentively to them because they didn't expect men to do so. "You seem to know about retail. What do you do?"

"Retail marketing management."

"For?"

"I know you're a customer. Go on, guess."

"So at some point you've got my attention and sold me something?" Her mouth was full so she nodded enthusiastically. "I'm very impressed because I consider myself immune to offers."

"Everyone thinks they are, but they're not. See if you can guess."

"My shoes?" she shook her head. "Jacket? Trousers? What? I give up." He was warming to her, and could feel that it was mutual.

"Your book. I work for BookShelves. You fell for this month's Three-for-Two offers."

"Damn, I bloody *hate* those stupid offers," he said, without thinking, too much of his real feeling coming out. "Drive me bloody mad."

It was only much later, on the tube back home, that he'd realised his comment had been the tipping point. It was a 'neg' of sorts. She'd been stunned for just a fraction of a second before bursting into laughter. "Gotcha!" she'd said, licked a finger and chalked up a point on an imaginary board between them.

They argued over the bill, which – such was his happiness – he insisted on paying. As they took another cup of coffee back in the café, he realised the time. "You should have been meeting your friend about half an hour ago," he said.

"That? Just a get-out in case we weren't getting along," she said. "A trick of the dating game. Relax – you're up to scratch."

He couldn't have been happier. Neither of them had anything planned for Sunday, so they'd agreed to meet again the following day. Since she'd arranged the first one, he agreed to plan the second.

There was an extra vigour to his evening's run: he wanted his body to be in as good a shape as possible for what he felt was imminent use. He congratulated himself for having come so far in a fortnight. This was just the beginning of Ian re-Bourne.

Of course he had his doubts on Sunday morning. How old was Hazel really? She was attractive, certainly, but she wasn't quite as attractive as Sarah. And he'd rather enjoyed the cachet of having a lawyer as a girlfriend – what was a marketing manager by comparison? Although he knew they had their contribution to make to the economy, he felt that their discipline lacked the intellectual rigour of the traditional three professions. And what if they started a much longer-term relationship – was she really what he was after? She lived out in High Barnet, which was a bit of a trek and in a different fare zone for the tube, which would mean the hassle of topping up his travel card on two consecutive days if he were to stay overnight there. He tried to put all these worries aside, reassuring himself that his primary objective – that of putting his sex-life back in order — was in hand (or rather, was no longer going to be a matter for his own hands). And now that he had a definite objective in his sights, he was determined to achieve it. He called her at half-nine with final arrangements, and headed for the tube.

Meeting as they did at Pimlico tube station, there could only be one place they were headed: Tate Britain. Ian had researched the reviews online painstakingly and managed to secure tickets for the half-past ten entry to the Turner Prize. To his delight, she pecked him on the cheek as a greeting, then tucked her arm in his as they headed to the gallery. Once inside, they didn't have to queue at all to enter the exhibition area.

It offended Ian's sensibilities that such work could be called Art. But he put aside his prejudices and did his best to engage with her and the work. In fact, although he couldn't bring himself to call it Art, he did find himself amused by some of it –

– particularly an exhibit that consisted of a robotic male mannequin simulating sex with the exhaust pipe of a luxury car.

What amused him most was the idea that it could be taken so seriously: seriously enough to attract collectors' money. But he comforted himself with the thought that these artists probably knew little about financial planning, and would soon be parted from their riches.

They stayed less than an hour and although it was worse value than a trip to the cinema, he felt he'd proved a point with regards to his cultural credentials. And it was far better to have participated in something than to have sat mute and fidgeting through a screening of an art house movie.

"What was your favourite piece?" she asked him as they left.

"There was this old bloke in a security man's uniform standing in the middle of the room with the rotten garden table in it. Him."

"Oh, *Ian*," she said, giggling, and squeezed his arm.

He'd meant to be sarcastic but, thrilled by his success, he went on. "Seriously, how do you know he wasn't part of the exhibition? Or perhaps he was a former *avant-garde* artist who was hijacking it as a protest?"

She laughed some more – genuinely, he thought.

They walked along the Embankment towards Westminster, enjoying the sun. The river was on the ebb, and a rescue launch growled upriver against the current.

The timing of the second half of the date had been something he'd fretted about, but they reached Westminster pier in good time for the noon trip to Greenwich. The river cruise was something he'd done a couple of times with friends up from Bristol for the weekend. What was more quintessentially London than a trip through its heart on Old Father Thames? The workaday blue and white boat had rows of plastic chairs laid out on the roofless upper deck. Down below there was a bar serving hot and cold drinks, and cramped seating for perhaps half the number accommodated outside.

It transpired that, like most Londoners, she'd never taken a boat down the Thames. It was a perfect day for the trip – the breeze too light to blow the unseasonable warmth away. With the current so strong in their direction of travel, the engine was throttled back to a gentle thrum, and they only caught the occasional whiff of diesel fumes. The gaps in conversation were filled by the commentary, which also served to provide Ian with ammunition for further sarcastic asides.

He brought out his phone and took a couple of shots of her. Sarah's hair was straight, and he decided he liked the way Hazel's red-brown hair cascaded in gentle waves down to her shoulders. He wondered if they'd look back on these photographs together in years to come and recall with fondness the magic of their second date.

"*Very* nice phone," she said. "I'm surprised a firm of accountants would fork out for one."

"Yes," he said. It's essential for work. A high definition camera is essential in my game. No forensic accountant should be without one."

"God," she laughed. "You really are the James Bond of the accounting world, aren't you?"

When they alighted near the dry-docked *Cutty Sark* at Greenwich he took her straight along the river to the Trafalgar Tavern, a grand early Victorian building whose front was directly onto the Thames, and which was famous for its seafood menu. They were in luck, taking a table in a bay window, where the muddy-brown river washed by just a few feet below them. Boats from the nearby rowing clubs gave the view an interest that he could tell she enjoyed.

He ordered a pint of real ale as a reward to himself for having done so extraordinarily well on this second date. He was relieved that she had a white wine, because the last thing he'd wanted was to be stuck with a prude who'd tut-tut at his drinking. She was making all the right noises and he was enjoying her company. After some polite disagreement, he let her pay the bill. His spirits rose – not only was this a sure sign of commitment on her part, but the costs of dating her and getting to the all-important objective of sex were falling. He revised his figures downwards by thirty-five percent.

They walked up the hill to the Royal Observatory. The sun and the gentle breeze had put paid to the last vestiges of haze that had hung over the capital, and the view was magnificent. He stood behind her and pointed out landmarks over her shoulder, his chest against her back. He couldn't help noticing how phallic London was: from the skyscrapers of Docklands on the opposite bank, to the fat stub of the Gherkin in the City and the cigarette outline of the BT Tower in the west. When she leaned back ever so slightly to increase the pressure of the contact on his body, he knew he was on a roll. Perhaps she'd picked up subconsciously on this forest of phalluses laid out before them? He tipped his head forward and down so that her soft red-brown hair brushed against his cheek. The smell of her hair was different to Sarah's and it flushed away all of his previous reservations, aroused as he was at the prospect of what he was sure would be sex with this woman in the next two weeks, which would cut his estimated costs of dating by half again.

On the way back down the hill to Greenwich he wondered how different sex would be with someone other than Sarah. He felt himself panicking a little about what she might be like in bed. Would she be interminably slow to come? What position would she prefer? How compatible would they be?

"I've been on a few dates through M—.com but I must say that I've never had as good a second date as this one," she said as they boarded the boat for the trip back upriver. "It's been so romantic and well thought-out."

"You're worth it," he said, meaning it with a sincerity she would never fully understand. The engines roared into life as the boat pulled away from the pier and headed into the current.

"I'll go and get some coffee," she said. "How do you take yours?" She got up and squeezed past him.

"No, please. I'll get them." He rose from his seat and took out his wallet. As he opened it to fish out a five-pound note, the wash from another boat threw him off-balance slightly. He pulled the note out and made a grab for the back of a chair with the same hand. A receipt fluttered out onto the deck. The breeze caught it and blew it past Hazel, who was already in the aisle.

"It's okay, I've got it," she said, catching it with remarkable dexterity. Her eyes opened wide, then her nostrils flared and her mouth set in fury.

Ian reached for the receipt but she snatched it away.

"What the hell's *this*?" she said through gritted teeth, glowering at him.

"Give me that receipt."

"Porno Emporium, Brewer Street," she read loudly.

The blood drained from Ian's face and his knees felt rubbery.

"I…"

"Special offer – half-price on second DVD. Christ, this is even *signed* by the manager. Just how much of this stuff are you watching?"

"Hazel," he said. "Just give me that receipt."

"What, so that you can buy more of this filth?" she shouted. "Your sort absolutely *repulse* me. Oh, you put on such a good act. What have you got in your flat – hidden cameras, you sick weirdo?"

"It's a mistake, really," he protested, aware that the boat's commentator wasn't bothering to compete with this unbilled entertainment.

"You're bloody right it's a mistake, you *pervert*," she spat.

"I can explain everything," he said.

"Get away from me. You *disgust* me." She crumpled up the receipt and threw it at him.

"No!" he yelled. He jumped up to catch the receipt as a gust of wind caught it. But his hand closed on thin air and he saw ten pounds of pornography discounts head for the water.

"It was going so *well*," she sobbed, shoulders collapsing. She looked at him, tears smudging her mascara. "I was really beginning to like you. And then… Then *this*."

"Hazel, really," he said, reaching out to touch her shoulder.

"Get away from me," she hissed, stepping back. "Don't come *near* me."

"I suggest you leave the lady alone, mate," said a burly member of the crew, stepping in front of him. The man guided her up some steps to the wheelhouse, where she collapsed, sobbing, into a seat.

Ian sought shelter from the stares and smirks of the other passengers by sitting in the downstairs bar area for the rest of the trip, cursing his bad luck and stupidity – it would surely be weeks, and yet more expenditure, before he would have sex. The forty-minute journey felt like an age. Burning with shame and humiliation, he looked out of the portholes, to avoid the stares of the passengers who came down for refreshments. When they reached Westminster he waited until the rest of the passengers had disembarked before poking his head out onto the deck again.

"All clear, guv," said the commentator over the public address system, and the crew fell about themselves laughing. One of them pretended to cough, instead spitting out the word "Tosser!", and there was a fresh bout of laughter. He hurried down the gangway, reddening in the stares of the crowd waiting to get on.

When he logged into M—.com that evening all trace of WhichHazel's entry had disappeared – no profile and no emails. Instead there was a message from the system administrator informing him that she had blocked further communication from him, and that only two more such blockings would be tolerated before his membership was automatically suspended, pending an enquiry. There was no further interest from any of the women on M—.com.

The light on the answering machine was blinking, and he felt there might just be a chance she'd had a rethink. But it was only Marina.

'Only Marina', was not what he thought after he'd replayed the message twice. The line was faint and her English faltering. But he was quite sure he heard something like "I am to come at London... visitch yew". After his initial panic, he realised that she only had his phone number. Even if she could afford to travel, she couldn't track him down from his phone number, could she?

Chapter Eight

"And how was your date with the lovely Hazel, may I ask?" said Rose in her *faux* posh accent, leaning over the top of his cubicle.

"No luck," said Ian, flatly. He was having one last check through the report on Elmer before submitting it to Peterson.

"What, crashed and burned, didya? Spectacularly, or did you just fizzle out?"

"I'd say it was a Jimmy Dean of a wreck. But at least *he* was lucky enough to have died quickly."

Rose giggled. "Well you obviously jumped clear of the wreck. What was she like?"

"Lucky escape. Nutter. And if you want my advice you won't move to High Barnet – something in the water there ages the skin rapidly. Either that or she put anti-wrinkle cream on the lens of her camera."

"I'm so glad you're not bitter, love. Got any more lined up?"

"Nope. Besides, up to Newcastle this week. Now, is there anything specific I can help you with, or are we going to keep up this jolly badinage until lunchtime?"

"That was what I came over for. Your humble presence is required in St Swithin's Lane."

"Oh, really? To what do I owe this dubious pleasure?" St Swithin's Lane was where the rest of Woodcock and Tweed was housed.

"Three things. First, they've got your tickets to Newcastle. Tomorrow morning at – wait for it – six-fifteen from King's Cross." Ian swore under his breath. "Now, now. Mind your blood pressure."

"I hope that was the bad news first. And the other two things?"

"If you could just introduce yourself to the two lovely young ladies you'll be working with, Jess and Louise. And then if you could pop into personnel to have a quick word."

"Personnel?" he didn't like the sound of that at all. "What

does she want?"

"For a professional investigator, you don't half ask the bleedin' obvious, love. A previously high-flying executive is ditched by his girlfriend, loses a ton of weight and collapses at his desk. Why d'you think she wants to see you?"

He took the short walk over to St Swithin's Lane at three. When he'd started his career at Woodcock and Tweed he'd been based there doing standard audit work. He vaguely recollected the two young trainees – Jess and Louise – from the Christmas party. They were fresh-faced and hopeful, working long hours to impress, and spending their spare time studying for exams. He knew what that life was like and didn't envy them.

They had roughly the same build and wore their hair and make-up the same way – and they were even wearing near-identical charcoal-grey skirt suits. He vaguely wondered if there was some genetic propensity towards accountancy which was expressed physically, and whether the pair of them were perfect female specimens. He thought that in a less well-lit environment he could easily mistake one for the other. Thankfully, Jess had light brown hair and Louise's was darker. Jess's face was also slightly thinner. Of the two, he thought Jess was slightly more attractive. He made polite conversation for a couple of minutes, and reflected that it would be quite a big deal for them to be working with someone of his standing and speciality. They'd be eager to please, desperate to pick up his touch. When he'd seen them at the Christmas party who could have guessed they'd be working together on an audit job?

His mind drifted back to the party. How could he forget it? God knows, he'd tried.

He'd been put in an uncomfortable and unusual position. It was unusual, in that it was he – a male – who felt he'd been molested by a member of the opposite sex. And it was uncomfortable for three reasons. The first was that he didn't at all like the person doing the molesting. If it had been the likes of Jess or Louise – and here he allowed his mind to think big, to replay DVD scenarios in his head – or Jess *and* Louise, then he would have had no cause for complaint. The second was that, as with his undergraduate days, he would never get involved with a colleague. The third was that it would have been the personnel department to which he would have complained. But in his case it was the personnel department in the guise of its manager, Barbara Metcalfe, who had molested him.

He had been on fine form that evening, having just been told by Messrs Woodcock and Tweed themselves that his move into partnership was on the cards. He'd drawn the short straw and sat next to her at dinner, where she'd clearly been impressed by his quick wit. A few glasses of wine later and she'd begun to get amorous, dragging him to the dance floor. He'd escaped after a couple of tracks but she'd caught up with him at the bar and squeezed his bottom before he'd managed to break away. As the event was finishing she'd actually grabbed him in an embrace. Cleverly, he thought, he'd had the presence of mind to tap her firmly on the shoulder and – whilst she broke off to speak to whoever she thought was behind her – break free. He walked briskly, almost at a run, until he flagged down a cab. As he slammed the door he heard her calling his name.

For one thing, he'd not been single then – and he did feel proud of himself for the fact that he'd been faithful to Sarah for four years; seven, if you counted the fact that he'd not even dated anyone else when they were separated. Those four years of missed opportunities with the girls on his course still hurt him – and who would remember them now, and what would it have mattered how he'd behaved? So in order not to be reliving his regrets in another few years, ought he not to change his stance on affairs with colleagues? And besides, he was quite sure the rest of the world was at it.

But in Barbara Metcalfe's case he'd continue with his policy of not involving himself with colleagues. It wasn't necessarily that he found her physically unattractive. Indeed, he could see how some men would like that kind of fleshy, big-breasted woman. It was her whole character he disliked. Everything had to be done precisely according to some specific process. For example, procedures more appropriate to a multi-national had now transformed the simple matter of recruiting staff from having a handful of candidates in for a few interviews, to a painful three-month series of hurdles during which Woodcock and Tweed lost most of the best candidates to other firms. And there was nothing anyone could do, because she was the personnel manager and was thus the only person who knew how to fire an obstructive employee. Peterson's cowering concern with Ian's health, as well as his reporting of Ian's loss of consciousness at his desk, had at its root this officious woman. Equally irritating was that her endless appetite for form-filling gave extra work to Rose and her equivalents in St Swithin's Lane. Ian knew the value of good administration staff in the smooth running of the firm, and had no time for those who obstructed them. And Barbara had even got her own office, even though she was junior to him and earned not a penny in revenue for the firm. He knocked and pushed open the door to her office, which had been slightly ajar.

"Ian, how good to see you. Thanks for popping over," said Barbara. She came out from behind her desk and they both sat at the small circular meeting table. He took an instant dislike to the fact that she had quarter of an inch of dark root beneath her auburn hair. No self-respecting accountant would ever appear like that in front of clients: personnel was simply not one of the real professions.

"Yes, good to see you too. You wanted to see me?"

"Just making sure you're alright. You do understand that last week did give us cause for concern. Particularly the weight-loss. Though I must say you're looking very well on it."

"Thank you. I'm alright now, really."

"I understand you lost your girlfriend a couple of weeks ago," she moved in closer over the table but Ian leaned back a little further to keep the distance the same. "We can understand that you must be feeling the strain. Four years, wasn't it?"

"Yes." He wanted out. Badly.

"I know you've had the one appointment with Dr Patel," she continued. "But if you need help on a more personal front, then I'm also a trained counsellor myself."

"Barbara, there's no end to your talents."

"And of course Raj can't take you out for a drink and get to the bottom of it. Only a good colleague, a friend, can do that sort of thing."

He noticed that her right calf was up against his left. An atavistic part of his brain woke his penis, urging him that he had to start somewhere if he was to reinvigorate his sex life. Fleetingly, he imagined what it would be like on top of her in bed, what colour her areolae would be, and how big. He drew his leg away from hers.

"Unfortunately I'm off up to Newcastle tomorrow morning."

"It could just be a quick one." Ian wondered if she had meant the statement to be quite that open to a loose interpretation. He didn't want to find out, though he was tempted to goad her by saying that it could also be a stiff one.

"You know me, Barbara – work before play. I have to be bright and fresh. Perhaps when I'm back in town."

"Yes, of course. When do you think you'll be back?"

"Hard to say with audits. Thank you so much for your time." He got up and went for the door.

"Ian?"

He turned back.

She flushed red. "Just bear in mind that my door's always open."

The caveman in Ian flashed him an image of frenzied, pounding sex with Barbara. "Yes, will do." He breathed a sigh of relief when he was five feet from her office.

He went up a flight of stairs to the floor where all of the senior partners except Peterson had their offices. "Good afternoon, Jean," he said to the PA they shared. He and Jean

Budd had always been on the best of terms. She was the same age as his mother, and he often wondered what she'd have been like as a surrogate one. In a way she'd been a midwife to the firm, having been Woodcock and Tweed's first employee when the partnership was formed.

"Ian, you're looking rather svelte. Doesn't Donald let you out at lunchtime?"

It had been a while since they'd seen one another, and he knew that time spent chewing the fat with her was well invested. She was Rose's boss, and he always made sure that he spoke highly of Rose to her. This was the kind of relationship with women that Ian understood well, and he'd always capitalised on it. He knew Jean had greased the wheels for him over the years. She tut-tutted over the news of Sarah's departure but – unlike his real mother – remained firmly on his side over the matter.

She handed him his train tickets when they'd done talking. "I think Mr Timothy would like to see you for a minute, dear," she said. It was one of the patrician characteristics of the firm that the founding partners were known to those beneath them as Mr Timothy and Mr Jonathan, a slight concession to a less formal society. Only upon graduation into the ranks of partnership was one allowed to address them solely by their first names. It had the effect of making Ian feel like a butler, and made him look forward more keenly than ever to moving from staff to part-owner.

There were two thick oak doors beyond Jean's desk. He knocked gently on the one on the left.

"Come." Woodcock and Tweed's air of anachronistic paternalism was somehow conveyed perfectly in that one word.

He twisted the brass handle and went into the oak-panelled office.

"Good afternoon, Mr Timothy," he said. "How are you?"

"Fine form, thank you." Woodcock rose to shake his hand across his large walnut veneer desk, his piercing blue eyes drilling into him from a six-foot three frame. In spite of his grey hair he always struck Ian as looking much younger than his sixty-five years, perhaps helped by his dapper dress-sense. "Do take a seat, won't you?"

Ian thanked him and sat in one of the leather seats. Would he, one day, be sitting where Woodcock was sitting, the managing partner of a modernised Woodcock and Tweed? He'd always had a suspicion that the founders would remain active in the partnership long after retirement, and would stipulate that it was to remain at least fifty years behind other firms in its attitudes.

"You're off up to Newcastle tomorrow, I understand." Ian nodded, keeping the airwaves clear for Woodcock's message. "This Armstrong business is a key account, you understand. Good piece of business to have, opportunities to network for other business up there, so on and so forth.

"Now, chap up there – the FD – absolutely first class fellow, name of Ed Watkins. Damned workaholic, excellent grasp of the numbers, trained with us way back in the earliest of the early days. With me?"

"Yes, absolutely." Watkins, the finance director, was to be treated with the utmost respect. Ian knew the type and didn't much care for it.

"Good. Now, just remember that it's not Armstrong who pays the bills, it's Watkins."

"Understood."

"Very well. Thanks for taking this one on board. Steer a steady course, there's a good man." Woodcock transferred his attention to a report on his desk: meeting over.

"Cheerio, Mr Timothy."

Woodcock raised his right hand off the desk slightly, but kept his attention on the report. Ian shut the door behind him gently, twisting the handle to avoid making the mechanism click, in the manner of a butler.

He said goodbye to Jean and left the building by the nearest exit.

The ten-minute walk back down the hill to D'Arcy House was perfect for cooling him off. There were times when he was blisteringly angry at the firm's attitude to clients, which was badly out of date and not what he'd regard as being in the spirit of the Ethical Standards guidelines for Chartered Accountants. He could understand a small firm's need to differentiate itself from larger competitors, and that niche marketing was good for the economy. But this patronising attitude was something he'd change if he were controlling the firm. Perhaps it was because he was a small businessman's son: a chip off the old block, after all?

It simply wouldn't do to say that the finance director was king. It was Armstrong's business, and his alone. He'd built it from nothing, and by the age of fifty-three had constructed a regional conglomerate. A great business in Ian's opinion. Indeed, what he would describe as a *beautiful* business, with the integral components each playing their part in supporting the whole. He couldn't care less whether the FD was a workaholic or an alcoholic: it was Ian's job to audit those accounts for the *owner*.

He calmed himself down: partnership before the end of the summer. He'd smile and grit his teeth for Watkins, but if Armstrong wanted impartial advice on the side then Ian would make damned sure he got it.

He packed a bag after his evening run. He'd be back home on Friday night, then off up to Newcastle again the following week.

There was nothing doing at all on M—.com – no women had viewed him, and even Marina had given him a break. He had a few moments' contemplation as to whether to bother with internet dating during his time in Newcastle. He should have spare time in the evening, but he had plans for that. Big plans. And when he logged into his Hotmail account he saw that those plans were coming to fruition.

He'd registered on the university's alumnus website at the

end of the previous week, requesting permission to contact Patsy, Debbie, Tamara and Valerie. There was an email from the alumnus coordinator, who had heard back from two of them already. He scanned further down the email.

Valerie and Patsy had given him permission to view their current contact details. He was conscious of his heart beating faster. He logged into the alumnus website and was able to see their details.

Valerie was now a senior manager in a financial services company. Patsy was working for the local council. He thought Val's job suited her well, but that Patsy's was a little beneath her – last time he'd heard, she'd been in marketing. Valerie had always been good at numbers, which had been part of his attraction to her. He was pleased for them both.

This was a moment of truth for him. For four years as an undergraduate, he'd let girls slip through his fingers. This was his chance to relive those student days, and to take what was rightfully his before he slipped into regretful middle age.

Valerie Craven. The night that Sarah had thwarted him at the party in Jesmond still burned a hole in him – especially the way she'd cut him off for the rest of their final year after Sarah had made him spill his drink all over her at the black and white party.

His recent failure with Hazel still stung. He had to start somewhere. Patsy was a less complex creature by far. He remembered the old axiom they'd learnt at business school: KISS – Keep It Simple, Stupid. Let one success build off another. He told himself that it didn't matter so much if he failed with Patsy or Debbie – they were just small fry compared with someone like Val.

He reminded himself of another business adage: remember your objectives. Doubts crept into his head. Could he really not become emotionally involved with these women? And supposing he succeeded in lighting a fire with Val? Wouldn't he be getting himself into another relationship like the one he had with Sarah? But the downside would be that she'd be in the North East and he'd be in London.

His objective was to get out there and have the sex he'd missed on account of Sarah. Who did he think he was more likely to have sex with – Val or Patsy? Val was more prim, that was for sure. Patsy was one to let her hair down and party a bit. Patsy it was, then.

His hand hovered over the phone. He checked the time: nine o'clock. He didn't want to get into some over-long conversation this late. Better to leave it all to an actual meeting.

He copied her email address and pasted it into a new message in Hotmail.

> Hi Patsy,
>
> Long time no see! I'm up in the Toon this week. Fancy getting together after work one night?
>
> Ian xx

KISS. He added his mobile number and clicked on send before he could change his mind.

But then he realised that it would strike Val as rather odd if he didn't contact her and she heard later that he'd been up in Newcastle. Besides, this was a numbers game too, surely? The bottom line was that he should be hedging his bets. He hovered the cursor over her email address but decided against it. There was still too much emotional baggage there for him. She was surely a long-term project.

Chapter Nine

He loved being on site with clients. There was a certain thrill in watching money flow through an organisation. It would come in from the customers, flow through the sales ledger, to the heart of the profit and loss account, from where it would be pumped through budgetary arteries to the vital organs of the business: sales, marketing, R&D, admin, fixed costs, depreciating assets. But a haemorrhage, a clot, or an injudicious budget cut meant death. At times, walking the corridors of an organisation made him feel like he was a doctor or surgeon on the wards. Except that he had sometimes saved the life of a business – and the livelihoods of hundreds of employees – rather than the lives of individuals. And – in his view at least – it was considerably easier to diagnose circulatory problems in a human being than a company, where electronic money could travel at the speed of light all over the world.

But he hated the early starts that client visits sometimes entailed. King's Cross Station at six-fifteen had meant getting up at five. As he'd taken his taxi across London he'd comforted himself with the prospect of relaxing in the relative peace and comfort of a first-class carriage.

He had been surprised and more than a little put out to discover that he was travelling second-class. An employee of his seniority was supposed to travel first-class – it was supposed to be an immutable part of the client service agreement. He assumed that this was due to Armstrong keeping a tight lid on costs: he was a canny businessman who knew everything would be recharged at a higher rate to his audit invoice. He cursed Armstrong silently, though he respected his tight rein on expenses. He dreaded what the hotel would be like.

His hopes rose fleetingly when two attractive young women greeted him as they took the rear-facing seats opposite him. Then he recognised them as Jess and Louise and his heart filled with dread at the thought of having to make small talk with them for over three hours. He'd been looking forward to a snooze but felt he couldn't do so in front of junior staff.

As soon as the buffet car opened he offered to buy them tea and coffee, so that he could at least escape quarter of an hour of conversation whilst he queued. However, his plan backfired when they took this to be a social offer on his side and talked with him for half an hour after he returned with the drinks. He was disconcerted when he felt a foot brush slowly up and down his calf once, for a few seconds. It was impossible for him to tell which of his colleagues it had been, because neither Jess nor Louise's face betrayed any hint of guilt; nor was there an apology for what must have been an obvious mistake, if it had been unintentional – a man's leg in trousers must surely be unmistakable when brushed by a stockinged foot. This lack of either guilt or apology both troubled and thrilled him. Which of them had it been? Was it time for him to revise his views of office romances? After all, they were in a different division to him. Again, he thought about which of them he preferred and decided it was Jess. Would the owner of the foot make another move later in the week, and how should he respond?

Eventually, they got out their revision notes for their forthcoming exams. He managed to disengage from them completely behind a copy of the *Financial Times*, periodically staring at the changing countryside. As they headed north the grass lost its fertile lustre and changed to the lighter green of plants used to hardier climes. He enjoyed a burst of sun over Durham Cathedral, the haunting outline of Anthony Gormley's Angel of the North winged giant on the skyline, then the spectacular view of the Tyne Bridge and its sisters as they made the final approach to Newcastle Central.

In the huge stone portico which served as a vehicular entrance to the station they got into a dark blue saloon car bearing the Noda Taxi logo so familiar from his student years, and headed for Gosforth.

It was like he'd never been away. The air was noticeably

fresher than London's. The double-decker buses were yellow, rather than red. The cars were smaller, cheaper, older and less aggressively driven. A traffic jam here meant a couple of extra minutes on a journey, rather than an hour. They drove up the Great North Road, with the grassy expanse of the Town Moor on their left; the sight of a few dozen black and white cows grazing so close to the centre of the city a source of wonder to his two colleagues. But Ian's mind was on the suburb of Jesmond, to their right. It was a reminder to him of that night he and Sarah had first met, when she'd wrecked his chances with Valerie Craven. If there'd been a taxi available that night, how differently might his life have turned out?

The taxi dropped them at the three-storey office block on Regent Farm Road. No regent would want a farm there now, he thought. They received visitors' passes at reception and sat down to wait. How long an auditor was kept waiting in reception was, he felt, generally a good indication of how the whole audit would go. After ten minutes, he had his doubts about the days ahead. After another ten minutes, Jess and Louise started shifting uncomfortably.

A lift door opened and a middle-aged blonde walked briskly over to them across the polished grey tiles. "Hello, I'm Anne Salter," she said, beaming a plastic smile at them. "Sorry to keep you waiting." They introduced themselves and followed her into the lift.

He hated awkward silences, particularly when junior employees would be looking to him for leadership. "I was at university in Newcastle," he ventured.

"Ee, really? How lovely," said Anne.

"Yes," he said. "Great place. So much to do, and the welcome's always so warm."

"Ee, I know."

Ian despaired. The days ahead were looking bleak. They went up just one floor. Even in his lazier days, he would never have taken the lift for a single-storey journey. He idly wondered how much electricity was wasted on single-user journeys in this building. The door opened into a small lobby. There were doors leading to separate male and female toilets, and a windowed fire door into a large open-plan office. As they entered, Ian felt all eyes on them. It was something that happened only on the first day of an audit, but it never felt comfortable.

"You can put your bags in here. That's where you'll be working." She opened the door to a small meeting room with a pine table for six, with bare walls and a window overlooking the car park. "If you need a wireless connection, we'll get you sorted for that." They put their bags in the room. He'd seen worse.

They trotted behind her through the office, where the workers were arranged in two islands of four desks. What was evidently Anne's solitary desk stood beside a closed door. A sign on it said 'Edward Watkins, Finance Director'. Anne knocked and Ian heard the same patrician "Come" from inside that he so disliked.

"The auditors from Woodcock and Tweed to see you," said Anne, leaving them in the doorway. Ian led his troops fearlessly into Watkins' office. Anne had not closed the door: this was evidently meant to be a short meeting. He introduced himself and his assistants and Watkins shook their hands. He was exactly what Ian had been expecting – a slightly more relaxed version of either Mr Jonathan or Mr Timothy, and a few years younger. His suit was light, rather than dark, and his tie was brighter. His flyer's moustache would not have been tolerated at Woodcock and Tweed. He'd not aged as well as the senior partners, either – over-exposure to sun, Ian thought.

"Thanks for dropping in," said Watkins to Jess and Louise. "Anne will show you where things are." After Ian's colleagues had left he motioned Ian to close the door, which he did. Watkins sat back down behind his desk but didn't indicate for Ian to sit, so he remained standing.

"I understand you're up here as a replacement," said

Watkins.

"Yes, shortage of senior managers in auditing."

"Big shot forensic chap, eh?"

"I wouldn't say I was a big shot, but I do know my stuff."

"Well if you mind your stuff as quickly as possible then that'll be just fine," said Watkins, with a forced smile.

"Since we're on a fixed-price contract for the job, then it does serve us well to be as fast as possible," countered Ian, politely. "But, as you know, at Woodcock and Tweed we pride ourselves on a thorough job. And I can't sign off on any accounts until I've done a thorough job."

"I'm sure you'll find everything in perfect order. I take a close hand in preparing everything myself. As I'm sure Jonathan and Timothy told you, I was an excellent auditor. Still, I'm sure your thoroughness will be duly reported to your superiors. A good job deserves a good word, eh?"

"Thank you, that's very kind." Ian didn't like this type of supercilious finance director, nor did he like the threatening undertone.

The door opened and in stepped Armstrong.

"Morning Ian, good trip up?" he gave Ian a warm handshake.

"Good to see you again, Mr Armstrong," said Ian, catching a look from Watkins that told him his previous meeting with Armstrong was news to Watkins.

"William, please," said Armstrong. "You've met Steady Eddie then, have you?"

"He was just telling me what a tight ship he runs here," said Ian.

"Aye, works all the hours, and then some. He was highly recommended by your bosses."

"Oh, when was that?" asked Ian.

Armstrong looked at Watkins. "Getting on for three years?"

"About that."

"You'll be getting your first share options soon, eh?" said Armstrong. He turned back to Ian. "He doesn't need the options, mind – he's a real whiz-kid on the financial markets, apparently. Anyway, I'll leave the two of you for now. Ian, I'll be seeing you for dinner. Half-seven at the Gossie Park."

"Oh, right you are," said Ian, recognising the local vernacular for the Gosforth Park Hotel, which he assumed was where he'd be staying. The knowledge lifted his spirits. "I'm looking forward to it." Armstrong left Watkins' office and closed the door. Ian made a mental note to find out what Watkins had been doing between leaving Woodcock and Tweed and joining Armstrong.

"Well, well. Dinner with William Armstrong – you are doing well," said Watkins.

"He's the boss," said Ian, with a smile.

Watkins handed him over to Mary Ruffcorn, the one fully qualified accountant the company employed besides Watkins.

He and Mary went to join Jess and Louise in the office that had been set aside for them. As Mary talked them through the accounts, he kept having to stop himself from focusing on Mary herself. It wasn't that she was attractive – beneath her trendy black-framed spectacles she was moderately so – it was just that the task ahead was so uninteresting to him that he could do it with half his mind. He thought he'd finished with basic auditing years ago and the thought of spending a couple of weeks on it was daunting for its boredom.

There was no canteen, so for lunch they went to the shops on Gosforth High Street for sandwiches and ate them in their meeting room. Ian had the company's IT manager set up his laptop on the wireless connection. He hid the view of his screen from his colleagues whilst he checked his Hotmail account. There was an email from Patsy, inviting him to dinner at her house that evening, and asking him to call her to confirm. He cursed his bad luck to be having dinner with Armstrong, and for the lack of privacy to make the call.

He didn't want to be seen on his mobile, so the car park was out of the question. The only place he could think of was the toilets.

The toilet had two urinals and two cubicles, the doors of which were flush with the floor. He went straight into the cubicle closest to him and pushed on the closed door. He entered, put the toilet lid down and sat on it. He dialled Patsy's number. It went to voicemail – it would be typical of gossipy Patsy to be on the phone. With his years spent away, her Geordie accent sounded much stronger than he'd remembered. He decided against leaving her a message, terminated the call and pocketed the phone. Just as he was leaving the stall the external door opened and another man came in. Ian held back the open door and exited. As he stood outside he realised that it looked to the other man like he'd not flushed the toilet, and had not bothered to wash his hands. What would he think of Ian? In that moment of confusion, his phone rang and as he took it out of his pocket he accidentally terminated the call. He clicked through the options on his phone and saw that it had been Patsy.

The toilet door opened and the other man came out, giving him a strange look. He ducked back into the toilet and went back to the same cubicle. He dialled Patsy's number again. She answered on the first ring.

"Ian!" she screamed into the phone so loudly he held it away from his ear.

"Yes, Patsy. Hi, how are you?" he said.

Her tendency to run away with sentences had not diminished and he couldn't get a word in. Furthermore, he found himself having to concentrate hard to catch what she was saying, due to the speed of her accented speech.

"I'm really sorry, but I can't come round for dinner tonight," he said. "I've got to entertain a client."

"What I've got for you will keep," she said, with a naughty giggle. She'd always given him come-ons in the past. His interest was aroused. Free of the unassertiveness of his early twenties, would he finally have the pluck to fulfil his desires?

"I'm looking forward to catching up with you over dinner

too," he said, but couldn't resist adding his own *double entendre*. "It'll certainly be a mouthful. See you." She giggled her goodbye.

This time he flushed the toilet before leaving the cubicle and then went over to the basin.

His heart leapt as the toilet in the other cubicle flushed and the door opened. He turned around to see Armstrong.

"What is it with you and toilets, son?"

"Not much privacy," he blurted.

"Not with you around, no. I'm sorry if tonight's dinner's getting in the way of your love life."

"No, really. Just catching up with old college friends."

"Sounds more like you're about to catch something *off* them." Ian gave a little laugh at Armstrong's joke. The older man looked him straight in the eye. "Joking aside, for Christ's sake don't let me down, son."

"I won't, I promise. You've just been unlucky with me, that's all. Bit frustrated since losing my girlfriend."

"*Never* let your personal life interfere with business. I expect all your mental faculties to be concentrating on this. It's what I'm paying you for."

"Yes, of course. My apologies." Ian wanted to point out that Armstrong wasn't actually paying for the services of a forensic accountant; only for an auditor — but he let it drop. He held the door open for Armstrong. They parted and Ian went back to his meeting with Mary, Jess and Louise.

Mary had printed a set of accounts for each of the subsidiary companies that comprised Armstrong's business empire. Part of Ian's brain shut down to the insufferable pain of boredom: if he'd seen one, he'd seen them all. Of course, it was Armstrong BioDiesel that interested him most, but he couldn't show that to Mary. In a forensic accountant's world, everyone was a suspect. Indeed, on many occasions it was someone in the accounts department itself who had perpetrated the crime. He turned the problem over in his head. The fact that the subsidiary company was based several miles away in South Shields, and that Armstrong had his suspicions about its turnover, made it unlikely that the fraud was taking place in head office. Unlikely, but not impossible.

The afternoon yawned on as he stopped Mary to ask her routine questions, which she answered thoroughly. She showed them to the archived invoices. Those from the current year were kept in the office, older ones were archived for the statutory seven years in a basement vault – a sensible move instigated by Watkins himself. At five o'clock he noticed that Mary was getting fidgety. He reminded himself that he was in the North now: work would start and finish earlier than in London. As he closed the meeting he felt a pang of envy for the lifestyle: Mary and her colleagues would most likely be home in a matter of a few minutes, rather than facing the hour of cramped conditions on buses and tube trains that most Londoners did.

Anne Salter told them they'd been booked into a local three-star hotel. He kept his anger to himself: the contract for someone of his seniority stipulated a minimum of four stars. He'd been expecting to stay at the Gosforth Park, and had been looking forward to running in the open countryside. "Do you want me to book a taxi, or are you happy to walk?" asked Anne.

"I'm pretty sure I know where it is, thanks." He turned to his two colleagues. They nodded their assent to walking.

When they were out of the company car park, Louise said: "I thought the North East was famous for its warm welcome?"

"It was in my day, but I think it's just a departmental thing," said Ian. "Watkins is a very domineering man, and he's no Geordie. Mary Ruffcorn's the only accountant who's stayed on there after qualifying. Must be hell working for him."

"But isn't Watkins ex-Woodcock and Tweed?" asked Jess. "I expected that to count for something with us."

"Apparently not," said Ian.

They reached the hotel and he took charge of checking in.

"So, are we going to see some of Newcastle's famous nightlife?" asked Jess. "I've heard it's supposed to be pretty wild."

"Yes, it is pretty wild," said Ian. He cast his mind back to the snowy winter nights when the 'lads' would wear short-sleeved shirts with no jackets, and the 'lasses' would parade in skimpy two-pieces more suited to summer on the Costa del Sol, tottering on four-inch heels. "I'm having dinner with Mr Armstrong tonight, so I'm afraid you're on your own for now. But shouldn't you be studying for the June exams anyway? I found that these sorts of hotel were pretty conducive to work."

Louise and Jess looked at each other. "I suppose," said Louise. "How about tomorrow night?"

"Dinner with an old university friend. Maybe Thursday? Thursday night here is like a Friday night anywhere else in Britain."

They nodded their assent and he congratulated himself for having managed his juniors so well.

His cramped room wasn't quite as bad as he'd feared, but it certainly wasn't to his satisfaction. The bed was a single one – presumably to deter business travellers from sleeping with colleagues – and there was no bath: only a shower. The luxuries consisted of a twelve-inch colour television, and a tiny kettle with two tea bags, two sachets of coffee, two plastic milk cartons and two gulp-sized cups. He turned on his laptop and found that there was at least a wireless signal. He charged the fee for the next three nights to his company credit card and found that there was a golf course nearby that he could run on.

Although the air was noticeably cleaner than in London, once he reached the small golf course he discovered that it was thick with balls and abuse. He received so much hostility from the players that he gave up after ten minutes and ran along towards a nearby housing estate.

Two minutes later he realised he'd made a mistake. Within that time, the local kids had discovered that there was an unfamiliar jogger on the loose. A pack of four cycled around him in circles, occasionally mounting the pavement, as he tried to ignore them. Initially, they were just curious, but then Ian made the mistake of telling one of them to get out of his way and they caught his accent.

"Are ye from the Sooth?" asked the oldest, probably about twelve.

"Bristol, originally."

"Bristol, *awriginarly*," mimicked the boy.

"Fuck off," said Ian, as politely as he could.

"Nah, *yeez* fook off, ye Soothern *coont*."

"Look, just piss off, will you?"

"Piss *orf*, will *yew*?"

Ian felt his blood rise. "Look, just fuck off."

"Ye ganna mek us?"

"I said fuck off."

The boy screeched his bike to a halt in front of Ian. "Are yeez ganna fookin' mek us, ye fookin' poof?"

Ian did what he knew he should have done minutes ago. He turned tail and began running the other way, out of the estate.

"Fookin' coward!" shouted the second-oldest boy, missing him by a whisker as he rode past at speed.

Ian was determined to stay calm and kept running at the same pace.

"Stop an' fight like a fookin' man, will yeez?" said the ringleader, punching him on the buttock. Ian knocked the boy's arm away. The boy lost his balance and fell off his bike. One of the younger boys collided with the downed rider and there were two yowls of pain. Ian saw his chance and began sprinting for the main road.

"I'll fookin' have ye noo, ye bastard!" yelled the leader.

Ian heard the sound of four bicycles accelerating. He looked back to see the ringleader out in front, just ten yards behind him. The intersection with the main road was just five yards ahead. He found a reserve of wobbly-kneed energy and rounded the corner onto the main road. He heard the gang skidding their tyres and slackened off his pace, exhausted.

"Fookin' gerrim!" said the leader, mustering his troops.

Ian checked back for cars and crossed the road at a sprint, inciting the ire of drivers in both directions, who sounded their horns angrily. The cyclists now had the traffic against them, unless they chose to cross the busy road and ride on the pavement.

"Stop him! He's a paedophile!" shouted the second-in-command at a pedestrian who was coming Ian's way. He looked at the man pleadingly, who shifted off to the side to let Ian pass. "Paedophile! Paedophile!" chorused the boys. He looked back – they were at least unable to cross the main road... for now.

He sprinted along the main road a hundred yards, then turned down a road in a more well-to-do neighbourhood, where he slowed his pace. He jogged on warily for a couple more minutes until he realised he was lost. He looked around and over the roofs of the houses recognised the top of a tall building on Regent's Farm Road, next to Armstrong's. Relieved, he soon found himself at the edge of the estate of offices. Reoriented, he began jogging in the direction of the hotel.

A police car overtook him slowly and pulled in a few yards ahead. The officer in the passenger's seat opened the window and beckoned him over.

"Yes, officer?" said Ian.

"A group of lads is complaining about a paedophile fitting your description," said the officer. "They say he beat a couple of them up and tried to steal their bicycles."

Ian hesitated before answering. It was a no-win situation. His own crime-fighting experience had taught him that the truth always came out in the end, and it paid to be deferential. "In that case, I'd like to report a group of four lads aged eleven to twelve for assault."

The driver harrumphed and tapped on the steering wheel. His colleague's expression was half-grimace, half-smile. They'd both heard Ian's accent and guessed the rest. "We do have to investigate these things, sir. There is actually a known paedophile on parole in the area but he's about thirty years older than you and wears spectacles. There's been a bit of media hysteria about him."

"It's alright, I do understand."

"Can we just take your details for the record? It's just that you might want to file a complaint against those lads in the future."

"Sure." Out of the corner of his eye, Ian saw an expensive saloon car pull up behind the police car but ignored it. "Ian Bourne. I'm an accountant up here on an audit at Armstrong's across the road there." He ignored the figure getting out of the driver's side of the saloon – if he wanted to speak to the police he could wait his turn: Ian had to be at dinner with Armstrong in half an hour.

"What's going on here, officer?" asked a familiar voice. Ian and the officer looked round at the man from the saloon car: it was Armstrong.

"Mr Armstrong. Hello, sir," said the officer. "This gentleman says he's here on business with you." Ian felt himself redden. He smiled weakly at Armstrong.

"Aye, right enough. Is there a problem, like?"

"Just some local kids up to mischief," said the officer.

"I see," said Armstrong. "I can vouch for this lad if you need me to."

"That won't be necessary, Mr Armstrong, but thanks for your help."

"Hadn't you better be running along, son?" said Armstrong to Ian. "We've got dinner in half an hour and I'd hate you to be late."

"Of course," said Ian, and ran off, feeling very self-conscious under Armstrong's gaze.

A few minutes later he stumbled, exhausted, into the hotel lobby.

He almost collided with Jess and Louise, who were in casual

attire. "Are you alright?" asked Louise.

"Yes, fine. Just pushing myself hard." He gave an unconvincing laugh and told them to enjoy their dinner. He went straight for a shower without his other exercises, and noticed that he was still shaking slightly from the adrenalin. He cursed his bad luck loudly.

The Gosforth Park Hotel was only a short taxi ride away and he arrived just before half-seven. He checked the lobby before going through to the lounge bar, where he found Armstrong. And he was sitting with—

"Hello Ian," said Armstrong. "I'd like you to meet Valerie Craven."

Ian felt himself flush from head to foot. His head swam. Valerie looked just as attractive as that fateful night he'd been ambushed by Sarah, seven years before. He reached out a hand towards her, as if it were down a long tunnel.

"Good to see you Ian," she said with her gleaming smile, blue eyes sparkling above her high cheekbones. "You're looking fit and well."

"Great to see you too, Val. You're looking terrific."

She turned to Armstrong. "We were in the same year at uni." She brushed a lock of her short black hair back behind her left ear. Ian's heart skipped a beat with desire.

"How lovely," said Armstrong. He motioned Ian to sit down with them. "Anyways, she's in charge of our leasing operation, which is doing very well indeed." Ian realised that this would be the finance company that the alumni association said she was working for. "Every quarter I treat my best-performing manager to a slap-up meal and this is her third in a row. She earns a very tidy bonus."

"Because she's worth it," Ian blurted, quoting the punch line from a beauty advertisement.

"Was he always a comedian at university, Val?"

"No, he was a very serious student. Why?"

"Oh, maybe I've just caught his humorous side."

Ian curled his toes. "So, Val," he said. "Great to hear you're doing so well. You were always the cream of the crop. I trust you're as successful in the rest of your life?" He tried to make his glance at her ring finger surreptitious, but was sure she caught him looking. He was delighted to see that her finger was ringless. An untamed part of his brain told him he'd cancel his dinner with Patsy tomorrow night, and even his weekend return to London to pursue Valerie.

"Work is my top priority right now," she said, primly enough for him to think she was telepathic.

Armstrong finished his drink. "Right, let's go and eat." He got up and led the way through to the Park restaurant. Ian followed the other two, hanging back a couple of paces to make sure he could catch a sly look at the calves and buttocks he'd thought of so often during the intervening years. Hers was certainly one bottom line he never believed he'd get to scrutinise again. The restaurant was crammed with diners but they were shown to an empty window table by a fawning *maître d'*. Dusk was settling in over the manicured grounds, the trees still bare due to the later spring of the north.

Valerie was a mistress tactician, keeping Armstrong interested in the brief catching-up that she and Ian carried out. It was made easier by the fact that Armstrong was very much a people-person who took a genuine interest in his employees' backgrounds. Ian envied Valerie working for someone of that ilk and entrepreneurial ability, rather than the crusty elitism of Woodcock and Tweed. Armstrong listened intently as she described a group project where she and Ian had collaborated to produce an innovative solution to a seemingly intractable business problem. They had then presented the proposition to a local company, which had gone on to implement it. The story was an excellent choice. It showed Ian in an much better light for Armstrong, talked up his abilities, and encapsulated the story in a witty and succinct way that engaged her employer expertly.

Ian fell madly in love with her.

His thoughts turned back to that night that he'd met Sarah, the night that he was supposed to get this beautiful woman, his dream partner. The night he met Sarah. The night that Sarah *hijacked his life*. The night she *ruined* it. She owed him seven years of sleeping with this vision – or at least the carnal knowledge of her to sustain him in later years. He still wanted Valerie. He wanted that toned body, forged in thousands of sweating hours of county-level squash. He wanted that dazzling smile, that advert-perfect black hair, the two beautiful blue eyes set above those finely sculpted cheekbones. He wanted other men to envy him for the delicate way she held her glass, wanted them to be as transfixed as he was by her mellifluous laugh. He wanted her now more than he ever did back then. It was his right – the world owed him, and he was desperate to collect.

Ian used the rest of the conversation to understand Armstrong's businesses better, and Armstrong suggested that Valerie might work more closely with him if he needed the inside track on any aspect of the business. To Ian's delight, she readily agreed to do it. His imagination began to run away with him – time alone in a car with her as she drove him around the outposts of Armstrong's empire, and secretive conversations over intimate dinners.

Towards the end of the meal Valerie excused herself. Now that they were alone, Armstrong changed tone. "I need you to sort out ABD as soon as you can."

"ABD? Oh, you mean Armstrong BioDiesel. Well, I do have to perform the audit first."

"Fuck the audit, son. Watkins is great at that stuff, and that's what I pay him for. Get your arse down there next week and get it sorted. I want results."

"First I'd like a detailed look at the accounts. After all, that's where the problem lies – a disconnect of some sort between your forecast figures and the actuals." He shifted uncomfortably. "Look, in a lot of these sorts of cases we find it's someone inside the accounts team itself. If you think this is an ongoing problem, then I can't just wave a flag to the person committing the fraud that I'm interested in ABD because they'll hide the evidence."

"Bollocks. That's the tightest accounting team I've ever had, and they've all been with me for years. Rock Steady Eddie's been over the accounts and found nothing. Something's going wrong on the ground."

"Fine, but then I've got to explain why I'm down in South Shields. You should hire a private investigator for that."

"Nah. Don't trust 'em. A lot of them are bent. Something doesn't add up and I want *you* to find out what it is."

"Okay. Well, it's not unheard of for an accountant to go and look at some of the fixed assets."

"Fine, do it. Whatever it takes, you have my authority."

Valerie returned to the table. "You two are as thick as thieves. What *have* you been talking about?" she said.

"Golf," said Ian.

"Aye, I'd watch Ian – I think he'd like to play a round with you," said Armstrong, and banged the table in merriment. He signalled for the bill.

"Can I offer you a lift back, Ian?" asked Valerie. "Or are you staying here?"

"If it's not out of your way, I'm staying at the VentureLodge across the way from the office."

She wrinkled her nose. "Shame on you, William. You've beaten down the accountants so badly that they have to put their staff up in a place like that."

"Don't blame me," said Armstrong. "It's Eddie who deals with all that stuff."

"Come on, Ian, let's get you back," said Valerie. They thanked Armstrong for the meal and headed for her car. It was a good quality company car, as he'd expected from someone working for a man whose empire encompassed the motor trade. They got in.

"So what did William *really* talk with you about so enthusiastically?"

"Fixed-asset depreciation," he replied. She looked at him for a moment. "Seriously. I know your leasing and finance division just occupies an office, but the petrol stations and the BioDiesel plant, for example, are substantial assets. How you write those down can make a massive difference to the bottom line."

She rolled her eyes. "That's just so you, Ian. You always had the answers and you're no different now."

"Ah, but now I get *paid* to have the answers." They both laughed, and he felt himself move a little closer to his objective.

"Listen," she said. "Why don't I take you for a quick tour of the Armstrong empire on Thursday afternoon?"

"That'd be great – I'll be halfway mad with the accounts by then."

He had desperately hoped that the relative earliness of the hour – ten o'clock – meant that she'd invite him back to her place for a coffee, but she took him straight to the VentureLodge and dropped him off.

Back in his room he checked his Hotmail. Nothing at all from M—.com, but he didn't care. Valerie was in his sights now and he'd use Patsy tomorrow night as a warm-up.

Chapter Ten

Jess and Louise's bleary eyes over breakfast told him they'd not spent the night studying. He didn't pass comment but downgraded his people-management capabilities. Conversation was muted on the walk to Armstrong's headquarters: the only thing less enjoyable than auditing was auditing with a hangover. For his part, his muscles ached from the previous night's sprinting.

The morning was spent looking at the details of the accounts, asking Mary Ruffcorn about the treatment of balance sheet items in the various subsidiaries. He had to give it to her – she knew her stuff, and he respected her for that, and could see that she was frustrated at not being given more responsibility by Watkins.

In the late afternoon they had scheduled the task of checking the profit and loss account of one of the subsidiaries. It was a process they would carry out on all of them, but there was the vexed question of which was to be first. He didn't want to pounce on Armstrong BioDiesel for the reasons he'd given Armstrong, but he wanted the man off his back and saw a way through. "Let's do it alphabetically. What's first? Whatever it is, I bet it begins with an 'A'," he said. The humour broke the torpor.

"You're right, it does begin with an 'A'," chirped Mary. "Armstrong…" she paused and adjusted her trendy black glasses for effect, "BioDiesel. We call it ABD in the company."

"Well, let's hope it's as easy as ABC," said Ian.

Mary fetched a thick printout of the nominal ledger – a list of all the transactions for the company, split on a monthly basis. This was grist to the auditor's mill, but superficial data to a forensic accountant. Any company could produce a fictitious set of accounts and a bogus nominal ledger – though it would require some applied intelligence to make them both appear genuine. It was far more difficult to present a convincing set of invoices that tallied with the rest of the accounts. What was almost impossible was to produce a convincing set of documents for two or more years running. He'd seen it done, but he'd caught it on those occasions. He was quite sure such a thing had never got past him.

Mary returned to her desk at last, leaving them to pore over the twelve months of nominal ledger and the file of invoices, as well as the bank transactions. So far this was entirely normal procedure, and no suspicions would be raised. On his trips through the office to fetch a glass of water or use the toilet, Ian checked for abnormal behaviour amongst the staff – nervous glances, red faces, sudden absences – but could see none. Perhaps Armstrong was right and this accounting team really was watertight? It begged the question as to where the fraud was – if, indeed, there was any. He began to wonder whether it was a dark imagining brought on by greed and ego on Armstrong's part. After all, what self-made millionaire likes to admit that his pet division is not performing to his expectations? Financial forecasts for operations in new markets were notoriously inaccurate, as many ruined investors could testify, and the man had invested millions with an expectation of a return that hadn't materialised.

The invoices were neat, clean and in order. Everything checked back perfectly to the nominal ledger. He called time on the proceedings at half-five. On any other job, he'd have called in on the finance director as a simple courtesy to let him know what stage he was at, but he wanted as little contact with Watkins as possible. As he walked back to the hotel that evening with Jess and Louise, he kept a nervous eye out for kids on bicycles.

"Out for another run tonight?" asked Jess.

"Dinner with an old uni friend. Not seen her in years."

"Very nice," said Louise, with a knowing smile. "See you at breakfast?"

Her cheekiness flummoxed him, so he just smiled and went

red. He showered and changed into casual clothes. He remembered Patsy's petite figure and tendency to sexual innuendo, and wished he'd chanced his arm years ago. Tonight was his big shot at redemption.

Patsy lived in Jesmond, barely quarter of a mile from the house where he'd met Sarah. Rather than use the Metro, he decided to take a taxi. Her house was in the middle of a terrace between Osborne Road and the Metro track – always the cheapest housing stock in the area. After he'd paid the driver he realised his oversight and walked back up to the main road. He bought a bunch of flowers from a petrol station forecourt and a mid-priced bottle of red wine from an off-licence. He was just a few minutes late when he knocked on her door. There were hurried footsteps from inside.

"Ian!" squealed Patsy, throwing her arms around him. His hands being full, he reciprocated with a kiss on her cheek. He found himself breathing in the fragrance he'd so often imagined himself waking up smothered in after a night of passion. She stepped back and invited him in. "So good to see you," she said in a curiously hushed tone.

"Wonderful to see you, too. You're looking so *well*." His last word hung in the air. She had put on weight. Gone was the petite figure of his fantasy. Her hair – although still highlighted – lacked the lustre and bounce of her youth. But her fingernails were still manicured, and varnished a passionate red.

"Ee, I'm so excited to see you," she said. "And you've brought flowers – how sweet. Come on through." He followed her past the stairs, into a room that had been knocked through into a sitting room and dining area. Although her mini-skirt had been traded for one that reached her knees, as was befitting the modesty of a middle manager, he was pleased to note that her calves were still as he remembered them.

He could smell cooking, but something niggled at him – something was out of place. He'd not thought to ask whether she was still single. He'd just assumed by the nature of her welcome that she was. A quick glance revealed no trace of another male. Patsy had clearly devoted a great deal of time and effort to the décor – as much as she had done to her own appearance when she was a student. The lounge area was tastefully modern, with a stencilled motif of musical notes between the dado rail and ceiling, whereas the dining area had a more traditional feel to it. Ian realised that there was just one item missing from Patsy's dream home: a man.

She poured the red wine into two glasses and handed him one. They drank to absent friends. "There's something I've been dying to show you," she said. With a conspirational smile she took his hand and led him upstairs.

His heart raced and his mind boggled. They reached the top of the stairs, where he could see a bathroom door and two bedroom doors leading off the landing. All three were slightly ajar. Was it really going to be this easy? "It's been a long time, Patsy. And I've certainly missed you," he said. Still grinning, she pressed a finger to his lips and slowly opened the door to one of the bedrooms.

"There," she whispered. "Isn't she beautiful?"

Ian's heart sank. In one corner of the room was a cot. The floor was littered with toys.

"How lovely," he whispered, struggling for words. The child looked like any other. "How old?"

"Ten months. Her name's Samantha." She pulled him forward for a closer look. He thanked his lucky stars that the child was asleep — he hated holding babies.

"She's as beautiful as her mother," he whispered. Patsy squeezed his hand and they crept back downstairs. He realised that she'd taken great care to keep the downstairs living area free of a child's clutter, but now that he was savvy he could see that there were some brightly coloured DVD boxes in her collection, similar to the those he'd seen at Stu and Nina's.

"So, who's the lucky father? Don't tell me his name. Let me

guess – it's Sam."

"Ee, good guess!"

He shrugged – it was hardly a deduction worthy of Sherlock Holmes. "Is Sam joining us for dinner?"

"No," she said. "The dirty bastard upped and left a couple of months after she was born. I get maintenance, like. And there's a free crèche at work, which helps."

"Local authority job. Of course."

"Aye, I work at the Civic Centre. It's ideal for us – just a couple of stops on the Metro. And the hours are great – thirty-seven hours a week and there's flexitime."

"You've landed on your feet, then. Much easier than working in marketing." He thought of his arduous working week and imagined his massive tax bill going to pay armies of single mothers to work in plush public sector employment.

"Too bloody right. I still do marketing, but it's for the local authority."

He wondered what could be so difficult about marketing services that were forced upon an unwilling and captive populace. The evening was not conforming to his expectations. For another thing, she wasn't as attractive to him as she'd once been. It wasn't just that she'd put on weight, but her face had sagged noticeably – bags under her eyes and a double chin. She no longer did anything for him – her mystique was gone. He thought back to his own state a few weeks before and realised how lucky he'd been that Sarah had kept her figure all those years as his own had deteriorated.

But dinner was delicious; she'd clearly taken her time over it. He supposed she didn't get much chance to entertain. He helped her clear the dishes and then they sat on the double sofa. Still being in the area, she was much more tuned in to what had happened to their peers and he was surprised at how well some of those he'd regarded as no-hopers had fared. He mentioned that he'd dined with Valerie Craven the previous evening.

"You always had a little something for her, didn't you?" she said, neutrally. "We all thought something might come of it, but you never did go out together in the end, did you?"

"No, there was nothing between us," he said.

"Oh, that's funny. We thought you were two of a kind. Always dead serious about your studies and that."

"So," he chose his words carefully. "Was she keen on me?"

"I never knew her that well. To be honest, I thought she was a stuck-up cow."

"Oh, right."

"And very materialistic."

"I see."

"So what about your love-life? Getting on for thirty. Are you still with that Sarah lass?"

"Split up last month. We'd been living together for about four years."

"Ee, what a shame. She was a bonnie lass, her. Brought you out of your shell a bit. Why did you split up?"

"I guess there was a lot of stuff that wasn't right."

"So... back on the market again then, eh?" Her voice had taken on a lower tone.

"In a manner of speaking."

She shifted on the sofa. "I've been on the market for quite a while now meself."

He could see where this was going, and didn't want a ticket. "You're an attractive woman, Patsy. You must have plenty of fellahs after you."

She put a hand on his knee. "You've no idea how hard it is to meet a man who isn't a bit spooked by a woman with a kid. Well, a decent bloke, anyways."

He straightened up. "I'm sure there's someone out there for you."

She bit her lower lip. Her hand slid slowly from his knee and up his thigh. There'd been a time when he'd longed for those red-varnished nails being so intimate, but now they looked like talons. "There's someone in here who can give me what I need right now."

What he'd fantasised about all day had become a reality he couldn't stomach. "I'm right in the middle of a really important job at the moment, Patsy. Very busy schedule, and I have loads of paperwork to go over tonight."

"Ian, for Christ's sake. Just drop the friggin' work for once, will you?"

"I'm in line for a partnership in the summer."

"Are ye fookin' serious?" she asked, her voice slipping deeper into Geordie. She took her hand away and clasped it to her chest, as if it were injured.

"I was always serious, you know that. I was notorious for it."

"Not the way you were talking on the phone yesterday." Her lips pouted.

"That was just our usual badinage, surely?" he stammered.

"Well you could have fooled me."

"I'm sorry if I gave you the wrong expectation."

"It's not like we're kids or something," she said. "All I'm asking is one fookin' night." He raised his hands in protest. "One fookin' night Ian. Ye divvn't know how lonely I get. I've got emotional and physical needs."

He got up. She was becoming emotional, and he couldn't deal with emotional women. "I'd better go."

"Ye *bastud*," she said.

"Look, I'm sorry if—"

"It's me, isn't it? I knew yous used to have a little bit of a thing for us. It's this motherhood thing, isn't it? Be honest, what would have happened if I'd farmed Samantha off for the night? Would yous have slept with me then?"

"Patsy, for crying out loud—"

"So it *is* me then, is it? Am I too fat for yous? Have I lost me figure?" She was on her feet now, standing between him and the living room door.

"Patsy, please." He tried to edge past. He panicked at the realisation that he'd just used a nickname for her from deep in his brain. What next?

"Am I *soiled* or something, am I? Not good enough for yous, with your big fookin' City job?"

"No, it's not that." He managed to push past and made for the door.

"This is what men do to women," she shouted as he unlocked the front door. She pulled up her blouse to reveal a mound of spare flesh, crossed with angry white stretch marks. He shuddered. "You knock us up and then leave us when yeez divvn't like what it does to us. Bastuds, all of yous."

The 'All men are bastards' refrain: being a civil servant had turned her into a radical feminist too, he thought as he stepped out onto the tiny front path. "Patsy, I'm really sorry this happened. You've got a beautiful baby girl and you're a wonderful person. You need a stable relationship, not a… not a one-night stand."

"Look where a stable relationship gorrus," she said, her voice trembling. "What I need is a really good shag and you're not man enough to do it. Now *fook off.*" She slammed the door, and he heard crying – both adult and baby – from behind it.

A couple of youths had stopped on the other side of the street. "I'd fookin' give 'er one," said one of them.

"Fookin' poof," said the other at Ian.

He snapped out of his shock. He had to get away, but had no idea where to get a taxi. He headed west, to where he knew the Metro station should be. He ran into the railings beside the track itself but it took him a few minutes to find West Jesmond station. One of the yellow and white two-carriage trains took him the three stops to the Regent Centre in Gosforth. The contrast to London's packed and stifling tube couldn't have been more striking. Again, he cursed the quality of life in the capital.

He got off at the Regent Centre, and as he walked disconsolately away he heard a male child's voice some distance behind him.

"There's that bastud! Oi, paedophile!"

Against his better judgement, he looked back. There was the ringleader of the gang of children who'd hounded him the previous night. The recognition was mutual. But he wasn't with his younger friends – he was now with four much taller youths, their faces in shadow from the hoods of their sweatshirts.

"That's him, alreet. Let's gerrim."

"Fuck," muttered Ian. He had a good fifty-yard start on them but didn't fancy his chances. An elderly passenger was getting into the back of the one taxi at the rank. Ian jumped in beside him.

"Hang on, mate," said the driver. "This gentleman was here first."

"They're after me." He pointed to the youths running their way. "Here." He took out a twenty-pound note. "I'll pay double the fare to my hotel and I'll pay this man a tenner for his trouble."

"He who pays the piper," said the taxi driver, and shifted the vehicle into gear.

"Make it twenty for me too," said the old man.

"Paedophile!" shouted the boy.

"What's that he's saying?" asked the taxi driver, slowing down.

"He's not saying nowt," said the old man. He glanced awkwardly out of the back window and slunk down into his seat. "A tenner'll do me, son. Yer alreet." The grey-haired man's spectacles glinted in the streetlights. Ian eyed the old man suspiciously but said nothing more.

His cramped hotel room was a welcome sanctuary. He turned on his mobile phone. It beeped. There was a message from Patsy:

Do you not want dessert next week? Patsy xx

He was dumbfounded. "Women," he muttered. He thought deeply whilst his computer booted up. Was this really what life had in store for him? Was he going to be trapped between the beautiful and unattainable and the faded and tired? It didn't bear thinking about.

He'd not been this long without any kind of physical companionship or comfort for four years. She'd just always been there. Even her slightest touch, he now realised, had been an important part of the way he felt about himself. He held the mobile phone face-up in his hand, hovering over the autodial for Sarah.

But the cheap hotel room pressed the idea of sex into him – not lovemaking, but sex, pure and simple. Well, maybe not pure... He scrolled through the menu to Patsy's message and hit reply. If there wasn't anything much on offer, then shouldn't he hedge his bets? And if this was the taste of things to come, perhaps he'd better get used to it. He typed in: 'Thanks for a lovely meal. Might be round next week for the next course. Ian xx.' He hesitated before sending it – he'd never have had the courage to be this blatant a few years ago, but sex without strings was what appeared to be on offer. And wasn't this what he'd wanted? Wasn't this the ideal he'd mapped out for his future? Couldn't he just close his eyes and imagine Patsy as she'd been when he'd found her so alluring? He pressed Send and the deed was done. Nothing came back to beep at him over the ether.

There was an email from Debbie.

> How r u? Call me and let's get together. Fancy seeing some of the old crowd as well? Deb xox

She'd put her mobile number on the bottom. He logged into the alumnus site and saw that she'd given him permission to view her details. She managed a fashion shop in the city centre. His heart lifted: she'd be fair game for evenings during the week if she had to work weekends. Dumb Debbie with her Do-me-Debbie eyes. He smiled automatically as he recalled the Debbie-dee-*Dawg* nickname, and once more imagined her colossal breasts swinging free beneath her as she was taken from behind. He imagined himself in the image, hands on her hips as he thrust hard and deep into her, watching the two of them in a mirror by the side of the bed, his loins slapping on her buttocks.

> Very well, thanks. Great to hear from you! Was thinking of seeing you first and then maybe the old crowd a bit later on. Fancy going out on Tuesday night next week?
>
> Ian XX

He had a quick look around M—.com but didn't have the inclination to start anything off – he had one sure thing for next week and another one in line. And tomorrow he had a chance to charm Valerie.

Chapter Eleven

Jess and Louise were as surprised to see him at breakfast as he was surprised at their chirpiness. One night on the town had been enough, evidently.

"So how was dinner with your friend?" asked Louise on the way over to Armstrong's offices.

"Great. People do change, though. There she is with a baby now."

"Happens," said Jess. "It's how the human race perpetuates."

"Well when your friends start perpetuating it feels a bit different," he said.

"It must have been a disappointment," said Louise. "They say babies are the ultimate contraceptive."

Again, he couldn't believe the innuendo. "Not at all. I'm very happy for her."

So far as he could see, there was nothing inconsistent in the nominal ledger for ABD. It was just another year of relatively poor growth after a promising first couple of years. He couldn't help feel that this indicated Armstrong's business model was wrong. After all, if this was supposed to be a high-growth market the logical conclusion was that Armstrong was losing market share.

They moved on to the next business just before lunch: Armstrong Civil Engineering, or ACE, for short. He had to give it to the man: he sold new cars, traded used ones, lent people the money to buy them, sold the fuel to run them, manufactured biodiesel to make them appear 'greener' — and even built and maintained the roads they ran on. Looking further down the lists of businesses, he could see that he even owned a scrap yard. Andrew Carnegie himself would have been proud of the man for his integration of the product lifecycle.

Anne Salter interrupted them shortly after lunch. "Valerie Craven's here to see you," she said. "She's on her way up."

"Thanks," said Ian. "I'm off to make a physical check of

some of the fixed assets," he said to Jess and Louise.

Valerie appeared in the doorway, looking as gorgeous as she had two nights before. "Hi," she said to the three of them, giving them a dazzling smile. "Shall we?" she said to Ian, dangling her car keys. She turned and walked over to the exit for the lift.

"I'll probably be gone the rest of the afternoon," said Ian. "So I don't know whether I'll be back for dinner this evening."

"Enjoy the fixed assets," said Louise.

"Yes," giggled Jess. "We'll look after our own figures if you mind the bottom line."

He checked over his shoulder to see that Val was out of earshot. "Appreciating assets is one of the perks of seniority." He closed the door behind him, thrilled that his two charges had acknowledged his sexual potential.

"Where to first?" asked Valerie, buckling her seatbelt.

"I'd like to see a bit of everything," he said. "But I'd quite like to see the BioDiesel plant in South Shields, if that's not too far."

"Why's that?"

Could he trust her? Armstrong had sworn him to secrecy on that first meeting. "As I was saying the other night, how you treat fixed assets has a dramatic effect on the balance sheet. And because it's the only manufacturing plant in the group it stands out like a sore thumb. Whilst I'm only doing an audit here, Woodcock and Tweed does offer sound accounting advice as standard practice."

She laughed a bubbling laugh that delighted him. "You're such a company man, Ian."

"The other thing," he said, taking his heart in his hands, "is that I thought I'd enjoy the drive with you."

She looked over at him, her smile more fixed now, examining him.

"No," she said. "You haven't changed. You're still the Ian I knew at uni."

"I hope that's a good thing," he said, remembering how she'd cold-shouldered him for months after Sarah intercepted him in the kitchen at that party.

"Yes," she said. "Yes, that's a good thing." He felt his spirits lift.

She took him via the scenic route, over the Tyne Bridge and into Gateshead. After they'd turned left towards South Shields, she pulled into a garage forecourt. He got out of the car to continue the conversation with her as she filled the tank. "This is one of the most profitable ones," she said.

"A rare thing to see an independent petrol retailer," said Ian. "I thought they'd all been forced to become tied to the big producers years ago. Especially with all these loyalty cards they have."

"Will's a smart man," said Val. "Loyalty and community — he understands that. People here would rather trade with one of their own, and they know he supports local jobs and charities." She signalled for him to follow her into the shop, where she greeted the person behind the counter. "He also lets them pay on tick. See this?" She pointed to the credit card reader. "He's adapted it to take his own pre-pay system. A bit like those pre-pay cards you get for gas and electricity. Total genius. It locks the customer in to your filling stations. Of course, you couldn't roll it out nationally because of anti-competition laws. But he's not about that. He's about creating an unassailable business here in the North East. The only thing he'd like to scale into a business outside the area is that." She pointed to a pump labelled Armstrong BioDiesel.

Armstrong BioDiesel was not what he'd expected. For one thing, it was very clean – there were none of the smoking chimneys or gas flares he'd seen in the refineries on a student field trip down to Teesside. On the opposite side of the road to the site there was a park, and beyond that some housing. The premises of every one of the businesses on the industrial estate were surrounded by high-security galvanised steel fencing. The bars were flattened, their sharp edges making climbing impossible.

Val stopped the car at an entry phone. After it was answered and she identified herself, they were let in. Even the car park was relatively clean, and there wasn't the acrid petrochemical smell he expected of a fuel plant – if anything, there was a sweetness in the air, with a hint of alcohol. A plume of water vapour rose from a bright metal chimney and evanesced in the wind. It was also surprisingly quiet, with just a mechanical humming from inside the three-storey steel building. There was a large, cylindrical tank on one side of the building, from which a fuel tanker was filling up. There was another, smaller, tank on the other side of the building. From the number of cars parked, Ian enjoyed making his own estimate as to the number of employees – though he conceded some might travel on public transport. He worked his calculation through to include three sets of shift-workers and hit on a figure of around twenty.

At the reception door, Val rang once again and they were let in. She signed them into the visitors' book in the deserted reception area, which consisted of a few cheap plastic chairs and an office desk. On the desk sat a computer terminal and a dot-matrix printer with a feed of quadruplicate paper with its white, yellow, pink and grey sheets, which Ian assumed would be to log shipments in and out of the plant. This was all as it should be. He followed her through a door and into a narrow corridor. She knocked on an open office door and went in without waiting for a reply. A man in his fifties rose up behind his desk. He was short and stocky, with a head of grey hair.

"Hello, pet," he said to Val. "How are you?"

"Hi Trevor, how are you?" They shook hands warmly. "This is Ian Bourne. He's from the accountants. Will's asked him to check out some of the fixed assets. Ian, this is Trevor Horsley, who manages the plant."

"Aye, welcome Ian," said Trevor. "I'll give you the two-bit

tour, if you like." They nodded their assent and followed him into a changing room at the end of the corridor. "No real danger, but you have to get kitted out," he said, giving them each a white coat, safety goggles and a yellow plastic safety hat.

They went out onto the factory floor. The humming they'd heard outside was much louder now, but not overbearing. Through the maze of steel pipes of criss-crossing a few feet overhead, Ian could see a large upright cylindrical tank which dominated the centre of the plant. It was covered in insulating padding. There was a smaller tank to one side, which was also insulated, and at various points around the building there were three brushed-steel cylinders about six feet long and four feet wide. Up on a gantry, a worker in a white, boiler suit tipped his safety hat to them and smiled. Trevor raised a hand back in greeting.

"It's a little-known fact that when Rudolph Diesel invented his engine in 1897, it was designed to run on castor oil," said Horsley, in what was obviously a well-rehearsed spiel.

"You're kidding," said Ian.

"Aye," said Horsley. "The oil industry was in its infancy and they had this heavy oil they had to get rid of from the refining process. What they did was they called it diesel oil and sold it alongside their kerosene and petrol, so people didn't have the choice of castor oil. And it's stuck in the public mind since that the right fuel for diesel engines is a mineral oil, not vegetable. In fact, any diesel car can run on cooking oil — but it needs a little adjustment to make it more efficient. And biodiesel is actually a lot kinder to the engine because it's not as corrosive as mineral oil."

Ian had to admire the marketing genius of those pioneering oil industry men. But he could now see why Armstrong had staked so much of his future on this plant – there would be a tipping point in favour of this technology and he would have a commanding lead in the market.

"You'll have seen the small tank on the outside of the

building," said Trevor, his voice raised above the noise. Ian nodded. "We pick up waste vegetable oil and it goes in there. We also take delivery of vegetable oil by ship from Africa, which comes into the docks. You wouldn't have seen the tanks from the car park, but they're massive and they're built down in one of the disused dry docks." He saw Ian raise an eyebrow. "That achieves two things – first, no one objected to them on planning grounds because they're out of sight. Second, if there's a leak then it's contained." Ian nodded his approval. "We also use methanol in the chemical process. That's volatile so we keep it in underground tanks. A lot of it we get as a by-product from the manufacture of spirits – it comes off first in the distillation process."

They were walking slowly through the plant. Besides the man who'd tipped his hat from the overhead gantry, they saw just two other workers: Armstrong had invested heavily in plant to keep the workforce to a minimum. "But why not build this down on Teesside?" Ian asked.

"Better subsidies for the brownfield site up here. When I was a lad this area was all shipbuilding and dry docks. That's all gone now, and the jobs with it. So they've needed new industries to come in. And it also reduces the transport costs. Margins in this business are wafer-thin, and we're bringing the stuff right to where it's sold and we're doing it by ship, rather than by road. That also reduces the mileage the product travels, so we can stake our claim to being even 'greener'. A lot of the oil we buy in is the low-end waste from palm oil used in the manufacture of cosmetics and food."

"And the other waste vegetable oil you get locally?" said Ian.

"Aye," said Horsley. "From little take-away restaurants serving fried food, right through to large food-processing plants. Used frying oil's always been an environmental hazard, so people are pleased to get it off their hands. Plus it makes their business look that bit 'greener' and makes everyone happy all round." Horsley gave them a broad smile.

They had come to a stainless steel workbench with several large single-lever taps above glass beakers. "This is quality control, where we can sample oil from all around the plant," Horsley continued. He held up a beaker of dark oil for Ian to sniff. It smelled foul, with a burnt note to it. "Used frying oil," said Trevor. "Here." He held up a beaker of lighter oil from the opposite end of the row. "This is after it's been purified." Ian sniffed it. "Sort of a sweetish, nutty smell to it, eh?" Ian nodded. "The palm oil can have an almost vanilla note before it's processed — quite pleasant. And none of this is toxic, either. It's less toxic than salt and it degrades in the environment faster than sugar."

"So how do you turn that stuff—" Ian pointed to the first beaker he'd sniffed "—into this stuff?"

"Your traditional crude oil refinery uses high-temperature catalytic cracking to break long oil molecules down into shorter ones for, like, petrol. Then you distil off the different products. We do some proper chemistry here, but it's nothing that you can't do at home if you know what you're doing. If you did advanced chemistry at school then you'll have done something similar. Those things," he pointed to the six-by-four brushed-steel cylinders, "are centrifuges. We adapted them from ones designed for separating raw milk into skimmed milk and cream in dairies. We use them to get rid of impurities at various stages of the process. People who make this stuff at home have to leave it to stand for a day, and time is money for us."

"So what's the schoolboy chemistry?" asked Ian.

"You've heard of saponification of an ester to make soap?"

"Did it in chemistry at school."

"This is esterification, which is very similar. We clean the incoming oil by filtering it, removing the water by using a patented aeration and centrifuge technique. We titrate a sample of the oil and some isopropyl alcohol – the stuff you use to clean your laptop screen — with some sodium hydroxide – caustic soda to you and me – to determine how acidic it is. Then we add the right amount of sodium hydroxide into a tank of meths," Horsley pointed to the smaller of the two insulated tanks. "That reacts to produce sodium methoxide, which is not very nice stuff – and is why you're wearing goggles. In the meantime, we heat up the vegetable oil in the big tank. Then we add the sodium methoxide to the oil. The two react and you get methyl esters, which is the biodiesel, and glycerine as a by-product. And maybe a bit of soap. We use the two centrifuges to separate all that stuff out. Make it at home and it's another day of waiting for it all to separate."

"There must be some waste oil from the process, surely?"

"Just a bit of grease that gets separated out at the first stage by the centrifuge. There's maybe ten tonnes of waste oil a month, which we store in barrels. But it gets burnt in a 'clean' power station that incinerates household waste and produces electricity."

"Great. I suppose that's another part of the Armstrong empire?"

Trevor Horsley and Val laughed, and she answered him. "If only. But I bet it's at the back of his mind somewhere."

"What about the waste glycerine?"

"You can use it as fertiliser, for soap-making, whatever. We heat it and it gives off methane, and we use that to heat the waste oil. The actual soap we just sell on – it's the liquid industrial stuff that mechanics use."

The tour over, they took off their safety gear, thanked Horsley for his time and walked back to the car.

Ian was hugely impressed by the rigour with which the operation had been planned, reminding himself that, on top of all this, Armstrong would be getting favourable grants for this environmentally-friendly operation. His first thought was that he'd love a slice of this action, but reminded himself that it wasn't performing well at all. And it was a simple goods-in, goods-out operation – not much room for fraud there.

"So where does the biodiesel go from here?" he asked Val,

as he reached for his seatbelt.

"Either straight to the filling station, or to Armstrong Distribution."

"Distribution? I've not come across that one yet."

"Fuel distribution. It's only quarter of a mile away. Come on, we might as well go."

They drove to the other end of the industrial estate and went through the same procedure to gain entrance. This time, she didn't bother to go to the small wooden prefabricated office. There were just a couple of cars in the car park, and she waved at the two men inside the office, who waved back.

The wind blew across the concrete expanse and ruffled her black hair. She brushed it back behind her left ear, eliciting a twinge of desire in him. "Not much to see," she said. "We buy conventional diesel and petrol on the spot market and bring it in by road for redistribution to our own forecourts. We stock biodiesel here as well. Over there are the underground tanks that store the diesel." She pointed to a row of six widely-spaced pumps with wide-diameter valves set on the concrete. Some are for biodiesel, the others for conventional. On the other side of the yard you have six for petrol. And that's your lot, Ian."

"Who's the gaffer, or are these lads on their own?"

"Trevor's responsible for this site too." Ian nodded – it made perfect sense for Horsley to be responsible for this small operation.

He looked over at the diesel valves. The difference was apparent. Under three of the valves the concrete had a black stain, from what he assumed must be conventional diesel, whereas the concrete under the three biodiesel ones had a light brown stain. They got back in the car.

"Where to next?" he asked.

She looked at her watch. "We can swing past one of the showrooms, if you like. I make spot checks on the sales staff to make sure they're plugging the finance option. There's one in Gateshead, so it's on the way back. Then it'll be home time."

Twenty minutes later they parked outside a showroom in Gateshead. He listened in on Val as she talked to the sales staff individually, between customers. Her success in promoting her finance schemes seemed to be down to the good rapport she had with the salespeople, as well as the incentives she'd put in place to encourage them to sell more. She seemed to be well-liked throughout the company, and he wondered if she might some day be its CEO.

"Great," she said, finally. "Now, shall I take you back to your hotel?"

"I'd prefer to take you to dinner by way of a thank-you," he said.

"Oh," she said, a trace of awkwardness in her voice. "I've got another commitment tonight, sorry." She paused for a couple of seconds. "Are you still with that girl you were dating in our final year? What's her name — Susan?"

"Sarah. No, we split up a few weeks ago after living together."

"Oh."

"You still single?"

Again she hesitated a split second before replying. "Yeah."

"We could have dinner next week sometime, if you like," he said.

"Sure." She didn't sound over-enthusiastic, and Ian was crestfallen. But he reminded himself that she'd not said no. There was a little awkwardness for the remainder of the journey.

"So," he said as they pulled up. "I'll maybe see you next week sometime?"

"I'm sure we'll meet up. You're off back down to London tomorrow?" He nodded. "Well, safe trip –and have a nice weekend." With that, she was gone. He'd had his chance and blown it.

"We were just going out for dinner. Care to join us?" It was Louise, accompanied by Jess.

"Sure, let me get showered and changed," he said. He knew

that a night alone ruminating was the last thing he needed.

"We'll be in the pub across the road," said Jess.

Ian joined Jess and Louse twenty minutes later. "Do you want another here, or shall we go and eat? I'm pretty hungry." He felt awkward at having accepted their invitation, and hoped they wouldn't hold him to his promise of a night on the town.

His colleagues tipped back their pints of lager. "Let's have the next one in town," said Louise, standing.

Before he could protest, they were heading for the Regent Centre Metro. His mind started playing scenes where he was taunted or chased by gangs of youths accusing him of molestation. "Look," he said, "a Metro's going to take forever. Let's get a taxi. I'll pay." He spotted a taxi office nearby and the operator radioed a car for them. It pulled up thirty seconds later. Ian thought it looked vaguely familiar.

"Y'alreet, mate?" said the driver.

"Erm, hello," said Ian, hesitating to get in. It was the driver who'd helped him escape the previous night.

"Come on, Ian," said Louise, and gave him a tug. He joined her on the back seat, with Jess in the front.

"Doin' a bit better the neet, eh?" said the driver, winking at him.

"Erm, yes. Much better. Thanks."

"You two know each other?" asked Louise.

"I took a taxi the other night."

"You sound well acquainted."

Ignoring Louise, he addressed the driver. "Can you take us down the Quayside please?"

Ian marvelled that at this time of night they could drive from the northern suburbs of Newcastle to the trendiest part of the city so quickly. In London they'd have taken three times as long for the same distance, and London's buildings wouldn't have been so consistently beautiful as the neoclassical Georgian architecture of Newcastle's Grainger Town. For Jess and

Louise's benefit, he asked the driver to take them down the grand sweep of Grey Street, towards the river, taking a peculiar pride as they cooed at the grand design funded by the city's early engineering prowess. The taxi dropped them outside the polished pink granite of the law courts at the Quayside. Ian gave the driver a good tip, though not as generous as the previous night's.

"Isn't it fantastic?" said Jess. The three of them looked around. Dusk was coming in and the bridges were already lit. "You wouldn't believe a place could have this many bridges in such a short stretch of river. And they're all so different."

Ian pointed at them and named the ones that he knew – the High Level, with its railway on top and road underneath; the Swing Bridge down at the Quayside level; the famous green arch of the Tyne Bridge and, finally; the twin white arcs of the Millennium Bridge furthest downstream. Just over the river was the huge, curved metallic shell of the Sage Music Centre.

Ian had hoped a pre-dinner stroll might have been on the cards, but his companions had other ideas. They headed straight for a restaurant full of twenty- and thirty-somethings, where they waited ten minutes to be seated. He marvelled at the ostentation of the locals, a characteristic they were famous for: designer clothes, flashy watches and the latest mobile phones. On Friday and Saturday nights the shirts would all be short-sleeved and the women's skirts would be little more than belts because they'd all have been home to get changed after work. Being a Thursday night, the air of Newcastle festivity was what would pass for a Friday night elsewhere in the country. When he'd been a student he'd watched from the sidelines, lacking the freeness of spirit to throw his caution to the wind – another regret he harboured.

They sat on leather benches in a booth, Ian facing his two colleagues. In casual clothes, Jess and Louise looked less identikit than their professional personae. Both allowed some cleavage to show – Louise noticeably more than Jess. Their make-up was somehow more exciting, and they smiled more. Of the two, he thought he still found Jess the more attractive, and realised that it might be her slightly thinner face reminding him somehow of Val, and her light brown hair of Sarah. Their drinks arrived what seemed mere seconds after they'd ordered them. The food took longer – a showy attempt at Mexican. As he took his first mouthful of a dish zesty with lime juice and hot with pepper, he felt a foot rub against his right calf. He tried to keep a poker face as he looked up. As with the previous occasion on the train north, here wasn't a hint of anything untoward on either of his colleagues' faces. He put it down to an inadvertent rubbing this time, and remarked how good the food was.

The conversation flowed more freely than before, and they talked about their lives back in London. Then again during the main course he felt the unmistakable brush of a foot on his calf. This time it was firmer, reaching up towards his knee. Still he could not work out which of them it was. He'd not thought through what his reaction should be. The raw memory of Patsy's anger the previous night caused him to panic, and he tucked his legs back as far as they would go under the bench. But whichever one of them had intended to plant the thought of sex in his mind had succeeded, and he began to see them for who they were outside of their office lives – attractive young women out on the town. At the back of his head he remembered hearing that two-thirds of couples met through work. His professional side warned him off any involvement – particularly with anyone junior, even if they were from a different division. But the alcohol was working its way through his system.

They split the bill equally. "Where to next?" he asked as they made their way out.

"We thought you'd know some of the clubs," said Louise.

"I didn't do much of that whilst I was a student," he said. "I suppose for sheer novelty then there's the *Tuxedo Princess*." He didn't much like nightclubs, but the thought of not having to make small talk appealed to him. If the worst came to the worst, he could take a taxi back early by himself.

"Where's that?" asked Jess.

"It's over there." He pointed to a large white ship on the Gateshead side of the river, berthed under the Tyne Bridge. "It's an old ferry. They call it 'The Boat' here. If I remember, it has three levels of dance floors, with each one playing a different era so that there's something for everyone."

"Now *that's* my idea of a nightclub," said Louise. He led the way as they walked upriver and crossed over the Swing Bridge.

A scantily-clad young woman in heavy makeup greeted them on the other side. "It's free entry for yous if yous gerrin before eleven," she said, and put stickers on their forearms.

"That seems to be settled," said Ian. They walked over to the gangplank, where they were inspected by the bouncers before being let onboard. It was just after nine, and Ian thought he might give it until eleven at the latest – enough to make sure his colleagues had a good time without letting them get too drunk, or into anything they might regret in the morning.

He bought the first round of drinks up on the top deck, then accompanied Jess and Louise down through the decks, spending only a couple of minutes at each to get the layout and check out the atmosphere. They were sparsely populated, with only a handful of people dancing on each floor. But when they reached the bottom deck, with its loud, thumping chart music, Jess and Louise lit up. At first, he couldn't see what had caused the sudden change in their demeanours.

Then he saw the revolving dance floor, which was already packed with clubbers. The next thing he knew, he'd been pulled onto it by Louise, and she and Jess were gyrating their bodies to the music. He began to dance awkwardly, trying not to spill his pint of lager. There were a couple of scantily-clad professional dancers at the side of the floor, and he could see that there was room for more of them. He tried not to ogle them for fear of offending his colleagues, but at the same time he didn't want to give either one of them the idea that he was warming to an advance from whichever one had made it earlier. But wherever he looked he saw attractive, available women. And after his period of relative abstinence, the alcohol was loosening him up.

After a few tracks he gestured his intention to Jess and Louise whilst trying to shout over the music, before carefully leaving the revolving floor. He finished his drink and went off for a look round the rest of the boat before buying himself another. In his solitude, he found himself drinking faster than usual, and was more than halfway through his drink before he re-entered the bottom level, which was now packed. He found Jess and Louise sitting at a table, with a couple of sharp-looking young men chatting them up. His colleagues looked relieved when they saw him, and shut the men out of the conversation. The men gave Ian a filthy look before leaving the table. Jess and Louise downed their drinks – he noticed that they'd been drinking shorts — and he did the same. He needed no invitation this time to get onto the dance floor, although it was a squeeze for the three of them to do so. The clubbers closer to the middle were defensive about their space, so they remained close to the edge.

The DJ made a muffled announcement over a track and then the crowd began to count down loudly from ten. He gave Jess and Louise a questioning look, but they each returned the same puzzled expression.

Three, roared the crowd. *Two. One!*

At first Ian thought there'd been a fire because the dancing broke down into a melee. Something cold slapped against the back of his head and he reached around to feel it just as he realised that they were being sprayed with foam. Jess scooped some off her head and flipped it into his face, laughing. Something in his system overrode his normal self and it finally clicked in his head that this was exactly the sort of experience he'd been missing out on in his adult life. He bent down to gather a large dollop of foam off the floor and threw it at Jess. At last the game was afoot, he thought – he knew who'd been rubbing his leg during dinner and this was foreplay from his wildest fantasies. He felt a plop of foam on his left ear from Louise, who was also laughing. He flicked the foam back at Louise and then focused his attention on Jess – he wasn't going to be thwarted now that he'd thrown caution to the wind. The jet of foam sprayed back over them again and he held up his hands to catch some more. If there was something he'd learnt in the last few weeks, it was that he had to take opportunities when they arose, and push the advantage home when he had it. He took the foam and smeared it down the front of Jess's blouse, feeling her nipples under her bra. Enthralled, he gave her breasts a squeeze.

Jess's smile turned to rage. She slapped him hard across the left cheek. He leapt back and held up his hands in apology and felt a kick on the back of his knee from Louise. It was in that instant that he realised he'd got the identity of the under-table leg-stroker wrong. Badly.

Chapter Twelve

It could have been far worse.

For one thing, the bouncers hadn't beaten him – they'd just frogmarched him away from the dance floor and down the gangplank onto the quay.

He'd taken a taxi straight back to the hotel and left an apologetic note under each of his colleagues' doors before going to bed. He'd had a sleepless night, contemplating the future of his once promising career, beating himself up and replaying the incident in his head. He now knew what it must feel to be a politician caught in the spotlight of an infidelity. Would the long train journey south on Friday evening be an opportunity to smooth things over, or a silent hell? What disciplinary action would be taken – a caution, a suspension, a forced resignation? He was sure that his meteoric rise to partnership was over. How would he explain it to his father? Would he now be consigned to a provincial life, working in the family business?

Louise explained matter-of-factly at breakfast that Jess had called in sick to head office and taken an early train straight back to London. Louise herself was in no mood to talk as they worked silently through the accounts that morning. She declined his invitation to take her lunch break with him, and he ate his sandwich whilst they worked through the accounts for another Armstrong subsidiary. Looking over invoices was bad enough, but the unspoken discussion of the previous night's events turned it into purgatory.

She broke the stony silence when she returned from lunch. "I called the office and I've asked to be taken off this job. Sorry."

"I completely understand. I'm sorry." He let too many seconds pass, but had to ask. "Did you give a reason?"

"No."

"That was kind of you. Thanks."

Louise sighed. "I hope we'll remain friends."

He'd not been expecting this sort of comeback, and felt a

little flutter of excitement. "Yes, I'm sure once this thing blows over then we could maybe go out for dinner. A couple of weeks, perhaps?"

"*What*? I meant me and Jess. Christ, I just can't believe you. You have this reputation as an archetypal boring accountant and you've just got a one-track mind."

"Sorry, I…." He hid the anger he felt for her. After all, she'd been the one who'd started it by stroking his leg. "Forget it," he said.

Anne Salter tapped lightly on the door of the meeting room. "Sorry to disturb. I've got Mr Woodcock on the phone for you, Ian. I can transfer it through here, or you can take it in Mr Watkins' office if you want some privacy – he's out for the afternoon."

"Thanks," said Ian. His heart filled with dread as he walked into Watkins' office. He closed the door behind him and picked up the phone. "Good afternoon, Mr Timothy. How are you?"

"Never mind that, what's going on with this audit?"

"The audit's going very smoothly, Mr Timothy."

"Not from next week it isn't – you're minus two assistants. Mind telling me what's going on?"

He cleared his throat. "One's ill and the other doesn't want to be on the job with me." He felt dread at the unintentional *double entendre* in his last sentence.

"Doesn't say much for your people management skills, young man."

"In my defence, I would like to point out that I'm a *forensic* accountant, sir. This is very much an auditor's job. Not my cup of tea. And these staff were Hendricks' – I felt I had little authority over them." He knew it was dangerous even to hint at a partner's ability to manage his staff, but he had no respect for Hendricks.

Woodcock harrumphed down the phone. "As one moves up the hierarchy, one must learn the ability to manage a variety of staff – both in the office and on a client's premises. Do you understand me?"

"Yes, Mr Timothy. My sincere apologies."

"Now, as for next week, we can't get anyone up there until Wednesday morning, so you're on your tod." Ian closed his eyes against what he knew was coming next. "I've already asked Eddie Watkins' assistant, and they've cleared it for you to come in over the weekend to keep things on track with the audit. I'm sure you'll have to work some late nights on Monday and Tuesday, too. Jean's had your return ticket pushed back to next Friday, if that's alright with you."

"Yes, Mr Timothy."

"Very good. I'm sure we'll talk further about this dedication at your review."

"Thank you. Have a good weekend, Mr Timothy."

"Thank you. Cheerio."

He put the receiver down, nestled his head in his hands and growled. He hated this. He was over a barrel. But at least Jess and Louise had kept quiet about their reasons for leaving the job, and he was grateful for that.

He walked back past Anne Salter, who smiled at him. He felt a surge of resentment for her too – she must know full well that he was staying in over the weekend.

"How did it go?" asked Louise, with a hint of compassion.

"Better than expected. They're sending someone else up in the middle of the week but I have to work the weekend."

"I'm sorry to hear that."

"A small price to pay."

"For groping a girl's tits? I should say so."

"Stroking a man's leg is harassment too, you know." He felt his anger begin to boil over.

"Hardly the same thing," she spat.

He could see the way things were going and wanted back from the brink. "Look, I'm sorry. Can we just chalk it down to experience?"

She glowered at him for a moment. "Alright," she said.

She left with a murmured "Goodbye" at four, and he wished her well for the weekend. He worked out that she'd be back in London by half-seven, and envied her.

At six, when Ian left the office, the security guard was on his final check around the building. Having decided that he needed a run to clear his head, Ian ran south on Gosforth High Street, in the opposite direction from the golf course. He found himself on the Town Moor, running up the path through the trees alongside Grandstand Road, where he and Sarah had bonded on that walk back to Fenham all those years ago. Again, he wondered how she was and where she was. This misfortune wouldn't have befallen him if she'd still been in his life. But then he wondered how his life might have been if he had been successful with Val Craven that night. Would he have settled up in the North East with her? They were the same age and she was also apparently single, so did she harbour the same disease of perennial regret and singledom that he did? A light rain fell, like the one he and Sarah had experienced on that late-night walk.

After dinner, he turned on the television in his room and booted up the company laptop. Again, nothing in his Hotmail account, and no interest whatsoever from anyone on M—.com. He did a few searches, but his heart wasn't in it.

His thoughts turned back to London, where his newest porn DVD was gathering dust. He remembered the previous night's events, and how he'd first had his leg stroked under the table by Louise, and how Jess's firm nipples – he was quite sure they had sprung erect – had felt under his foamy fingertips. If only he'd turned his attention to Louise, everything would have been alright: he'd not be spending this miserable weekend alone in Newcastle – he might be spending it in bed with her in London instead.

The internet bludgeoned its way into his bored but salacious mind. At first he hesitated to do it, but he was bolstered by the fact that no one had mentioned anything about his logging into M—.com during working hours. And, he reasoned, half-past nine on a Friday night a couple of hundred miles from the office hardly constituted normal working hours. He went to a search engine and soon found what he was looking for – a couple of sites showing short but explicit samples of porn movies and amateur porn. His Friday night was transformed, and he thanked God for giving his creation a strong enough moral turpitude to create the miracle of free online pornography. He also thanked God for the insane pride of foolish men as he watched them have sex with their girlfriends, many of the women apparently unaware that they were being filmed – uncurious about their partner's desire for unusual positions and sudden desire to ejaculate externally. The low-grade footage, played in a matchbox-sized area of his screen, wasn't to his usual standards – but it was enough to satisfy his needs.

He was in the office by half-eight on Saturday morning, lest he be accused of sloth. The security guard made him sign in, since it was outside normal business hours.

He was now onto the audit for Armstrong Distribution – the tiny operation they'd visited down in South Shields that held fuel supplies for the filling stations. It was a straightforward goods-in, goods-out operation, without any value added to the products. The matter of reconciling the quantities of the various fuels in stock was nothing more than simple arithmetic – there should be a quantity in the tanks at the start of the year, plus all of the incoming fuel, minus the outgoing fuel to leave a quantity at the end. It all seemed to add up about as well as could be expected, allowing for spillages and — he thought this was an excellent feat of memory on his part – the difference in volume accounted for by expansion and contraction due to temperature differences between the cooler underground tanks and the warmer lorries.

During his perusal of the invoices and nominal ledger, he turned over the problem of ABD in his head. It was not quite the simple goods-in, goods-out operation that he'd originally thought it to be. The volumes going in would come from three separate sources – the vegetable oil from West Africa, the methanol to thin the oil, and the waste oil that was recycled. But there was only one output so far as he knew – the biodiesel. Trevor Horsley had talked about other products, but they were in development and were of low volume – so the opportunity for fraud had to be with the high-volume biodiesel production.

The guard waved him away from the register as he left to get a sandwich at lunchtime, telling Ian that he was the only person in that day. He wandered off down Gosforth High Street. The sandwich shop they'd been using all week was closed, so he walked a little further south. He saw a Pizza Hut restaurant on the corner and recalled how Hazel from M———.com had been amused by his story of the restaurant that had been operating two tills and buying extra ingredients to make extra pizzas to cream off the profit.

Then it struck him that the same scam could be worked on a plant like Armstrong BioDiesel. He did one of his favourite things as a forensic accountant: he put himself in the fraudster's shoes and thought through the practicalities of executing such a scam successfully.

The entrance was locked when he got back. He looked around and found a buzzer, which he pressed. After half a minute the guard appeared in the lobby, hurrying a little. "Sorry, sir," he said as he let Ian in. "Answering a call of nature."

Ian went back upstairs, to the nominal ledger of ABD. He couldn't see how it could possibly be done – but that didn't mean that it was impossible. The thief was always one step ahead of the honest businessperson. He would sit on the thought and let it germinate.

At half-five he called it a day and said goodnight to the guard. That was when he had the Gestalt that he needed: the weekend. Any fraud at the plant would be done at the weekend. Trevor Horsley, the plant's manager, was no shift-worker. The weekends would see the way clear for illicit production. And it was unlikely that any other deliveries or pick-ups would disturb the fraudsters.

He took a bus straight into town to the Eldon Square shopping mall, where he bought a pair of cheap blue jeans and a hooded sweatshirt. It was attire that was repugnant to part of him – he'd long felt intimidated by hooded youths on the streets of London — but its rebellious connotation and the delicious irony of wearing it gave him a frisson of excitement.

The thrill of the chase was in him as the Metro train crossed over the Tyne and into Gateshead, and it grew as the train went east along the banks of the river. None of the other passengers gave him a second glance because he was in character – a bored man on a train heading back home after a day at a menial service sector job in 'the Toon'. An internet search had shown him that he should get off at Chichester, rather than South Shields itself.

It was night now, and he hid his fear of being a Southerner in this downtrodden area at this time on a weekend by pulling the hood of his sweatshirt over his head. He was now one of them: unapproachable, tough – trouble if you wanted it. His sense of direction took him northwest from the Metro station, feet crunching on glass fragments from broken car windows. He found himself at the large roundabout on the dual carriageway where Val had turned off for ABD. Quickening his pace, he took an exit down a road called Laygate, past houses with graffiti tags on their walls and windblown litter in their gardens. A couple of minutes later he could see the edifice of the biodiesel plant over the park on his right in Commercial Road, gleaming in the orange tint of the sodium vapour lights.

The plant was silent and there was only one car behind the high security fencing – almost certainly that of the security guard, he thought. He realised what a fool he'd been – if the plant wasn't running to capacity then they'd not be working night shifts on weekends. Mindful of the CCTV cameras, he kept moving along the fence. He glanced in again and something caught his eye. There were several barrels by the waste oil tank on the east side of the building. They looked old and battered, and were of different colours. It would be out of character for a business like Armstrong's to collect waste oil in tatty, unbranded drums like those. They were so out of place that he knew in that instant that he had found the evidence he had been looking for: someone was using the plant to recycle waste oil on the side.

He thought it through quickly. Oil – either palm or waste – accounted for by far the biggest volume of raw material going into the process. If someone could put some extra oil in one end of the plant it would be relatively easy for them to piggyback on the conversion process, then take the excess volume out the other side. The relatively small amount of extra chemical reagents used would probably be overlooked as wastage, or put down as being due to a particularly bad batch of waste oil going into the plant. Whoever was piggybacking the production was probably picking up the waste oil for free. They would then be able to sell the biodiesel for nearly the full market price, bypassing fuel duty, and netting themselves one hundred percent profit.

He was ecstatic. These were the moments he lived for. He slid the camera phone out of his jeans' pocket and hit the zoom before bringing it to bear on the barrels. Just as he was about to take a photo he remembered to disable the flash, which took him a couple of eternally fumbling seconds. He took three photos in quick succession before making his way back to the Metro station, his torso slick with sweat.

It was ten o'clock before he got back to the hotel via a Chinese takeaway and an off-licence, where he picked up a celebratory four-pack of cold lager. When uploaded onto his laptop, the pictures were quite decent, but he knew he needed more conclusive evidence than these alone. The thieves would have to be caught red-handed, but he was confident he had enough to convince Armstrong to investigate further.

He was up a bit later on Sunday morning, but the office door was still locked at half-nine and he realised he'd never made any specific arrangements with the guard – not even a "See you tomorrow". He didn't want to risk Woodcock's ire by not working on the audit, especially when he was in such a potentially precarious position, so he went back to the hotel and out for a run. When he got back an hour later, the office was still closed. His years as a forensic accountant had taught him to take evidence, so he photographed the locked door with its distinctive Armstrong logo on it, knowing that the time and date would be recorded on the image. He sent it to his email account so that he'd have an extra time stamp on it as proof.

There was only one thing to do: he changed into his jeans and hooded sweatshirt and took the Metro to Chichester. It was quiet, and the few people on the two-carriage train were subdued. A stiff breeze from the North Sea pushed up the steep cut of the Tyne valley and buffeted the carriage as it crossed the river.

The day was overcast; the light from behind the clouds so diffuse that he cast no shadow as he walked down Laygate. The wind carried the hum of the plant to him as he left the last of the houses to his right and it came into view across the park. He was more nervous this time because he was without the cover of darkness. The guard from last night should have been replaced, but if anything fraudulent was happening the perpetrators would be vigilant.

The park was a good cover, so instead of walking on to the T-junction with Commercial Road and walking past the plant, he took a right into the park and walked towards a manicured set of hedged pathways in the centre. The path ran parallel with Commercial Road, about fifty yards from the plant. A couple of kids – perhaps twelve or thirteen years old — were kicking a football around.

There was a flatbed truck in the yard on the east side of the building, next to the waste oil tank, and a couple of men were hefting empty barrels onto it. He stopped and pretended to tie his shoelace, and instead took a couple of pictures with full zoom. He checked them as he walked on: they would do, and he emailed one to himself. But this could be anything – it could well be that this was legitimate waste oil, and that his theory was quite wrong. However, he knew that a business with thin margins wouldn't be conducting such a low value activity on weekend rates of pay. It was getting on towards noon and he couldn't hang around for fear of attracting attention. The path he took deposited him onto Commercial Road, just past the plant, and he walked on past Armstrong Distribution along to the next roundabout.

He could see he'd missed the best of South Shields, if there was such a thing. It was all industrial land that had been redeveloped for office use, and the only thing of any interest was the Shields Ferry, carrying passengers and vehicles across the river between North and South Shields. He turned sharp right up Station Road, back in the direction of the Metro in the hope of finding somewhere to grab a bite. A couple of hundred yards up he saw a very large, modern police station. The sheer gall of the crime being carried out less than quarter of a mile away made him smile. He had nothing at all to go to the police with, but he was reassured to know the station was there. Back towards Chichester Metro station he bought a packaged sandwich, as well as a cheap biro and a local newspaper.

He took his time on the way back to Armstrong BioDiesel, and an hour had passed since his first visit. The kids were still playing football. There was a much larger patch of empty ground off Laygate just before the park, and it annoyed him that they might draw attention in his direction. But for the accent, he could have been back in South London, although the level of swearing was noticeably worse. It wasn't just rugby that he didn't get – football was something he'd spurned as a youngster; further alienating him from his peers. He'd been so hopeless with a ball that even a casual kickabout had held a special dread for him.

The truck was now on the west side of the building, next to the tank storing the finished fuel. The back of the vehicle now had over a dozen fifty-gallon barrels standing upright on it. One of the men had stuck a funnel into a barrel, over which he held the end of a fuel pipe. The other man controlled the flow of the fuel. Ian could see it would require some skill to keep the spillage to a minimum. Still, he realised, any spilled evidence would degrade quite quickly. He took his mobile phone out and zoomed in. He took a picture – perfect. He emailed it to himself. This was the clincher – this was not a legitimate activity related to the business. But he had to get closer to get overwhelming evidence. He wanted a clean kill on this one.

He made for the exit onto Commercial Road. A football rolled across the path in front of him.

"Hey mister," called one of the lads. "Pass us the fookin' ball will yeez?"

This was the last thing he needed, but cover necessitated it. He jogged after the ball and stopped it by placing the sole of his foot on top as he passed it. Not bad, he thought. He jogged round and kicked it in the direction of one of the lads. A gust of wind caught it and it veered off badly to the right.

"You're fookin' shite!" said the other boy.

"Piss off ye fookin' little fookin' *coont*," said Ian in his best Geordie accent, spat at the ground and bared his teeth. His heart was so far into his mouth with fear he thought he might have spat it out. He stared the lad down then tucked his fists into the pockets of his sweatshirt and walked to the exit of the park, knees weak with fear. With relief, he heard the kickabout resume behind him.

He crossed Commercial Road, over to the fence outside the plant. He took the newspaper out and casually wrote down the license number of each of the four cars and the truck as he walked along, trying to make it look as if he was making notes on the classified ads. Everyone in the plant at the time had to be in on the scam. Even if they just ignored it they were just as guilty – in Ian's view at least – of the same crime. He took out his mobile again and switched it to movie mode, his heart beating fast. He kept it at hip level in his right hand for the first few steps, checking the LCD display to see that it was working. Then he stopped, brought it up to eye level and pointed it through the railings. It couldn't be clearer what was going on.

"Dad! Watch oot!" shouted one of the kids. One of the men he was filming looked up and saw Ian.

The kids were lookouts. His cover had deceived them just long enough. He stopped filming and began to jog off down Commercial Road, where he knew there was a shortcut to the police station. His brain was screaming at him to sprint but he clicked through the menu on his mobile to the email function. He glanced round and saw the two kids racing towards him, almost at the edge of the park. He kept hold of the page of the newspaper he'd written the license numbers on and threw the rest of it behind him as he ran on. He crumpled the page up and stuffed it down the front of his trousers with his left hand.

"Ye fookin' bastud!" yelled one of the boys.

He selected his email address and then navigated his way to the movie file. Their footsteps on the road behind him were getting louder. He selected the file. The little hourglass told him the file was uploading. Slowly: it was a big file.

"Fookin' gerrim, Bazza!" he heard one of the men shout. "Gan fer 'is fookin' mobile, son!"

Ian stepped up his pace as much as he could but he knew the lads were almost on him. He held the mobile in front of him and looked at the screen. The hourglass disappeared. He clicked on Send and another hourglass appeared. *Time will tell*, he thought.

The shove from behind sent him sprawling, tumbling into the security railings of the neighbouring property. He felt the stunning blow of the metal on the top of his head. The mobile was still in his outreached hand. He saw a training shoe stamp down on his wrist and he let it go. A foot connected with his

stomach and he gasped. He saw the mobile snatched up.
Time will tell, he thought as he blacked out.

Chapter Thirteen

Ian felt hands arranging his limbs, the rough tarmac cold on his face. He was in pain, plenty of it, but the blows had stopped.

"He's coming round now," he heard a man's voice say. "Can you hear me, sir?" it asked gently.

Ian assumed the voice was referring to him and slowly opened his eyes. It was still daylight. He groaned and looked up into the face of a policeman bending over him.

"Lucky we were going past," said the policeman. "They saw us and scarpered."

"Did you get them?" Ian's first thoughts were of the evidence, and whether the file had had time to send.

"You were our first priority and we've got a couple of cars out looking. But to be perfectly honest there's not much chance of catching them. There's an ambulance on its way and then we'll get a statement from you when you're feeling up to it. Just lie there. How many fingers am I holding up?"

"Two and a thumb."

"Aye, you're alright," said the policeman.

A second voice spoke from behind him: a woman's. "Not from around here, are you, Mr Bourne?"

He felt for his wallet. It wasn't in his pocket. Of course: the policewoman had it.

"That's exactly what doesn't fit, Mr Bourne. It doesn't look to me like you were mugged if they didn't rob you."

"I'm a forensic accountant investigating a fraud at Armstrong BioDiesel up the road. I was gathering evidence."

The male officer tut-tutted. "Law enforcement's for the professionals, Mr Bourne. Still, at least you've lived to learn that."

"I *am* a professional," said Ian. "I'm a forensic accountant."

He heard the female officer snigger. "So you're the man to see if I have a problem with my books, eh?" she said.

"I've got the license numbers of the cars," he said, putting his hand down the front of his trousers. "They were all in on it. The truck they were using to steal the diesel is the number on the left." He pulled out the sheet of newspaper and held it up for the male officer. "I'll need that back as evidence." He twisted onto his back and rubbed gravel and dirt from his right cheek.

The smile dropped from the officer's face. "It's our evidence now, sir," he said. He keyed his radio and called in the truck's number.

"I'll have those details as part of my statement, will I?" The officer nodded at him. "I filmed it on my mobile. I assume you didn't find it nearby?"

"No," said the female officer. "Is Giacomo Travelli your boyfriend? Nice looking guy I have to say. Bit of a waste if he's gay."

"*What?*" Ian saw that she was had pulled Giac's 'call me' card out of his wallet and was looking at his picture. "No, he's my personal pulling trainer, a shagger beyond compare, actually." He squinted up at the woman. "I'll put in a good word for you if you like."

"I'm not that desperate," she said. She caught the look on Ian's face and could read the words forming on his lips. She raised her finger. "I should warn you that it's an offence to—"

The male officer's radio crackled into life and the three of them listened intently. Ian couldn't make it out. "Your story stacks up alright," said the male officer. "Graham Neilson's known to us. It's his truck."

The mention of Armstrong's name had turned his ordeal around. The police were quick to take a statement from him as he waited just a short time in the A&E department of the local hospital. He'd identified both of his attackers from a large photograph album: the sons of criminals, as expected, each with their own record of juvenile offending. A detective drove him back to his hotel, where Armstrong met them in the lobby.

"How are you, Ian?" Armstrong made to shake Ian's hand,

but then saw the bandage on it. "Christ, you've been through the wars, son."

Ian smiled weakly – his head was throbbing. The cut from the railings had required three stitches, so part of his scalp had been shaved and was covered with a white dressing. His ribs were sore and every breath was painful. "I was lucky — the cavalry came in the nick of time," he said. "The officer and I need to get the evidence off my laptop if you want to join us."

"You're staying in the Gosforth Park tonight, Ian," said Armstrong. "I'm paying. I'll give you a lift over when we're done here."

"Thanks."

Armstrong and the detective were quiet as the laptop booted up, tense as the internet connection took its time logging in. Ian opened up his email account and checked for new messages.

The detective insisted on him opening up all of his email from the preceding twenty-four hours. The first was the picture he'd taken of the front door of Armstrong's head office on Sunday morning, and he was embarrassed to explain the reason for it being there. The second photo was of the barrels on the flatbed beside the waste oil tank.

"Those aren't my barrels," said Armstrong.

"You ain't seen nothing yet," said Ian. "This email was the one I was sending when I got attacked." He downloaded the file and played the video, which clearly showed the biodiesel being taken from the tank of finished fuel.

"Bastuds," muttered Armstrong. "Bloody bastuds."

The detective took copies of Ian's photos on a flash drive and left. Armstrong helped Ian pack his few belongings and took him to the Gosforth Park Hotel, and called his wife to tell her he'd be dining there with Ian.

"It's the *betrayal*," said Armstrong over dinner.

This was the part Ian didn't enjoy. When he'd started as a forensic accountant he thought he'd be greeted as a hero by those whose money he'd saved. But it wasn't always like that:

he was the bearer of bad news. "But William," he said. "At least it's stopped now."

"But how long did it go on for? And who was involved? Was it just that shift, or did everyone down there have their hands in the tin?"

"You have to assume the worst in these situations, but you can only prove what you have evidence for. In some respects you're lucky because it's a police investigation now. If it had just been me with the evidence it would have been purely a disciplinary matter."

"You don't understand the law," said Armstrong. "It wasn't my guys who were caught, so we're lumbered with an internal investigation and all that personnel stuff."

"Ah, but I wasn't the only person filming that weekend," said Ian.

"What do you mean?"

"You had CCTV. You could reasonably assume that any worker in the vicinity of the truck and barrels was at least guilty of not reporting the operation."

"Aye, you're right, son. Good thinking."

Ian chose his next words carefully. "The good news is that this going to reduce costs and have a positive impact on the profitability of the biodiesel plant."

"The bad news?" asked Armstrong.

"You originally told me the problem was low account sales of biodiesel. We're no further forward with that. Yes, you might see a slight uplift in overall sales because your product's no longer being sold on the black market. But that's marginal, surely?"

Armstrong chewed thoughtfully before replying. "Maybe my forecasts for the business were over-optimistic."

Ian knew it was a big step for his client to have said that. "I looked at the market and I think you should be selling more. It could be that your strategy's wrong."

"Aye, could be. Are you going to sell me some consultancy

work now?" Armstrong laughed for the first time in hours, and Ian joined him.

It wasn't the sort of stiffness Ian liked in the morning. He fought against the pain to be in the office by half-eight, because he felt he still had a point to prove to Woodcock. Peterson called him at nine in the meeting room. His boss was concerned, but couldn't hide his glee that Ian had cracked the case so quickly. "But look here," he said. "There's this business of these two girls. I hear from Jean that the drums are beating in the background on this one. You know what personnel's like – bloody dog with a stick."

"Christ, Donald. You saw Barbara go for me at the Christmas party. She'd have to sack herself."

"That's the whole point, lad. Just watch yourself, that's all I'm saying. Goodbye and good luck."

The meeting room door opened a few minutes later. It was Watkins. "Well, well. I understand we had quite a busy weekend," he said dryly. "Hail the conquering hero."

"Thanks," said Ian, looking up from a pile of invoices from the leasing company.

"How much do you think your amateur dramatics are going to delay the audit?"

Ian was stunned by the openness of the man's hostility. "They're sending an extra person up here on Wednesday: Brian Stead. I understand he's very fast. The job's been going well so far." His own nickname for Brian Stead was 'Brain Dead', although he often used his name as a statement, pronouncing it "Brian's Dead". The man was very competent, but had no personality. It would be like sitting in a room with a mannequin.

Watkins harrumphed and left the room. Ian made a rude gesture at the closed door. He guessed he'd shown the man up to a certain extent, and it reminded him that he'd not checked on Watkins' career since leaving Woodcock and Tweed and joining Armstrong's company.

In the afternoon he was party to a two-hour meeting with Trevor Horsley, Armstrong and the personnel manager. Horsley looked both scared and angry. Ian assumed it was because he'd just waved goodbye to a large bonus. If ever there was a man who wished he'd popped into work on the occasional Saturday or Sunday, it must be Trevor Horsley, he thought.

Despite having attended dozens of disciplinary hearings, he found their unpleasantness wore him deeply. A feigned headache let him off the one that had been set up for the employees who'd apparently turned a blind eye to the crime. He excused himself with the justification that the evidence was hardly of the type that required a forensic accountant's expertise.

The plush room in the Gosforth Park was a special kind of torture that evening. He was in no state to run, nor was his right hand in any condition to pleasure himself. Debbie had written him an email complaining that she couldn't get hold of him on his mobile number, so he called her and they arranged a date for Wednesday evening. She didn't sound as overjoyed at the prospect of meeting him as Patsy had. It was disappointing, but meant that he wouldn't get his hopes up any higher. Besides, he was sure he'd heard the interruption to her breathing caused by the smoking of a cigarette, and he wasn't sure if the taste of her smoker's kiss would put him off sex if the opportunity occurred.

On Tuesday morning Valerie Craven called into the office to see him, full of praise and admiration. She suggested dinner on Wednesday, which he eagerly accepted.

That evening he called Debbie to cancel their date.

"What, have you found someone more interesting, like?" she asked in her husky voice.

"No," he said, but he'd hesitated just too long.

"Aye, you have. Haven't you?" Her voice took on a deeper, more menacing note.

"Debbie, it's not like that. I'm up here on work after all."

"Work? Well you failed to get *on the job* with Patsy last week, that's what I heard." There was a heavy click and a long intake of breath as she lit a cigarette.

"I don't know what you mean."

"The rest of us do keep in touch, you know. Just up here for the chance of a shag, are you?" He heard smoke being blown forcefully out of Debbie's lungs. "Who's next after me and Patsy? Is it that Valerie Craven? You always had the hots for her, didn't you?"

Again, he hesitated before saying "No," and the silence fingered him.

"So me and Patsy aren't good enough for you. Is that it?"

"Debbie, please—"

"You're so superior and you think we're all stupid, do you know that? Well we're not. We've known for *years* all these nicknames you had for us."

"Debbie—" his heart sank at the ghastliness of this knowledge.

"We had nicknames for you too, you know."

"I—"

"Ian the Iguana was one of them."

"*What*? I don't get it."

"You know, them lizards that have the eyes that roll around in different directions looking for insects. They have geet big tongues that are longer than their fookin' bodies. You know the ones."

"I don't see the allusion," he said, knowing in his heart of hearts that he did.

"You're *exactly* like one of them," said Debbie. "Your fookin' eyes are always rolling all over the shop, leching at women. And your tongue practically hangs out. It's fookin' disgustin'."

"It's *chameleons* that have rolling eyes," he growled.

"No, we checked. It's iguanas. Iguana Ian, that was one of the nicknames."

"*One* of the nicknames?" He could imagine now the ranks of women laughing behind his back.

"Ian *Bore* was the other."

He terminated the call. Who else had been in on these nicknames? Were there other nicknames lying around waiting to blow up in his face? Had they carried over into his professional life? Hadn't Louise said he had a reputation as an archetypal boring accountant? Were his colleagues laughing at him now in a City pub? What about his mates at the Derbyshire?

His first instinct was to seek solace on the internet, but then he remembered his reputation for lecherous behaviour.

He turned instead to his Hotmail account. There was an email from Tamara. The subject line was 'Holding out for a hero'

> Hi Ian,
>
> Great to hear from you! I read about your crime-busting exploits in the Chronicle. I've been looking for a hero like you! Fancy dinner at my place? Every hero deserves a rewards and I've got something VERY special planned for you……
>
> Tamara xx

He grew turgid almost immediately. She'd not hung around much with anyone else on the course, so she might not know his nicknames. How he'd envied those lucky engineering students she'd enslaved.

There were no reservations in his mind as he wrote back. This was exactly what he'd been looking for – straightforward sex without the complications of a relationship. Even Valerie Craven held no fascination for him as rampant lust swamped his imagination. After all, Val would require wining, dining, flattery and more before he even stood a chance of sex. And there was no guarantee that the sex itself would be any good.

> Hi Tamara,

> I'd love to be the man to give you that something special. You have to be the most amazing woman in Toon. I'm ready when you are!
>
> Ian xxx

No longer having a mobile, he added the hotel's number to the bottom of the message and clicked Send. It was at that moment the doubt set in. Was she another Patsy, ruined by childbirth? He'd not seen her in years. And why would such a desirable woman be after him when she could have the pick of any man? Or maybe she was genuine – his mind went back to the time when he'd danced with her at a rock nightclub when she was wearing her skin-tight leather trousers. He realised she'd have given him permission to view her entry on the alumnus website, so he logged in and looked her up. She ran her own new media company in Newcastle. She'd taken the trouble to upload a picture of herself, and she looked even more gorgeous than the last time he'd seen her nearly seven years ago – her features were more toned and she looked professionally made-up.

His wrist was just about back in action, but he decided against self-pleasure, saving himself for what he was sure would be an end to his sexual drought on Friday night.

Brian Stead arrived mid-morning on Wednesday. He was in his mid-thirties, tall but with a pot belly: uncommunicative, even for an auditor. What Ian found odd was that the man was married – happily, apparently – and with kids. And yet he displayed less character than a corpse. Ian supposed it was some mild form of Asperger's, or perhaps it was what one ended up like working for a dolt like Hendricks? If it weren't for Stead's lack of social skills, he'd have been a senior manager or partner at an early age. It was unnerving at first to have someone sit and work so quietly, but when he saw the speed with which the man was doing it, he was thankful. This hellish audit would be over by the end of the week, he was sure.

But his commitments in Newcastle would drag on for months. That afternoon he attended an identity parade in South Shields, where he easily picked out his two attackers. At the tender age of thirteen, they already had a history of offending – it was the family business. Their fathers had both been bailed for the theft, and he'd have to appear as the star prosecution witness when the case came up in a few months' time. He had no fear of it because he'd done it many times before. But it was an annoyance: in a criminal prosecution such as this one that he wouldn't be able to charge his time at the high rate he would were he appearing on behalf of a client.

His annoyance turned to depression when the detective in charge of the investigation told him that it would have been much better if Ian hadn't got caught, because the investigation would never fully uncover every aspect of the crime. There was the question of whether the men had been part of a larger organisation, who the biodiesel was being sold to and what quantities were involved. So far, they'd only found the firms who'd been disposing of their waste cooking oil through them. Those organisations had done nothing illegal.

The detective had dropped him back at the hotel at five. He checked his work email and then his Hotmail. There was a reply from Tamara:

Hunky Boy,

I'll expect you over on Friday night. Don't plan anything strenuous for Saturday…

T x

He rang the office to speak to Rose.

"Ian!" she said. "How are you, me darlin'? Have you recovered from your little crime-busting adventure?"

"I'm fine thanks, Rose. You okay?"

"Christ, boy. You been gettin' yourself into all sortsa

trouble, ain't ya?" She lowered her voice. "Watch your back, buddy. I'm not sure what it is, but there's something I don't like going on here, and it's to do with you. What the hell have you gone and done?"

He thought twice about doing it, but then told her the truth about what had happened under the table and on the dance floor in the *Tuxedo Princess* the previous week.

"Oh, *Ian*," she tittered quietly. "I shouldn't laugh about it. But only you, mate. You total plonker. Mind you, I always thought you must feel a right tit sometimes."

"Look," he said, losing the fight against her infectious snigger. "It's really serious and I'm very sorry for what I've done."

"Don't bleedin' tell *me* that," she said. "Anyway, how's the love life? Any chance you might feel a left tit too?" She gasped for breath between muffled cackling.

He let her laughter die off. "That's the reason I'm calling. Hot date with a lass from my old course on Friday night. I need to come down on Saturday instead."

"You old dog, you. I'll get your ticket changed. Oh, and the insurance is sending a new mobile to you at the office tomorrow. Don't go picking no more fights over it, eh?" She broke into giggles again. "I'm sorry. Do you think you'll be up to it on Friday night with those injuries?"

"Thanks," he said. "I'm sure I'll be just fine. Look, I have to go – I've got a dinner date."

"My *God*," said Rose. "You little devil. Good luck with it, and let me know how it goes, eh?"

"Thanks, I will." He felt reassured now that Rose had the truth from him: she would do her best to defend him on the quiet, and to silence the drums that Peterson had been so worried about.

"Here's to our handsome hero," said Valerie, clinking her glass on his. She'd picked him up from the hotel and they'd gone straight to a restaurant in rural Northumbria; a gem of a place kept secret by its location.

"Nothing much heroic about getting beaten up," he said.

"Not disagreeing with the 'handsome', though," she said, coyly.

He flushed, feeling guilty about keeping his options open with Tamara. He sipped his wine. She'd ordered a full bottle, even though she'd said she'd only have the one glass, telling him it was too good to miss. The waiter topped up his glass periodically through the meal and he told her about Sunday and how the case was progressing. She listened attentively and made the right noises.

"But what made you suspect something was going on down there in the first place?" she asked over dessert, leaning closer to him. "There can't have been any evidence up in the office. And it can't have been something at the plant because Trevor Horsley would have spotted it ages ago."

"Intuition," he said, feeling the effects of most of the bottle of wine. "I thought something like that had to be going on."

"But there can't be something going on at *every* place you audit. So what made you suspect ABD?" Her right leg brushed against his left and stayed there. It had the effect of jarring him back to sobriety, remembering the last time he'd had a few drinks and felt someone do that. But perhaps this was different? He was confused because the conversation didn't match her body language. He inched his leg away from hers.

"Things just seemed a little off, that was all. A few figures didn't add up," he put a spoonful of tangy lemon tart in his mouth, to give himself some thinking time. "A little too much meths being used. The proportions of raw materials were a touch out. I looked up the process on the internet."

"Oh," she said. "I find that pretty amazing. To have spotted that sort of detail. It's a big operation."

"I'm a forensic accountant. Besides, you know me – good old Ian with his attention for detail," he laughed awkwardly and caught her looking at her watch. He knew he'd blown his chances with her.

He offered to pay the bill. "No," she said. "I'll put it on expenses. Ed'll be fine about it."

"Shouldn't say that in front of the auditor," he joked.

The conversation was muted on the way back, and he kicked himself for not having responded to the contact with his leg under the table. Had he just delivered a rebuff similar to the one that had ended their friendship seven years earlier? Was the conversation supposed to have been sincere flattery to match her move – a topic appropriate for Ian *Bore*?

She stopped the car in front of the hotel. "Thanks for a lovely evening," he said. "Do you fancy dinner again next week?"

She hesitated. "But won't you be back in London by then?"

He shrugged. "Who knows?"

"Ed said—. Look, I'll probably see you at the end of the week. Cheers, Ian." And with that she was gone.

Women, he thought. There was no understanding them. He knew he'd not get a third chance at Val, but couldn't understand how he'd managed to blow his second — if that was what he'd done. But he was glad he'd hedged his bets on Tamara,

Chapter Fourteen

He had a hangover on Thursday morning from the bottle of wine he'd consumed with Val over dinner. Deep down, he felt quite hurt that talk the previous evening had only been about the biodiesel fraud. Armstrong must have known about Ian's soft spot for Val, and had arranged the dinner with his top manager to try to find out Ian's *modus operandi* so that he could replicate that sort of investigation in his other businesses without the expense of hiring forensic accountants. Ian had a good mind to bill Armstrong for his services at the full forensic rate — including weekend working allowance – which would be a pretty penny.

He thought about it some more and realised it was Watkins who must have arranged the dinner with Val. It was obvious now that he saw it: Watkins had to work long hours because he was incapable of delegating to Mary Ruffcorn. As a result, he had failed to spot the fraud, and Ian had humiliated him by being the one to uncover it.

Even arrival of his new mobile – the latest model, with faster internet surfing – failed to lift his spirits. So far as he was concerned, it was just another tool of the job. Apart from his parents' number, the only other ones he could remember were Sarah's parents', and her old mobile number. And what irritated him all the more was that Brian Stead either failed to notice, or simply refused to respond to, his mood.

"Bloody clients, eh Brian?" His colleague looked up blankly at him from his paperwork. "I said bloody clients, eh Brian? They can't do things right, can they?"

"Auditors are a legal requirement to ensure that an independent party is able to certify that an organisation's accounts meet the appropriate levels of accuracy," said Brian.

"Well, quite," said Ian. "Sorry for interrupting." Stead was, he thought, probably mildly Aspergic – it was almost commonplace amongst certain accounting specialists.

But at least the hotel grounds and the neighbouring sporting facilities were away from the hoi polloi, and that evening he went out for his first run since his beating. The pain disappeared after a few minutes as he jogged gently around the deserted racecourse. It was eerie to be somewhere so quiet where such public events took place, and he couldn't help but feel somehow spied upon — as if hordes of spectators might suddenly appear to cheer or jeer his performance on the soft sward.

His resentment for Woodcock and Tweed burned deeper for having been so cheap as to send him to the first hotel, and for the subsequent hassle he'd had with those children on his first run. Like the priceless stallions that had rode these furlongs, he deserved better surroundings. He couldn't wait to get back to London.

He checked out of the Gosforth Park on Friday morning with a tingle of excitement in his body. A month ago he could never have imagined himself checking out of a hotel with plans to stay overnight with a female acquaintance he'd not seen in so many years. A month ago, sex with a woman other than Sarah had seemed an impossible dream, but in the taxi to the office he reminded himself that it was still not reality. Pictures posted on the internet meant nothing – appearances were too readily faked.

True to her word, Val did pop in to see him, although she seemed distant – even awkward. He wondered if they might try a third time, another seven years hence.

"Next time you're down in the Big Smoke just give me a call," said Ian.

"I'm sure I'll see you when you're up here for the trial," she said. "'Bye."

"Yeah, 'bye." And that was that: not even a peck on the cheek. Brian Stead hadn't lifted his eyes from his work.

Armstrong asked him up to his office in the late afternoon.

"I just wanted to thank you, Ian," he said. "I'm sorry you went through what you did, but I'll always be grateful for it."

Ian felt like hitting him with a large invoice. "Of course, there's little I can do in reality, except to say that I've put the word out amongst the business community here about you personally. You're a bloody weird one at times, son, but you're a good accountant. Every man's got a weakness, Ian. But just watch it with all this stuff with the ladies because it can be highly distracting – and not to say prejudicial to your career."

"Thanks, I appreciate your advice but it was all an accident, I assure you. I'm very grateful for your recommendation to your peers. Good luck with Armstrong BioDiesel, by the way."

"Thanks, son. I'll be revising the forecast down a bit. For the time being we'll be sticking with just the two tanks for distribution."

"No, you can't win 'em all," said Ian. They shook hands warmly and said a final goodbye.

On his way back downstairs he congratulated himself for a mission accomplished – at least professionally. He could tell Donald Peterson on Monday that they'd be getting more business up in Newcastle, which should secure his promotion to partner — providing the incident with Louise went no further.

In a brief meeting with Watkins at five o'clock Ian told the finance director that he'd finished his on-site work and would be prepared to sign off on the accounts within the week. There was no handshake, just a muttered farewell.

He took a taxi down to the station to drop off Brian Stead. He asked the driver to stay whilst he got a bunch of flowers from a stall. Once back in the taxi, Ian gave the driver Tamara's address. He felt a gigantic burden lifted from him as they drove out of the station and down towards the Quayside. The excitement built in him as they passed the law courts and halted at a warehouse that had been converted into luxury flats. Tamara was no Patsy: she was clearly doing well for herself. There was even a concierge, a necessity rather than a luxury, Ian thought, given the proximity to so many bars and clubs. The concierge directed him to the lifts, and told him to take it to the top floor.

Tamara was doing more than just well.

There were doors to four penthouse apartments. The closest one, on the river side of the building, opened. It was Tamara. He felt the breath sucked out of him. She looked stunning. Her long brown hair cascaded over her shoulders and she locked him with her blue eyes and beaming white smile. She wore black thigh-length suede boots, a black mini-skirt and a red silk blouse.

"Ian," she said softly. "Won't you come on in?"

"Tamara," he squeaked, then cleared his throat. "Tamara, you look terrific." He bumped his bag off the doorframe as he entered her apartment.

She closed the door behind him and locked it. She took the flowers, gave him a kiss on the lips and then stepped back to look him up and down. "You've looked after yourself well, Ian. Often one meets people a few years on and they've let themselves go. Do you exercise regularly?" He nodded. "Oh, that's excellent," she said. "Wine?"

"Yes. Yes, please," said Ian, kicking himself for not having brought a bottle of champagne. She walked off into the open plan kitchen area. Deprived of the sight of her legs by a counter, he took in the rest of the apartment. It offered a spectacular, sweeping panorama of the river and the bridges through full-length windows on two sides. He took off his shoes before going any further on the deep cream-coloured carpet.

"Do sit down and make yourself comfortable." She handed him a glass of red wine and patted an area of plush sofa next to her. "Dinner will be ready in just a little while."

"I must say, you've done incredibly well for yourself," he said.

"Thanks."

"What exactly do you do? I know it's new media or something, but what?"

"It's sort of educational documentary and performance art. I'm lucky – I just spotted a trend and went with it. Cheers, here's to us."

They touched glasses and he repeated the toast, spirits lifting. "So how and when did you get into it?" He couldn't help but glance at the naked thigh above the top of her boots. She smiled, and he flushed.

"In my last couple of years at business school, actually. That's why I was always so busy. It started looking like a full-time occupation, so I just went with it. I've a tremendous passion for it."

"May I see some of your work?"

"Later, perhaps. Let's eat."

Ian was delighted with the food. It was delicious, and she'd kept the portions to a size that didn't make him feel full. They talked warmly about their student days, even though they'd not shared a close friendship at the time. He felt himself at ease, but continually had to stop himself from ogling her body when he thought she wasn't looking. Being aware of his lecherous lizard nickname made it even worse.

"You must be exhausted," she said after they'd cleared away the dishes. "I've got a great all-body shower I know you'll just *love*." Before he could object, she led him by the hand to the bedroom. The bed was larger than any he'd seen in a private home. One wall of the bedroom was formed by the sliding, floor-to-ceiling mirrored panels of a wardrobe. He thought there was a lot of height to the room until he realised that there was a large mirror over the bed. She led him straight through to the large *en suite* bathroom. "You'll feel totally re-energised after five minutes in there," she said, pointing at the shower cubicle. "Or you could have a bath," she said, patting the large circular tub. It looked more like a Jacuzzi to Ian. "But I always think it's a bit of a waste unless there are *two*," she said with a grin. "There's a clean bathrobe in the cupboard for you. I'll see you in five. *Ciao*."

His mind boggled. Was he really reading the situation correctly? Could he really be so lucky? He reminded himself of all those opportunities lost over the years through indecision or a lack of follow-through. If it was on offer tonight, then he was damned well going to make sure he was going to have it. This was a dream come true.

He put his suit on a hanger, took off the rest of his clothes and showered. Tamara was right – just a couple of minutes in the powerful shower jets invigorated him. Indeed, they invigorated him just a little too much and he had to wait for his penis to detumesce before he stepped out of the bathroom in the thick white robe. He half-wondered whether he ought to wear his underpants under it to keep himself strapped down.

She was sitting on the sofa with her back to him. She turned as she heard him open the bedroom door.

"I was getting worried," she said. "I was going to come in and get you." She had a television remote control in her hand, but Ian was at the wrong angle to be able to see the screen as he walked over to her. All he could hear was cheesy background music and some guttural dialogue.

"Oh, you caught me," she said. As he sat back down on the sofa he was shocked to see that she was watching hardcore pornography. She clicked the pause button. "I do hope I've not offended you. It's one of my little indulgences at the end of a really hard week."

"No, I…" He stared at the screen.

"Do you like this kind of thing, Ian?" She patted the sofa and he sat down, feeling naked and vulnerable in his robe next to her.

His brain felt like it would short-circuit. "I," he said. "I've seen a few and quite liked them, yes." He regretted not wearing his underpants as he felt his penis stir.

"So you won't be offended if I just watch to the end, then?" She restarted the movie before he could say anything. "I mean, these images are everywhere now. But it's still so taboo, and I think that's just so *wrong*. Don't you agree?"

"Well, yes." His throat was rather dry, he noticed.

"It's just a natural act. Everyone does it, so what's the

problem?"

"Yes," he said, more firmly, taking a sip of a replenished glass of red wine. He felt his penis pressing against his robe, hoping it wasn't noticeable.

"I'm so glad you're okay with it," she said. "A lot of men look at it – lad's magazines, the internet and all that stuff – and yet they just won't admit it. But since it's one of the biggest industries in the world then there are an awful lot of hypocrites around. Have you ever bought any?"

"Well, I... I have a couple of DVDs, yes."

"Oh, only two?" she said, turning to him. "What titles?"

He told her and she nodded. "Not bad."

They watched on in what to Ian was an awkward silence. This was just too surreal for him to take in. At once a fantasy, but also an exquisite torture. It was way out of his experience, and he hadn't a clue how to respond. He watched as beautifully tanned and toned bodies writhed on the screen, the cameras zooming in on erect penises and flushed vaginas, which were sucked, licked or masturbated before intromission in athletic positions, and the inevitable external ejaculation.

"Did your girlfriend let you watch these?" asked Tamara.

"Christ, no. I mean, no. She didn't."

"Didn't approve?" Ian nodded. "You did used to have *sex*, didn't you?"

"God, yes." Ian was sure he'd never blushed this much in his life.

"Any good?" asked Tamara absently, replaying a cunnilingus shot in slow motion.

"Yeah, I think so."

"Hmm," said Tamara, squirming her bottom on the sofa.

He glanced at his reflection in the windows. It was dark outside now, and the lights of the city were the only evidence of the rest of the world outside this bubble of strange reality. The Millennium Bridge was a twin, violet arc – not so much a winking eye as a gaping neon vagina on its side, he now thought.

"I'm sorry," she said. "It's a terrible distraction, isn't it? But it's rather fun to think who might be looking in, don't you think?"

"It's, um. It's a great view, though. But a little distracting, you're right."

She clicked another control and blinds consisting of strips of material moved out from the sides of the windows. Another click and they swivelled, shutting off the view. "I suppose you're right," she giggled. "People should at least pay to see this kind of stuff."

The movie finished in an orgy a few minutes later, but Ian couldn't see a resolution to whatever thin storyline the action was supposed to have been tied to. "So what did you think?" asked Tamara.

The question threw him completely. He'd expected something more physical, like a hand casually slipped onto his thigh. Surely he wasn't going to be thwarted yet again? He reminded himself that she was a professional producer. "Low on plot, but excellent action sequences. Good, um... Good use of close-ups. I thought the cast were really into it: very well acted. Good production values. Very professional."

She stared at him. "Jesus, Ian. I meant 'Did you *enjoy* it?'"

"Sorry. Yes. I did. It was great."

She sighed. "For crying out loud. Did it put you in the *mood*?"

He realised just in time that only he, *Ian Bore*, could steal defeat from the jaws of victory. "God, I feel so *horny*," he said, sounding ironic to his own ears.

"Me too," said Tamara. "And tonight I'm going to show you just how much." She stood up and took his hand again. He rose, his robe bulging. In her boots she was almost the same height as him. She pulled him close and they kissed. The silky sensation of tongue on tongue – a tongue not Sarah's – was as fresh to him as if he was a teenager again. He slid a hand round and caressed her firm buttocks, not daring to reach under the mini-skirt but feeling the texture of lace through the material. She broke off the embrace and led him through to the bedroom, where she used the control to close the blinds.

"Do you mind just brushing your teeth first," she said, going into the bathroom. "We've both got red wine stains on our teeth and it looks a little gross."

"Sure," he said, skipping back through to the living room. He punched the air in victory as he retrieved his toothbrush from his bag. This was it: this was what he'd been missing out on all these years. Tonight he would banish all the ghosts of his wasted youth. Valerie Craven was a prude, Patsy wasn't even a shadow of her former self, and Debbie's breasts were probably now too floppy to turn him on. Tamara's body was perfect and he was happy to be joining the ranks of the enslaved engineers, on his way to a glorious burnout.

Contraception. He'd forgotten to bring condoms. She'd had all those sexual partners. Doubt crept into the back of his mind. She would have some condoms, surely? The doubt spread as to whether he could maintain an erection wearing a sheath. It had been years since he'd used one. His erection began to falter at the prospect.

She'd already finished brushing her teeth and was tinkering with the control again. "Sorry," he said, and went past her to the bathroom.

When he got back into the bedroom she was lying on the bed, leaning back on a pile of pillows. She still had on her thigh-length boots. She had removed her blouse and mini-skirt, and a diaphanous black negligee covered her black lace bra and panties. She motioned him to lie beside her. There was another film playing on a flat screen in the corner of the room. For one awful moment he thought they were just going to watch pornography all night. "Just a little background indulgence," she said. "I hope you don't mind."

"No. No, not at all."

They turned their bodies towards each other and kissed, slower this time. He reached out a hand and stroked the few inches of bare thigh above her boot and below her underwear, then moved his hand up over her panties and under her negligee to her midriff. She undid the knot of his robe and slid her left hand underneath against his chest, pushing the fabric away.

"My," she said, seeing the bruises. "We'd better be careful with you, hadn't we?"

"Speaking of careful," said Ian. "I forgot to bring condoms. Do you have any?"

"I got a test just last month," she said. "And I'm clear. I should imagine you're pretty safe too after seven years of monogamy."

"Well, I suppose. But we really…" She'd had a test, he thought. That sounded responsible. It was already awkward enough asking about contraception and he didn't want to push his luck. Just a month ago he'd thought it might be years before he fucked without a condom again, and now here he was with this stunning, sexually charged woman. To hell with it.

"I think we ought to just relax and enjoy the moment, don't you?" She slid her hand down his stomach, and stroked her open palm gently against his penis, which recovered its stiffness. "But I'd like to keep my boots on, if that's okay."

"Uh… Yes," he said. She rose to a kneeling position and he helped her off with the negligee. She flipped the robe off his shoulders and suddenly he was naked with a woman for the first time in weeks; naked with a new woman for the first time in years.

He luxuriated over her body, taking his time to remove her bra, kissing and tonguing each nipple as he set it free, noticing a small birthmark a couple of inches above and to the right of her right nipple; what would have perhaps have been called a beauty spot in more innocent times. Unlike Sarah, her tan did not diminish anywhere on her firm breasts. She gasped and moaned as he worked his way down her stomach with his tongue. He flicked it in and out of her navel, whilst stimulating her right breast between his moistened index finger and thumb. Then he put his hands on her hips and kissed around her inner thighs and above the top of her panties.

"Oh, *please*, Ian," she moaned.

He slid the panties slowly down to discover that she was neatly shaved apart from a small crop of hair, which had been left as if to point to her engorged clitoris. The skin was as tanned as the rest of her body. She raised her legs and he pulled the panties over the tops of her boots and down over her feet. He kissed around the inside of her thighs again and she moaned. He gave a full lick of his tongue onto her clitoris and she spasmed, gasping his name. "Yeah, right there. Go to it, baby," she said. And Ian kissed, licked and fingered her moist cleft with a passion that he'd never felt before. Only on a very few occasions had he ever known Sarah be so wet. Tamara's scent was different; sweeter, somehow – less pungent. God, he thought, this was like being a porn star. Only in his wildest imaginings had he ever dreamt he'd get to do this with a girl like Tamara. She writhed beneath his touch before raising her pudenda to his mouth one final, juddering time. At the back of his head he remembered that drunken afternoon in the Trent long ago. *Tamara Never Comes* was a myth finally put to rest.

He elbowed his way back up to the top of the bed and they kissed again. "It's always the quiet ones, isn't it?" she said. "Now, lie across the bed with your feet towards the mirror, will you?"

He did as he was told, putting a couple of pillows under his head. The bed was massive and she went head first down his body with her tongue, taking him in her mouth after a few licks. From his position lying back against the pillows he caressed her buttocks and alternated his attention between the movie and the sight of her sucking him. He noticed that the soles of the boots were smooth, having never been worn outside the apartment – or at least never worn on anything other than carpet. Then he saw the head-spinning perspectives of him and Tamara provided by the mirror on the ceiling and the mirrored wardrobe. Now he understood why she'd repositioned him: he could see her sucking him from three different angles, as if in their very own porn movie. "Oh, *God*," he moaned. He was in heaven.

"Oh," she said, "I'll have to lay off a little. I want a lot more action out of you before tonight's over." She swung herself around and straddled him, clamping his body between her black suede boots, stroking her slippery vulva along his penis. She took his member in her hand, and Ian gasped at the ecstasy of the warm, wet enclosure as she gently lowered herself down on it. She rocked her hips back and forth, not in the big body-thrusts that he had been used to with Sarah, but with the subtler movement of a dancer. And then, just as he was getting ready to come, she dismounted and changed position so that she was facing away from him now, towards the mirror. Their eyes met in their reflections, her breasts bouncing, and her beauty spot setting her nipples off perfectly. She stopped to masturbate herself, whilst keeping the rhythm going with muscular movements deep within her vagina. She came, gasping, juddering, stopping for a minute to catch her breath. Then she ushered him to the end of the bed, where she bent over with her hands on the mattress for support as he took her from behind. She flicked her hair away from her face and looked in the mirror as he pumped vigorously, his loins slapping loudly against her buttocks. He felt invincible, knowing that this must be how it was done in the films, how it must feel to be a porn star.

Finally she settled back on top of him, thrusting faster and faster, looking at him intently, cheeks flushed. As he felt himself finally ready for orgasm, she slipped off him to one side. She watched herself in the wardrobe mirror as he ejaculated into her mouth and on her face. She let it dribble and then rubbed it onto her breasts, admiring her work in the mirror.

"Christ," he said. "That was the best sex I've ever had in my life. You were magnificent."

"Thank you," she said, switching off the television. "You were pretty good. But I should tell you that I slipped a little something into your drink."

"*What?*"

"Cialis. It's like Viagra but longer lasting. Come on, let's get washed. I've got your cum all over me."

It was all so matter-of-fact that he couldn't find the words. She took her makeup off in just a matter of seconds, he supposed because she was a professional presenter or actress. His erection came back to him in the shower as they soaped each other and he began foreplay again, but she brushed off his advances. "Please, not in the shower," she said. "There's a time and a place for everything." Again, he was lost for words.

Back in the bedroom she put on some panties and an old T-shirt, climbed into bed and wished him goodnight. She gave him a quick kiss on the lips and then rolled over. He lay awake for a while wondering whether it had all been a dream. He was happy – over the moon, in fact – with his experience. It was everything he'd hoped for on a physical and erotic level, but her matter-of-factness left him cold. He'd always enjoyed it when Sarah had lain her head on his chest after love-making, and he missed that.

He woke with an enormous erection, images of the previous night's sex still burning in his head, and reached out a hand towards her. "Oh," she said. "Good morning." She looked over at the alarm clock on her bedside table. "Hmm. It's quite early for me for a Saturday."

She pulled back the sheets and examined his body. "My, those bruises are still quite prominent, aren't they?" She thought for a few seconds. Ian felt like a piece of meat, but his erection had its own ideas, and pulsed expectantly. "I've got an idea. You go and brush your teeth and get yourself refreshed. I've got just the thing."

When he came back into the bedroom she was dressed in a black bodice, her hair was tied back and she was wearing stilettos. She tapped her left palm impatiently with a riding crop. "I suspect you've not tried bondage before. Am I right?"

He nodded, aghast.

A minute later, he found himself face down on the bed like a giant X, his wrists and ankles strapped in place by leather cuffs on chains. The speed of his transition from free man to bound at Tamara's expert hands was startling. And how right he'd been about his nickname for her: Tie-me-up-Tamara. She walked around each of the four points, and with a tug on an unseen mechanism tightened his bindings so that he couldn't move. Just as he was getting over the shock and beginning to feel the thrill of the forbidden, he felt her weight press on the bed either side of his body and her knees clamp on his ribs.

"If you could just look forward and raise your head," she said. He did as he was told and the world suddenly went dark as a rubber mask was slipped over his face. He felt it tighten as it slapped tight on the back of his head. He panicked, straining uselessly against the cuffs, unable to breathe. "If you just breathe normally you'll be fine," she said. He realised that he had no option but to put his trust in her: that this was exactly what this game was about. He stopped struggling and felt her expert hands adjust the rubber on his face – he could breathe through his mouth and see through narrow slits.

"I'm not going to hurt you, but you do look like you've been through the wars. Just indulge me and yelp a little from time to time, will you?" He nodded. "Oh, and call me Mistress. Okay?" He wasn't in a position to disobey, and he didn't want to find out what would happen if he did.

He wasn't sure whether he enjoyed it or not. Certainly it was something he'd remember for the rest of his life – though not something he could see himself telling his grandchildren on a lazy Sunday afternoon. She hit him on the buttocks with the riding crop, and he cried out on cue, calling her Mistress and begging for more. She changed his position a couple of times, once almost suffocating him under her vagina as she cried out in pleasure. She finished the act by straddling him whilst he was strapped face up on the bed. His lack of control in this position was the most curious thing of the whole experience. Again, she spread his ejaculate over herself.

She unstrapped him. "So, how was your first experience of BDSM?"

"Not quite what I expected. I suppose it's quite... *specialist*, isn't it?"

"Again, it's nothing to be ashamed of, Ian. You'd be surprised how many people have it as their little private fantasy. As with all pornography, the numbers speak for themselves."

They showered separately; her first. He felt quite alone with her, almost abandoned, such was her nonchalance. It had been a strangely disappointing experience – though he had stored up the images in his head.

Having been expecting to go back to London at the end of the working week, he'd not thought to bring a suit bag, so he put his suit on. As he entered the living room he realised he'd only brought one bag with him from the office. "Damn!" he said.

Tamara was dressed and had makeup on, and had laid out a light breakfast. She looked even sexier with her clothes on. "What's up?" she asked.

"I've left my laptop at the office."

"Where's the office?"

"Gosforth."

"I'll give you a lift, but we have to hurry – I have a meeting at ten."

He wolfed down his breakfast and they took the lift down to the underground garage. Driving as a passenger in her black Porsche with the top down was another realised dream for him; other men looking twice at her as they sped past. They reached Armstrong's offices in no time. Ian bounded up to the door whilst Tamara sat in the car listening to loud rock music.

Fortunately, the same guard was on duty as the previous weekend. He recognised Ian and waived the signing of the register, so long as he was quick.

Ian reached the meeting room they'd used for the audit. He had left his laptop and bag on the table, but they weren't there. He panicked, thinking of all the confidential material stored on it. Then he realised from the smell of furniture polish that the cleaner must have been in. He hunted around the room and discovered them out of sight on a spare chair between a filing cabinet and the far wall. They were sitting on a suspension file full of invoices. With just himself – and latterly he and Brian Stead – in the room the previous week, that end of it hadn't been used. He picked up the suspension file. The plastic tag had fallen off so he looked inside to see what the invoices pertained to. The first one he came across was a crisp, clean invoice for palm oil. It had to be the file for ABD: Armstrong BioDiesel. Something was still nagging at him about this whole ABD business. Val's behaviour over dinner on Wednesday night, the company's falling market share in a growth market, and other, smaller things – things he couldn't put a finger on, but which burrowed into the back of his brain. If the accounts team hadn't missed these invoices for a week, then they'd not miss them for another, would they? It wasn't that uncommon to take files away for further study during an audit. And he was sure Armstrong wouldn't mind, even if Watkins kicked up a stink about it. He stuffed the file into his laptop bag – reading for the journey home.

"Get what you wanted?" asked Tamara as they drove off.

Ian laughed, and she laughed too, realising the *double entendre*. If only she'd not been so clipped about the sex, he thought. "Yes," he said. "Will we be seeing each other again? I mean, I really enjoyed myself. I'd love to… you know."

She glanced at him, smiling, her hair blowing over her face. "You're sweet," she said, squeezing his thigh. "I suppose part of it's this thing of heading for thirty. You must be feeling that too, surely?"

"Mmm?" Half his mind was on ABD.

"Come on," she said. "It's worse for guys. You wonder about all the great sex you never had. Or even the lousy sex. You always think about the ones who got away."

She had his full attention. "God, I thought that was purely a *guy* thing," he said. She rolled her eyes. "And if you don't mind me saying, you seemed to do pretty well when we were students," he added, hoping it wouldn't offend her.

"Oh, that was different. I always regretted not shagging anyone on the course."

He thought for a few seconds. "You don't mean to say…"

"Yeah, you were on my list. I was always a bit disappointed that I didn't shag you that night at Rock City. You were kind of cute. Sorry, you still are, I should say."

"So." He leaned his elbow on the lip of the door and rubbed his head. "So I was just on some list or other in your head?"

"Sure. But it was all a bit more than that."

The tables had been turned and he'd not suspected for a moment. He chuckled. She glanced over and they both laughed.

"Well I'd love to see you again," he said.

"I'm sure you will," she replied. "Here's the station. I'm quite late for a business meeting, so no big farewells, okay? There's a train in nine minutes." He gave her a questioning look. "I get distributors up from London all the time."

She took a ticket from the barrier and pulled up, engine thrumming, under the huge stone portico. "Your business," he said, getting out of the car. "I never even asked about your business. If you need any accounts done I'd be happy to help, *gratis*."

She grinned. "I'm sure you'd expect *some* kind of payment in return, Ian." She gave him a quick kiss on the lips and tugged his door shut. "I'll send you a link by email. *Ciao*!"

"*Ciao*," he called after her.

Rose had done her work. He presented his old ticket at the office and was issued a new one.

He settled back into his seat and peered out at the view of the

Tyne as the train passed over it. He could see Tamara's penthouse apartment, and felt a warm glow of satisfaction. Then that ugly duckling of a ship, the *Tuxedo Princess*, caught his eye, bringing him back with a bump to thoughts of London and Monday morning in the office, and the possibility of recriminations over the incident with Jess.

The lump of his new mobile phone weighed in his suit pocket. He turned it on and navigated through to the internet function before realising that it would take a half-hour phone call to turn the service on.

He'd not had time to buy a newspaper, so he turned his attention to the pile of invoices from ABD. Without the nominal ledger, he was able to concentrate on the documents themselves. After a few minutes, he was left with a burning question that made him angry.

How could he have been so stupid?

The rush of the capital on a Saturday compared to Newcastle blasted his senses and he was quite sick of it by the time he got home.

His initial anger had turned to excitement. Now, sipping a beer and having eaten a low calorie frozen meal, it turned to fear. If he'd been beaten up over a few thousands of pounds worth of theft, there'd be murder to pay for a fraud this size.

Providing, of course, that he was right.

The invoices for the palm oil were fake, and so were those for the methylated spirits. The numbers had all tallied back to the entries on the nominal ledger – no doubt about that. What had alerted him to the questionable authenticity of the invoices was that the bank account being invoiced for the goods was different to Armstrong's – a number quite familiar to him by now – and a different number even from that which was used to pay the company's substantial electricity bill.

A closer examination of the invoices had found that those for the palm oil and meths were on the same watermarked paper.

Yet these were invoices supposedly produced in different countries. The chances were slim for this to have happened, but they were real. But the paper used for both had changed in the same month. The odds against that were so small as to be negligible. He'd looked at the invoices themselves and then it had become glaringly obvious. The paper hadn't been folded. He felt a fool when he'd noticed that. Practically every invoice he'd ever seen had been folded to fit into an envelope. Companies which produced larger numbers of invoices tended to use a single-fold because it was cheaper and was less likely to jam the industrial laser-printers used for the job. The trade-off was a larger, more expensive envelope. Companies issuing smaller numbers of invoices – for example, bulk industrial goods — tended to use double-folded invoices. But even where companies didn't fold their invoices, they still showed signs of having been through the mail. The invoices for these two goods were clean and uncrumpled.

The clincher for him was that the dates on the meths and palm oil invoices were the same, and one of the dates was a Saturday. Someone had been re-invoicing for the goods into the factory. Presumably, they'd been paying the supplier directly and then picking up the payment from Armstrong using the fake invoices.

There was only one possible explanation: the factory was producing biodiesel at a higher capacity than was being declared. He had no way of telling just how much it was producing – he would need the original invoices for that, and copies would be with the supplier.

Who was in on it? Watkins, for sure: he alone had the authority to nominate which accounts to pay invoices to. And Horsley? Horsley would be the one person with all the figures to hand. Were the suppliers also in on the scam? If so, going to them for the duplicates would alert them.

He thought back to his experience the previous weekend. Thanks to his surveillance being interrupted, the police had been left with a lot of loose ends they might never tie up. This one needed to be watertight. He would keep it quiet at work. One thing was for sure, though: cracking a case this size by himself would guarantee him that partnership.

Chapter Fifteen

Ian walked tall as he parted the ribbons of the sex shop on Sunday afternoon. He now felt a certain kinship with the stars of naked flesh. Indeed, the lasting effects of Friday night's Cialis had woken him with a reminder that the life of a sexual superstar was his for the taking if he chose it.

He'd rejected a return to his normal life of Sunday lunch with friends at the Derbyshire, despite the invitations on his answering machine. They were nowhere people, sinking without protest into the mire of the middle of their lives. He could have bragged about Friday night's adventures but they just wouldn't have got it. They thought small: porn to them was an indiscretion, a furtive activity to be hidden from their girlfriends. Ian was a superior being now: fit, single and sexually active. He was done with them: they belonged a past life. Whilst they were getting pot-bellied in the pub, he'd taken a run on Clapham Common and ogled at the first sunbathers of the season. There were four million women in London, and if they knew what he was capable of, he'd have them queuing round the block. Maybe gym membership and an all-over tan were his next steps? And perhaps Iguana Ian might actually be quite a decent *nom de coq* for the all-new Ian Bourne? There must be ten thousand Tamaras in London, and he would find a way of tracking them down now that he knew what a stud he really was.

He met the shop manager's eyes with a friendly "Hi," which surprised the man.

"Oh, I remember you," he said, scratching his thick stubble. "That discount still holds if you've got the receipt."

"Lost it."

"Never mind. I'll do you a special. How about four for fifty quid?"

Ian knew a bargain when he saw it: the normal price was twenty pounds each, or three for the price of two. He checked his watch and calculated he had at best half an hour, though he should allow more for the ailing tube network if he wanted to drop them off before getting to Stu and Nina's for dinner. "Great," he said. "What would you recommend?" He was kicking himself for not having asked Tamara for a list of good titles, and made a mental note to drop her an email to that effect.

The manager laughed. "Whatever you can think of, we've got it. Everything from the bizarre to the amateur to the professional – with every fetish between thrown in."

Ian stood in front of the racks and took an unhurried look. The Amateur section didn't take his fancy at all. Perhaps he'd been spoiled by his sex with Tamara, but the women's bodies were mostly not up to her standard. Besides, he considered himself somewhat of a professional now. He lingered over the Bondage section – his experience had been interesting, but he might have enjoyed it more if it had been less one-sided. The two other mainstream categories were Movies and Compilations. He took his time selecting a couple of movies which featured stars whose names he was familiar with through his earlier purchases before moving on to Compilations, which had the appeal of variety. He scanned the titles and picked out a third DVD. One more to choose. His eyes stopped on the cover of a compilation and his brain screamed at him.

Tamara.

It was her picture. Younger, perhaps, but it was her, he was sure. With a trembling hand, he picked the DVD up and took a closer look at the three women featured on the front. There was no doubt about it – Tamara's unmistakable beauty spot was there on her right breast.

Thoughts collided in his head, bounced off the inside of his skull and collided again. His first reaction was one of excitement and pride. He really *had* qualified as a porn star of sorts. For a few amazing hours he, Ian Bourne, had enjoyed the kind of spectacular sex that other men had to pay money just to view, with a woman who was out of the league of most of them.

The thoughts collided again, congealed, and sank to the

bottom of his cerebellum.

Disease. Aids. Death.

The matter of her having had a test the previous month was explained. Anything could have happened between that test and having sex with him. There had been newspaper stories about porn stars contracting HIV in spite of regular testing, hadn't there? And couldn't the body take several weeks before producing the antibodies to HIV that the test relied on?

He calmed himself. This was a much younger Tamara. She had a respectable new media company now, with distributors – and meetings at ten o'clock on Saturdays. Sure, her personal taste in the bedroom was a little adventurous, but everyone was entitled to their own penchants. She'd obviously done this sort of work to get the seed capital – he smirked to himself at an accounting term with a *double entendre* – and he took his professional hat off to her for making the most of her assets. Again, he smirked at his diction, then again at *dic*tion. Good for her, he thought. No wonder she'd questioned him about his tastes so closely the other evening.

Yes, he was a liberated man now: a new man of a new order. The new order of the pornographic age. He was damned if he would condemn anyone for it. It was a natural act, as Tamara had insisted, and it had spawned – there was no end to his puns today – a multi-billion dollar industry. This DVD would almost be an heirloom. He checked his watch – he was running late.

The shop manager wrapped the DVDs in an anonymous brown paper bag, which he stuck shut with tape, then put it in a blue plastic shopping bag. "That'll be fifty quid. Nice choice, by the way."

"Thank you." Ian brought out his wallet. He didn't have any cash. Damn the rest of the world, he thought, piously, and handed over a credit card. He tapped the PIN into the machine and took the receipt with a cheerful goodbye. The fronds of plastic ribbon at the door didn't feel like fingers of guilt now – they were the garlands of a champion: tickertape on a hero's parade.

He stopped in his tracks at the entrance to Leicester Square tube Station. He'd been so used to living off his company credit card the last fortnight that he'd used it to buy the DVDs. A wave of fear washed over him as he turned and ran back to the shop. How could he of all people have been so stupid?

"You have to reverse this transaction," he said, panting, to the manager. "*Please.*"

"A deal's a deal. Technically they're second-hand now," he pointed to a sign that said *No refunds or exchanges*.

"I do want them. I just have to pay you with a different card. Please, can you just reverse the sodding transaction and I'll use a different credit card."

The man scratched his stubbled cheek slowly. "Alright, but so long as you pay using the other card first. I'm not having you running off."

"Sure, sure." Ian checked his watch. He'd be quite late now, even if the tube was running on time.

The process took several painful, precious minutes. The DVDs had to be scanned through the electronic till again, and the system insisted that one of the titles couldn't be being sold because the last one in stock had just been sold in the previous transaction – which had been to Ian in his initial purchase. Then the previous transaction on his company card had to be reversed.

He left the shop sweating, the ribbons pulling him back, reminding him of the exit of an unfunny House of Fun he'd gone to at a fairground as a boy.

The tube was clammy. He couldn't drop the DVDs off at his place before heading for dinner at Stu and Nina's because it would make him forty-five minutes late. Being teachers, at weekends they ran their lives to an unheard bell. He picked up a bottle of more than decent red, but there were no flower shops open. He popped the bottle into his bag alongside the DVDs.

He was twenty minutes late. "Sorry," he said to Stu as he entered the house. "Bloody tube. Much better up in Newcastle, let me tell you that."

"Hell's bells, Ian," said Stu. "Look at the state of you. You said on the phone this morning you'd never been better. Here, Nina, come and look."

Ian took off his jacket and was just able to make it stick onto one of the overloaded pegs next to the front door. He took out the bottle and dumped the blue plastic bag of DVDs on the floor.

Young Jeremy staggered through to the hall to greet him before his mother could. "Hello," said Ian. "Look who it is." He lifted the boy up and they went through to the living-cum-dining room. Jeremy was a miniature of Stu – a blond mop and an already powerful build. Ian plonked him down by his train set.

"God, Ian," said Nina, seeing the shaved patch and the plaster on the side of his head where the stitches had been put in.

"It's nothing, really," he insisted. But the complications in the sex shop had flustered him, and he was sweating. Then he realised that it was a chance to paint himself into an heroic picture for his friends. And if his parents heard of his adventure through Stu then there'd be a chance they'd lay off him for a while.

Nina had roasted a turkey, which Stu carved: this was food for a functional family; not single-serving bachelor fare. Over dinner he told them about his triumph in having uncovered the scam at ABD, and the assault that had been a direct consequence of him putting the safety of the evidence before his own well-being. With his father being a policeman, Stu had a good grasp of the court procedures that would block Ian's time in the coming months.

Jeremy had been sitting in his highchair quietly but now began to bang his spoon on his tray. Nina lifted him out and put him down on the floor. "What about this internet dating business?" asked Nina. "Did you give it a go?" Jeremy staggered off out of the room.

"Er, yes. It's overrated. Some right nutters on it." He took a sip of wine. "There was a reason I didn't return until yesterday afternoon, though," he said, putting his palms on the table. "I met up for dinner with an old friend from my course and one thing led to another."

"Oh, yeah?" said Stu, smiling "What's she like?"

I've got a DVD in the hall that would give you a bloody good idea, Ian wanted to tell him. "Very attractive, has her own new media company and drives a Porsche." Stu whistled.

"God," said Nina. "You're so materialistic. You're seeing her again soon, I hope."

"Oh, yes. I'm seeing her very soon," he said, realising what Tamara must have been hinting at when they parted.

There was a rustle from the hallway and the sound of tearing. Nina rolled her eyes. There was more tearing and then the sound of plastic hitting plastic. "I'd better see what he's up to," she said.

"No!" said Ian, getting up. But he was on the opposite side of the table and Nina was already out into the hall. Stu looked at him curiously.

"Leave them, Jeremy," he heard Nina say. Then there was silence.

"You alright, love?" called Stu.

Nina came back into the room slowly, looking at the backs of the four DVDs in her hands. She handed them to Stu The Policeman and fixed Ian with a teacher's stare. "I'd rather you kept this stuff out of my house, Ian Bourne," she said. "Stu, I think you need to talk to him. But not in here. Not in my house."

Jeremy hugged his father's leg with one arm and reached up for the DVDs, yelling. Nina picked him up and thudded upstairs.

Ian had to endure another of Stu's patronising monologues as they cleared the plates: hobbies and interests; the curse of free time given only to oneself. "And you were looking so fit and well, mate," he said as they left the house. "At least physically. But you're dying in here," Stu tapped his head. "I've a good mind to confiscate those. What am I going to tell your parents?"

Something snapped in Ian. "Look, fuck off with your

moralising and mollycoddling. I'm no worse than anyone else. It's one of the biggest industries in the world because — guess what? – there's a demand for it."

"There's a demand for heroin too, sunshine," said Stu, stopping him with a hand on his shoulder. "Doesn't mean to say you have to go and shoot up, though – does it?"

"Hardly the same thing. And you're not my moral guardian, nor are you a surrogate parent. Alright?"

"I've got your best interests at heart. No good comes of this sort of thing, you know."

"How the *fuck* would you know?" asked Ian. "The sum total of your biggest thrill was moving to London. My life's bigger than that. I've got dreams."

"Fine, bugger off yourself," said Stu. He went back into the house and slammed the door behind him.

Ian sighed: he'd call him later in the week to make it up. Tamara was right: people were too uptight about porn.

He was taking the cellophane wrapper from Tamara's compilation DVD when the phone rang. He let it go to voicemail as he loaded the disc into the player. In a voice that would have sounded chirpy in any accent Marina said, "So, finally I to looking see you forward, Forensitch. Am come to Ball-ham shortly. Goodbye!" When he'd got back from Newcastle he'd chosen to erase the four messages she'd left without listening to them. What were her plans? Where was she? Was she already in London?

He turned his computer on and logged in to M—.com and saw that he'd deleted all her emails but still had the replies he'd sent her. He opened one and clicked on the link to her name. An hourglass appeared and after a few seconds the screen changed to a message which read, 'Sorry, this subscriber is no longer a member of M—.com'.

The panic began to snowball within him. How could she possibly have tracked him to Balham? A quick search of the internet found a couple of sites from which it was possible to determine the local exchange using the first four digits of phone numbers.

He calmed himself down and dismissed his concerns. She couldn't possibly afford a trip to London. Even if she could, it was impossible to track him down any further from his phone number. Or was it? He turned his thoughts around again. What if she turned up? She'd need a bed for the night, or perhaps longer.

His mind boggled at the possibilities: weren't the papers full of stories about Eastern European women being exploited for sex? He'd certainly make sure she did nothing against her will, but the allure of a visa was bound to make her pliable.

He chastised himself for having behaved like an amateur – he was a super-stud in the making, and this would be another situation he could turn to his advantage. The key was to relax and make the most of the possibilities life threw at him.

He settled back into his settee to enjoy the last of the weekend. The copyright on the DVD was three years old and, since it was a compilation, he assumed that the actual footage must predate that by at least another couple of years. That proved he'd been right about her having only been in porn only to make some seed capital to start her business. He relaxed.

Tamara smiled bare-breasted at him from the menu screen – one of three women featured. He moved the cursor over her image and pressed Play.

Tamara serviced – or was serviced by – two young men for half an hour. Judging by the editing, they must have been at it for much longer than that. And by the standards he was accustomed to viewing, she was a magnificent performer.

It was the most disconcerting experience of his life to see a woman he'd made love to – *had sex with*, he corrected himself – just forty-eight hours before, sharing that most intimate and sacred of experiences with two strangers. He hadn't so much envy, as empathy with the men. It was they who should envy him because he'd been part of her life for her four student years, and his experience had been within the temple of her home, rather than under the glaring lights of a studio. She'd taken him because she lusted for him, and she'd been paid for their pleasure. However, he considered it a pity that it was they who were the ones to bask in the public glory of having enjoyed her most passionate delights.

He rewound, paused and replayed selected scenes a few times, overlaying his own images from Friday night into his imagination as he masturbated his tired penis one final time that weekend. If only they knew, he thought. If only his friends could have seen what he did on that glorious night.

Then he remembered she'd said she would email him a link to her site. If he wanted to see her again – and he most certainly did – he realised he'd better show an interest in her work. He logged into Hotmail. There was an email from an unknown source with the subject header 'Your subscription to Tamara's People'. He opened it to find a link and a user name and password. His account settings prevented the email's graphics from displaying, so he just clicked the link. A fresh window opened with a black background. Pink letters to the left of the two white spaces indicated where he should enter the details he'd been sent, which he did.

Tamara's People formed on the screen in large, electric-blue letters. *People like YOU* appeared slowly underneath. There was a warning that viewers had to be aged eighteen or over to view the site. She must have moved into production, he thought. He'd heard about porn actresses taking control of the supply chain, and he admired them for it. He clicked the box to certify that he was over eighteen and then hit Enter.

There was a full-screen picture of Tamara, viewed from the side, being taken from behind. The focal point was her gasping, ecstatic face, eyes closed, and nothing of the man was even in shot above his biceps. 'Welcome, Ian Bourne' it said next to the Log Out button. He clicked on the Latest Content button. What was she doing, he wondered, remarketing her old titles or paying for new content? Was she producing and directing, or...?

His question was answered as a small video frame opened up, with a shot showing Tamara having sex with a man on a large bed. She was sitting across the bed, facing the camera, the man's feet in front of her as she straddled him. She stopped and began to masturbate, her lover still inside. The blind in the background looked very familiar, as did the man's face as he leered round from behind her.

Oh, *fuck*, thought Ian.

His own delighted face looked back at him from the TV as it stared straight into the camera that must have been hidden behind the two-way mirror of the wardrobe in Tamara's bedroom.

"Oh, fuck, *no*," he said loudly, as the two figures made their way to the end of the bed and began to fuck doggie-style, her hands on the mattress for support. He watched in frozen horror as the video sample cut to the 'money shot', where he ejaculated and she spread the resulting mess over her breasts, moaning. Text on the screen offered him the chance to download the full-length, full-screen movie.

He was paralysed, hands cupped over his nose and mouth. He looked at the text underneath.

> Main category: Friday Night Fuck
> Sub-categories: Old times BDSM

Friday Night Fuck was clearly a link. Gingerly, he moved the cursor over it and clicked. The screen refreshed to show six thumbnails with dates underneath. His was the most recent, and the one before that was a couple of weeks earlier. There was a paragraph of text above the thumbnails:

> Now and then I like to take an unsuspecting cute-looking guy and give him something he never dreamed possible. No names, just a great time in a no-rules romp in my

> luxury apartment! This is invitation-only and a party just for one. But if you meet a beautiful stranger on a Friday, who knows what might happen?

His dry throat stopped him from swallowing. He didn't deserve this. It wasn't fair.

He hit the Back button and looked at the Sub-categories under his thumbnail. He clicked on Old Times and another half-dozen thumbnails filled his screen.

> We all have our regrets, and mine was not to play to a wider field during my mad college days. Watch me as I try to catch up on my revision! I give you a little background on each of my lucky 'revision subjects'.

He looked at the thumbnails in more detail. Tamara was with a woman in one them – though no one he recognised. Ben Fingal was in there. God, he'd hated Ben; a smug, rugby-playing loudmouth. And the fact that he'd enjoyed Tamara before Ian made him sick. There were other faces he recognised. As with the previous set of thumbnails there was a button on the bottom right signalling More>> but he resisted the temptation, frightened of what else he might find.

He hovered over his own thumbnail and then clicked.

She was speaking into camera, dressed as she had been on Saturday morning. "What can I say about Ian?" she said. "He had two nicknames at college: Ian Bore and Iguana Ian. Seven years ago he was a quiet, hard-working student who went on to become an accountant. He's been with the same girl all that time and I don't think she once 'cooked his books'. Keep watching for some 'double-entry' like you've never seen in book-keeping. Oh, and watch that iguana tongue go! Who said accountants were boring?"

He breathed out a sigh. That was at least something. In his heart-of-hearts he knew that she was being generous – she had to up-sell these videos to the audience. But even so, he had it there in sound and vision for the whole world to see.

A fresh claw of fear gripped his heart. He calmed himself: this was a members-only site. He'd been through these anxieties when he'd joined M—.com. No one could say they'd seen him without admitting that they themselves had logged in.

Then he remembered there was something else he had yet to see. He clicked the Back button twice on his browser and clicked on the BDSM Sub-category under his name. There were six more thumbnails, and he could see that the people in them were bound in various positions, with Tamara in shot wearing dominatrix outfits. She'd certainly made the most of him — he was the most recent star. He navigated back to the Friday Night Fuck page, and felt a chill. She said she'd had an Aids test the month before, but there she was having sex with another man just two weeks prior to Friday. He clicked on the thumbnail and watched the action closely: the man was not wearing a condom.

He was nauseous with panic. He'd heard there was some kind of morning-after treatment for rape victims, some kind of pill to suppress the virus in its early stages. It had already been forty-eight hours since he'd first had sex with Tamara. Was it worth taking a taxi to a local A&E department?

He glanced at his watch. It was nearly eleven o'clock. He went to his Hotmail account and found Tamara's number.

"Hello?" said a sleepy female voice.

"Tamara? Hi, it's Ian." He was shaking. Was it a touch of fever already?

"Ian, do you know what time it is?" He heard her bedclothes rustle as she rolled over. "It's eleven o'clock for God's sake. I've got a long day tomorrow."

He felt the blood rise to his ears. "You didn't tell me you'd fucked all those men," he said.

"What do you mean?"

"You know, on your website. I had no idea you were a porn star."

"But I thought you liked porn?"

"I do, but…"

"So what's the problem, baby?"

"The problem is that you filmed me secretly and have put it up on a website."

"I gave you free lifetime membership, so that's fair isn't it? Look, I really do need to sleep."

"You never told me you had another man just two weeks before."

"Christ, what's with all this jealousy?"

"My point is that you said you'd been tested a month before. But you screwed this guy without a condom just a fortnight ago."

"Did I say that? I'm sorry. Really, I'm fine. He was safe, I checked. Besides, you'll see that it was an external cum-shot, which is safer."

"But you can't be sure."

She paused. "You know, you're right," she said casually. "I should be more careful."

"But what about me?"

"You should be more careful too."

"Well it's a bit late now."

"You're right. It's five-past eleven."

"That's not what I meant."

"Oh, sorry. I'm tired. You didn't object, did you? Isn't it *caveat emptor*, or something like that? You can get a test in the morning, but I'm sure you'll be fine."

Caveat fornicator, Ian thought of saying. "And I'd like my videos down off the site."

"Oh, come on, Ian. I have a living to make, you know. There's an expectant audience."

"You never sought my permission."

"Isn't that a little hypocritical? I bet you've seen amateur spy-camera stuff of men fucking their wives and girlfriends and enjoyed it. Come on, don't be such a prude."

"I'm not being a prude. I have a professional reputation."

"Well so do I, Mr Accountant," she said, and hung up.

He stared in disbelief at the phone then hit the redial button.

"What *now*?" said Tamara.

"I want those videos down *immediately*," he barked.

"Well I can't do it 'immediately'," she said sarcastically. "It's late on Sunday night, I'm tired and the access to the internet server's in my office. It'll have to wait till the morning. And I shall expect compensation for lost revenue."

"*What?*"

"Fresh content's what it's all about. If my punters don't see fresh content then they don't resubscribe, do they? Then there's the syndication sales."

"*Syndication?*"

"Yeah, those clips get sold on and on and on. Like I told you – I've got loads of distributors. I'm on DVD, websites, even stuff you can download to your mobile. I told you I was into new media. Those clips are worth a good thirty grand each in the first year alone. I've got a limited time to make my money – looks do fade, you know."

"But that's *blackmail*."

She paused. "You know, I'd never thought of it like that. But I must say you're the first to complain. That's the magic of internet porn, you see."

"What do you mean?"

"You don't get it, do you? It's a magic roundabout, Ian."

"You're right: I still don't get it."

"When I said it's one of the biggest businesses on the planet, I meant it." The tiredness had gone from her voice, and there was the enthusiastic edge of an entrepreneur to it. "It's bigger than the airline industry. Isn't that amazing? You think of an airport like Heathrow and the tens of millions of people passing through it each year. And you know why the porn industry's better?"

Ian thought for a moment. "Most airlines don't make a

profit?"

"Bang on. It's a magic roundabout because the customer pays as the content goes round and round. And the more there is, the more the punters want. The more they want it, the more they get. And it's an elephant in the corner because everyone knows it's there, everyone knows they're buying it, but no one says a thing. Do you know what proportion of men look at porn on the internet every month, Ian?"

"No," he said, quietly, marvelling at the genius of the business model.

"About eighty percent of men aged twenty to forty-five admit to looking at internet porn at least once a month."

"Christ."

"And the other twenty percent are probably liars. Either that or they don't have private internet access."

Ian pondered a few moments. "But what's that got to do with me wanting my videos down?"

"It's all to do with other people *not* wanting to. God, you're slow. Most guys are quite proud to know there's a bit of them out there for posterity, that they were part of this revolution. The industry was like this when *Deep Throat* became a mainstream movie in 1972 – most porn stars said they were like social campaigners. But now it's back under the surface again, except that it's so much more pervasive. Now, think of the elephant in the corner: if someone sees you then they can't say a thing because they'd be stigmatised for having watched porn."

Ian was silent.

"You still there, Ian?"

"Yes," he mumbled.

"You poor thing," she said softly. "You're really out of your depth, aren't you?"

"Yes," he said.

"That really was your first time doing anything like that, wasn't it?"

"Yes."

"I'm sorry. But you did enjoy it."

He sighed. "I'd not have done it if I'd known the consequences."

"Just think of the innocent women in the sex trade," she said quietly. "The Eastern European or Filipino girls who're sold as slaves – right here in this country. I give part of my profits to run a refuge for them."

Ian felt a wave of guilt about his earlier fantasy about Marina turning up. "How about I donate a couple of grand to your charity?"

"Oh, Ian. You're actually a very good man at heart. Okay, I'll take down the straight sex video, but the BDSM one stays up — those bruises gave it incredible authenticity and it'll be a great earner. You're wearing a mask the whole time and you don't say anything that could give you away."

He hesitated. "So long as there's nothing whatsoever connecting me with it."

"It's a deal."

"Thank you," he gushed. "Thank you, Tamara. Look, I'll even do the charity's audit for free."

"You're very sweet. I'm sorry about all this. Now get some sleep and get a test in the morning if it makes you feel better. Goodnight."

What was the expression? *Tart with a heart.*

He turned back to his laptop and downloaded the full-length video to his pocket flash drive for posterity. With meticulous care, he wiped the History from his browser, deleted the offline content and erased the cookies on his company laptop. If only it were so easy to ensure his own health.

Chapter Sixteen

"Thank you for calling St Bartholomew's Sexually Transmitted Disease Clinic," said the recorded male voice. It then slowly and meticulously reeled off the opening hours for every day of the week before telling Ian that he was number eleven in the queue. He wondered how many hundreds of men and women across the capital were in his predicament, if this was the volume of calls at just one clinic. Was it something they'd been sweating over for months – or, like him, had they made a rash decision to have unprotected sex with an unknown partner that weekend? Rash, he thought – if only it were just a rash.

He'd felt feverish most of the night. The darkest part of his mind told him that he was infected; the more rational side that he was just scared. On the tube he'd felt every glance from strangers, wondering if they'd seen him on the internet. The fact that most of the other men in the carriage had a secret porn habit was of no comfort. He'd felt naked and diseased. *The Word of the Lord Endureth Forever* carved on the pages of the open bible above the door to D'Arcy House had triggered youthful fears of eternal damnation as he'd entered the building.

He moved to position ten in the queue and estimated he had perhaps half an hour to wait at this rate. He pulled the receipts out of his wallet and began to do the expenses for his fortnight in Newcastle.

A computer technician arrived from the main St Swithin's Lane office. "Laptop needs to go back for maintenance," said the nerdy-looking youth, avoiding eye contact.

Ian checked the pockets of the laptop bag. The ABD invoices were at home. There was nothing else in it, so he handed it over. He remembered how many happy hours he'd spent alone with that computer late at night and congratulated himself on having remembered to erase all traces of them. He smiled confidently. "When do I get it back?" he asked.

"Dunno. Depends."

"Look," Ian said, irritated by the lack of a clear answer. "That device is critical to my job. If I'm asked off-site then I'm stuffed. Do you understand me?"

"Sure. Maybe tomorrow." The youth slouched off.

Ian smiled. They might check it for viruses, but it was more likely that samples of his DNA were spattered over it.

He had the two receipts from his transaction at the sex shop to deal with, one cancelling out the other. There was no avoiding the twin entries in his monthly credit card statement, but at least they'd be side by side. Fortunately, the shop's name — Porno Emporium – wasn't on the transaction receipt for the card. Instead, the operating company's trading entity — X-Star Retail – had been used, probably to help customers make their bank and credit card statements look less incriminating. The mistake would be evident and surely no one would bother to find out who X-Star Retail were. An educated person would surely assume the X was a Roman numeral and infer that 'Ten-Star' retail was some top-class outfitter. He had finished his expenses sheet by the time he got a live receptionist at St Bart's. The first free appointment was that afternoon at half-four. He was warned that he'd still face a long wait, and told that he should not urinate in the preceding two hours. He handed his expenses to Rose.

He and Peterson took lunch at *Les Trois Voleurs*, a restaurant frequented by corporate lawyers – something they did after every successful case.

"You prepared to sign off on the audit?" asked Peterson.

"End of the week," replied Ian. "Armstrong's really pleased and says he'll be recommending us to all his mates."

"Great, great," said Peterson. "Shame we can't bill him any extra."

"Yeah. But it'll look good for me, won't it?"

"Christ, yes. I shouldn't be surprised if our PR chaps get you a spot in *Accountancy Age* for your heroics. We've been looking to – what's the term for it? – 'reposition' ourselves away from our stuffy image."

His boss insisted on splitting the bill. It had been Ian's win and, in theory at least, his pay packet would be boosted by the earnings from the job, and so he should have been the one to have paid. But the reality was that he'd probably lost out by taking the auditing job because he might have missed a more lucrative forensic one.

The choice of a restaurant populated primarily by lawyers was deliberate: after a successful case, one was always on the hunt for more business. Peterson consoled him over the episode: Ian's promotion was up for discussion at the next partners' meeting, which was on Friday. He was quite sure it would be rubberstamped; the loss of Ian's two female subordinates from the job overshadowed by his uncovering of the fraud.

Ian spotted a woman with red hair entering the restaurant as they stood up to leave. It was Karen Goodman, Sarah's former colleague. She was with an older woman who looked familiar to Ian. He caught her eye and she signalled that it was okay to interrupt. "Karen, hi," he said, and gave her a peck on the cheek, which he thought was acceptable. "May I introduce Donald Peterson? Managing Partner of Woodcock and Tweed's Forensic Accounting division. Donald, this is Karen Goodman, of Perky Bottom," he stopped himself deliberately. "I mean, *Perkins Botham*." It broke the ice.

"Suzanne Meadows," said Karen's older companion. "Senior Partner, Corporate, Perkins Botham."

"My boss," chirped Karen in her Scottish accent.

They swapped cards and talked shop for a few minutes. The men had been early, and the women were having a late lunch.

"Perky Bottom? I'll say she does," said Peterson, as soon as they were outside the restaurant. "Tell you what, why don't we double-date them? Suzanne's not got a wedding ring."

"I seem to remember she went through a divorce a couple of years ago," said Ian. "You do at least have that in common."

"How'd you know that?"

"Karen's Sarah's old colleague."

"Ah. Kind of precludes you from taking a stab at Karen, as it were."

"Not my type, actually. Feel free with Suzanne, though."

"I will, thanks. Have you heard from Sarah?"

"No. I wish I'd had a chance to ask Karen."

"Never mind. How's your love life? Rose mentioned you'd been dating."

Ian hesitated before answering. "Still nothing doing. Look, I have to go and see Dr Patel again this afternoon. You're right: it really does help. I've got an appointment at half-four."

"Oh, good. Glad Raj Patel's proving to be a help. Take care."

Ian had less than three hours to kill, which he spent on Armstrong's accounts. He took care of one transposition error he'd missed earlier through sheer boredom. His thoughts turned to the fraud, and he wondered about Watkins' career after Woodcock and Tweed. He kicked himself for not having questioned Peterson over lunch. Knowing his boss's habits, he wandered into the man's office just after three with a cup of coffee for him. Peterson thanked him, and broke away from his work.

"Was Ed Watkins here during your time?" asked Ian, sipping his mug of tea.

Peterson scratched his pepper-grey beard and leaned back with his hands behind his head. "Yeah, left about ten years ago. Some small oil company up in Middlesbrough. What did you make of him?"

Ian thought before continuing. "Flashy, arrogant. Did Messrs Timothy and Jonathan like him?"

"Liked him a lot, so far as I could tell. I thought he was an arse, personally. An intelligent arse, though. Bit too smart for his own good if you want my opinion."

"And this oil company he worked for – what about that?"

"Some small-cap. Didn't do at all well – not as well as Watkins had expected. Big price hikes and they couldn't compete against the big boys. Expensive tastes, Watkins. Greedy bugger. Thought he'd do much better there than here. Believe me, you're better off with a professional firm, lad. All these glittering share options don't count for squit when you're a partner in a firm with a good reputation."

Ian finished his tea and went back to his desk. Oil. That was the connection to Trevor Horsley. And it would give Watkins enough knowledge – or at least enough self-confidence – to attempt a fraud on that scale. The man had clearly had expectations about the share options at this small oil company, and had been disappointed.

He went to the toilet and was just about to urinate when he remembered he hadn't to do so two hours prior to his appointment. It was five to three and his appointment was at half-four. He cursed himself for having had that cup of tea with Peterson.

By four o'clock he was desperate for a pee. At ten-past he waved goodnight to Peterson and told Rose he was off to Dr Patel's. No one would know the difference, but he felt like he had the first time he'd entered the porn shop on Brewer Street. His full bladder made walking uncomfortable, but he couldn't take the fastest route past the Old Bailey – too many people he might know there, not to mention the chance of wandering into shot behind a TV journalist.

He'd not appreciated the size or complexity of St Bartholemew's hospital and had no option but to circumnavigate it, noting the nearby Cock Lane with a wry smile. Eventually he saw the small notice with STD Clinic in black type on a white background. An arrow pointed to a gap between the old buildings and he ducked in, feeling unseen eyes on his back. The alleyway led to the modern innards behind the Victorian outer buildings. There was the thrum of ventilation units and a plume of water vapour from a small metal chimney. Around another corner he came to a sign that simply said STD Clinic, Male Entrance. He ducked through the adjacent doorway and into the linoleum-floored hallway. The first door on the left was marked Reception. He pressed a button on the entry phone and was buzzed in without question.

There was seating capacity for fifty, and a dozen men sat waiting. Two white-coated women sat ignoring them in a nurses' station. He was five minutes early. "I've got an appointment at half-four," he said to the nurse at the station's window, glad he'd be able to relieve himself soon.

The nurse pointed at a sign that told him to fill in a form before doing anything else. He apologised and took a clipboard with a stack of forms on it. He filled in the questionnaire – name and address, GP's details, age, current state of health. Was this his first visit to this clinic? Was the test result of this visit to be passed to his GP? He filled it in and handed it back. "I had an appointment at half-four," he said.

"You have to wait your turn," said the nurse.

So much for all the taxpayers' money pumped into the health service, thought Ian as he sat down. There was a ticket counter of the kind used in supermarkets, and some other people held stubs. He approached the nurses' station again. "Excuse me," he said. The nurse eyed him wearily. "Don't I need a ticket?" he asked.

"I thought you said you had an appointment?"

"I do. But don't I need a ticket?"

"You only need a ticket if you're a drop in patient."

"I had an appointment at half-four. It's—"

The nurse sighed loudly. "I said you'd have to wait your turn."

Fortunately, he'd brought a novel with him. His name was called after quarter of an hour. He was given a note and sent up to the next floor. He told himself that quarter of an hour hadn't been too bad – and booking in advance did appear to have got him ahead of some other people. So long as he was ahead of someone, he felt better. He should be able to pee in the next few minutes and could look forward to getting home early.

The upstairs waiting room had another dozen men in it. Disheartened, he took the only spare seat. Sitting in such close proximity to the other patients unnerved him. He took out his novel and crossed his legs against the pain of his distended bladder.

After a minute, curiosity got the better of him and he looked around at his companions. One obvious City type, looking stony-faced, white knuckles clutching a briefcase for support, staring at the sky out of the high window. The others were mostly dressed more casually than Ian or the City man. Only two men were older. One pair of men was clearly well acquainted, and talked quietly. Ian vaguely wondered if they were a gay couple.

He realised that Death was hovering in that room, pointing his bony finger at one, two, or – who knew? – perhaps all of them? Everyone's circumstances must be different. Some might have been sitting on the decision to have the test for weeks, months, or years.

A male, white-coated nurse came into the room and called an ordinary-sounding name. A young man in his twenties got up and followed the older man. Something about it reminded Ian of the anteroom at a magistrate's court on a Monday morning: petty criminals being brought to book for the weekend's sins. The hospital's location on the opposite side of Newgate Street to St Paul's wasn't lost on him – a halfway house between prison and piety; hell and heaven. Inside his head, he muttered a prayer to the God he'd abandoned at the age of fourteen. He checked his watch: he'd not urinated for three hours.

Another name was called, this time by a woman. The man who'd left with the orderly reappeared. He deduced that it was a two-stage process. Slowly the people in the waiting room were shuffled, with a fresh entrant from downstairs every few minutes to replace someone who disappeared after his appointment with the orderly.

After about half an hour, the woman called his name. His

knees felt week and his bladder ached as he rose to his feet. He walked silently behind the woman, who walked wearily. She took this walk scores of times a day, hundreds of times a week, thousands of times a year. He followed her into an office and she motioned him to sit down. She was in her forties, wore spectacles, but no white coat.

She introduced herself as Dr Paignton. He sat upright, confident, in spite of the acute pain from his abdomen.

"Have you ever had sex with anyone from Sub-Saharan Africa, or someone you have known to be injecting drugs, or have you ever paid for sex?" asked the doctor, holding a pen over a form on her desk.

"No," he said.

She ticked a couple of boxes. "When did you last have sex?" she asked.

"Friday night."

The doctor made a note. "With a man or a woman?"

His confidence shook. "A woman."

She ticked something with her pen. "Have you ever had sex with a man?"

"No," he said.

She ticked again. "What sort of sex was it?"

"No, I said I never had sex with a man."

"I meant Friday night. What sort of sex did you have on Friday night?"

"Well, heterosexual."

The doctor sighed. "Vaginal, oral, anal?" her tone was clinical, clipped. He hesitated and she looked up, her face bare of emotion.

His toes curled. "Vaginal and oral," he said.

"Was it a new sexual partner?"

'It', Ian thought, was a 'she'. "Yes." And he still felt a little proud of that. And the 'it' was, if anything, an 'It-Girl': a porn star, he wanted to tell her.

"And did you wear a condom?"

He felt himself blush, his confidence ebbing away. "No," he said, sheepishly.

She met his eyes again, more coldly this time. "And before Friday night, when was the last time you had sex?"

"A few weeks ago."

"And what were the circumstances of that?"

"A monogamous relationship of seven years."

The doctor looked up at him again, her face more relaxed. "You're relatively low-risk, you'll be glad to know. Now, what do you want to be tested for?"

"Everything," said Ian, thinking how thin the veneer of his apparent risk-profile was.

"Everything?"

"Please," he said.

"Very well," she said. "An Aids test'll take two weeks, if that's the one that worries you."

"Two *weeks*?"

She shrugged. "And you might want to have a follow-up another ten weeks from now. You can get what we call a false-positive on the first test. Then, of course there's Hepatitis C."

"*Hepatitis C*? I didn't think…"

"No, you *didn't* think, did you? Hep C can kill you just as easily as Aids." She grimaced at him like a teacher.

"Isn't there something you can give me now, some drug?"

"You hardly fit the risk profile for that, Mr—" she checked her form, "—Bourne. It's extremely expensive and we reserve it for rape victims, not those who've had careless consensual sex. Besides, it really is a morning-after treatment at best. Now, if you'd like to go back to the waiting room, someone will call you."

"Can I go to the toilet now?"

"Not until after your tests."

"I'm really quite desperate. Will it be long?"

The doctor shrugged.

He trudged back to the waiting room, leaving Dr Paignton

with his paperwork, conscious of the eyes on him – had his news been good or bad?

"Hello, mate," said a voice from the corner. Ian recognised the stubbled head and face of the porn shop manager. The only spare seat was beside him, and the man patted it. The other patients stared. "It's me second time 'ere in six months. I think I've got a bit of the old weepin' cock. I oughta be more careful, like. But you know – heat of the moment, and that. You've obviously been busy yourself, eh?" the man winked at Ian.

"Sorry, I don't want to talk about it," said Ian. He eased himself down into the chair, crossed his legs and leaned forward to relieve the pain from his bladder.

"Don't worry about it," said the manager. "You can last for years on these new anti-virals. Gawd, I remember the herpes scare back in the Eighties. I guess you was too young to remember that. This makes it look like a bleedin' scratch, eh?"

"I suppose it does put it in context, yes," said Ian. He was spared further philosophising by the orderly calling his name. "See you," said Ian, wincing with pain as he got to his feet.

"Yeah, cheers, Ian," said the manager.

Ian's heart sank at the realisation that the man didn't just know his first name but, thanks to the orderly, his surname too. And if he checked his records he'd see it spelled correctly on the transaction details from Sunday, along with his employer's name. And the guy seemed now to consider him a friend.

The orderly led him into a small room that smelled of disinfectant, with a backnote of urine. "Hop up on here and pull your trousers and pants down," said the man.

Ian lay on the elevated examination table and did as he was told. The orderly put on some latex gloves. "Now, we're just going to take a couple of swabs from your urethra. When was the last time you urinated?"

"About two o'clock," said Ian. "I'm really quite desperate."

"Good," said the orderly. "If there are any bacteria in here then they'll have built up." He took the end of Ian's penis and pulled back the foreskin. "This shouldn't hurt too much," said the man, picking up a thin steel rod with a tiny bud on the end. He pushed it into Ian's urethra. Ian winced. "Oh. Did that hurt?"

"Of course," said Ian.

"Hmm. Well I can't see any discharge or redness, so I think you're perhaps a little sensitive." He smeared the swab against the jelly in a Petri dish. "One more," he said, and took another, gentler stab down Ian's Jap's eye. He took out another Petri dish and smeared the swab on it. He looked at the form Dr Paignton had filled in and copied a number onto the dishes. Then he scribbled the number onto two beakers – one large, the other small. "Now, just a quick look on the glans for warts." He pulled back Ian's foreskin and gave his penis a thorough inspection. "No, nothing. You can get dressed now. I want you to go into that room," he pointed to a door, "and urinate into each of these containers, then place them on the shelf."

There was no lock on the door. On the back of it there was a notice which said 'Strictly No Defecating'. Ian urinated into the first beaker but was so full that he couldn't stop his flow when he switched to the other one, splashing urine all over the toilet. The second beaker overflowed whilst he placed the first one on the shelf and in his panic he let a burst of urine go down his trousers. He swore under his breath as he mopped up his urine from the smelly floor, which must have seen a hundred such incidents that day.

As soon as he opened the door, the orderly entered, blocking Ian's exit. The man picked up the beakers from the shelf. He held one up to the light. "Well," he pronounced, "you don't have what used to be known as the clap."

"That's something," said Ian.

"It is," said the orderly, locking him with an earnest look. "Nasty business. And on the increase. You really wouldn't want it."

"No," said Ian. "I wouldn't. So, what's next?"

"Just roll up your sleeve, please."

Ian did as he was told, and the orderly took a sample of blood from his left arm.

"That's it," said the man. "You're free to go."

He called Tamara later in the evening.

"Did you take down the video?" he asked.

"Of course," she said. "I got it down just before noon."

"*Noon*?" he said.

"I wouldn't worry about it. Mondays are very slow, particularly during the day."

"Yeah, well it was up from Saturday, wasn't it?"

"In terms of actual downloads, only a few subscribers chose to take that option. I hope you're not disappointed. I think all those bruises put people off. The bondage one's doing pretty well, though – you looked rather, shall we say, 'authentic'."

"Thanks for taking it down. Let me know the account details for your charity and I'll send the money tomorrow." He thought for a moment. "I don't suppose there's any chance you can recall the video clip?"

"No way, I just have IP numbers. I don't track individuals – all my payments are taken by a company specialising in credit card payments. They take a cut and pass the profit to me. Remember the old business-school lesson: KISS – Keep It Simple, Stupid. How did the test go, by the way? I assume everything was fine."

"Result in two weeks."

"Two *weeks*?" she said.

"Well, yes," he said, trying to keep the air of suspicion out of his voice. "You should know that – if you've been having them."

"Christ, you didn't use the NHS, did you?" she asked.

"Sure. Why?"

"Private clinics can give you same-day results. Good ones can do it in under five minutes."

"But—"

"Those NHS tests are cheaper because they take longer, plus you're heaped in with everyone else and the system's at breaking point. Oh, Ian — you really can't afford to scrimp when it comes to your health. Just do a Google and you'll see there are loads of private clinics."

Chapter Seventeen

"Ian," called Peterson. "Here please."

Ian's guard went up – he'd only just walked in, and the hard tone in Peterson's voice rang alarm bells. "What's up?" he asked as he went to the door of Peterson's office. His boss looked ashen-faced. Barbara Metcalfe was sitting beside him at the round conference table. The roots of her hair were still dark – she was the polar opposite of all he aspired to in a sexual partner. He gave her a weak smile and she grimaced back at him. What could have turned her so cold?

"Come in and close the door, please," said Peterson. Ian did as he was told, taking the only seat available, next to Metcalfe.

"I have to caution you that I'm taping this conversation," said Metcalfe. A knot tightened in Ian's stomach. "You're charged with gross misconduct. Amongst other breaches of staff regulations, we have evidence that you've been accessing pornography using your company laptop. The purpose of this interview is to give you a chance to defend yourself, prior to a disciplinary hearing. You don't have to say anything now, and you may wish to have someone else present to advise you."

Ian's brain slammed into a brick wall. How could they possibly know? He'd covered his tracks by deleting all the evidence at the weekend. "I didn't."

"Ian," said Peterson. Metcalfe opened her mouth to protest, but his boss waved her to be quiet. "They've got evidence. Spyware, you bloody fool. It's not a question of cookies and all that – this stuff reports your every keystroke. The evidence is compelling, if not conclusive. For God's sake, man – don't make it any worse."

"Okay," said Ian. He was sweating now beneath his jacket. "I did, but it wasn't on the company's time. It was after about ten o'clock at night, and mostly at the weekend."

Metcalfe, a look of disgust on her face said, "And you also accessed a dating site during your working hours."

"*Dating*, for God's sake," he gave a pleading look to Peterson, who closed his eyes slowly.

"Where were you yesterday afternoon?" asked Metcalfe.

"I went to see Dr Patel." Peterson pulled back from the table slightly, behind Metcalfe's field of vision, and shook his head at Ian.

Metcalfe sneered. "You actually *missed* an appointment with Dr Patel last Monday, which cost the firm money. And there was no appointment with him yesterday. Where did you go after you left the office yesterday afternoon?"

Ian knew that someone – more likely a team of people – had done their work thoroughly. He'd done this work himself; been one of the brutal interrogators who'd confronted fraudulent employees with the damning evidence against them. He must assume they knew everything.

"I went to the STD clinic at St Bart's Hospital. I had reason to be concerned that…." He put his palms on the table. "I had unsafe sex on Friday night and wanted to have an Aids test." Playing the health card might just work.

"My dear fellow," said Peterson. He turned to Metcalfe. "Doesn't this put a different perspective on things?" he asked her.

"If you had unsafe sex on Friday night," said Metcalfe, "why were you buying pornography in Soho using your company credit card on Sunday afternoon?"

Bitch, thought Ian. Hell hath no fury like a woman spurned. "I used it by accident. The transaction was reversed, so there was no malfeasance." He looked at Peterson for support.

"It builds into a pretty compelling case," said Metcalfe.

"This isn't a court."

"It's a formal disciplinary hearing," countered Metcalfe.

"I've not received written notice of it."

"There's no need for notice: this is gross misconduct, and you could be dismissed instantly."

"I want representation from a colleague. Donald?"

"Ian, I—" began Peterson.

"I wouldn't put you in that position, Donald. I meant that you're a managing partner, you can stop this meeting right now."

"Ian, I really c—"

"Very well," said Metcalfe with a grim smile. "We'll halt proceedings here whilst we gather more evidence. Not, frankly, that we need it. Of course, you do have the option of resigning at any time, Ian. In the meantime, you're suspended. Here's the formal notice of your suspension." She handed him an envelope. "I shall be taking your credit card and staff ID. We will send you formal notice of the date of your disciplinary hearing. Now, if you would care to accompany me from the premises. If you have anything in your desk you'd like to take with you, you may remove them in my presence within the next fifteen minutes. You won't be allowed to log in to your computer under the circumstances – it will be taken away for examination later this morning. And the same goes for your phone. I'll take it off you now, please."

Ian glanced at Peterson, who gave him an almost imperceptible nod. He reached into his trouser pocket and handed his phone to Metcalfe, who looked almost triumphant. She got up and held Peterson's door open. "Your fifteen minutes starts now," she said with a thin smile.

"He's staying with me as a visitor for a while," said Peterson. "Thank you, Barbara. That will be all." Metcalfe stared hard at Peterson. "I said that will be all, thank you," repeated Peterson sternly.

"Right," said Metcalfe, hovering at the door.

"Rose?" called Peterson. "Could you bring me the visitors' book, please?"

Metcalfe stalked out of the office, brushing past Rose, who gave her a dirty look.

"'Ere," she said. "What's goin' on?" She gave the visitors' book to Peterson, who handed it to Ian to sign.

"Please, ten minutes, okay?" said Peterson. Rose hurried out of the room.

Ian sat with his head in his hands.

"Well?" said Peterson.

"No, not at all," said Ian, dryly.

"For fucking crying out loud, lad."

"Spare me the bollocking, Donald. Tell me what the score is."

Peterson blew out a long sigh. "You're in a world of shit. Messrs Jonathan and Timothy are not best pleased with you. No one wants to see you trip and fall, but you've made it pretty hard for everyone concerned. Current thinking is that you could get away with some unpaid suspension, bonus disqualification, a delay in your promotion, that sort of thing. Or, as Babs says, you could just leave."

"What would you recommend?"

"Whatever they do, don't fight it. They don't like that. Come clean, see what happens. The good thing is that you weren't dismissed automatically for gross misconduct."

Ian sat and thought a moment. "I think I can see a way back."

"Go on."

"I have evidence of a massive fraud at Armstrong BioDiesel." Ian told Peterson everything he'd figured out about the fraud — the invoices that hadn't been through the post, and the ease with which raw materials could be processed into finished biodiesel without being booked into the system.

Peterson heard Ian out, but was quick to respond. "Ian, it's conjecture on your part. Nothing you've given me is incontrovertible evidence."

"Unless you go to the suppliers and check the quantities with them."

"True. Look, you're suspended. Give the invoices to me and I'll take it from there."

"But then my name's not on the case."

"But we'll all know. You'll see."

"So what do I do now?"

"Take a holiday, take up golf. I'm sorry, Ian. These things happen in one's life and one just has to get through them as best one can. I've a busy workload right now. Post those invoices to me, or pop them in at reception and I'll get someone assigned to it."

Ian was glad that only Rose was in the office to witness his departure. She was shocked. "I'll be fine," he told her. "We'll do that dinner later this week, eh?"

It was strange to be in his flat at eleven on a Tuesday morning. He flicked through the ABD invoices, but was repelled by them.

He felt completely isolated without his phone. The only numbers he could remember were his parents' and Stu's landlines. There was no one he could turn to, he realised. He'd not seen the Derbyshire bunch in several weeks now, and had no desire to see them under these circumstances. What would his family say if they found out the reason he wasn't to become a partner? If Sarah had been with him he'd not have got into this trouble in the first place. And even if he had, she'd have been able to get him out of it. What felt so unjust was knowing that such a large percentage of the male population was as guilty as he was. His only crime was to have been caught. What galled him the most was that he hadn't even committed the offences on company time.

He booted up his own laptop – how he wished he'd used it instead – and checked his email. There was one from Tamara giving the bank details of her charity for abused women from the sex industry. Two thousand pounds was a great deal of money to a man in his precarious financial position. But he had enough on his conscience without feeling he'd defrauded some victims of abuse – besides, he felt this sacrifice might somehow absolve his sins, or appease whatever gods he'd angered. He wrote back to explain that his circumstances had changed, but said he would honour the commitment.

On Wednesday morning he went to his local printing shop and had copies made of all the ABD invoices. He couldn't face going up to town, and so sent the invoices by registered mail. The postman was delivering his own mail when he got back, and the irony of having to sign for receipt of formal notice of his disciplinary hearing wasn't lost on him. There was a message on his answering machine from Rose, saying how sorry she was, and wishing him the best. He called her back and they arranged to meet for dinner that night.

She gave him a hug as they met in Leicester Square tube station. She'd insisted on meeting in the West End, because she said he needed cheering up.

"You don't strike me as a perv, Ian," she said.

"Thanks."

"Not a *real* perv, anyway," she said.

"Really, you're too kind. Where are we going?" They had walked through Leicester Square and were heading up Wardour Street.

"I've not seen any of this stuff," said Rose. She put her arm tightly around his and steered him down Brewer Street. "I'm curious. I want to understand what's going through your head."

"I'd rather not go down here." But he knew Rose better than to resist.

"Come on," she tightened the grip on his arm. She looked through the ribbon curtains. There was a blown-up picture of a veinous penis at the point of entry into a glistening vagina. "*Euh*," she said. "It's disgusting. How could you look at this stuff?"

"You have to understand that I'm no worse than the next man," protested Ian, reddening.

"Hello, Ian," said a figure smoking a cigarette outside the neighbouring shop. It was the manager. "How'd the test go? Alright?" He nodded his head in Rose's direction. "She's worth it though, eh?"

"Fuck," said Rose, reversing their direction and hurrying away. "You really *are* a perv: the next man was a filthy bastard."

Over dinner she told him that Barbara Metcalfe had re-interviewed Jess and Louise on Tuesday afternoon, forcing out of them the truth about what had happened on the *Tuxedo Princess*. Jean had seen the reports and passed the information to Rose to give to Ian. "Barbara might send you another disciplinary notice for that incident," she said. "Sorry."

Rose offered to share the bill, but he covered it. She gave him a big hug and a kiss on the cheek as they parted company. "Good luck," she said.

On Thursday morning he went to a private practice in Harley Street and had an Aids test. It was negative, but he was advised to have a follow-up test in ten weeks' time. Since he was up in town, he called Peterson and asked him out for lunch at a discreet pub.

"Not looking good for you," said Peterson. "Jess and Louise aren't pressing any disciplinary charges, you'll be glad to know. But Barbara's putting pressure on them to do so. I must say, she's a total bitch. She really does have something against you."

"Yeah," said Ian, sipping his pint. "It's always the personnel people who're trouble, isn't it? Anyway, how's the case going?"

"Case? Oh, ABD? Passed it to Hendricks over in Auditing. He's taking a look at it."

Ian didn't much like Hendricks. He'd made partner at an early age, though Ian couldn't understand why because he wasn't much good in Ian's view. "Is he making much progress?"

"He says he's been in touch with the suppliers and everything's fine."

"*What*?"

"Ian, you've been under a great deal of pressure. Losing Sarah, boring auditing job, this Aids business. And then there's this bang on the head. The trouble is that when one's in the middle of all this stuff, one simply doesn't recognise that one's behaviour's a bit, you know, ill-judged."

"If you're trying to say my judgement's gone, you're wrong, Donald."

Peterson waved him down. "I had a chat with Doc Perry, yesterday. Strictly confidential, you understand. He knows a bit about occupational health law and all that gubbins. Your behaviour has been way, way out of the ordinary the last few weeks. Just look at yourself then and now, for God's sake."

"No, I don't accept that," said Ian. He'd only seen Dr Perry, the firm's physician, once a year for his check-up, and didn't have a high regard for him.

"Denial's the other thing," continued Peterson. "Hear me out. The Doc says you can probably plead some kind of temporary mental illness due to stress – that sort of thing. He also says that your bang on the head could be what's driving this nonsense about the fraud. Remember: you were investigating a fraud when you got that knock. It's like a scratch on a vinyl record – if you're old enough to understand the concept. The thought's been indented into your head and you can't let it go. D'you see?" He patted Ian on the shoulder. "Go and see the Doc. Clear this whole mess up. What do you say?"

That was another thing Ian missed about Sarah. With both of her parents being doctors, he could always get clear and rational advice. He made an appointment to see Woodcock and Tweed's occupational health physician the following Monday. His disciplinary hearing would be on the Thursday.

He'd meant to call Stu that week to make it up to him and Nina, but he was now too ashamed to do it by phone. Instead, he dropped a card and some flowers outside the house when he knew they'd be out.

By Saturday morning he was agitated by the question of his judgement. He refused to accept that he'd been wrong. But with the original invoices presumably now back at Armstrong's headquarters, some of his evidence had gone – namely the fact that the invoices hadn't been folded, and showed no signs of having been through the mail. He was sure that there was a story in the invoices, but he couldn't figure it out.

On Monday, Dr Perry examined him and took the stitches out of his head wound. Ian had quite forgotten to see his local GP to have it done. Perry took that as evidence that the blow to Ian's head had resulted in more than mere physical injury, and assured him that he'd send a letter to that effect to his employer.

Ian had never felt so utterly alone as he waited in the reception area outside the boardroom on Thursday morning, and wished he'd asked for someone else to accompany him. He'd toyed with the idea of asking Karen Goodman, but was too ashamed of the charges against him. Jean wasn't at her desk to talk to, and he assumed she'd be taking notes in the boardroom. He was ashamed at the aspects of his personality she'd now know: a friendship would be ruined.

He had reassured himself that, if he kept it quiet, there was a good chance he could keep the whole matter secret from his friends and family. Peterson had seemed quite sure that he'd just face some kind of delay – indefinite or otherwise – to his promotion to partner. Ian had already played through in his head the story he'd tell to prospective employers – that there'd been budget cuts or a personality clash. Then he'd wait a year or two and move to another firm. He'd already got a shortlist in his head and, if he were honest with himself, he'd be glad to be somewhere less stuffy than Woodcock and Tweed. He reassured himself that he just had to sit through this mud-raking hour or half-hour, take his punishment with good grace and he'd be fine.

He was kept waiting until nearly ten o'clock – by which time he was a bag of nerves.

Jean emerged solemnly from the boardroom. "I'm sorry, Ian," she said. "This way."

There was silence as he entered the room and Jean directed him to a seat at the end of the long oak table. With a thin smile, she handed him a glass of water on a coaster and then sat at a chair away from the table, taking up a pad of paper. The seats either side of him were empty.

As he looked down the table he realised that in a different world he'd have been sitting in this room a few weeks from now, participating in his first partners' meeting. Timothy Woodcock was at the head of the table, Peterson to his right and Jonathan Tweed to his left. In all, there were five partners, with Hendricks one of those in attendance – enough for a quorum. Metcalfe sat closest to Ian, to his left, a smug look on her face. He tried to catch Peterson's eye, but his boss was looking down at his pad, chewing on a pencil.

The IT manager was called. He had a thick sheaf of paper detailing Ian's every move on the internet for the last few weeks, and in a monotone described the content of some of the sites Ian had visited. Ian vaguely wondered how much fun the IT department had had in collating the evidence – a real perk of the job. After several minutes, Woodcock dismissed him. Ian was relieved – now for the verdict. Peterson glanced up and met his eye, but he couldn't read his expression.

"And now the other charges," said Woodcock.

Metcalfe slid a piece of paper down the table towards Ian. "Sexual harassment," she said. "Gross misconduct, second count. We don't actually need to serve you with this."

The tightness in Ian's stomach turned to nausea. How could they be doing this?

"We've decided to spare the ladies concerned the indignity of facing you," said Woodcock. "Apologies for the late notice but it was only this morning they decided to press charges. Now, we're looking for your resignation. Do we have it?"

Ian was stupefied. He looked to Peterson for support, but the man wouldn't meet his eye. "You're joking," he said.

"Please, watch what you're saying," said Peterson into the

table. The other partners looked at him.

"We're quite prepared to go ahead with a separate action against you for sexual harassment," said Woodcock. "As it is, we'd prefer to leave it with gross misconduct over the pornography. We can't tolerate this kind of behaviour, especially in someone of your seniority."

"Can I speak to you in private please, Mr Timothy?"

Woodcock glanced around the room. "Barbara, what's the law on this?"

"Nothing, Mr Timothy."

"Very well," said Woodcock. "If the rest of you leave the room, please."

The others shuffled out quietly. Peterson gave him a querying look, which Ian ignored. Jean left last, closing the door silently behind her. Woodcock and Ian faced each other down what seemed like a hundred yards of table.

"Now, what's this all about, young man? You shouldn't be afraid to resign in public, you know. We would all think better of you for it."

"I have evidence of a big fraud at Armstrong BioDiesel," said Ian. "If you let me stay on I can prove it. It'll be a big case for us. The biggest."

Woodcock shook his head. "Doc Perry warned me about this. And I must say," he sneered at Ian, "that I can understand why you wanted the others out of the room. Resigning in public is what real men do. Begging is beneath a gentleman. You have no place in this firm. I would like your resignation, and I would like it *now*." The old man slammed his fist on the table.

"With respect, sir. I don't think Hendrick's investigation can have been thorough enough."

"Mr Hendricks is a highly-respected partner in this firm and I would caution you not to slander him."

"That's not slander."

"I'm losing my patience, young man. Will you resign?"

"You're losing a very good, hard-working employee who—"

"An employee who appears in pornographic movies," hissed Woodcock. "If you don't resign I shall *ruin* you. I will order that video to be circulated and you will be *finished* in this profession."

Ian was stunned into silence for several seconds. Of course, the IT department must have looked at his records on Monday morning. The video hadn't been taken off the website until noon, so they'd taken the opportunity to download it. There was no way out of this mess.

"If I resign, do I have your word that you'll order that video and any copies of it to be deleted?"

"You're in no position to bargain. Resign, or I'll make you wish you'd never been born."

The pun on his surname – albeit accidental – had been one he'd grown accustomed to over the years, and brought back happy memories of the playground. Shrieks of childish delight echoed between his ears, and the real world seemed distant, down a long tunnel. He was aware of giggling, if just for a moment. "Sure," he said. "I resign."

Woodcock relaxed his shoulders. Ian rose quickly to his feet, the smile gone. The sudden movement made the older man flinch back. He walked to the door on jellied knees and turned to face his former employer for what he thought would be the last time. "By the way, you've got a great surname for a porn star. And you'd need no practice at all to make a very convincing *cunt*." Woodcock's face was a picture.

He caused consternation as he brushed past his former colleagues outside the room.

"Ian," said Peterson, grabbing his arm. "I'm sorry."

"Do us a favour and sign me out in the visitors' book, *Donny*," he said, using a cheeky nickname he'd never dared used before. "Be in touch. Probably see you in hell. *Lad.*"

Chapter Eighteen

The void in Ian's life was massive, and his nature abhorred the vacuum.

Alcohol, anger, bitterness, self-hatred and self-pity rushed in to compete to fill it. What made it worse was the isolation, and he'd seen enough men destroy themselves at this sort of juncture in their lives to know better.

He'd gone straight from the tribunal to the Derbyshire, where he'd eaten the kind of lunch that had been off-limits for the last few weeks. He'd drunk his first three pints alone before falling into conversation with an old soak, to whom he'd poured his heart out about his travails. As he'd angrily gone over the events, encouraged by his drinking partner — who had also apparently had more than his fair share of injustice – it had become clear to him that all the partners at Woodcock and Tweed were crooks.

He had fled the Derbyshire at half-four, realising drunkenly that he couldn't be caught there by his former friends. There were messages from Peterson and Rose, which he deleted, cursing his former boss loudly.

Ian was now convinced his boss had been complicit in defrauding clients. He saw it all now. Woodcock and Tweed were in on the ABD scam, which Ian had inadvertently discovered. That was why they'd fired him. Peterson was at least complicit: after all, he'd handed the investigation over to Hendricks, who was a lynchpin in the operation because he was in charge of the Armstrong account. Woodcock's threat to ruin him was the clincher: no reputable firm would wish to see a former employee exposed in such a way – especially if they'd been a senior member of it at the time.

He turned to his only friend that evening: pornography. His boyhood dream of becoming a partner in an accounting firm was now over. Maybe there was a career in porn – if not as an actor, as an accountant?

He picked himself up on Friday morning with a renewed sense of purpose. With money enough to survive several months without employment, he had ample time to plan his next career move. If the worst came to the worst he could take temporary assignments or, dread the thought, take over the family business.

In his drunken stupor the previous evening he'd written to Tamara to tell her what had happened, being careful not to blame her. She phoned him back that morning to say that she knew there was demand for good accountants in the sex industry, and she could put the word out if he wanted. It was certainly a consideration he took seriously, though he'd never be able to tell friends and family what, exactly, he did for a living.

"Just one thing's bugging me," said Ian. "What prompted you to pick me for a Friday night shag?"

"You fitted the bill – you were a guy I'd not shagged in my college days, and it was a Friday night."

"No, who put you up to it?"

"No one put me up to it – you emailed me, remember? Mind you, Val Craven mentioned you were finishing off that job at Armstrong's and would be heading south on Friday. She said you'd really changed."

"I see. Thanks." That explained Val's behaviour at dinner the previous week. To think he'd once fallen for her charms. He could trust no one.

A self-help book Sarah had bought some years earlier had a chapter on goal setting after a career crisis, which he read over breakfast. He took out a clean sheet of paper and wrote:

> Aim: To live a dazzling life free from assorted shitheads, with ideal female <u>partner</u> who will enhance my life. This to be achieved through the following goals:
> 1 Regaining self-respect, reputation, etc., namely by:
>   a) Proving I am right about ABD
>   b) Ruining Woodcock and Tweed, and all its

       partners
       c) Seeing Ed Watkins go to jail
2 Being fit and healthy, making most of self, etc., by:
       a) Keeping fit
       b) Not over-indulging in vices
       c) Finding said loving partner, who must be an equal to me, understand me, etc.

He looked at what he'd written, tapping his pen on the kitchen table. Part 1 was perhaps not as positive as the book's authors might have wished, but they were tangible, short-term goals that would deliver a high degree of satisfaction if — *when*, he corrected himself, taking the book's advice in affirming goals as certainties – he was to achieve them.

His plan hinged on 1 a) being implemented immediately, and so he brought out the pile of photocopied invoices for ABD. He was about to call the palm oil company when he realised that a fraud of this size would be 'immunised' against this sort of investigation. Someone in the supplier would be complicit in the fraud, and would have the ability to shut down any investigation at the first hurdle – or at least to alert the perpetrators to it. The likelihood of him getting valuable information from a supplier was slim, and the risks were high. He'd already been beaten up over a few barrels of illicit biodiesel, so the consequences of blowing a multi-million pound scam like this didn't bear thinking about. Wouldn't he be better off going straight to the authorities and letting them take it from there?

Peterson had been right – he didn't have sufficient information to warrant an investigation. Besides, he decided, he needed the redemption this case offered him, and he needed it quickly.

That left him with one focus for investigation: the delivery end of the operation. He berated himself for having been so stupid. Horsley was also in charge of Armstrong Distribution, and that was what made the whole thing possible. Away from head office, Horsley could control every piece of paperwork pertaining to the plant. Never mind a flatbed truck with a few barrels of oil in it: with his connivance, fleets of tankers could fill up almost any time they wanted.

Then he realised that Horsley must have known all along about the illegal activity that Ian had uncovered. It was a 'throwaway' operation that would distract any serious investigation. Perhaps Horsley and Watkins had even encouraged the crime?

There was only one thing for it: he would go back up to Newcastle.

The weekend's low point was a call from his father on Sunday evening.

"Are you alright, Ian?" his father asked in a tone that told him his father knew it wasn't.

"Yes, fine."

"I called you at work on Friday and they told me you'd resigned. Your PA seemed very upset about it, let slip that it wasn't entirely a time of your own choosing."

"No, it wasn't."

"So," his father said wearily. "I called Stu to see how you were."

"I had dinner with him and Nina last weekend."

"I know all about last weekend, Ian." He let a few moments of silence hang. "What am I going to tell your mother?"

"You can tell her anything you like."

"Don't be cheeky with me."

"What you choose to tell her is exactly that: your choice. I'm trying to dig myself out of a world of shit and the last thing I need is a lecture in morality, either from you or Stu. I need support. I'm working on a big case that's going to vindicate me."

There was silence on the end of the line. "You'd better be at your nieces' christening on Sunday. Good luck."

"Thanks," said Ian, but the line was dead by the time he'd said it.

The colossal Angel of the North Statue – its wingspan equal to that of a jumbo jet – stood black against the sky on its lonely hilltop over the approach to Newcastle. Ian imagined himself animated into the statue — gigantic, solid, cold steel. In his mental image he flapped his dark wings and cast a shadow of fear over Watkins and the partners of Woodcock and Tweed before he dropped a huge stone bible on them: *The Word of the Lord Endureth Forever*.

He'd bought a train ticket for Tuesday because it was cheaper, and he arrived in Newcastle in the middle of the morning. A few calls had secured him the rental of a second-hand car and a cheap room in a modern hotel. He would have gone for a cheaper bed and breakfast, but he needed the anonymity and the internet access.

By one o'clock he was heading south over the Tyne Bridge. He glanced back over his left shoulder and saw Tamara's penthouse. In different circumstances, he'd have called in on her – he really liked her, and not just for the sex. But this was a solo trip and no one could know he was there.

Over the Tyne Bridge, he turned left towards South Shields. His own weakness and lack of attention had been responsible for his downfall. Now he would rise like an avenging angel and smite his enemies with his own hand. This was a dangerous game and he'd lodged an envelope detailing his suspicions and itinerary with his solicitor, to be opened in the event of his death. There was nothing more he could do – this would either be very easy or very difficult.

He had no doubt that ABD was producing more biodiesel than Armstrong knew about. Without access to the real invoices, there was little he could do to prove that there was an excess of supply into the plant. However, the biodiesel had to be shipped out to customers. His game plan was beautiful in its simplicity:

to follow the money, he need only follow the biodiesel. It had to go somewhere. He had no idea how much over the declared capacity the plant was operating at, but suspected that an arrogant and greedy man like Watkins would be ambitious. Watkins was, after all, an accountant: he knew that if you were going to perpetrate a fraud, then the risk was only worthwhile if the returns were exceptional. And it was similar to Tamara's elephant in the room analogy. If it was truly colossal, it was almost above board – any government could vouch for that, in his opinion.

As any investigator knew, the biggest danger was himself: he had to remain under cover – hence the cheap and anonymous second-hand rental car.

On Monday he'd gone up to Tottenham Court Road and equipped himself with a small digital recorder and a microphone with a sucker to record telephone conversations, as well as a small video camera. He'd also gone to a novelty shop, where he'd bought a stick-on moustache and fake glasses. After some searching, he'd found Armstrong's card in the top pocket of one of his suits – access to the man would be easier via his personal mobile number. Monday night had been spent plugging important phone numbers into his new pay-as-you-go mobile phone, which had a digital camera as a backup for the one he'd bought.

He came off the roundabout and down Laygate. At the bottom, he turned right onto Commercial Road and drove slowly past ABD. The yard was empty apart from employees' cars – at least the plant was operating. He continued on down past Armstrong Distribution. Again, the yard was empty. It was a waiting game, and that was the difficulty – the longer he had to wait, the more likely he was to be spotted. He circled around in a giant loop back to the roundabout and came back down Laygate. This time, he took a left along Commercial Road, turned the car around and parked it. From there, he'd be able to see any tankers coming down Laygate. It was the most logical route because it cut a sharp right turn out at the other end of Commercial Road.

He only had to wait half an hour before an Armstrong-branded tanker growled slowly to a stop at the bottom of Laygate and then down Commercial Road, where he saw it swing into the yard of Armstrong Distribution. He noted the license number. Half an hour later, it emerged. Ian waited a few seconds before starting his car and following it back to the roundabout, where it headed towards the Gateshead. It stopped in the forecourt of the petrol station where Val had refuelled. He drove past to the next roundabout, doubled-back and pulled into a parking spot in the station. He bought a sandwich and a local A-Z and went back to his car. He watched as the tanker filled all three of the underground tanks. Filling up Armstrong's own tanks didn't look like fraud to him: the biodiesel had to be taken completely away from Armstrong's operations for the fraud to work. When he caught his second glance from the vehicle's driver, he decided he'd been there too long and drove back to his position in Commercial Road.

This was not a good development, and he was confused and concerned. He could easily spend days tailing these tankers. In his ignorance, he'd not realised that they could carry mixed loads in their compartments. And while he was out trailing one, anything could happen. It could take him a fortnight to track each of the fleet of trucks just once.

He put himself in the fraudster's shoes and began to think it through. As he did so, another Armstrong tanker stopped at the bottom of Laygate before turning right. He took its license number. This time, it pulled into ABD itself. Twenty minutes later it pulled out of the yard, but instead of going out along Laygate, it went to its left, along Commercial Road. Ian started his car and followed. It pulled into the distribution yard quarter of a mile further down the road. Ian drove past and parked the car. He waited a few minutes and put the fake glasses on before walking back past. The tanker's load was being emptied into one of the underground biodiesel tanks.

That's when he remembered that Armstrong had told him he'd continue to have just two tanks at the yard dedicated to biodiesel. Ian had seen with his own eyes that there were three. Indeed, he now recalled from doing the distribution yard's simple goods-in goods-out calculations during the audit that there had only been two tanks dedicated to the fuel. He kicked himself again for not having realised something so obvious. The third tank was the elephant in the living room that he'd been looking for – or at least its trunk.

He worked through the economics and practicalities because even theft obeyed the laws of maximising profit and minimising risk. Ian appreciated the simplicity. It was far easier for Trevor Horsley to have appointed the two men in the distribution yard than the many workers in ABD. Taking large quantities by tanker from ABD would have been riskier – far easier just to siphon the product off and into one of the three fuel bunkers, from where it could be picked up at any time. And Armstrong had said that the deficiencies had been in the account sales to other distributors. It was unlikely, though not impossible, that Armstrong tankers were being used to distribute the fuel. But it was a complication. Ian was a great believer in Occam's razor – – keeping his assumptions to a minimum. A good fraud had to be simple.

This sort of surveillance job would take a team of investigators. The first step to getting his proof had to be to admit to himself that he was gathering his evidence the wrong way. Unless he could find a simpler method, he was looking at a task that would stretch him to his limit.

He started the car and began the drive back to his hotel in Gateshead before the rush hour could lengthen the journey. After getting nowhere by following the product into the plant, his assumption that he should follow the product down the supply chain had been the right one. Now he had to look at the supply chain in a different way. Supposing he turned the logic on his head? He was convinced that he'd found the fraudsters:

Watkins and Horsley. If he now worked it through on the basis that they were guilty, he could shorten his search. But how? Follow the product: the pair of them had to be selling the fuel to end-users to get their money. And to sell to end-users, they had to have a legitimate company, and every company had to list its directors.

And there could only be a limited number of fuel distribution companies in the North East of England.

Within ten minutes of getting back to his hotel room he had a list of just thirty-two independent fuel distributors within the whole of the North East, thanks to the online Yellow Pages. Take away duplicate entries and he had twenty-six. Economics dictated that he would eliminate those in rural Northumberland, towards the Scottish border. Twenty was still a lot of work, so he decided to concentrate on those in Cleveland, where he knew Watkins and Horsley would have had been able to recruit former colleagues from their previous company. He was left with eleven: an eminently manageable number for a man of Ian's expertise and enthusiasm.

He broke off for a celebratory dinner by himself at an Indian restaurant on the high street. Of course, the evidence wasn't conclusive, but he had a company name at last. A simple online search using a paid-for website specialising in information on the 1.8 million directors in the UK had been an excellent investment. Watkins and Horsley wouldn't have been so stupid as to have registered their own names as directors, but they'd had to trust someone: their wives. He'd cross-referenced their addresses against the online phone book for the area. Watkins was ex-directory, but Horsley's address matched that of Sally Turner, director of Can-Green Fuels of Cleveland. Turner would be the maiden name of Trevor Horsley's wife. He would stake his life on it.

He set off for Cleveland before seven on Wednesday morning, chuckling with delight. As he drove south, past the towering

Angel of the North statue, he visualised himself again as an avenging angel from the south.

His journey ended on a small industrial estate. Can-Green Fuels was a much smaller operation than Armstrong's, but from a couple of expensive cars parked outside, it looked a lot more profitable. As with the previous day, he had to be careful not to give himself away. He parked up along the road and waited for a tanker to set off. At twenty to eight, one did, and he followed it on its route, keeping at least two cars between it and his own, sometimes allowing up to half a dozen. He noted down the names of the petrol stations it stopped at on a pad of paper.

In the early afternoon the driver headed north on the A1, his vehicle faster now that it was empty. Rather than risk being spotted, Ian overtook it, drove ahead and parked up opposite Armstrong Distribution. He took out his small video camera and turned it on. Sure enough, the tanker went into the yard and began filling up from one of the biodiesel bunkers, filling all but two of the compartments with the fuel. But to his amazement and dismay, it took petrol in the last two.

He thought through his assumptions again. This looked legitimate – was he at square one again? Self-doubt crept in. Had Doc Perry been right about his knock on the head?

No: he was certain of his assumptions.

An Armstrong tanker drew into the yard as the Can-Green one was leaving. He had no further interest in the Can-Green tanker, but realised he'd never seen an Armstrong tanker in the yard at close range.

He was excited to see that it filled up from a different tank to the one that the Can-Green vehicle had. There was his proof – the chances were minimal that the first tanker had precisely drained the tank. It was self-evident that Can-Green was a legitimate customer of Armstrong's, as well as a fraudulent one. The operation was breathtakingly simple.

That third tank was the equivalent of the second cash register at the pizza restaurant. It was all the evidence he needed for now.

It was just gone four o'clock. He headed back to the hotel and began writing his preliminary report. He'd finished it by six and sent the email to himself: his solicitor would have access to his email account if he were to die.

He'd worked it all out. Can-Green was taking the biodiesel out of Armstrong using their tanker fleet. They filled compartments in their tankers with biodiesel whilst they were collecting legitimate loads of petrol. When stocks were high at Armstrong Distribution there would be more frequent visits by Can-Green tankers, which would then off-load the fuel back at Can-Green for further distribution. Little wonder Armstrong hadn't been able to expand outside the North East with a cheap supplier like Can-Green blocking the route to the south. With such thin margins, Armstrong couldn't afford to hop over Can-Green's sales territory to explore sales to the south. The beauty of Can-Green was that it was a legitimate business. Ian suspected there'd be invoices from another front company, purporting to supply them with biodiesel, and that that company would be the one that was creaming off most of the profit.

Yes, Watkins was a very good accountant. But Ian was better.

On Thursday morning he felt confident enough of his case to call Armstrong on his mobile. This was it: he was on the road to redemption.

No – he corrected himself – he was on the *expressway* to redemption. He stuck the microphone of his digital recorder onto his mobile and dialled Armstrong's number.

"Hello, William?"

"Aye? Who's this?"

"It's Ian. Ian Bourne."

There was a hollow laugh on the other end of the line. "Oh, aye?" said Armstrong. "Sexually frustrated of south London. Listen, if you want a reference from me, you've got to be fucking joking. I'd never want my name associated with you, son. I warned you about all that business with women, didn't I? Do yourself a favour and get some professional help."

Ian's felt his heart pounding – nothing travelled as fast as bad news. "I'm not after a reference. "I've got the evidence that ABD's being defrauded. It's huge, believe me."

"Aye, they said I'd probably be hearing from you, son. Don't *ever* call this number again. Do you hear me?"

"How many tanks of biodiesel are there at Armstrong Distribution?" blurted Ian.

The line went dead.

Chapter Nineteen

Ian thought better of calling Armstrong again. He sat, disconsolate, in the cramped hotel room. Checkout was by eleven, and the car had to be back by noon. He had twenty minutes to come to a decision.

Was there any sense in pursuing this case on his own? He needed to see records that he couldn't possibly access. There was a remote chance he could complete the investigation, but it would be months of painstaking work.

He could be back home by mid-afternoon. He missed the predictable comfort of the life he'd had two months ago – simple, unassuming friends, a girlfriend he could rely on for support; boozy and carefree weekend afternoons spent in the Derbyshire. There had been no looming threat of disease, violence or danger.

He packed his bags, checked out and drove the car to the backstreet garage behind Newcastle Central station. They fleeced him on the half-empty tank – his contract had been to return it full. He had half a mind to report them for hinting that a cash payment would be cheaper than running it through his card, since it would avoid VAT. But he'd probably need their services in the future.

He was sitting on the London train, waiting for it to depart, when his phone rang. It had to be a wrong number – no one had it yet. Except—

The screen identified Armstrong's mobile number. He felt a frisson of excitement, and stuck the recorder's microphone onto the phone.

"Three," said Armstrong. "I just paid a visit to check and there are *three* tanks containing biodiesel." He was short of breath.

"Would you agree that there should be two?" said Ian.

"Aye. Two. Care to tell me what the *fook* is going on?"

The train pulled out of the station. "You're being robbed

blind, William. Think big. Think big, and it's so much bigger than that."

"You're hired. But you'd better bloody be right."

"I wish I was wrong. By the way, who else knows?"

"No one. The lads are used to me dropping in on them out of the blue and I didn't let on what I was looking for."

"Good. Keep it that way."

"I want your arse here right away, and I want a fookin' explanation. Where are you now, son?"

"Next stop York."

"What?"

"I'm on the train south."

"You're under contract to me now and I want your arse back up here this instant."

A switch clicked in Ian. He straightened his back and spoke in his professional voice: calm, confident and authoritative. "I've got some interesting paperwork back down in London that I couldn't risk bringing on this trip. I'll be back up tomorrow morning. I'll be charging you at the rate Woodcock and Tweed hire me out at. And I shall be travelling first class. You and I will be in the office at the weekend. Tell no one about this. And I mean *no one* – not even family."

"Aye," Armstrong choked. "Right you are, son. But you'd better be fookin' right."

"I am. Just make sure you're not busy this weekend."

Things were looking up. He made his way to the buffet car for a celebratory beer. Woodcock and Tweed charged for his services at an exorbitant rate, and he would keep the full amount for himself on this job. He toasted silently his new life as a freelancer.

On Friday morning, Armstrong was waiting to pick him up from Newcastle Central in his expensive saloon car, but at first didn't recognise Ian in the glasses and fake moustache. They put his luggage in the boot and Ian got in the front passenger seat.

"Right, tell me who it is and how they're doing it," said Armstrong, starting the engine.

Ian switched the car's hi-fi on, turned up the volume and leaned over to Armstrong before answering. "There's a chance your car's bugged. Transmitters are very cheap these days. They'd have to have a receiver within a couple of hundred yards of us, but there are also devices that record for later transmission. Let's go for a walk somewhere."

Armstrong drove down to the Quayside but Ian advised him against it. "Too public for a man of your stature," he said. "You can't go anywhere on Tyneside without being recognised. Why d'you think I had to wear this ridiculous disguise? Didn't you even notice it?"

"Son, I just took it to be another one of your eccentricities." Ian looked at him and they both laughed. He peeled off the moustache and pocketed the glasses.

They got out of the car at Wallington Hall, a stately home in rural Northumberland whose grounds were open to the public. Ian took the file of photocopied invoices out of his bag and they strolled off towards the gardens, gravel crunching underfoot.

"I could be wrong," began Ian. Armstrong gave him a look that suggested a swim in the Tyne was on the cards if he was. "But ABD is producing a good twenty to thirty percent more biodiesel than you think it is – maybe more." Armstrong opened his mouth, but Ian held up his hand and continued. "You're getting shipments of raw materials – palm oil and meths – into the plant at a much higher quantity than your books show. The paperwork goes to Horsley, and he passes it – as he should – back up to the accounts department. Your *workaholic* Finance Director has substitute invoices produced for a smaller amount, which he then files. They're perfect in every way."

"Rock-steady Eddie?" said Armstrong. He stopped and stared at Ian.

"Yeah. A control-freak Finance Director's a major warning sign in corporate fraud – they can hide just about anything from their staff. Watkins has complete control over all the accounts that are paid. He never lets Mary Ruffcorn get a look-in."

Armstrong grabbed Ian's lapels, pulling his face close. "That man's been a *bedrock* to my company's success over the last three years. And the suppliers would have shouted out long ago if they'd not been paid the full amount." He let Ian go and marched back in the direction of the car. "You fookin' time-waster," he spat. "Make your own way back to town."

"That's the cunning bit," called Ian. "Watkins pays the suppliers the full amount from a separate bank account he controls, so they think they're being paid by ABD. He is meticulous with his payments so they never even chase an invoice. In the meantime, Watkins invoices ABD for *smaller* amounts of raw materials, and ABD pays into Watkins' account. Remember: your workaholic Finance Director controls all the bank payments. The accounting team and the auditors see a perfectly balanced set of books. There's never any need to check bank details for any of the payments because it's all tickety-boo." He jogged after the older man. "The upshot is that the plant is receiving much more raw material than you think it is. It's converting that into biodiesel. So you're manufacturing much closer to capacity than you realise. There are two bottom lines – one for you and one for Watkins. And his has all the profit."

"Bollocks!" said Armstrong without looking round.

"Okay," said Ian. "Ask yourself this: if you're operating way below capacity, why are you running shifts on the weekends?"

Armstrong stopped in his tracks, breathing heavily, face red as he turned to face Ian again.

Ian jogged to a stop a few yards away. "What sort of bullshit excuses has Horsley, the experienced oil man, given you for the electricity costs being so much above the forecast?"

Armstrong stared at Ian, breathing deeply. Ian kept his distance. He could almost hear the cogs whirring in Armstrong's bald head. He saw the point at which the penny dropped.

"That fookin' *bastud*," said Armstrong through clenched teeth.

"I think we'd better go and have something hot and sweet to drink, don't you?" said Ian quietly. "There's a tea-room over there. Come on." He put a hand on Armstrong's back and guided him towards the café.

"But what happens to all that excess production?" asked Armstrong, nursing a cup of sweet coffee.

"Watkins and Horsley have a fuel distribution company down in Cleveland."

"*What*? What's it called?"

"Can-Green Fuels."

"But they buy petrol off us, and a bit of regular diesel too."

"Yes, but they also fill up with biodiesel free of charge from that third tank. I'll show you a video if you like. I'll bet you've never sold any of that to them, have you?"

"No, they have their own brand that they buy from overseas. Our rep says he can't get in the door. And they undercut us to the retailers down south."

The economics were precisely as Ian had thought. "Can-Green, or a front company connected to it, must pay the suppliers. There's a load of work I need to do tracing bank accounts, et cetera – but that's the long and short of it."

Ian showed Armstrong the copies of the invoices, pointing out the coinciding dates, and the invoices that had been dated on a Saturday. "Basically, what ABD is doing is manufacturing biodiesel free of charge for Can-Green. You pay all the electricity and staffing costs. As well as the capital costs of the plant and buildings, of course."

"Bastuds," said Armstrong. He ran his finger along the rim of his plate and licked the cake crumbs off it. "So how come your colleagues didn't spot this going on? I thought Woodcock and Tweed were good?"

"That's the sorrier part of the tale, in my view," said Ian.

"Woodcock and Tweed are also Can-Green's auditors. Everyone's making a profit out of that biodiesel plant except you. I suspect my former employers are covering for Watkins. I'd stake my reputation on it."

A vein throbbed on Armstrong's right temple. He breathed in deeply and closed his eyes. He breathed out after a few seconds. He looked straight into Ian's eyes. "Thanks, son." He cleared his throat. "I'm sorry I didn't believe you."

"That's alright," said Ian. He felt a surge of affection and admiration for Armstrong for his apology.

"But it doesn't say much for what Woodcock and Tweed think of you, does it son?" Armstrong laughed.

Ian smiled back: Armstrong always had him off-guard with his ability to see the humour in the blackest of circumstances. "Piss off, William. They put me on the job by mistake. And I got there in the end, didn't I?"

"What's our next step? I want them nailed. I want every one of them in jail."

"Invoices, accounts. I'd also like to see itemised phone bills because I think at least one of the reps is dirty. We need access to the office tomorrow."

"We?"

"No one else I can trust. Even Valerie Craven's in on it somewhere along the line."

"No way."

"She was pumping me for information on Watkins' behalf over dinner the other week. I never had access to your management accounts, but I'd expect her targets were manipulated. She's good, but I bet she's not as good as you've been led to believe."

Rather than risk the high profile of the Gosforth Park, Ian had made do with another three-star hotel – though he couldn't risk the one near Armstrong's headquarters because it had been Watkins' choice, and might therefore have moles amongst the staff. Armstrong picked him up in his wife's car at nine on Saturday morning and they drove to the office. The security guard was instructed to close the building and let no one else in.

"What about him?" asked Ian.

Armstrong fixed him with a stare. "Terry? Mates since school. I fixed him up after he was invalided out of the army. He's *family*."

The filing cabinets were locked, but Ian retrieved the key from the top drawer of Anne Salter's desk and they set to work. Ian was conscious of his need to demonstrate a quick win and fished out the itemised phone bills for ABD's sales reps. Armstrong told him the name of the rep covering the southernmost territory. He took out his notepad from the previous day.

"What's that?" asked Armstrong.

"A list of petrol stations one of Can-Green's tankers delivered to last week. I looked up their phone numbers." He studied the rep's itemised mobile bill. "Look at this: Can-Green have even got this guy selling for them. You're not just paying for their production, you're even subsidising their sales operation."

They worked until three o'clock. Ian had shown Armstrong more than enough to convince him by then. Although Armstrong didn't know Watkins' and Horsley's wives' maiden names, he recognised their addresses because over the years they'd become family friends and been dinner guests at each others' houses. That the bank account numbers on the invoices for the palm oil and meths matched Can-Green's was the most damning evidence of all. "You'll also find that those invoices were printed on one of the machines in your office, or one at Can-Green's."

"Aye, is that right, son?"

"Every printer and photocopier has its own distinct fingerprint – a unique pattern of random dots from imperfections on the roller that takes the electrical charge. The police will get forensic scientists to determine that one."

"Okay, I'm convinced you've got all the bases covered on my lot," said Armstrong. "Now, what about them snooty bastards down in London? What do we have on them?"

"First, you can't audit these records and not know what was going on in my view. So there's signing off on fraudulent accounts for a start. Just a quick glance at this file," Ian slid an open folder over to Armstrong, "shows that they've been overcharging for their services, so that's at least one count of fraud. The invoice for the audit I carried out looks like it's for one senior and four junior staff. Of course, it was issued after I'd left so that I didn't see it. That would be about normal for a firm of this size, but I'll give Watkins his due – he really is a very good accountant, so the audit could be done by fewer people."

Armstrong sighed and leaned back. "I'm in your hands, Ian. Where do we take it from here? Do we gather all this evidence up and take it off-site for safekeeping? When do I get to sack those bastuds and sue your former employers?"

"We do nothing for the moment," said Ian.

"*What?*"

"We need to calculate how much meths and palm oil you actually have in stock, versus what the fake figures say you should be holding. Obviously, there should be a big surplus. That gives us grounds to go to the police."

"Do we have to? They'll take forever, surely."

"The great thing about the forces of law and order is that they can arrest on *suspicion*. We can only do so much ourselves. The real paperwork has to be somewhere, and they can get warrants to search for them and we can't do that without bringing a major legal action. We'll also need samples of the biodiesel in Can-Green's tanks to establish that it has the same chemical fingerprint as yours. Ideally, we need to catch the perpetrators when a new consignment of palm oil has been delivered."

Armstrong sighed. "Well, you're the professional."

"We also need the services of a good lawyer."

"I assume you know one."

Ian had known the best, but he'd settle for her former colleague. "Karen Goodman of Perky Bottom."

"*Perky Bottom*? This isn't another one of your sexual things, is it son?"

"I'm sorry, I mean Perkins Botham. Mid-sized City firm. I've worked extensively with them."

"Great. Hire them. Now, can I drop you anywhere?"

"Shit," said Ian. "I have to be in Bristol tonight for my nieces' christening tomorrow morning.

"No problem, son. I've got a spare car or two at home. I'll lend you one for the weekend."

Armstrong drove them to his estate, on the North Tyne valley. The period house and stables sat in a hundred acres of arable land. He clicked a button on the car's sun visor and the metal shutters of the stable doors opened to reveal a Bentley and a Jaguar convertible. "They're both nice for motorway cruising," he told Ian. "Which would you prefer?"

"If it's okay with you, can I just take your wife's car? It's a little more discreet. Just."

"You're a funny one, son. She'll not object to driving the Jag in the meantime, though."

The Mercedes convertible got him to Bristol in four and a half easy hours, and he braked it gently to a stop outside his parents' house in Clifton. It was a three-storey Georgian pile that spoke of its owner's seniority in the city's independent business community – a status he himself had never wanted to inherit.

He rang the doorbell and recognised his father's footsteps in the hall. The light came on in the porch. Ian prepared himself for the worst.

"Where the *hell* have you been?" asked his father as he opened the door. "We left messages for you. You were supposed to get a lift down with Stu. We wanted you here for a family dinner at six."

"I'm sorry, I was on a job in Newcastle. I came down as soon as I could. I'm here now, okay?"

His sister and her husband were preparing to leave with his two nieces, Hannah and Natasha. He kissed the girls and his sister goodbye. He kissed his own mother, who shuddered at the patch of stubbly hair over the angry scar on his head as she examined it. "My baby," she said.

"Nice car, Ian," said his sister's husband.

"Perk of the job," said Ian.

He ate microwaved leftovers from the family dinner, glad of his mother's fussing because it prevented his father from having another go at him. "I don't see a suit," said his father.

"Forgot it. We're near enough the same size, aren't we? I can use one of yours."

He slept in his old bedroom that night. As a teenager, he'd lain in bed and fantasised about the kind of sex he'd had just eight days before. He wanted to reach back and touch that other, younger self and tell him he'd get it in the end; to tell him to relax and take life in his stride.

As Ian swore to renounce the Devil and all his works the image of *The word of the Lord Endureth forever* engraved on the open stone bible flashed into his head, and he imagined himself as an avenging angel once more. He would smite his enemies. D'Arcy House and St Swithin's Lane would be purged of evil. Woodcock and Tweed would be a smoking ruin redolent with the smell of brimstone.

There was a buffet lunch after the photos. Ian found Jeremy, his mini-nemesis, staggering around with a piece of squashed quiche in his hand. He picked him up and used him as a human shield as he made up with Stu and Nina.

He allowed himself only half a glass of champagne because he was driving, but saw his parents take more than they were accustomed to. He gave them a lift back to their house and got changed out of the suit. His father came into his bedroom as he was putting his casual clothes back on.

"You're mother's bawling her eyes out downstairs," he said.

"Christ, what have I done now?"

"It's what you *haven't* done. For Christ's sake, you're nearly thirty years old and you've not even got a steady girlfriend. It's a good job she doesn't know about all this pornography Stu caught you with. And God knows who you're hanging around with if you're out of a job and able to drive a car like that after being fired. Are you a crook now, is that it? Is *that* why you were sacked?"

"Quite the opposite, Dad. I told you before: I'm on a job. Look, plenty of guys who're thirty don't have girlfriends."

"What about us? We're not getting any younger. I love Hannah and Natasha to bits but we need someone to carry on the company name. Jane doesn't want any more kids and you're no bloody use. We were expecting you to marry Sarah this summer."

"You mean *family* name," said Ian. "You said you needed someone to carry on the *company* name. I'm different to you, Dad. I want to live a little, and I don't want to take over the family business, alright?"

"You need a woman, that's what you need. Without a stabilising influence in your life you're just going to become some sad, selfish old soak sitting in his local snug bar."

Ian managed to tear himself away, arriving back up in Newcastle in the early evening.

He was ready for the showdown.

Chapter Twenty

"Good morning, Perkins Botham, Karen Goodman speaking," said the Scottish voice.

"Karen, hi. It's Ian. I've got a case for you. A big one."

"Ian, are you alright?"

"What do you mean?"

"I heard through Suzanne that you resigned last week. You should *never* have resigned without asking me first."

"Wow, bad news travels fast. How'd you hear? And what makes you say I should never have resigned?"

"Your old boss, Donald Peterson, is going out with my boss, Suzanne Meadows. Donald's apparently quite upset about it. He said they threatened to fire you if you didn't resign, but that there were medical grounds for your suspension. Even if you did resign you've got a solid case that it was under duress and that you weren't *compos mentis*. I'd be quite happy to take the case on a *pro bono* basis. Didn't you get my message?"

"They took my work mobile, and I've not been back to the flat, sorry." Ian was confused – Peterson was a managing partner in Woodcock and Tweed: a sworn enemy he'd vowed to destroy. "I'm not bothered about that. Look, I've got a client who needs a solicitor to stand in to check we're following procedure. The client isn't in a position to trust his own at the moment. We're at the preliminary stages. We'll need you on site in about a week."

"Great, thanks for the job. But what about suing Woodcock and Tweed? I think on the evidence you could get them for unlawful dismissal, which carries far better compensation than for unfair. What do you think?"

"I'm really not fussed, for reasons you'll understand soon enough." Ian shifted his mobile. "How's Sarah?"

"Sarah…. She's doing fine."

"Please send her my love."

Later that morning he called a contact in the fraud squad.

The machinery of the law swung slowly into action.

Trevor Horsely and his wife were arrested at home, on a Thursday evening in late June. Together with officers from Revenue and Customs, Ian had been through the fake records of the goods received at ABD, which had matched – a little too well – the volume of biodiesel produced at the plant. In turn, that had matched the volumes booked into Armstrong Distribution. Fortunately for the investigators, there had been recent deliveries of raw materials, and an audit of the tanks of unprocessed palm oil and meths at ABD had shown an excess of over thirty percent. A similar audit of the tanks at Armstrong Distribution showed a surplus of biodiesel.

As had been hoped, Horsley had no resolve in the face of the law, and chose to turn Queen's evidence as soon as the opportunity was given.

On Friday morning Ian was pleased to be seated in Armstrong's office, along with Karen Goodman. Armstrong sat at his large desk, with the forensic accountant and solicitor to his right and left respectively. Ian and Karen were both a little tired, having been up half the night observing Horsley's interview. Ian's mind was in the grip of the second wind that comes with the closing on the quarry.

"Eddie," said Armstrong into his phone. "Could you come up and see me for a moment, please?" There was a gruff reply from the receiver. Armstrong dialled another number. "Terry, those two policemen in reception. Can you show them up here in five minutes for me please?" The three waited silently for a minute before there was a tap at the door and Watkins entered.

"Hi William, I—" Watkins caught sight of Ian and took a quick step back. "Excuse me, I thought the auditors were done," he said, hovering at the door, eyeing Ian and Karen.

"Close it behind you," growled Armstrong.

"How can I help?" said Watkins, insouciantly. He took a seat in front of the desk.

For a moment, Ian wondered whether he'd have to stop Armstrong from leaping over the desk and strangling his finance director. Armstrong relaxed his clasped hands and coughed lightly. He breathed out and sat back in his chair. "There seems to be a small problem with the accounts, Eddie," he said mildly. He coughed again. "Ian, perhaps if you were to explain?"

Ian hadn't been prepared for another of Armstrong's strange changes of mind, and hesitated. Although he'd been at numerous disciplinary interviews in his career, none had involved a fraud of such audacity and magnitude – nor a man of Armstrong's nature.

"Actually, I don't see how this young man has anything to do with the accounts any more William," said Watkins, his confidence returning. "Do you know he was fired for gross misconduct only the other week? He's lucky not to be on the Sex Offenders Register by all accounts."

Ian's distaste for such proceedings evaporated. Watkins was a thief and a bully. "I'm freelance now, Watkins," he said. "I've been back over the figures for Armstrong Leasing. There was just no need to manipulate Valerie Craven's performance figures."

Watkins reddened and glanced at Armstrong, who gave Ian a quizzical look.

"Just no need to do it," said Ian, leaning back and stretching. Watkins was done and he couldn't be bothered to give him the third degree.

"I don't know what you mean," said Watkins.

"It was over-egging the pudding," said Ian. Watkins reddened some more. "She didn't need to win some management prize every quarter. Don't get me wrong: she was always good as a student. But making sure she always got the prize by manipulating the accounts.... Weakness on your part."

"I don't know what you're driving at," said Watkins. "William, I've got a lot on my plate, so if you'll excuse me."

"Sit *down*, Eddie," growled Armstrong. "Go on, Ian."

"Amateur would be a better word for it," said Ian. "Rank amateur."

"How *dare* you?" said Watkins, purple.

"*Bungling* amateur, even," said Ian. Armstrong's shoulders began to shake, and he let go a stuttering hiss.

"You go to all that length. Years in the planning – the investment in Can-Green – a brilliant operation, and you let it all go because you're smitten with a young woman. It's tragic. Yet you really fancied yourself as the criminal mastermind, didn't you?"

"You can't have found it all out from just *that*," squealed Watkins. "She told me you got it just by *chance*."

"No, but thanks for the tacit admission." Armstrong was now sniggering uncontrollably by Ian's side. "I think William can see the tragic comedy in you. It's not just that it's another crime. How's this affair with Valerie Craven going to play with your wife during the trial? I really don't envy you at all: you've not got a friend in the world and everyone else's defence is going to lay everything at your door. You're an incompetent oaf, Watkins." Karen Goodman cleared her throat. "Just my opinion, of course," said Ian. "I mean no professional slander: you're a very good accountant."

Watkins collapsed in his chair and Armstrong burst into open laughter, slamming the table with his fist. He was still laughing as Terry the security guard let in the two plain-clothes detectives, who arrested Watkins and took him away. Ian supposed it was something to do with the years of stress over ABD suddenly being relieved, rather than the insults he'd heaped upon the fraudster.

"How do you fancy being my new finance director?" asked Armstrong. "I can offer you an excellent package. And you're no stranger to the excellent quality of life here in the North East."

"Thanks, but no. I'm toying with the idea of my own firm."

"Well, I'm a bit buggered now, son: it could take months to

recruit one. Can you not at least take it on a temporary basis?"

"Weren't you the one who always said never to underestimate your own staff? I think Mary Ruffcorn is long overdue for a promotion."

"Touché: you're absolutely right. I hope you'll take on the contract for auditing my group?"

"I'd be delighted to, William."

"Excellent," said Armstrong. "Right, it's Valerie Craven next." Ian looked away. "It's alright, son." Armstrong put a hand on Ian's shoulder. "There are some things I'd never ask you to do. Maybe if you go and tell Mary about her promotion and brief her team – make sure morale's alright, systems are in place, get the paperwork back in order, that sort of thing."

"Thanks."

"Right," said Karen, reaching for a file. "Valerie Craven. Ian says there's no evidence she was involved *directly* in the operation, though she must have known about it. However, what we can say with certainty at this stage was that she was party to the fraudulent management accounts concerning her performance. Whether or not you choose to press *criminal* charges, is of course at your—"

Ian closed the door behind him and nodded to Armstrong's secretary, who raised her eyebrows at him from behind her desk in the anteroom to his office. Val was standing, head bowed, waiting to be called in. He touched her on the upper arm. "I'm sorry," he said.

She looked up, eyes red, mascara smudged. "No," she said. "*I'm* sorry, Ian." She paused to blow her nose. She flashed a faint smile at him. A strand of hair had fallen forward and stuck to her damp cheek, and she brushed it back behind her left ear.

"I always wondered...." she said. "Do you remember that party in Jesmond? You know. The one where you met Susan?"

"Sarah. Yes. I remember."

"I always wondered. For *years*, I always wondered if...."

"Yeah. So did I," he sighed. "It's a question of choices, isn't it? I suppose chance plays a part. But mostly it's choices."

Armstrong's secretary's phone rang and she picked it up. "Mister Armstrong's expecting you in now, pet," she said.

"My advice is to come clean – it's the best option in the long-run," said Ian. "Well, good luck."

"Thanks." She leaned over to kiss him but he turned his back and walked away, his heart hardened.

As Ian addressed Watkins' former staff a few minutes later, it was clear that their morale was – if anything – too high. Even Anne Salter was chatty with him. Mary Ruffcorn rose to her new challenge and she and Ian worked on overhauling Watkins' systems.

At lunchtime, Ian's liaison officer at Revenue and Customs called to tell him they had shut down Can-Green's operation. There was little doubt that an assay of their biodiesel would prove it to be from ABD, and that the missing fuel would tally with the quantities sold on by Can-Green. The genuine quantities of palm oil and meths that had been processed over the years would take longer to determine, since the suppliers were overseas – but it would all piece together to complete the picture, he was sure.

The only truly upsetting thing that happened to him on Friday was a call from a tearful Rose. "They've closed us down, Ian," she sobbed. "They arrested Donald. Jean called to say they'd taken Woodcock and Tweed, and the other partners too." She paused to compose herself. "'As this got anything to do with you? I mean, this is for real, ain't it? I just don't know what I'm going to do. If they's all in prison, how am I even goin' to get references?"

Ian felt a pang of guilt. "Rose, you'll be just fine. If you need any references, I'm your man. Don't worry: I'll see you're alright. You have my word on that."

When Ian got back to his apartment on Saturday, he deleted two messages from Marina the Marauding Ukrainian – he hadn't the patience to listen to her wittering. The phone rang and he thought twice before picking it up. It was Peterson. He sounded tired and suggested they meet for lunch. Ian decided he had nothing to lose. They met in a pub in Charing Cross.

"I'm on police bail," said Peterson, handing Ian a pint of bitter. "Suzanne's been a great support with all this legal stuff. She sprang me from jail, as it were, this morning. I really owe you for the introduction." They sat at an empty table by the window.

"You'll need all the help you can get where you're going," said Ian, flippantly. He wondered what Peterson was after – a character reference for the court, possibly. But if it was Ian's sympathy, he'd never get it.

"No, you don't understand. I'm innocent, you silly arse. I'm only on police bail because they want to continue to interview me. It's a right bloody nuisance."

"Oh, yeah," said Ian, shifting awkwardly on his wooden chair. "Yes, I thought you might be innocent. You were just too caught up in your own work to notice any of this, weren't you?"

"Why the hell do you think they located the forensic division, away from the main office? They couldn't trust me to be dishonest, if you follow me. And despite my blameless past I'm out of a bloody job. It's a real bugger. Of course, the firm's wrecked – who the hell would ever trust the name again? Any assets will be seized, so my partnership's worth nothing. And I still have to pay my bloody ex-wife alimony. Sixty-one years old and I'm bloody *ruined*."

Ian looked pensive for a moment. "I'd say your own name's pretty good," he said. "Though you'll face a professional disciplinary hearing from ACCA."

"Well, thank God for the famous Chinese walls between us and Auditing. I should be okay. But don't think you're going to get off scot-free, lad. ACCA will want a word with you, too."

"Why?"

"Woodcock had that video of you emailed to every man Jack

on our client list, and some more besides. You'll face charges of bringing the profession into disrepute. And the publicity over this trial's going to see the media getting maximum titillation value out of it. Now that video's out, there's no putting it back. That's the way of the internet: the content is there for eternity."

Ian shrugged. "It's funny, I'm not that bothered now it comes down to it. I knew when I decided to go after them that it would be released. It was clearly not intentional on my part, so ACCA can't discipline me for it." He sighed. "It's just my parents I feel sorry for. I'm not sure my mother ever realised Sarah and I were having sex even when we were living together."

"Everyone's buggered, Ian. The whole lot of us are out of work, including Rose." They sat in silence. Peterson stroked the condensation off the side of his pint and stared out of the window. Ian's gaze wandered round the pub. It was empty apart from the barman, who was hunched over some receipts, totting them up on a calculator.

"I've got an idea," said Ian. "How about Peterson Bourne, Forensic Accountants? Rose can be our office manager."

Peterson looked at him for a couple of moments and pushed his glasses back up his nose. "Yes," he said, beaming. "Here's to Peterson Bourne. Cheers."

"What have you got to say for yourself now?" Ian's father's voice on the phone had a dead tone to it; angry but controlled, with an edge of sadness, something simmering.

"I'm not sure what you mean," said Ian. This wasn't the sort of call he'd expected early on a Monday morning.

"I asked you the other weekend where you got that fancy car. And it's obvious to me now that you're involved with criminal elements."

Ian sighed. "I told you: it's a client's car. What are you on about?"

"I got an email from Andrew Bishop, our accountants. The

ones you worked for in your student days, if you're not too big to admit your roots. It seems you're quite a celebrity."

Ian's heart sank. No amount of preparation could have readied him for this. The countless times he'd simulated this conversation had failed to reach a comfortable conclusion. The speed the email had reached his father was amazing, but he decided he'd been through too much in the last couple of months to care. He was an adult now, teetering on the brink of thirty. "Yes, I suppose that email was about the raciest thing to have happened in accountancy in a decade."

"Is that what you think? The *shame* you've brought on the family. How am I going to tell your mother?"

"Dad, look. Get it in perspective. It happens all the time and I was just unlucky to be caught *in flagrante*, that's all.

"Unlucky to be caught?" spluttered his father. "You make it sound like it's perfectly acceptable."

"Sure, everyone's at it."

"I can assure you they're not!"

"Of *course* everyone's at it: it's natural. So it was filmed and I inadvertently became a big internet porn star. These things happen. Big deal."

"*What*?"

"Ah," said Ian, the light dawning on him. "Look, that story Andrew Bishop emailed you from *Accountancy Age* about me being dismissed from Woodcock and Tweed. That's old news, and it's not true. Now, that's the *good* news…."

Karen Goodman had invited him to lunch at *Les Trois Voleurs* on Monday to celebrate the arrests. He usually celebrated successful cases with accounting colleagues; but only occasionally with lawyers he'd worked with. And certainly never one-on-one. He hoped Karen didn't have anything other than work-related matters on her mind. She was attractive, certainly – but she just wasn't his type and he wouldn't know what to say to her if the situation arose.

The *maître d'* told him Karen was waiting, and beckoned him to follow. He glanced around the restaurant, but he couldn't see that striking head of red hair.

There was a woman sitting at a table on her own, facing away from him. The back of her head looked familiar. So did her jacket. He felt his pulse quicken.

The woman heard the footsteps behind her and turned round. "Hello, Ian," she said.

"Sarah."

"*Pardonnez-moi*, there 'as been a mistake?" asked the *maître d'*.

"No mistake," said Sarah, dismissing the *maître d'*. "Well, you recognised me. That's something."

Ian felt giddy. Memories of warm lovemaking and laughter came flooding back. "Sarah," he said. "Of *course* I do, don't be silly." He took in the sight of her. She had grown her brown hair to shoulder length, and the sun had lightened it to that blondish colour he loved. He felt a strong urge to reach out and stroke it. "You're looking… fantastic," he said. And she did – her complexion was somehow more vibrant, her eyes were a deeper blue against ultra white eyeballs, and he couldn't help noticing that her breasts had never looked firmer. Of course: she'd given up drink and was eating well and exercising regularly. He leant over and kissed her on the cheek, then sat down opposite her.

"You've been busy," she said. "I've heard all sorts of things from Karen. And you're in the papers, too." She toyed with the straw in her cranberry juice.

"Some of it's not that good. I… I made a mistake." He ordered a mineral water from the waitress, who handed them their menus.

"*One* mistake?"

"Well, you know. One thing led to another." He looked down at the table.

"Jesus, Ian. In the great internet shopping experience of mistakes it looks like you downloaded a fucking lifetime's worth."

"Look, it all just spun out of control."

"I'm sorry," she said, laughing. "Only you, Ian. You're just too sweet and innocent sometimes."

He smiled sheepishly back at her, and they held their gaze. She put her hand on his for a moment and squeezed it. "We both made a mistake," she said.

"Well…." he wasn't sure where this was leading. "So what have you been up to?"

"After I left Perky Bottom I went back up to my parents' place in Nottingham. I've been doing some work in the voluntary sector — human rights stuff. The pay's not great but I feel like I'm a better person for it. You lose contact with real people when you work for a big firm."

"Yeah, it does feel great to get out of the corporate machine and be doing something more worthwhile, doesn't it?"

"Oh, and congratulations on forming your new firm. That's quite a move."

"Yeah, me and Peterson, eh? Who'd have thought it?" he gave half a laugh. "And we've got good old Rose to keep us in order."

"You've done a lot of growing up, from what I've heard. And you look ten times fitter."

"Well," said Ian, looking away, into his menu. "I'm sorry. You know, about me. Back then." He felt embarrassed about his past life as a denizen of the Derbyshire. "There's so much more to do with one's life, isn't there?"

"I'm sorry too. All those times I chucked you. No wonder you used to call me your default girlfriend."

He looked up, embarrassed. "Ah," he said. "Yeah, I suppose you got to hear about that."

"Oh, it's okay. I used to tell people you were my default boyfriend."

He felt a twinge, but it faded: fair was fair. "So, are you down in London for long?"

"That depends," she said.

"Christ, I think we're more than three times lucky now, aren't we?" he joked.

"I think things have changed. We've changed."

"Yeah, we're both at the arse-end of our careers and I'm inadvertently the star of the most emailed porn video on the internet," said Ian. Sarah pushed back her chair and rose to her feet. She had a stomach like the one he'd exercised off. "Looks like you put on the weight that I lost," he said, feeling superior.

"No," said Sarah. "I'm pregnant with our child. Nearly four months."

He opened his mouth to speak, but no words came.

"It happened about five weeks before I left you," she said. "I wasn't sure you were up to being much of a father. But that was back then."

Ian stared at her belly, then up at her. "Sarah," he said. And then he hugged her to him, rocking her gently, surprised to find tears welling in his eyes. "Oh, *Sarah*." It all made sense to him now – giving up alcohol and eating well.

She broke off. "Bugger the lunch," she said. "I've been so *horny* the last couple of months."

"I'll get us a cab," said Ian, fumbling for his wallet. He left money on the table for the drinks. They picked up the overnight bag she'd left in the cloakroom and made their way out into the buzz of Holborn Circus. "Look," he said, "I'm embarrassed to say this, but I'll have to wear a condom. I did get a new test last week, and I was negative. But I really should wait until I have another test at the end of July." He helped her into a cab and closed the door behind them.

"Tamara's clear," said Sarah. "I spoke to her yesterday. She says we should be fine."

"Tamara? I didn't know you knew her."

"Men," Sarah sighed, leaning back. "You think women don't have their regrets, and their sexual fantasies? Tamara has that whole category on her site devoted to it."

"I know that only too well, but what are you talking about?"

"Unlike you, I worked out all my sexual fantasies in my college days. Did you think I was celibate the whole time? Tammy and I had a bit of a thing, but I wasn't so stupid as to have it on video."

Ian's jaw dropped. She lifted his chin and looked him in the eyes. "Now, is that it?" she asked. "Have you worked all those regrets out of your system?"

"Yeah." He looked into her eyes. "Yes, I'm done."

When the cab dropped them off outside his apartment there was a strangely familiar-looking female hanging around the entry phone. She had two battered suitcases with her. As soon as she saw Ian, her face lit up. "Forensitch! London field trip!" she said in a heavy accent.

Sarah raised her eyebrows at him. "One of the lifetime of mistakes I downloaded," he said to her.

He turned to face Marina. "*Nyet*," he said. "Forensitch kaputski." He reached for his wallet and pulled out Giac's card. "Here," he said, placing the card in her hand. "Top London model agent for Ukrainian good-looking girls. Big contract, much money. Give call."

Woodcock, Tweed, Hendricks and two other partners were committed for trial, as were Watkins and Horsley and their wives. Those involved in the investigation joked that Watkins was glad to have been remanded in custody because his wife might have torn him to pieces for the affair he'd had with Valerie Craven. It emerged that the two of them had double-crossed Mrs Watkins, and had planned to elope to South America, leaving her to face all the charges alone. He heard through the grapevine that Armstrong hadn't prosecuted Valerie, and that after she'd been fired for gross misconduct she'd gone to work in the voluntary sector.

After its founders were exonerated by their professional body, Peterson Bourne enjoyed a highly successful first year's trading. It was Ian's decision to meet his sexual notoriety head-on. Using the advertising straplines 'Making accounting sexy' and 'Accounting with attitude', their success was assured.

Christopher Bourne emerged screaming into the world on the second of December, named after his delighted paternal grandfather, who had just sold his printing business to William Armstrong, whom he'd met at his son's wedding four months earlier.

Ian's parents had wanted an early christening for their first grandson. Ian and Sarah's secret revenge was in their choice of godmother. "She's a good looker alright," Ian's father told him at the reception. "But I've never seen so many men fawning over a woman. It's astonishing."

"She's got a certain *je ne sais pas*," said Ian. "It's a generational thing you'd not understand." Tamara saw them looking across at her, and waved.

Sarah didn't return to work for Perkins Botham. She followed her husband's example and teamed up with Karen Goodman and Peterson's girlfriend, Suzanne Meadows, to form the City law firm Meadows Conway Goodman. "No question of glass ceilings for mothers with young children," chirped Sarah when she told him.

Often, as Ian lay in the dark, trying to get back to sleep after being woken by his default son, he used to thank the circumstances that had brought him his default family. If that default backup software hadn't been quietly running in the background, he'd have been a poorer man by far. He might have had more sex with more women; that was true. But as he drifted off to sleep he would smile at the thought of his digitised self, preserved forever in its state of arousal, endlessly copulating in the ether: a pioneer of the pornographic age.

He appreciated the assets he had. He was more than satisfied.

About the author

Mark Speed's comedy writing has been broadcast on BBC Radio 4 Extra and appeared in newspapers as diverse as the *London Evening Standard* and *The Sun*. He performed his solo comedy, *The End of the World Show*, at the Edinburgh Fringe in 2011 and 2012.

He's been writing novels since he was fifteen, and has an MA in Creative Writing from City University, London. In 1995 a chiropractor told him he'd never run again. He chose to give up chiropractors instead, and has since completed several marathons and a couple of Olympic-length triathlons. He has been diagnosed as a 'polarity responder'.

Please review!

If you've enjoyed this novel, please leave a review. As an independent author, word of mouth recommendations and the kind reviews of readers are my only means of publicity. Thank you so much – I really appreciate your help! ☺

Other works by the same author:

The Doctor How series:

Book one: *Doctor How and the Illegal Aliens: The Doctor Who is Not a Time Lord*

Book two: *Doctor How and the Deadly Anemones*

Book three: *Doctor How and the Alien Invasion*

Apocalypse Later: A guide to the end of the world by Nice Mr Death

Britons in Brief (anthology)

Author information and more writing:
www.markspeed.co.uk
http://www.amazon.com/author/markspeed

Acknowledgements

My sincere thanks to Harriett Gilbert – course director, mentor and midwife on the MA in Creative Writing at City University – for her patience, guidance and friendship. Thanks also to Shannon Falk, for her enthusiasm, love and encouragement – when I was writing this, at least. I'm also grateful to Dr Liz Miller for teaching me how to ask a better question in the search for solutions to life's questions. My thanks to the forensic accounting team at Baker Tilly for background research.

Printed in Great Britain
by Amazon